Bedtime Stories for Kids

Vol 1+Vol 2 + Vol 3

A Collection of over 100 Short Meditation Stories

to Reduce Anxiety, Learn Mindfulness, Increase

Relaxation, and Help Children Fall Asleep Fast

(Ages 2-6, 6-12, 3-5)

Giuly

Gabriell

Thompson

Table of Contents vol .1

Table of Contents vol .2

Table of Contents Vol.3

Introduction

Congratulations on purchasing *Bedtime Stories For Kids Vol 1 +Vol 2 + Vol 3: A collection of over 100 short meditation stories to reduce anxiety, learn mindfulness, increase relaxation, and help children fall to sleep fast (age 2-6, 6-12, 3-5)* and thank you for doing so.

The following chapters each contain their own meditation story. Each meditation story has been specially designed to both grab and keep your child's attention, and as they listen to and follow along with the fun and immersive stories in this book, they will also be learning mindfulness meditation and relaxation exercises that will help to reduce anxiety and let them drift off to sleep quicker each and every night.

Feel free to skip around in the chapters. They do not need to be read in any specific order.

The benefits of learning and using mindfulness meditation and relaxation techniques cannot be overstated. The following chart is just a sampling of the many behavioral, emotional, and physical benefits of employing mindfulness meditation and relaxation techniques.

Benefits of employing Mindfulness Meditation and Relaxation Techniques:

- ➢ Improved quantity and quality of sleep
- ➢ Improved overall mood
- ➢ Improved academic performance
- ➢ Improved work performance
- ➢ A reported decrease in daily anxiety
- ➢ A reported decrease in daily stress levels
- ➢ Improved chronic pain outcomes
- ➢ Lower blood pressure

This book is great when used both as an introduction to mindfulness meditation and relaxation techniques and as an integral part of continuing meditation practice.

There are plenty of books on this subject on the market, thanks again for choosing this one! Every effort was made to ensure it is full of as much useful information as possible, please do enjoy!

Chapter 1:
Carnival Fun

Have you ever been to a carnival? Even if you have never been to a carnival before in your life, you can go there any time you want to—in your mind! Really, you can. Your mind is capable of doing many great things, including something called Visualization.

Visualization happens when a person uses the power of their brain to create a picture so vivid and detailed that the person can actually experience it like they are actually there! In fact, if a person gets a special brain scan done while they are visualizing something, the exact same parts of their brain will be active, as if they were actually doing the thing they were visualizing. This means that your mind can be anywhere it wants to be at any time, with just a little guidance from you.

To begin your visualization practice, close your eyes. Really, close your eyes (unless you are the one reading this, of course!) To build a very strong visualization, it is usually helpful to first center yourself and be sure you are giving your brain the very best tools it needs to work with. In this case, that means oxygen, and oxygen means taking some good, deep breaths.

You are going to take some slow, deep breaths now, following along with my instruction: Breathe in very slowly, 1 - 2 - 3 - 4. Now breathe out, very slowly, 1 - 2 - 3 - 4. Excellent. Now again very slowly, 1 - 2 - 3 - 4 and breathe back out very slowly, 1 - 2 - 3 - 4 very nice. Once more, very slowly in 1 - 2 - 3 - 4 and back out very slowly, 1 - 2 - 3 - 4. Great!

Take a moment to review how you feel. Are you comfy and feeling good? Okay, great.

Take another big deep breath in, still with your eyes closed. Listen closely. What is that you hear? Is that... carnival music? Yes! Yes, it is. It's very faint and in the distance, but you can hear it. It sounds like the music you hear on the Merry Go Round, doesn't it?

Take another big deep breath in, what is that now that you smell? It smells sweet, very, very sweet! Oh, you know what that is! That's cotton candy! There's the cotton candy machine right there, now you can see it. The woman that is working the cotton candy machine is holding up two giant cotton candy sticks, one pink and one blue. They look so fluffy and soft, don't they?

Look, the woman is holding one out to you. Reach out and accept it. Wow, this thing sure is heavier than you expected, isn't it? Feel the weight of all of this cotton handy as you hold it in your hand. That's a lot of cotton candy!

Now give it a little taste. Wow! Feel the sticky sweetness on your tongue. The wispy and colorful spun sugar dissolves almost the exact moment it touches your tongue, doesn't it? How syrupy sweet it is! Delicious. What a lovely carnival treat.

You can still hear the carnival music playing, and you now look around to see exactly where it is coming from. Look, over there! Now you can see it. It's the Merry Go Round, and it's just across from the cotton candy booth.

You've finished your cotton candy now, and you'd like to go have a ride on the Merry Go Round. It is dusk out, and as the sun sinks down in the sky, the lights of the Merry Go Round provide a soft, warm glow to the carnival, and you walk towards it.

The light and happy music of the Merry Go Round is getting louder now as you get closer, and you can see the Merry Go Round is beautifully lit up with strings of lights, and now you can see the ponies that can be ridden on.

This Merry Go Round has ponies of all different colors. There's an aqua blue pony with a yellow saddle, and next to it is a tangerine orange pony with a cherry red saddle. Which pony do you like best? Would you like to ride on the aqua blue pony with the yellow saddle or the tangerine orange pony with the cherry red saddle? The Merry Go Round is stopped and waiting for you to get on and ride!

Climb on the pony you like best. You can feel the firm, sleek surface of the painted pony below you now, and the Merry Go Round begins to gently move. The lights above and all around you are soft and warm, and your colorful pony is beautifully painted, just like all the other pretty ponies on this ride. The lights and the colors together make you feel so happy inside.

As the Merry Go Round goes around, you can feel the gentle breeze on your face. The night is warm, and the breeze is perfectly cool and calming as it softly caresses your cheeks and nose. The music of the Merry Go Round is light and happy, and you enjoy listening as the colorfully painted pony you are riding on goes up and down and around and around.

Take a slow, deep breath in. The air still smells of light, sweet cotton candy, and you smile as you remember its wispy sweet taste and the way the wisps of spun sugar melted on your tongue with each bite. The Merry Go Round feels happy and warm as you continue to go up and down and around and around on your beautifully painted pony, listening to the light and happy carnival music.

The soft light surrounds you, and the sun is setting even further. You are still going up and down and around and around on your safe and happy Merry Go Round as the night grows darker still. The gentle breeze against your face feels delicious, and you close your eyes to take in all of the sensations.

The syrupy sweet cotton candy smell enters your nose again, and the light and happy music make you smile. You rest your head on your colorful painted pony and enjoy the light, cool breeze as you continue to ride up and down and around and around on the Merry Go Round, safely tucked under the warm glow of the strings of light above you. You are so thankful to be here at this awesome carnival.

You do not have to leave the carnival now. You can remain on the Merry Go Round if you wish, riding the beautifully painted ponies and enjoying the light and gentle breeze on your face, or you can get off and go explore other areas of the carnival.

You can create anything you want in your mind. Imagine where you want to go and build the picture in your mind. Be sure to imagine how you want it to smell, taste, hear, and feel. The more detailed you can make your mental picture, the more you will enjoy being there.

It is all up to you. Perhaps as you drift off to sleep, you will find yourself able to play at the carnival in your dreams.

Chapter 2:
Hay Maze with Friends

Have you ever been to a hay maze before? No problem if you have not, because you are going to go right now! Really, you are- In your mind! Your mind is capable of doing many incredible things, including something called Visualization.

To begin your visualization practice, close your eyes. Really, close your eyes (unless you are the one reading this, of course!) To build a very strong visualization, it is usually helpful to first center yourself and be sure you are giving your brain the very best tools it needs to work with. In this case, that means oxygen, and oxygen means taking some good, deep breaths.

You are going to take some slow, deep breaths now, following along with my instruction: Breathe in very slowly, 1 – 2 – 3 – 4. Now breathe out, very slowly, 1 – 2 – 3 – 4. Excellent. Now again very slowly, 1 – 2 – 3 – 4 and breathe back out very slowly, 1 – 2 – 3 – 4 very nice. Once more, very slowly in 1 – 2 – 3 – 4 and back out very slowly, 1 – 2 – 3 – 4. Great!

Take a moment to review how you feel. Are you comfy and feeling good? Okay, great.

Take another long, deep breath and see if you can notice any smells. What would that particular smell be? Oh, you know what that is. That's the smell of fresh hay! It smells like hay and fall weather. You know that smell, right? It is the crisp, clean smell of autumn as the heat of summer fades away, and the cool breezes of fall move in. The smell reminds you of jumping in freshly raked leaf piles and visiting pumpkin patches.

Notice the weather now. It is not cold outside, and you do not need a heavy winter coat, but your light jacket is just perfect for the cool, crisp breezes that are blowing around you and making the leaves on the trees flutter in the distance and blow off. The sun is still up, but barely. As the seasons change and the days get shorter, you get to witness some truly incredible sunsets as you watch the sun sink into the sky, and this is happening right now.

Look overhead at the sky and the light crimson reds and deep oranges that are streaking above you. It looks as though the sky is aflame with firelight, and you get a pleasant shiver up your spine as you feel the crisp, clean autumn breeze blow around you.

You are standing at the entrance of a hay maze. This is a hay maze that you have never been in, but you are not afraid. You know you are safe where you are, and there are many other kids running in and out of and all around the hay maze. Listen closely. Can you hear the laughter and the voices of the other children? Everyone sounds like they are having so much fun! You want to try it out too.

You see, a group of your friends nearing the entrance of the hay maze, and you follow them in. Kids are scattered all around, running in every direction as the hay maze opens into a large square that is entirely surrounded by hay bales stacked one on top of the other up higher than you can see over, and there are yellow gold string lights that have been hung on the top of every hay bale so as you step into this entrance, you are surrounded by the warm electric glow of the lights attached to the hay.

It feels safe here, and you take in another deep, slow breath, breathing in the scent of the fresh hay bales and the crisp, clear autumn air. You follow your friends as they take off at a quick pace through one of the doorways made by hay bales.

Feel your legs as you follow along. The quick pace means you have to use your leg muscles to keep up, and your legs feel strong and able. You spring along on your strong, capable legs, feeling proud that you can easily keep up with them.

You can still hear the chatter and laughter of all of the children all around you as they make their way through this hay maze. Everyone sounds like they are having a great time, and you are so happy to be here too. You look up and notice the sun is setting even further, and as the sky grows darker, the warm glow of the lights all around you makes you feel cozy and safe.

Suddenly your friends in front of you come to an abrupt stop! You've hit a dead-end in the hay maze, and you all laugh as someone has put a scarecrow with a funny face and crooked hat there. You can feel your lungs and belly go out and in as you all laugh together and turn back around.

Once again, you are quickly following your friends through the hay maze, back in another direction. The trail under your feet has been cleared and laid with loose straw from the hay bales, and you can feel it occasionally slipping below your feet. Notice the blood pumping through your legs as you move quickly through the hay maze. You feel strong and sure of yourself and your abilities.

You put your arms out to lightly graze the hay bales as you run through the maze; can you feel the thin, brittle bits of straw poking out at you? The lights are so comforting as the sky grows darker, and you feel perfectly comfortable and happy as you continue through.

You can see the exit of the hay maze ahead, and you and your friends all exclaim happily that you can see it, and you have made it through! You high five each other, feeling the satisfying smack of your hand against theirs as you triumphantly congratulate each other

Right before you finally exit the hay maze, you turn to look back and look once more in the warm and well-lit hay maze. It was great fun and the perfect fall activity, and you are so proud that you have made it through.

Take a deep, slow breath. Smell the freshly baled hay and the crisp autumn air. Feel the cool breeze as it whips past you and refreshes you as you stand comfortably in your light fall jacket. You can hear the sounds of delight and fun coming from all around you as kids laugh and chatter with one another. You are so happy right now and so confident in your capabilities. You are grateful to have had the opportunity to go through this awesome hay maze!

You do not have to leave the hay maze right now if you don't want to. You can stay and go through again if you like and enjoy the warm, soft glow of the string lights and the crisp and clear autumn air.

You can create anything you want in your mind. Imagine where you want to go and build the picture in your mind. Be sure to imagine how you want it to smell, taste, hear, and feel. The more detailed you can make your mental picture, the more you will enjoy being there.

It is all up to you. Perhaps as you drift off to sleep, you will find yourself able to run through the hay maze in your dreams.

Chapter 3:
Blowing Bubbles

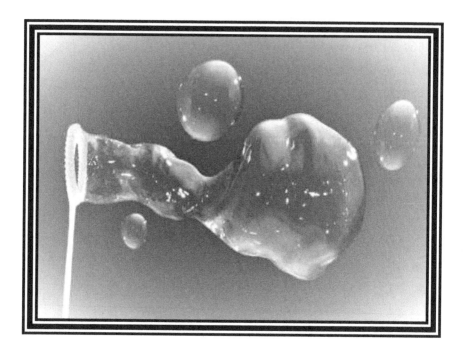

When was the last time you were able to blow bubbles? It is so fun to blow bubbles, isn't it? Well, guess what? You are going to blow some bubbles right now. Really, you are- In your mind! Your mind is capable of doing many incredible things, including something called Visualization.

To begin your visualization practice, close your eyes. Really, close your eyes (unless you are the one reading this, of course!) To build a very strong visualization, it is usually helpful to first center yourself and be sure you are giving your brain the very best tools it needs to work with. In this case, that means oxygen, and oxygen means taking some good, deep breaths.

You are going to take some slow, deep breaths now, following along with my instruction: Breathe in very slowly, 1 – 2 – 3 – 4. Now breathe out, very slowly, 1 – 2 – 3 – 4. Excellent. Now again very slowly, 1 – 2 – 3 – 4 and breathe back out very slowly, 1 – 2 – 3 – 4 very nice. Once more, very slowly in 1 – 2 – 3 – 4 and back out very slowly, 1 – 2 – 3 – 4. Great!

Take a moment to review how you feel. Are you comfy and feeling good? Okay, great.

You are barefoot in the grass. Can you feel the soft and squishy green grass underfoot? Let your toes curl and scrunch up a bit to really feel the grass as it crinkles underfoot.

It is a beautiful spring day, and the weather is absolutely perfect. The sun is shining, but you don't feel hot. It is warm but not warm enough to be uncomfortable, and there is a gentle breeze blowing around you. Take in a long, slow deep breath.

You can smell flowers from the flower bed next to you and the fresh-cut grass that you are standing on, but what is that other smell? It smells very fresh and clean and — soapy? Look around. Oh, there it is! A big tub of bubble solution!

My goodness, look at all of that bubble solution! It's as big as your kitchen sink! Oh my, look at the bubble wands for it. They have long stems, and the ends are as big as dinner plates! What kind of bubbles do you imagine you might be able to make with these?

You notice the label on the side of the bubble solution bin and read, "Everlasting Bubble Solution: Warning, Bubbles May Last Forever."

Hmm, you think. Forever??? You've never seen a bubble that could last forever before!

You pick up the long stem of the bubble wand and dip the end into the tub full of soapy bubble water, noticing the way the bubbles gather on the surface of the bubble solution. You let the wand soak in the bubble solution for just a moment before lifting it all the way out.

As you lift the bubble wand out of the tub with the bubble solution, a huge gust of spring wind blows through where you're standing and blows the first bubble for you.

This bubble is MASSIVE. It is the biggest bubble you have ever seen! This bubble is the size of a Golden Retriever puppy dog! You can't wait to see what comes next, and you dip the wand back into the bubble solution, breathing in the clean, soapy smell.

You lift the wand again, and this time use your arm to gently sway the wand back and forth, back and forth. This time, instead of one giant bubble, several giant bubbles are made! You excitedly dip the wand back into the bubble solution and begin the process again and make several more giant bubbles again.

You squish your toes even further into the soft, green grass underfoot and take a moment to look up and watch your bubbles drift away. But wait! These bubbles are NOT drifting away!

Instead of drifting up and away from you, these bubbles are instead floating down and around you. You are surrounded now by probably 20-30 giant bubbles. You reach one finger out to touch a bubble floating to your left, and you can feel the soft, slippery bubble just fine, but it doesn't pop! Maybe these bubbles really are forever bubbles!

You dip the bubble wand back in the tub of bubble solution and begin making bubbles even quicker now, ready to see how many bubbles you can create with this stuff. The sun warms your skin, and you can smell the fresh-cut grass and the soapy bubble mixture mixing together in the clean spring air.

This time when you look up to inspect your work, you realize you have so many bubbles swirling all around you that you can barely see around them and through them! They are everywhere! Some bubbles are giant, and some are regular-sized, but they are all floating around you, glistening, and sparkling in the sunshine as the breeze floats them around.

You spread your arms out wide and spin yourself around a few times, feeling the slippery soft texture of the bubbles as they glide over your skin, still never popping! You can't believe it! You've never seen bubbles like this before!

You are in a bubble wonderland. The spring day breeze gently swirls the forever bubbles around you, and you give a wide smile. The bubbles feel soft and slippery against your skin, and you think they are almost as soft as the lush green grass under your bare feet. The clean, fresh soapy scent of the bubble solution surrounds you, and you think that you are perfectly content at this moment. You are so grateful to have been able to experience these incredible bubbles!

You do not have to leave this bubble wonderland right now if you don't want to. You can stay and play with your forever bubbles in the gentle spring sunshine if you'd like.

You can create anything you want in your mind. Imagine where you want to go and build the picture in your mind. Be sure to imagine how you want it to smell, taste, hear, and feel. The more detailed you can make your mental picture, the more you will enjoy being there.

It is all up to you. Perhaps as you drift off to sleep, you will find yourself surrounded by slippery soft forever bubbles in your dreams.

Chapter 4:
Bendy and Stretchy Yoga Peace

Have you ever been to a yoga class or done yoga at home? Yoga is all about stretching and bending your body in fun ways so you can be more flexible. Guess what? You are going to do some yoga right now without moving your body at all. Really, you are- In your mind! Your mind is capable of doing many incredible things, including something called Visualization.

To begin your visualization practice, close your eyes. Really, close your eyes (unless you are the one reading this, of course!) To build a very strong visualization, it is usually helpful to first center yourself and be sure you are giving your brain the very best tools it needs to work with. In this case, that means oxygen, and oxygen means taking some good, deep breaths.

You are going to take some slow, deep breaths now, following along with my instruction: Breathe in very slowly, 1 – 2 – 3 – 4. Now breathe out, very slowly, 1 – 2 – 3 – 4. Excellent. Now again very slowly, 1 – 2 – 3 – 4 and breathe back out very slowly, 1 – 2 – 3 – 4 very nice. Once more, very slowly in 1 – 2 – 3 – 4 and back out very slowly, 1 – 2 – 3 – 4. Great!

Take a moment to review how you feel. Are you comfy and feeling good? Okay, great.

See yourself, in your mind, in a large room with huge windows all around. There is nothing in this room except for you and a light green cushioned yoga mat on the floor. Step forward and notice how pleasant and comfortable this room is! There is sunlight streaming through the windows, and you are perfectly comfortable in the loose-fitting and relaxing clothing you are wearing.

Take a deep breath in. You can smell something that is very light and fresh, what is that? Oh, now you see! This room has all the windows open, and there is a beautiful breeze that is coming through the room, and you can smell the fresh, natural scents from outside, like the piney freshness of the pine trees and the sweet floral notes from the rose bushes below the windows.

You can hear something now, too. It is very light but very relaxing. There is music in this room, a calm and relaxing piano melody that makes you feel very peaceful. What a lovely song.

You walk up to the light green yoga mat and sit down on it, stretching your legs out in front of you. You reach forward, stretching yourself down as far as you can until your fingertips touch the tips of your toes. It feels absolutely wonderful to stretch out your legs, arm, and back like this.

You hold this stretch and take in another deep breath. The relaxing notes of the piano music make you feel oh so peaceful as you stretch even further down. You can feel the muscles in your legs, arms, and back release their tension, and you take another deep breath along with the slow, relaxing pace of the music.

Now you release your toes with your fingers and slowly and gently move your body back up and stretch yourself back until you are lying flat on your back. Rest here a moment and feel the gentle breeze coming in the room through the wide-open windows. The fresh floral scent of the rose bushes is wafting through the room, and this makes you smile.

Now you are taking your left leg and stretching it over to the right side of your body. It is a looooong stretch, but it feels so good to make the muscles in your leg and lower back stretch themselves out, and you pause here a moment to take another deep breath.

The gentle wind blowing through the room keeps you perfectly comfortable as you rest in this stretch in your comfortable yoga clothing. You notice how soft your long sleeve shirt and pants are as they slide like silk against your bare skin. The sensation of the silky soft clothing against your skin makes you shiver with pleasure.

Now you stretch your left leg back to where it began and move your right leg now to stretch over and across the left part of your body, stretching now the muscles of your right leg and lower back. Stop here a moment, and let yourself relax into the stretch. You can feel the muscles in your right leg, releasing their tension, and the gentle piano music in the background seems perfectly synced to how you feel: peaceful and relaxed.

Another gentle breeze flits through the wide, open, naturally-lit room, and you can smell the fresh woodsy scent of the pine trees outside the window. You feel perfectly at one with nature and yourself at this moment. It is a wonderfully relaxing feeling to feel as if there is nowhere on earth that you would rather be.

You move your right leg back to where it began and lay still, stretched out on your back. The muscles in your legs, arms, and back have been well-stretched, and your muscles feel very relaxed. You feel peaceful and calm. There is nothing that you would rather be doing at this moment, and you are so happy with how you feel. You are grateful to be here in this calm and peaceful moment. You take another long, deep breath in and enjoy the fresh and clean scent of the room.

You do not have to leave this place of peace right now if you don't want to. You can stay and relax your body and mind here in this wide-open space with the gentle breezes and the peaceful music as long as you want to, and you can come back here anytime you'd like.

You can create anything you want in your mind. Imagine where you want to go and build the picture in your mind. Be sure to imagine how you want it to smell, taste, hear, and feel. The more detailed you can make your mental picture, the more you will enjoy being there.

It is all up to you. Perhaps as you drift off to sleep, you will find yourself back in this place of bendy, stretchy, yoga peace.

Chapter 5:
Swinging into the Sky

Do you like to swing on the swing set? Have you ever swung yourself so high it felt like you could swing right into the sky? Well, guess what? You can swing right now without having to go anywhere near an actual swing set. Really, you can- In your mind! Your mind is capable of doing many incredible things, including something called Visualization.

To begin your visualization practice, close your eyes. Really, close your eyes (unless you are the one reading this, of course!) To build a very strong visualization, it is usually helpful to first center yourself and be sure you are giving your brain the very best tools it needs to work with. In this case, that means oxygen, and oxygen means taking some good, deep breaths.

You are going to take some slow, deep breaths now, following along with my instruction: Breathe in very slowly, 1 - 2 - 3 - 4. Now breathe out, very slowly, 1 - 2 - 3 - 4. Excellent. Now again very slowly, 1 - 2 - 3 - 4 and breathe back out very slowly, 1 - 2 - 3 - 4 very nice. Once more, very slowly in 1 - 2 - 3 - 4 and back out very slowly, 1 - 2 - 3 - 4. Great!

Take a moment to review how you feel. Are you comfy and feeling good? Okay, great.

See yourself in your mind now. You are entering a sunny playground, surrounded by tall, strong trees. Take a deep, long breath in. You notice this playground smells of the fresh mulch underfoot and the grass surrounding the playground that must've been very recently cut. It reminds you of happy summer memories.

You step towards the swing set and notice it is the tallest swing set you've ever seen! Wow! Look at how tall this swing set is and how high this swing must be able to swing! You love to swing and know you want to try it out for yourself right away.

You hop on the giant swing and settle yourself into the comfortable, flexible rubber seat that is warm from being kissed by the summer sun. It is definitely the most comfortable swing you have ever been on, and you shimmy back and forth as you get yourself positioned in the perfect spot.

This swing has the softest rubber grips to hold on to, and you squeeze them in your hands a little. Everything about this swing set is absolutely perfect! You begin to kick your feet back and forth, back and forth, just very gently at first, your hands firmly holding on to the rubber grips.

Because this swing set is so tall, it feels like it takes a lot more work to get yourself going, but you don't mind because it feels really, really good to stretch your legs out in front and bring them back again as you pump back and forth, back and forth. Your whole body is getting into it now, and this swing is really getting going.

A warm summer breeze blows through the playground, and you watch the leaves on the trees flutter back and forth. You can hear the birds singing their summer songs in the trees. You take a deep breath in and think you can smell somewhere in the distance, someone firing up a grill for a barbecue. Wow, what a perfect summer day!

You continue to pump your legs back and forth, back and forth. The blood is really pumping in your legs now, and your muscles feel great from the workout! You notice how high you are swinging now! Wow! You feel as if you are almost as high as the treetops that surround you!

You look up at the bright blue sky overhead. It is a beautiful summer day, and the sun is now behind you, so you are able to see the clear blue sky and the fluffy white clouds in the distance perfectly. You keep swinging, higher, and higher still.

It almost feels as if you could swing right into the sky, you are swinging so high now! The summer breeze is warm and light, and you close your eyes for a moment to enjoy the sensation of the light breeze as it caresses your face. You take in another long, deep breath and can smell the fresh pine mulch below mixing in with the other scents of summer, the fresh-cut grass all around you and the barbeque in the distance.

You are so happy as you continue to swing back and forth, back and forth, listening to the cheerful chirping of the birds in the trees around you. Your legs are strong and keep you swinging higher and higher, and your hands are perfectly comfortable as they continue to firmly hold on to the rubber grips. You love the way the muscles on your legs and arms feel as they warm up. You realize you have a huge, happy grin on your face because you are so happy.

You open your eyes back up and see that you are swinging higher than the treetops all around you! Wow! You are swinging so high now it almost feels as if you are flying through the air, and you think that this must be the way it feels to be a bird soaring on the breeze.

You are flying through the air, back and forth, back and forth, feeling 100% happy and contented. Everything is absolutely perfect at this moment right now, and you let your eyes drink in the deep blue of the sky as you swing so high it feels as if you are swinging out in the wide-open summer sky. You are so grateful to be experiencing this wonderful summer day.

You do not have to stop swinging right now if you don't want to. You can keep swinging into the beautiful clear blue summer sky just as long as you want to, and you can come back here anytime you'd like.

You can create anything you want in your mind. Imagine where you want to go and build the picture in your mind. Be sure to imagine how you want it to smell, taste, hear, and feel. The more detailed you can make your mental picture, the more you will enjoy being there.

It is all up to you. Perhaps as you drift off to sleep, you will find yourself back in your giant swing, swinging yourself into a blue summer sky.

Chapter 6:
Walking the Dog

Have you ever walked a puppy dog before? Walking a dog is fun because not only do you get to hang out with a puppy dog, but you also get to experience some of their worlds and how they see it! Guess what? You are going to get to walk a puppy dog right now without having to step a single foot outside of your front door! Really, you are- In your mind! Your mind is capable of doing many incredible things, including something called Visualization.

To begin your visualization practice, close your eyes. Really, close your eyes (unless you are the one reading this, of course!) To build a very strong visualization, it is usually helpful to first center yourself and be sure you are giving your brain the very best tools it needs to work with. In this case, that means oxygen, and oxygen means taking some good, deep breaths.

You are going to take some slow, deep breaths now, following along with my instruction: Breathe in very slowly, 1 – 2 – 3 – 4. Now breathe out, very slowly, 1 – 2 – 3 – 4. Excellent. Now again very slowly, 1 – 2 – 3 – 4 and breathe back out very slowly, 1 – 2 – 3 – 4 very nice. Once more, very slowly in 1 – 2 – 3 – 4 and back out very slowly, 1 – 2 – 3 – 4. Great!

Take a moment to review how you feel. Are you comfy and feeling good? Okay, great.

In your mind, picture yourself standing on a sidewalk, holding on to a leash. The ground is firm under your feet, and the leash is a smooth, leather leash that feels very comfortable in your hand. Follow along with the leash, and what do you see? The tiniest, fluffiest snow-white puppy dog you've ever seen! This puppy dog looks like a little fluff ball with a poof tail and a tiny face, and she is precious.

You reach down to pet her, and she is the softest, fluffiest little puppy dog you've ever touched, and your hand almost completely disappears into her long fluff ball hair! She is a very sweet puppy dog and seems to be smiling at you as you pet her.

You are excited to be taking this precious little fluff ball puppy dog on a walk, and you straighten yourself back up and look down the sidewalk. There's a nice little winding sidewalk that you will walk her down, and you know it will be a great walk for you both. You set off, following this sweet little ball of fluff with legs in front of you. It makes you giggle as you watch her little fluffy tail bounce and bob all around with every step.

You've only made it a few feet before this fluffy pup pulls you off the paved sidewalk towards some bushes. You laugh a little to yourself and think, "alright, alright, pup, you want to walk over here, that's okay," as you follow her towards the low bushes. You are surprised when you realize there is a hidden path beside the bushes that you never knew existed!

The fluffy pup is pulling you along towards the hidden path, and you are excited now because you realize it might be a shortcut to the park that you never even knew about! You take in a big deep breath and realize you can smell magnolia flowers and birds singing. The park has huge, towering magnolia trees and tons of birds. This really must be a shortcut to the park!

You follow the little snow-white fluff ball in front of you, chuckling to yourself as you watch the fluff of this sweet little pup flounce around with every step. The secret path leads to the park, and the song of the birds is getting louder and louder now. The fluffy pup gives a few excited yips as she pulls you along down the path. Her excitement is making you excited, and now you are just as happy to be heading to the park as she is!

You make your way to the end of the secret path and look around you. The fluffy pup has led you to a section of the park that you've never seen before. It is absolutely beautiful, with a dense grove of magnolia trees surrounding a small wooden bench in a semi-circle. You think it looks like the perfect spot for a quick rest.

You take a seat on the bench, and the little fluffy pup hops up on your lap. The smell of the magnolia trees all around you is heavy and fragrant, almost intoxicatingly sweet. The little pup's fur is still the softest, fluffiest thing you think you've ever felt, and you pet this sweet little pup happily as she seems to smile back up at you. This section of the park is pretty quiet except for the song of the birds in the magnolia trees, and you smile to yourself as you realize that this is a hidden piece of heaven here that you never would have discovered if you hadn't had a fluffy pup to lead the way. You feel perfectly happy and content, and you are so grateful to have had this fun experience.

You do not have to leave this lovely little magnolia scented slice of heaven if you don't want to. You can keep petting this sweet little fluff ball pup just as long as you want to, and you can come back here anytime you'd like.

You can create anything you want in your mind. Imagine where you want to go and build the picture in your mind. Be sure to imagine how you want it to smell, taste, hear, and feel. The more detailed you can make your mental picture, the more you will enjoy being there.

It is all up to you. Perhaps as you drift off to sleep, you will find yourself back in this secluded section of the park, inhaling the intoxicating scent of magnolias while you pet a sweet, snow-white, fluffy pup.

Chapter 7:
Monkey Bar Mischief

Do you like to climb on the monkey bars at the park? The monkey bars can be so much fun because there are so many fun ways to play on them. Guess what? You can play on the monkeys right now. Really, you can- In your mind! Your mind is capable of doing many incredible things, including something called Visualization.

To begin your visualization practice, close your eyes. Really, close your eyes (unless you are the one reading this, of course!) To build a very strong visualization, it is usually helpful to first center yourself and be sure you are giving your brain the very best tools it needs to work with. In this case, that means oxygen, and oxygen means taking some good, deep breaths.

You are going to take some slow, deep breaths now, following along with my instruction: Breathe in very slowly, 1 – 2 – 3 – 4. Now breathe out, very slowly, 1 – 2 – 3 – 4. Excellent. Now again very slowly, 1 – 2 – 3 – 4 and breathe back out very slowly, 1 – 2 – 3 – 4 very nice. Once more, very slowly in 1 – 2 – 3 – 4 and back out very slowly, 1 – 2 – 3 – 4. Great!

Take a moment to review how you feel. Are you comfy and feeling good? Okay, great.

See yourself now, in your mind, standing on a playground. Under your feet is freshly laid pine mulch, and the smell of pine is heavy in the air. It reminds you of playground fun and Christmas. It is a crisp, clear day, one of those perfect days where it's not too hot, and it's not too cold, but rather just right. The sun is in the sky, but you can't feel its heat.

You can hear the songs of the birds in the trees around you, and you think they sound like they are also enjoying this crisp, clear, perfect weather day. You see that you are standing right in front of the monkey bars.

These monkey bars aren't like other monkey bars you've ever seen, though. These monkey bars are rainbow-colored and curved to look like a rainbow! Wow! You can't wait to give these a try.

You walk to the beginning and reach your hand up to grasp the cool metal of the ladder up. It is comfortably cool and refreshing to the touch. You climb up the ladder until you reach the first colorful bar of the monkey bars. It is a bright cherry red, and it is glistening in the sun.

Beyond it continues all the colors of the rainbow: first cherry red, then tangerine orange, followed by sunshine yellow, lime green, sky blue, and then finally pure violet. From where you are standing, the gently curving colorful bars really do look like a rainbow! You can't wait to make your way across it.

You reach out and grasp the cherry red bar, firmly gripping it in your hand, feeling the muscles in your right arm tightening and flexing before your body swings out, and you reach for the tangerine orange bar with your left arm, feeling the muscles in your left arm now tightening and flexing as you grasp this second bar.

You continue swinging down the rainbow to sunshine yellow, lime green, sky blue, and then finally the purest and deepest violet-purple you've ever seen before you make it to the other side. You leap off the end and look back up.

It feels as if you really did scale a rainbow! You are standing beneath the brightly colored rainbow, and you can hear the birds chirping their cheerful song. You put your hands on your hips and feel very proud of yourself.

You wonder what the rainbow would like if it were upside down! Hopping back up on the ladder, you decide you will make your way back up the rainbow, but this time you will swing your legs up so you can hang upside down and see the view from there.

Once again, you make your way down the rainbow, this time in reverse, your hands gripping each cool, smooth bar as you swing from each color to the next: violet to sky blue to lime green and then when you get to sunshine yellow, you decide to swing your legs up and hook them up above.

You flex the muscles in your legs to firmly attach yourself to the monkey bar, and you let the upper part of your body swing down as you release the grip of your hands. Your back and torso stretch out, and you can feel the hair on your head falling downward with gravity, tickling your scalp a little.

You look down the monkey bars and realize that from your new upside-down perspective, it really does look exactly like a rainbow! You are hanging from a rainbow, your body swaying gently back and forth as you hang by your legs.

You decide to swing yourself back up and sit on top of the rainbow now, so you use your abdominal muscles to bring your hands back up within reach of the bars. Once you are gripping the cool colored metal again, you use your arm muscles to push yourself up and through the bars. Once you've sat comfortably on top of the rainbow, you look down at a distance between you and the ground and feel very proud of yourself.

You are strong and confident. You are capable and wise. You can do the things you want to do as long as you stay focused and work hard. You smile because you know that this is all very true, and you lean back and listen again to the cheerful chattering of the birds. You are grateful to be here stretching your body, using your muscles, and enjoying this beautiful day on the rainbow monkey bars.

You do not have to leave your colorful rainbow monkey bars just yet if you don't want to. You can continue to climb around on top of it and test your capabilities as long as you want to, and you can come back here anytime you'd like.

You can create anything you want in your mind. Imagine where you want to go and build the picture in your mind. Be sure to imagine how you want it to smell, taste, hear, and feel. The more detailed you can make your mental picture, the more you will enjoy being there.

It is all up to you. Perhaps as you drift off to sleep, you will find yourself back on top of these rainbow monkey bars, climbing around to the best of your capabilities.

Chapter 8:
Off to Join the Circus

Have you ever been to the circus? You know, with the big red and white striped tent and the performers and the animals and all of the fun? Well, what if I told you that you could actually be in the circus if you wanted to? You can! You really can- In your mind! Your mind is capable of doing many incredible things, including something called Visualization.

To begin your visualization practice, close your eyes. Really, close your eyes (unless you are the one reading this, of course!) To build a very strong visualization, it is usually

helpful to first center yourself and be sure you are giving your brain the very best tools it needs to work with. In this case, that means oxygen, and oxygen means taking some good, deep breaths.

You are going to take some slow, deep breaths now, following along with my instruction: Breathe in very slowly, 1 - 2 - 3 - 4. Now breathe out, very slowly, 1 - 2 - 3 - 4. Excellent. Now again very slowly, 1 - 2 - 3 - 4 and breathe back out very slowly, 1 - 2 - 3 - 4 very nice. Once more, very slowly in 1 - 2 - 3 - 4 and back out very slowly, 1 - 2 - 3 - 4. Great!

Take a moment to review how you feel. Are you comfy and feeling good? Okay, great.

Picture yourself, in your mind's eye, standing outside of a giant red and white striped tent. It's a circus tent! You know it's a circus tent because you can hear the fun and festive circus music pouring through its door and the murmur and excitement of all of the people already inside.

You take a deep breath in and notice that you can smell all kinds of delicious circus foods! Something smells crispy sweet, and you know right away that it is funnel cake, with its powdered sugar sprinkled on top. Yum!

You take a step into the giant red and white tent, and the moment you step your foot into the tent, you realize that you are not just at the circus today, you are IN the circus! You are being ushered along by two beautiful circus performers wearing red glittery sequined outfits with tall purple feather hats. As you get closer to the ring, you look down and notice that you yourself are also covered from head to toe in red glittery sequins!

You and the two circus performers enter the ring, and they assist you in climbing up steps that lead to a giant bicycle! This bicycle is the biggest bicycle you have ever seen. It is as tall as a house! You climb all the way up the steps and are helped on to the giant bicycle's seat. You can feel the breathless anticipation of the audience as they watch you get into position high up in the air.

You take a deep breath in and then out and begin to pedal. You are amazed at how natural it feels to you to be riding this giant bicycle! The other two glittery costumed circus performers are back down below you and are doing flips and twirls all around the bicycle as it slowly makes its way around the performance area. The audience is clapping and cheering for you and the other performers!

Your bicycle comes to a stop, and you look down below you. There is now a giant pool of water below you! The other glittery costumed circus performers have set this giant pool of water below you and are now standing on the other side of the pool, motioning for you to jump. Again, you can feel the breathless anticipation of the audience as you stand yourself up on top of the bicycle seat and look down below at the pool you're meant to jump into.

Taking a deep breath, you gather your courage and leap off of the bicycle seat into the air. You instinctively know how to do a triple tuck fancy flip into the pool, and you land with a giant splash. As you swim your way back up to the top of the water, you can hear thunderous applause from the audience. You were a hit! The other two circus performers help you out of the pool and usher you off to the side where other circus workers are waiting with big fluffy towels for you to dry off with.

You are set up with giant fluffy towels and the biggest, warmest, sweetest smelling funnel cake you have ever seen in your entire life! Now that you have performed, you get to sit on the sidelines and watch the rest of the show while you enjoy a special circus treat. You first take your finger and gingerly feel the side of the funnel cake to see how hot it is. It is not too hot, but the powdered sugar has covered your finger, and you give it a little taste.

Your taste buds go crazy as you taste the light and sweet powdered sugar that you love so well. You pick up the funnel cake and give it a little nibble. It is deep-fried flaky goodness, so perfectly prepared that you don't think you've ever tasted anything so delicious before in your life!

As you sit and enjoy this delicious circus treat, the fun and festive circus atmosphere around you makes you so happy. You are so glad to be a part of this wonderful experience! You feel so thankful to experience this awesome circus that you will never forget.

You do not have to leave the circus just yet if you don't want to. You can stay here at the circus, performing your magnificent circus acts and enjoying your delicious circus treats as long as you want, and you can come back here anytime you'd like.

You can create anything you want in your mind. Imagine where you want to go and build the picture in your mind. Be sure to imagine how you want it to smell, taste, hear, and feel.

The more detailed you can make your mental picture, the more you will enjoy being there.

It is all up to you. Perhaps as you drift off to sleep, you may find yourself back here under the red and white striped circus tent, performing your magnificent feats of daring and sampling delicious circus treats.

Chapter 9:
Bubble Bath Blues

Do you like to take bubble baths? What if you took a bubble bath with so many bubbles that you almost got lost inside? Well, what if I told you that you could do this right now without having to even get wet? You can- In your mind! Your mind is capable of doing many incredible things, including something called Visualization.

To begin your visualization practice, close your eyes. Really, close your eyes (unless you are the one reading this, of course!) To build a very strong visualization, it is usually helpful to first center yourself and be sure you are giving your brain the very best tools it needs to work with. In this case, that means oxygen, and oxygen means taking some good, deep breaths.

You are going to take some slow, deep breaths now, following along with my instruction: Breathe in very slowly, 1 – 2 – 3 – 4. Now breathe out, very slowly, 1 – 2 – 3 – 4. Excellent. Now again very slowly, 1 – 2 – 3 – 4 and breathe back out very slowly, 1 – 2 – 3 – 4 very nice. Once more, very slowly in 1 – 2 – 3 – 4 and back out very slowly, 1 – 2 – 3 – 4. Great!

Take a moment to review how you feel. Are you comfy and feeling good? Okay, great.

See yourself now, sitting in a bathtub. This isn't just any ordinary bathtub. However, there is something very extra special about this bathtub. Not only is this bathtub absolutely humongous, but it is also a sparkling deep blue color. This tub is so large that you have to use a step ladder to climb up and over its edge to get into it.

You climb up and over into this giant bathtub just as it is starting to fill up with warm, toasty bathwater. This warm, toasty bathwater is a little different from the bathwater you are used to, however, because this warm and toasty bathwater is SPARKLING! It is shimmering and shining as it comes out of the water faucet, and once it hits the tub, it creates bubbles.

Relax back into the tub and take a deep breath. The air in here is warm and reminds you of being somewhere tropical, and you close your eyes to take it all in. It smells fresh and clean in here, and this tub already feels so relaxing.

You can feel the warm and toasty bathwater rising around you, and you open your eyes to take a quick peek. You are amazed and can hardly believe what you see! The bubbles in this bubble bath have multiplied so quickly. You are now almost completely surrounded by bubbles!

These bubbles aren't like any other bubbles you have ever seen. These bubbles are sparkling blue bubbles, and you feel like you are surrounded by twinkling blue bubble lights. The sound of the water splashing in the tub from the faucet reminds you of a waterfall, and you imagine yourself in a magical sparkling bubble world. Listen closely. You can almost hear the magical twinkling of these sparkling blue bubbles!

You are now completely surrounded by these sparkling blue bubbles. The water is perfectly warm and comfortable, and you feel like you are being given a soft, sweet, magical hug by these twinkling blue bubble lights all around you. The air in the room is warm and moist, just like you would expect to find on a tropical island.

At this moment, completely surrounded by magically sparkling blue bubbles, listening to the distant sound of rushing water faucet waterfalls, you feel totally and completely at ease. Your muscles are all relaxed and loose, and you let yourself sink even deeper into these twinkling blue bubble lights. You are completely relaxed and comfortable. You feel so thankful that you get to experience this beautiful and peaceful sparkling blue bubble bath.

You do not have to leave your sparkling blue bubble bath just yet if you don't want to. You can soak in this warm and toasty water with the twinkling blue bubble lights as long as you want to, and you can come back here anytime you'd like.

You can create anything you want in your mind. Imagine where you want to go and build the picture in your mind. Be sure to imagine how you want it to smell, taste, hear, and feel. The more detailed you can make your mental picture, the more you will enjoy being there.

It is all up to you. Perhaps as you drift off to sleep, you will find yourself back in this magically twinkling and sparkling bubble bath world.

Chapter 10:
Freedom to Fly

Have you ever wondered what it would be like to fly? Some people like to imagine what it would be like to be a bird or what it might be like to go skydiving and feel the air rushing all around you as you soar through the sky. Well, what if I told you that you could actually see for yourself what it was like to fly if you wanted to? You can! You really can- In your mind! Your mind is capable of doing many incredible things, including something called Visualization.

To begin your visualization practice, close your eyes. Really, close your eyes (unless you are the one reading this, of course!) To build a very strong visualization, it is usually helpful to first center yourself and be sure you are giving your brain the very best tools it needs to work with. In this case, that means oxygen, and oxygen means taking some good, deep breaths.

You are going to take some slow, deep breaths now, following along with my instruction: Breathe in very slowly, 1 – 2 – 3 – 4. Now breathe out, very slowly, 1 – 2 – 3 – 4. Excellent. Now again very slowly, 1 – 2 – 3 – 4 and breathe back out very slowly, 1 – 2 – 3 – 4 very nice. Once more, very slowly in 1 – 2 – 3 – 4 and back out very slowly, 1 – 2 – 3 – 4. Great!

Take a moment to review how you feel. Are you comfy and feeling good? Okay, great.

Picture yourself now, in your mind's eye, standing at the top of a mountain peak. You are surrounded by other mountain peaks and white, fluffy clouds. The air is cool and fresh, and you take a deep breath. You can feel your feet firmly planted on the grassy top of this mountain, but you feel much lighter on your feet than you've ever felt before in your life.

You feel so light, you decide to just jump up in the air a little bit, and you are amazed when your little jump actually becomes more like a boomerang leap, and you go shooting up into the air! Wow! You feel yourself drifting slowly back down to the mountain top, and you wonder what this all is in amazement.

As your feet gently come back to the grass beneath you, you decide to give it another little test. This time, you decide you will give yourself a bit of a running start and see how high you can leap. You take a few steps back and then begin to run, your leg muscles quickly pumping below you. Amazingly, you feel your feet rise up from the mountain top, and you stretch your arms out above your head.

It seems like as you raise your arms, you go up higher and higher! You are flying upwards towards the bright blue sky above you when you bring your arms back down to your sides, and immediately your body begins gently drifting back down towards the mountain top. Wow! You can control if you go up or down or not!

You bring your arms back up over your head to get a little height and then decide to lean your body over in the direction out beyond the mountain top and whoosh! You take off out over the cliff, and for a brief moment, you wonder if you really have this flying thing figured out, but then you seem to hit your stride, and you are soaring through the air across the valley below, and it all feels like second nature to you somehow!

The cool mountain air washes over you as you soar through the sky, and you feel refreshed and content. You are experiencing total freedom, and it feels incredible. You bring your arms down just a bit to fly lower towards the lush green valley below. You can see the thick groves of green bushes and wildflowers below you, and you don't know if you've ever seen anything so beautiful in your entire life.

You decide to head back up the mountain, so you raise your arms back up and over your head. This makes you shoot up to the top of the mountain, and as you near the peak, you decide to land for a moment. Bringing your arms back down to your side, you gently land and are finally back on the mountain peak.

Your feet firmly planted back on the ground, you find yourself with a huge grin on your face. Being able to fly is absolutely amazing, and you feel so open and free as you soar through the sky. You are so incredibly happy, and you think to yourself that even if you never fly again, you will never forget this feeling in your whole entire life. You are so grateful that you have been able to experience this!

You do not have to leave this beautiful mountain peak in the clouds just yet if you don't want to. You can stay up here and take as many flights as you want to for as long as you want to, and you can come back here anytime you'd like.

You can create anything you want in your mind. Imagine where you want to go and build the picture in your mind. Be sure to imagine how you want it to smell, taste, hear, and feel. The more detailed you can make your mental picture, the more you will enjoy being there.

It is all up to you. Perhaps as you drift off to sleep, you will find yourself back on this mountain top in the clouds, ready to soar off on another flying adventure.

Chapter 11:
Magic at the Magic Show

Have you ever been to a magic show? Better yet, have you ever been a part of a magic show? What if I told you that you could actually be a part of a magic show right this moment if you wanted to? You can! You really can- In your mind! Your mind is capable of doing many incredible things, including something called Visualization.

To begin your visualization practice, close your eyes. Really, close your eyes (unless you are the one reading this, of course!) To build a very strong visualization, it is usually helpful to first center yourself and be sure you are giving your brain the very best tools it needs to work with. In this case, that means oxygen, and oxygen means taking some good, deep breaths.

You are going to take some slow, deep breaths now, following along with my instruction: Breathe in very slowly, 1 - 2 - 3 - 4. Now breathe out, very slowly, 1 - 2 - 3 - 4. Excellent. Now again very slowly, 1 - 2 - 3 - 4 and breathe back out very slowly, 1 - 2 - 3 - 4 very nice. Once more, very slowly in 1 - 2 - 3 - 4 and back out very slowly, 1 - 2 - 3 - 4. Great!

Take a moment to review how you feel. Are you comfy and feeling good? Okay, great.

Imagine yourself, in your mind's eye, in an audience in a huge, dimly lit auditorium. Looking around you, you can see this place is packed! Up on stage, there is a spotlight and one person standing front and center with a small table in front of him and a single chair next to the table. Look closer, who is that person?

He is tall with dark hair, and he appears to have some sort of a cape and top hat on. He takes the top hat off and looks to be rummaging around within the hat… how deep is that thing anyway! It looks like his whole entire arm is in his hat! And what on earth is he pulling out of it now? Oh, my goodness, look! It's a fluffy white bunny rabbit!

You and the rest of the audience applaud this amazing trick. How cool! This person is a magician, and you are at a magic show. Wow! Take a moment and take a long, deep breath in. You can smell the old auditorium with its worn leather seats and its maple wood stage. Just then, you hear the magician asking the crowd for a volunteer to come up on stage.

You have never been on stage as a magician's volunteer before, and you have to think a moment; what do you think the magician will need the volunteer to do? Will you be nervous? You realize your arm is already going up as you are thinking through it all because your excitement wins out over your worry every time. Now the magician is looking directly at you and motioning for you to come up! Wow! This is incredible!

You get up and out of your seat and make y our way out of your row. The other audience members are congratulating you on being picked. Everyone is very excited to see what will happen next, including you! You can feel the excitement in the air as you make your way up the steps on to the stage.

The magician welcomes you up on the stage and asks you to sit on the chair beside the table. You take a seat, and he immediately hands you the fluffy white bunny that he had just pulled from his hat. He tells you his bunny's name is Fluffy and that it is your job to keep Fluffy comfortable during this next trick, so you will need to pet Fluffy and keep her calm.

The magician reaches back into his top hat and begins rummaging around again. Oh, my goodness, seriously. How deep is that thing? He pulls out a large blueish black velvet drape and brings it over to where you are sitting with Fluffy. You are petting Fluffy and smiling. Fluffy's fur is so soft, and the lights of the stage are so warm as you sit petting this fluffy white bunny rabbit.

The magician drapes the bluish-black velvet drape over you and Fluffy and reminds you that you must keep petting Fluffy and keep her comfortable during this next trick. You are feeling so excited now to see what this trick will be! The magician takes his wand and waves it around both you and Fluffy a few times and says some silly magic words and voila!

The magician pulls the drape off of you and Fluffy bunny in one swift motion, revealing that instead of Fluffy Bunny in your lap, you are now holding and petting a stuffed bunny rabbit toy! You and the audience gasp together.

Your mouth drops open in disbelief, how did this happen? What on earth is going on? Where is the little fluffy bunny rabbit you had been petting? The magician motions to your head, and you reach up to feel that you are now wearing the magician's tall top hat on your very own head. You pull the top hat off and guess what's underneath? Fluffy Bunny Rabbit!!!!

The audience erupts into applause as the magician scoops the fluffy bunny rabbit up off of your head and returns him to the table with the tall top hat. The magician motions for you to stand up and take a bow as he thanks you for your assistance. You are still in absolute disbelief on how on earth he did this trick when he tells you that you can keep stuffed bunny rabbit toy as a souvenir.

You make your way back off the stage and to your seat, with the other audience members clapping for you and the magician. Once you've sat back down on the cool leather seat, you realize you are grinning ear to ear. You are so happy to be a part of this magic show, and you know that it has been an experience that you will never forget. Plus, you have this soft fluffy bunny rabbit toy to always help you remember it by. You feel so thankful that you have had this incredibly cool magic show experience!

You do not have to leave this magic show just yet if you don't want to. You can stay here in the audience, watching these amazing magic tricks as long as you want, and you can come back here anytime you'd like.

You can create anything you want in your mind. Imagine where you want to go and build the picture in your mind. Be sure to imagine how you want it to smell, taste, hear, and feel. The more detailed you can make your mental picture, the more you will enjoy being there.

It is all up to you. Perhaps as you drift off to sleep, you may find yourself back here in the auditorium with the maple wood stage, waiting for the magician to ask for another volunteer from the audience.

Chapter 12:
Skydiving Adventure

Are you an adventurous person? Have you ever considered going skydiving? It's something that only the bravest and most fearless people do. What if I told you that you could actually go skydiving right this moment if you wanted to and you wouldn't need to move a single muscle? You can! You really can- In your mind! Your mind is capable of doing many incredible things, including something called Visualization.

To begin your visualization practice, close your eyes. Really, close your eyes (unless you are the one reading this, of course!) To build a very strong visualization, it is usually helpful to first center yourself and be sure you are giving your brain the very best tools it needs to work with. In this case, that means oxygen, and oxygen means taking some good, deep breaths.

You are going to take some slow, deep breaths now, following along with my instruction: Breathe in very slowly, 1 - 2 - 3 - 4. Now breathe out, very slowly, 1 - 2 - 3 - 4. Excellent. Now again very slowly, 1 - 2 - 3 - 4 and breathe back out very slowly, 1 - 2 - 3 - 4 very nice. Once more, very slowly in 1 - 2 - 3 - 4 and back out very slowly, 1 - 2 - 3 - 4. Great!

Take a moment to review how you feel. Are you comfy and feeling good? Okay, great.

Picture yourself, in your mind, in the back of a small plane. It is loud: very, very, loud as you can hear the plane engine through the open side door. That's right! The side of the plane is totally open! You look to your side and see what the other person with you is dressed in head to toe safety gear, including goggles and a very sturdy looking harness. You look down and see you are also decked out in all this same safety gear.

The other person with you is the skydiving instructor, and he is checking through his gear and is now attaching his gear to yours. He gives you the thumbs up, and you find yourself returning the thumbs up, although you're not quite sure if you're ready for this or not, but…

Too late! The skydiving instructor scoots you both closer to the open side of the plane, and you wonder for a moment if you're actually brave enough to do this when he kicks off of the side and you find that the floor of the plane is no longer beneath you because you are now soaring through the open air!

You are falling so quickly that the force of the air rushing up on you is making your lips shake and quake as you try to smile. You are almost in shock but in a great kind of shock. You have never felt these kinds of sensations before all at once.

You are still a little nervous, a little afraid, but you know that the skydiving instructor is right with you and very knowledgeable. You know there is nothing to worry about because this person is going to make sure that the cord is pulled at just the right time.

For the moment, however, you are free-falling! The air is rushing so quickly around you that you really can't get your lips to make a complete smile because the air is displacing them so quickly! You then feel the instructor moving his hand behind you, and you can feel the cord being pulled a nanosecond before you are suddenly feeling like you are being jerked upwards as the parachute above you is opened.

Once the parachute is open, and your descent towards the earth has slowed down, you are able to really look around you and take everything in. You are floating through the clouds, and you can hear laughter and joyous exclamations coming from someone, and it takes you almost a full minute before you realize that it is you making those elated and happy sounds!

The earth down below looks both humongous and oh so tiny all at the same time. It is so far away from where you are, and everything below seems to be far, far, out of your reach. You then take in a long, deep breath and notice how different the air smells all this distance above the earth. It smells cleaner and fresher than you have ever smelled it before. It feels like the freshest air you've ever breathed in!

Your body feels weightless as it floats on the air like it would out on the waves at sea. You are swimming in the wide-open oxygen of the atmosphere, and you feel so free as you float on the air currents. The clouds you are passing through are like wisps of soft white cotton candy, and you think that they are so much more beautiful from this viewpoint than you've ever seen them from down below.

Way up high above the earth, you realize that this life is so wonderful and so amazing. You will never forget this beautiful vantage point of seeing the earth looking both so big and so small. No matter what, you will remember what it felt like to float through the air and look down at the beautiful earth below. You are grateful for this awesome experience.

You do not have to stop skydiving just yet if you don't want to. You can continue to float through the air on a breeze as long as you want, and you can come back here anytime you'd like.

You can create anything you want in your mind. Imagine where you want to go and build the picture in your mind. Be sure to imagine how you want it to smell, taste, hear, and feel.

The more detailed you can make your mental picture, the more you will enjoy being there.

It is all up to you. Perhaps as you drift off to sleep, you may find yourself back up in the clouds, swimming through the air as you would on the waves out at sea.

Chapter 13:
Jumping in the Leaves

Do you like to jump in the leaf piles during the fall? The crisp and crunchy autumn leaves that have fallen to the ground always make the coolest noises when you jump into a pile of them! What if I told you that you could jump in a leaf pile right now, without having to leave this spot. You really can-In your mind! Your mind is capable of doing many incredible things, including something called Visualization.

To begin your visualization practice, close your eyes. Really, close your eyes (unless you are the one reading this, of course!) To build a very strong visualization, it is usually helpful to first center yourself and be sure you are giving your brain the very best tools it needs to work with. In this case, that means oxygen, and oxygen means taking some good, deep breaths.

You are going to take some slow, deep breaths now, following along with my instruction: Breathe in very slowly, 1 - 2 - 3 - 4. Now breathe out, very slowly, 1 - 2 - 3 - 4. Excellent. Now again very slowly, 1 - 2 - 3 - 4 and breathe back out very slowly, 1 - 2 - 3 - 4 very nice. Once more, very slowly in 1 - 2 - 3 - 4 and back out very slowly, 1 - 2 - 3 - 4. Great!

Take a moment to review how you feel. Are you comfy and feeling good? Okay, great.

Picture yourself, in your mind's eye, standing outside on a crisp, cool autumn day. Take a moment and breathe in deep and slow. What do you smell? Is that the smell of someone having a bonfire somewhere in the distance? I think so! Someone must be having a lovely fall bonfire, the perfect thing to do on a crisp, cool autumn day.

You look down at your feet where you stand and see that directly in front of you is a massive leaf pile. This is not an ordinary-sized leaf pile. This leaf pile is gigantic! It is as tall as you are and as wide as a car. You feel your body buzzing with excitement because you see this beautifully humongous leaf pile, and you know what you have to do... You have to jump in it!

You take a couple of steps back and then charge as fast as you can towards the pile, leaping up in the air at the last moment and coming down with a whoosh into the middle. As you land in the crisp fallen leaves, you hear a satisfying crunch of the autumn leaves as your body presses them down to the ground. Leaves fly up in the air all around you, and it is like being surrounded by and rained down on with natural autumn confetti. The leaves vary from golden yellow to deep crimsons, and you use your hands to dig deeper down into them.

You decide to flop back into this magnificent leaf pile, and you start making not snow angels, but leaf angels! The fallen autumn leaves make light crunching noises as they are moved back and forth with the movement of your arms and legs. You are giggling to yourself because the crunching noises and the squishy feeling of the leaves against your body are just so satisfying. You take a moment to close your ears and take another long, deep breath in.

You can smell the bonfire in the distance, but you can also smell the autumn scents of the leaves all around you. It smells like the seasons changing, and you are so happy that you were able to do this. There's only one time of year that you can make a humongous autumn leaf pile for jumping in, and you are in it right now. You smile and think to yourself that you will never miss an opportunity to play in leaf piles ever in your entire life. You are so grateful for this beautiful fall day.

You do not have to get up out of your autumn leaf pile just yet if you don't want to. You can spend as long as you want in your leaf pile, and you can come back here anytime you'd like.

You can create anything you want in your mind. Imagine where you want to go and build the picture in your mind. Be sure to imagine how you want it to smell, taste, hear, and feel. The more detailed you can make your mental picture, the more you will enjoy being there.

It is all up to you. Perhaps as you drift off to sleep, you may find yourself back in this colorful leaf pile made up of nature's autumn confetti, making leaf angels and enjoying the crunch of the fallen leaves.

Chapter 14:
Chef for a Day

Do you ever get a chance to cook? What if you could work in an actual huge chef's kitchen and create absolutely anything your heart desires? Wouldn't that be so cool? Well, you can- In your mind! Your mind is capable of doing many incredible things, including something called Visualization.

To begin your visualization practice, close your eyes. Really, close your eyes (unless you are the one reading this, of course!) To build a very strong visualization, it is usually helpful to first center yourself and be sure you are giving your brain the very best tools it needs to work with. In this case,

that means oxygen, and oxygen means taking some good, deep breaths.

You are going to take some slow, deep breaths now, following along with my instruction: Breathe in very slowly, 1 - 2 - 3 - 4. Now breathe out, very slowly, 1 - 2 - 3 - 4. Excellent. Now again very slowly, 1 - 2 - 3 - 4 and breathe back out very slowly, 1 - 2 - 3 - 4 very nice. Once more, very slowly in 1 - 2 - 3 - 4 and back out very slowly, 1 - 2 - 3 - 4. Great!

Take a moment to review how you feel. Are you comfy and feeling good? Okay, great.

Picture yourself, in your mind's eye, standing in a giant kitchen. This is the fanciest kitchen you've ever seen! There is a long, shiny stainless-steel counter in front of you, and you look down at yourself to see you are wearing a long, white chef's apron. You look up and down the counter and see that there are all kinds of different chef's tools like mixing bowls, spoons, spatulas, baking pans.

You take a step closer to the counter to inspect what else is there. It looks as if there is an area that is chock-full of ingredients. Hmm, wonder what might be there? You realize that the ingredients are actually just chocolate candy bars. That's right, chocolate candy bars! It literally looks like just about every chocolate candy bar ever made to man are neatly stacked here next to these shiny pots and pans.

Hmm, what are you supposed to do with these? You are wearing a chef's apron. You want to cook, not just eat candy bars. Wait a moment! You have just had a fantastic idea. You know that chocolate candy bars are delicious when you eat them one at a time, but what if you could mix them all together and eat them all at one time! That's it!

You begin picking up each individually wrapped chocolate candy bar and unwrap each bar, putting the chocolate into a pot that is on the stove. Each time you add a new chocolate bar, you give the pot a little stir and watch as the chocolate melts down from a hard solid to a melty, gooey liquid. You watch as the chocolate candy bar wrappers pile up beside the pot, and the melty, gooey chocolate gets higher and higher in the pan. Pretty soon, you have finished, and you take in a long, deep breath.

Oh, my goodness, the smell is downright heavenly! It is the sweetest, richest, most delectable chocolate scent you have ever smelled! You can smell hints of coconut, bits of peanut butter, a little caramel, but most of all. You can smell the rich and delicious chocolate of each of the chocolate candy bars that are being swirled and melted together. You stir the contents of the pan and think that it is the prettiest chocolate concoction you have ever seen!

You take the pot and pour the melted sweetness into a pan and let it spread out. Once you've transferred your melty goodness into the pan, you take it over to the nearby freezer and pop it in to set up. You are so excited about your new creation and can't wait to try it!

You pause a moment and think that because you are the chef, the sky really is the limit here. You have basically created what you are pretty sure will be the best and most delicious chocolate candy bar that the world has ever seen, but you know what would make it even more spectacular? Ice cream!

While the chocolate candy bar sets up in the final moments, you scoop yourself out some vanilla ice cream into a bowl. Once you have your ice cream ready, you pull your mega huge combination of every different kind of chocolate candy bar, new chocolate candy bar out of the freezer. You take a huge chunk from one side and admire your handiwork. You can see little bits and pieces of the original chocolate candy bar inside, but it is an entirely new creation!

You can barely contain your excitement as you take your new creation and dip it into the ice cream, using it as an edible spoon. You bite into it, the rich and dynamic chocolate flavors melding into the vanilla ice cream perfectly, and you can't help but lean back against the counter.

You have created the finest chocolate candy mega bar that you could ever imagine. You didn't even know that a chocolate candy bar could be so delightfully exciting! You are so happy that you were able to be a chef for a day! You feel thankful that you have been able to do this.

You do not have to take off your chef's apron just yet if you don't want to. You can spend as long as you want here and you can come back here anytime you'd like.

You can create anything you want in your mind. Imagine where you want to go and build the picture in your mind. Be sure to imagine how you want it to smell, taste, hear, and feel. The more detailed you can make your mental picture, the more you will enjoy being there.

It is all up to you. Perhaps as you drift off to sleep, you may find yourself back in this amazing chef's kitchen and able to create a new chocolatey delicious creation for yourself!

Chapter 15:
Teacher for a Day

Have you ever wondered what it might be like to be a teacher? What would it be like if you went to school, but instead of having to sit in your seat and follow your teacher's lesson plan, what if you were instead able to design your very own? Well, today you can! You can- In your mind! Your mind is capable of doing many incredible things, including something called Visualization.

To begin your visualization practice, close your eyes. Really, close your eyes (unless you are the one reading this, of course!) To build a very strong visualization, it is usually helpful to first center yourself and be sure you are giving your brain the very best tools it needs to work with. In this case, that means oxygen, and oxygen means taking some good, deep breaths.

You are going to take some slow, deep breaths now, following along with my instruction: Breathe in very slowly, 1 – 2 – 3 – 4. Now breathe out, very slowly, 1 – 2 – 3 – 4. Excellent. Now again very slowly, 1 – 2 – 3 – 4 and breathe back out very slowly, 1 – 2 – 3 – 4 very nice. Once more, very slowly in 1 – 2 – 3 – 4 and back out very slowly, 1 – 2 – 3 – 4. Great!

Take a moment to review how you feel. Are you comfy and feeling good? Okay, great.

Imagine this, in your mind's eye: You step into your classroom and begin to make your way over to your regular desk when your teacher suddenly rushes up to you and tells you that today, you will be the one leading the class. What's more, you are told that you get to do whatever you want as the teacher of the class!

Your teacher leaves, and you slowly walk to the front of the classroom, your head spinning as you try and figure out what you will do as a teacher. You take a long, deep breath in, smelling the chalk and dusty erasers from the chalkboard behind you. The fluorescent lights overhead are very bright as the light bounces off of the bright white tiled floor.

Your classmates are still wandering in and making their way to their seats, and someone points up at you, confused as to why you are at the front of the classroom. You decide that you will make today the absolute best day that anyone has ever had in this classroom before!

Everyone is sitting in their seats now, and you look around the room. How many students are there? Let's see, it looks like four rows with five students in each row, so twenty including yourself. Okay. What can you figure out for twenty students to do that would be fun in a classroom?

Suddenly, you realize that you know what would be a ton of fun to do in a classroom! You announce to everyone that today, you get to be the teacher. You tell them all that instead of doing a regular day of school, you all will be doing a super special extraordinary day of school because everyone will be making a special school fort built out of desks!

You tell your classmates that each row gets to construct their own special fort. They can use any materials from the classroom they can find. Your classmates cheer and jump up to begin their fort building.

You go to your row, and you start brainstorming. You all decide that you can easily use the desks to make the walls of your fort, but for the ceiling, you would need to do something extra special. You begin looking around for materials. Hmm, what would work to make your fort extra special?

Just then, you have a great idea! You remember that your teacher has a giant multicolored parachute that she pulls out on certain days for you all to play with. That would be absolutely perfect! What's more, it's big enough that it can cover the entire classroom. You know exactly what that means: Mega Fort!

You tell the rest of the class your idea and everyone cheers! Your classmates begin working together quickly to build the outer walls of the fort with the desks, and you and another classmate go to pull the multicolored parachute out of the desk drawer the teacher keeps it in.

The parachute is silky smooth, and as you and your classmate unroll it, everyone oohs and ahhs because they know it will be absolutely perfect! You stretch it out over the top of the desks, and once it is in place, everyone scrambles to get underneath.

Inside the fabulous school fort, space has been transformed into a colorful wonderland. The bright fluorescent lights overhead come through the colorful fabric of the parachute and make the inside look like a rainbow. All of the students clap and cheer with delight because it is the coolest fort that anyone has ever seen! You are having the best day at school because you are the teacher of the day. You are so grateful that you and all your classmates get to have this super cool experience!

You do not have to leave your amazing, colorful school fort just yet if you don't want to. You can spend as long as you want here and you can come back here anytime you'd like.

You can create anything you want in your mind. Imagine where you want to go and build the picture in your mind. Be sure to imagine how you want it to smell, taste, hear, and feel. The more detailed you can make your mental picture, the more you will enjoy being there.

It is all up to you. Perhaps as you drift off to sleep, you may find yourself back under your rainbow school fort with your classmates, happy and proud to be the teacher for the day.

Chapter 16:
Sandcastle Creations

Do you like to build sandcastles on the beach? It's always so fun to scoop and mold the damp and grainy sand into different shapes, isn't it? What if I told you that you could build a sandcastle creation right now? Seriously. You can- In your mind! Your mind is capable of doing many incredible things, including something called Visualization.

To begin your visualization practice, close your eyes. Really, close your eyes (unless you are the one reading this, of course!) To build a very strong visualization, it is usually

helpful to first center yourself and be sure you are giving your brain the very best tools it needs to work with. In this case, that means oxygen, and oxygen means taking some good, deep breaths.

You are going to take some slow, deep breaths now, following along with my instruction: Breathe in very slowly, 1 - 2 - 3 - 4. Now breathe out, very slowly, 1 - 2 - 3 - 4. Excellent. Now again very slowly, 1 - 2 - 3 - 4 and breathe back out very slowly, 1 - 2 - 3 - 4 very nice. Once more, very slowly in 1 - 2 - 3 - 4 and back out very slowly, 1 - 2 - 3 - 4. Great!

Take a moment to review how you feel. Are you comfy and feeling good? Okay, great.

Picture yourself now, in your mind's eye, at the edge of the sea. You can see the waves gently rolling into the seashore, bringing the foamy white waters closer to you. You feel the cool, refreshing wave of water splashing over your toes, and you curl your toes up a bit into the cool, wet sand. It feels marvelous!

You take a long, deep breath in and smell the salty sea air. You notice how moist and cool the air is here beside the sea. You can feel the sun warming your skin from above, and you feel perfectly comfortable here on the beach.

You take a few steps away from the water's edge and go over to where you have chosen the perfect sandcastle creation building spot! You kneel yourself down in the sand and begin by digging your hands into the cool, moist sand to gather it all together into a giant mound. The giant mound will be your sandcastle!

Your hands are warm from the sun, so immersing them in the cool, moist sand feels wonderful. The grains of sand rubbing against the skin on your hands almost feel like you are getting a hand massage. You use your fingers like little rakes and let the sand pass through them and feel the cool grainy sand squish in between each finger.

Once you've raked all of your sand into a giant mound, you sit back on your knees and determine where your first floor will be. You take one of the shells out of a pile of beautiful white and pink seashells beside you and use that you smooth out the first floor of your sandcastle creation. The seashell is smooth and cool to the touch, and it carves out your first floor beautifully. You decide this castle will have two main floors and a large turret, so you begin to carve out the second floor above the first, again using the smooth seashell to shape the second floor.

You now have a sandcastle creation that has two solid floors or stories, and now you just have to build the turret. You use both of your hands to mold the remaining sand on the top into a wide turret. Now you can begin the fun part!

You turn your attention to the many shiny seashells beside you and begin picking through them, looking for the perfect seashells to use to decorate your sandcastle creation. There a few smaller seashells that are smaller in size but are shiny and beautiful. You pick them up and notice how well they reflect the sunlight off of them. You know these are the ones you will use for the windows. You begin carefully placing each small, smooth, rounded, reflective sea shell as windows on the turret and the two floors of your sandcastle creation.

Once you have completed the windows, you know it is time to find the seashell that will be placed at the very top of the turret. You immediately settle on the largest and most stunning seashell in the pile. It is almost a tie-dye sort of pattern of glossy coral pink and pearlescent white. It is perfectly formed, and when you place it carefully on the top of the turret, it completes your magnificent sandcastle creation!

You carefully get up and take a few steps back to admire your creation. It is beautiful! You are so proud of yourself and all of the hard work you have done. You breathe in the salty sea air and think to yourself that you are having a lovely time here on the seashore. You are so thankful to be spending time on this wonderful seashore, creating cool sandcastle creations.

You do not have to leave your magnificent sandcastle creation just yet if you don't want to. You can spend as long as you want here and you can come back here anytime you'd like.

You can create anything you want in your mind. Imagine where you want to go and build the picture in your mind. Be sure to imagine how you want it to smell, taste, hear, and feel. The more detailed you can make your mental picture, the more you will enjoy being there.

It is all up to you. Perhaps as you drift off to sleep, you may find yourself back here by the salty sea, ready to build another fantastic sandcastle creation.

Chapter 17:
Meet a Mermaid

Do you think mermaids are real? Maybe they are, and maybe they aren't. No one really knows for sure, do they? Well, what if I told you that you could meet one right at this very moment? You really can- In your mind! Your mind is capable of doing many incredible things, including something called Visualization.

To begin your visualization practice, close your eyes. Really, close your eyes (unless you are the one reading this, of course!) To build a very strong visualization, it is usually helpful to first center yourself and be sure you are giving your brain the very best tools it needs to work with. In this case, that means oxygen, and oxygen means taking some good, deep breaths.

You are going to take some slow, deep breaths now, following along with my instruction: Breathe in very slowly, 1 – 2 – 3 – 4. Now breathe out, very slowly, 1 – 2 – 3 – 4. Excellent. Now again very slowly, 1 – 2 – 3 – 4 and breathe back out very slowly, 1 – 2 – 3 – 4 very nice. Once more, very slowly in 1 – 2 – 3 – 4 and back out very slowly, 1 – 2 – 3 – 4. Great!

Take a moment to review how you feel. Are you comfy and feeling good? Okay, great.

Picture yourself, in your mind's eye, standing on a seashore. You are dressed in your swimsuit, and you have your goggles and snorkels on. You want to explore the sea, and you have been looking forward to this adventure for a long time.

The sun is warm overhead, and the salty sea makes the air smell fresh and clean. You take a step forward towards the water and feel the cool seawater rush over your ankles and up to your feet. It is so perfectly refreshing on this hot summer's day!

Without another moment wasted, you take a few steps forward before you go ahead and leap out and into the sea. The water welcomes you in, and your entire body feels so comfortable and light in the salty seawater. You take a few strong strokes out towards the sea before you let yourself rest, floating face down in the water and looking around the sea bed with your goggles on.

It takes a moment for your eyes to adjust to the underwater scene. There is tall seagrass everywhere around you: long, thin, jade-green seagrasses that are flowing back and forth with each current. The languid back and forth underwater motion have a hypnotizing effect, and you feel your body relaxing in a way that you haven't felt it relax in a very long time.

You want to see sea creatures and wildlife you've never seen in person before, so you try to look around and are a little surprised that there don't seem to be many fish or sea creatures swimming around where you are. Just when you are starting to think that you should maybe swim out further, you are startled when you see two eyes peering out at you through the jade-green seagrass! It almost looks like a woman! Oh, my goodness, it is a woman, isn't it?

Her hair is long and golden brown, and it shimmers with the sunshine streaming through the water. She peeks her head out a little more and gives a tentative wave your way. You are amazed! How is she holding her breath so well? You have a snorkel on, and that's how you are staying down here, but how is she doing it? You wave back, and she shyly comes out from behind the jade-green seagrasses, swimming flawlessly.

Your eyes wide as saucers now, you notice that this is not just any woman here beneath the sea... This is a mermaid! Her long, emerald-green tail has a strong fin that she uses to effortlessly glide through the water. She is swimming circles around you now, almost performing for you! She can tell that you are surprised and amazed by what you see, and she seems to want to show you what she can do. She flips and twirls with ease in the water, and you watch in disbelief as she flashes friendly smiles at you.

You need to adjust your snorkel so you make your way back up to the surface of the water and adjust it so you can dive back down, hurrying as quickly as you can. You dive back under the water and look back and forth. Your eyes slowly adjust back to the underwater world, and you look all around you, trying to find your new mermaid friend.

You don't see her anywhere! You swim towards the long, thin seagrass and look through, but still can't find her anywhere. Where did she go, you wonder? You relax your body again in the water and decide to sit and enjoy the weightlessness of the sea as you wait for your mermaid friend to show back up again.

You can't believe you got to meet a mermaid! You are so pleased that you got to meet a mermaid. You hope she shows up again! It feels like an incredibly magical underwater dream. You feel so grateful that you have had this crazy and unique underwater experience.

You do not have to leave your underwater world just yet if you don't want to. You can spend as long as you want here and you can come back here anytime you'd like.

You can create anything you want in your mind. Imagine where you want to go and build the picture in your mind. Be sure to imagine how you want it to smell, taste, hear, and feel. The more detailed you can make your mental picture, the more you will enjoy being there.

It is all up to you. Perhaps as you drift off to sleep, you may find yourself back under the sea with the seagrasses, waiting again for your new mermaid friend.

Chapter 18:
The Incredible Shrinking Kid

Do you think it's possible for a kid to shrink down to another size? You know, like a miniature size, where they could go places they never could have fit before? Well, what if I told you that you could do that right now? You really can- In your mind! Your mind is capable of doing many incredible things, including something called Visualization.

To begin your visualization practice, close your eyes. Really, close your eyes (unless you are the one reading this, of course!) To build a very strong visualization, it is usually helpful to first center yourself and be sure you are giving your brain the very best tools it needs to work with. In this case, that means oxygen, and oxygen means taking some good, deep breaths.

You are going to take some slow, deep breaths now, following along with my instruction: Breathe in very slowly, 1 - 2 - 3 - 4. Now breathe out, very slowly, 1 - 2 - 3 - 4. Excellent. Now again very slowly, 1 - 2 - 3 - 4 and breathe back out very slowly, 1 - 2 - 3 - 4 very nice. Once more, very slowly in 1 - 2 - 3 - 4 and back out very slowly, 1 - 2 - 3 - 4. Great!

Take a moment to review how you feel. Are you comfy and feeling good? Okay, great.

You are standing outside on the edge of your lawn. It is a lovely spring day, one of those days where the weather is just absolutely perfect. The sun is shining, and it has just rained. You can smell the wet earth, and everything smells clean and fresh. You take a deep breath in, enjoying that lovely spring freshness.

You notice that there is a little bottle on the edge of a wooden lawn chair, and you pick it up and take a look. On it, the label reads "The Incredible Shrinking Kid Solution: Only Use If You Like Adventure." Hmm, you think. The Incredible Shrinking Kid Solution? You've never heard of such a thing, but you do like an adventure!

You decide to go ahead and give it a try! You open up the bottle and quickly drink down the Incredible Shrinking Kid

Solution. The solution is sweet, and you wonder if someone is playing a joke on you! Once you've finished the solution, you set the bottle back down on the arm of the wooden chair, but as you are moving your hand back, you all of a sudden feel the sensation of falling, very, very fast!

It almost makes you feel dizzy, and you have to take a moment to get your bearings because you feel as if you just fell out of a tree or something! You shake yourself off a bit and reach your arm out to use the chair beside you to steady yourself, but the chair isn't there! Instead, there is a huge wooden post! What on earth? You take a few unsteady steps back and realize you are staring up at a gigantically oversized wooden chair! Wait here a second; the chair isn't gigantically oversized... you are incredibly undersized! You have been shrunk!

Dazed and a little confused, you look around you. You are next to a thickly wooded area, maybe the densest forest you've ever seen. Wait a moment; those trees are really interesting looking... Those aren't trees, are they? Those are blades of grass! Wow!

You must only be about two or three inches tall because these blades of grass are towering over you!!! This is so cool! You decide to go explore the world from a miniature point of view, and you rush forward into the thick and lush lawn, raindrops still clinging to each blade of grass. Wow, you've never seen grass with such incredible detail before! A raindrop slowly slides off of a blade of grass next to you and lands beside you, making a giant PLOP sound, and the rain splatters and splashes you. You have to laugh because this is so cool!

Just then, you notice a pond nearby. Well, you realize it's not actually a pond, but a puddle from the rain shower. You don't care. It is the perfect size for the miniature-sized you to go for a quick dip! You head over and decide to do a cannonball in.

SPLASH! You land in the pond that's really a puddle and laugh as you splash around. You don't think you've ever swum in rainwater before. This is an absolute first for you! You look around at the tall and towering blades of lush green grass all around you and think how it almost seems like you are on another planet somehow. You take a deep breath in and appreciate how clean and fresh it smells down here, so close to the earth. You have never experienced anything like this, and you are perfectly content splashing around in your lovely little rain puddle. You feel so grateful that you get to experience the world from this new perspective!

You do not have to leave this rainwater pond just yet if you don't want to. You can spend as long as you want here and you can come back here anytime you'd like.

You can create anything you want in your mind. Imagine where you want to go and build the picture in your mind. Be sure to imagine how you want it to smell, taste, hear, and feel. The more detailed you can make your mental picture, the more you will enjoy being there.

It is all up to you. Perhaps as you drift off to sleep, you may find yourself back in this miniature form, exploring the world from an entirely new point of view.

Chapter 19:
North Pole Relaxing

Have you ever wondered what Santa's elves do all day? Would you want to visit the North Pole? Well, what if I told you that you could do that right now? You really can- In your mind! Your mind is capable of doing many incredible things, including something called Visualization.

To begin your visualization practice, close your eyes. Really, close your eyes (unless you are the one reading this, of course!) To build a very strong visualization, it is usually helpful to first center yourself and be sure you are giving your

brain the very best tools it needs to work with. In this case, that means oxygen, and oxygen means taking some good, deep breaths.

You are going to take some slow, deep breaths now, following along with my instruction: Breathe in very slowly, 1 – 2 – 3 – 4. Now breathe out, very slowly, 1 – 2 – 3 – 4. Excellent. Now again very slowly, 1 – 2 – 3 – 4 and breathe back out very slowly, 1 – 2 – 3 – 4 very nice. Once more, very slowly in 1 – 2 – 3 – 4 and back out very slowly, 1 – 2 – 3 – 4. Great!

Take a moment to review how you feel. Are you comfy and feeling good? Okay, great.

In your mind's eye, picture yourself standing in a deep snowy bank. This is a really, really deep snowy bank, but you don't mind because you are bundled up as warm as warm can be in your thick winter coat, fluffy snow pants, and thick winter gloves. There is snow swirling around you as you take a look around. There is a wooden door up ahead, but the rest of the building is completely covered in snow, so you can't really see what it is.

Well, you know you need to get out of this snow, so you make your way towards the door and knock. The door opens immediately, and you are being bathed in a warm glow of light and can immediately hear lots of cheerful, busy commotion from inside. The person that opens the door is very short and has a huge smile on her face. She invites you in and makes you feel very welcome.

You step through the door into the warmth and are immediately relaxed by the coziness of this place. It is all aglow with beautiful colored lights everywhere you look and not one, not two, but several roaring fireplaces along the walls of this gigantic room. The person who has opened the door for you is taking your coat and gloves for you and is explaining to you that she is an elf here at Santa's workshop and that they love having visitors!

Another elf comes forward and offers you a steaming mug of hot chocolate with whipped cream and chocolate shavings on top. You take it gratefully, nodding your thanks as you are led to a giant overstuffed armchair beside one of the roaring fireplaces. You are invited to sit and relax there for as long as you'd like and warm up.

Once you've settled in, the two elves that have helped you in scurry off, and you finally get a good look around you. There are twinkling lights and shimmery garland everywhere you look, and this room smells of cinnamon and nutmeg. You notice that there are several stations in this large place where groups of elves appear to be hard at work building toys. Wow! You really are in Santa's workshop!

One of the elves had set a pair of fluffy slippers at your feet for you to change into, so you go ahead and take off your cold boots and slip your feet into these new slippers. The interior is somehow silky smooth and fuzzy soft all at once! Your feet are immediately warmed by these snuggly slippers, and you stretch your legs out beside the crackling fireplace.

There is an air of festive excitement here, and you watch the elves as they scurry back and forth between stations. You take another sip of your hot chocolate and think to yourself that this is the richest, smoothest hot chocolate you've ever tasted in your entire life! You listen to the crackling of the logs in the fireplace and think to yourself that this is probably the most magical place you've ever been in your entire life. You smile as you lean back to relax in the chair and think that this is probably the coziest you have ever been. You are so thankful that you get to hang out at the North Pole like this!

You do not have to leave this cozy, toasty North Pole scene just yet if you don't want to. You can spend as long as you want here and you can come back here anytime you'd like.

You can create anything you want in your mind. Imagine where you want to go and build the picture in your mind. Be sure to imagine how you want it to smell, taste, hear, and feel. The more detailed you can make your mental picture, the more you will enjoy being there.

It is all up to you. Perhaps as you drift off to sleep, you may find yourself back in this overstuffed armchair, listening to the fire crackle while you sip on hot chocolate in the North Pole.

Chapter 20:
River Tubing Fun

Have you ever been on a river tubing trip? If you haven't ever been on one, then you are in for a real treat because guess what? You get to go on a river tubing trip right now without moving a single muscle! You really can- In your mind! Your mind is capable of doing many incredible things, including something called Visualization.

To begin your visualization practice, close your eyes. Really, close your eyes (unless you are the one reading this, of course!) To build a very strong visualization, it is usually helpful to first center yourself and be sure you are giving your brain the very best tools it needs to work with. In this case, that means oxygen, and oxygen means taking some good, deep breaths.

You are going to take some slow, deep breaths now, following along with my instruction: Breathe in very slowly, 1 – 2 – 3 – 4. Now breathe out, very slowly, 1 – 2 – 3 – 4. Excellent. Now again very slowly, 1 – 2 – 3 – 4 and breathe back out very slowly, 1 – 2 – 3 – 4 very nice. Once more, very slowly in 1 – 2 – 3 – 4 and back out very slowly, 1 – 2 – 3 – 4. Great!

Take a moment to review how you feel. Are you comfy and feeling good? Okay, great.

Picture yourself, in your mind's eye, standing on the bank of a river. The bank has soft, sandy soil, and your feet are bare. You let your toes squish into the soft and sandy bank as you take a moment to appreciate the scene.

It is a beautiful sunny summer day, not too hot but just perfectly pleasant for being outside and splashing around in the water. You take a deep breath in and can smell the muddy banks of the river and the trees and plants all around you. It smells like the woods, and you are so happy to be out here on this fine summer's day!

You dip your toe into the water of the river and are pleasantly surprised by how cool and refreshing it is. It will be absolutely perfect for your river tubing trip. You place your round donut-shaped inner tube into the water with a splash, and then you let yourself plop in it, behind first! As you hit the tube, the water splashes up around you and sprinkles you a bit. You grin widely because it is a perfect way to cool down on this sunny summer day.

You begin to drift down the river, and you relax back and look up towards the sky. There are trees that have grown wild and unruly on the banks of the river, and their branches and leaves extend over the top of the river like a natural canopy. You can lean back on your tube and feel the sunshine on your face, but there is enough shade from these beautiful tree branches that you never have to worry about the sun being in your eyes.

You can hear the sounds of the river banks all around you. There are frogs croaking in the distance, and critters scurrying through the underbrush that make the occasional twig snap beside you. A gentle breeze blows through and cools you off even further and causes the tree branches above you to gently sway and you listen to the rustling of the leaves high above.

The current of the river is not going fast. It just lightly carries you along. You are floating down the river slowly but steadily, and you even can feel yourself being rocked and swayed from side to side with the currents of the water below you. There is a rhythm to this tubing journey that is almost rocking you to sleep, and you close your eyes so you can relax even further into it.

You take in another deep, long breath and smell the freshness of the forest around you and the clear river below. You feel completely at peace here on the river as you are gently floating further down along the banks. You are safe, and you are content. You feel very grateful to be experiencing this peaceful, happy ride down the river.

You do not have to leave this lovely river tubing journey just yet if you don't want to. You can spend as long as you want here and you can come back here anytime you'd like.

You can create anything you want in your mind. Imagine where you want to go and build the picture in your mind. Be sure to imagine how you want it to smell, taste, hear, and feel. The more detailed you can make your mental picture, the more you will enjoy being there.

It is all up to you. Perhaps as you drift off to sleep, you may find yourself back in your tube, peacefully floating down the river on a sunny summer's day.

Chapter 21:
All Aboard

Have you ever had a chance to ride on a passenger train? Do you think that would be fun? Well, what if I told you that you could do that right now? You really can- In your mind! Your mind is capable of doing many incredible things, including something called Visualization.

To begin your visualization practice, close your eyes. Really, close your eyes (unless you are the one reading this, of course!) To build a very strong visualization, it is usually helpful to first center yourself and be sure you are giving your brain the very best tools it needs to work with. In this case, that means oxygen, and oxygen means taking some good, deep breaths.

You are going to take some slow, deep breaths now, following along with my instruction: Breathe in very slowly, 1 – 2 – 3 – 4. Now breathe out, very slowly, 1 – 2 – 3 – 4. Excellent. Now again very slowly, 1 – 2 – 3 – 4 and breathe back out very slowly, 1 – 2 – 3 – 4 very nice. Once more, very slowly in 1 – 2 – 3 – 4 and back out very slowly, 1 – 2 – 3 – 4. Great!

Take a moment to review how you feel. Are you comfy and feeling good? Okay, great.

Picture yourself, in your mind's eye, standing on a platform at a train station. Look around you. You can see the ticket counter behind you and the wide-open space of the platform. Directly in front of you is the track that the train will be coming along on. It is a beautiful sunny day, and you take in a long, deep breath, enjoying the clean, fresh air.

Wait a moment, what is that sound that you hear? It's very faint and in the distance, but you know it is coming closer to you as it gets louder and louder. It is a chugga-chugga-chugga-chugga sound, and as it gets louder and louder you hear a high-pitched whistling choo-choo sound just as you can see it coming around the corner!

This train doesn't look like any train you have ever seen before. This train is rainbow colored! Each train car has rainbow stripes painted on it. The train is bigger than you had imagined, and it pulls to a stop on the track directly in front of you, and you hear the conductor call from the front, "All aboard!"

The door nearest you opens up, and you approach excitedly. You can hardly wait to see what the inside looks like! You realize as you step up and on to the train and realize that it is even better than you ever could have imagined. The entire top of the train is a skylight, and you can see directly through the roof to the sky!

The seats of the train are covered with a light blue fluffy fabric, and when you sit down, you sink into the soft, fluffy cushions. Your seat reclines back, and you are looking out into the clear blue sky above.

The train begins to move, and now you are reclined back on the rainbow train in your fluffy blue seat with a spectacular view of the sky above. It is a beautiful spring day, and the sky is a deep blue. There are fluffy white clouds that are dotting the sky above, and you are watching them pass by as the train moves quickly along the tracks.

A steward stops by your seat and offers you a complimentary lollipop for your journey, and you accept it graciously. The lollipop is a rainbow swirl, just like the train you're on! You can smell its combination of fruity flavors before you even take the first taste; there's banana, watermelon, cherry, orange, strawberry, maybe even pineapple! You give it a little lick and immediately smile. It is deliciously, fruity, and sweet!

As you enjoy your rainbow swirl lollipop, you watch the scenery outside of your window. You are passing by wide-open country fields, and you can see cows and horses grazing in the distance. It is all so beautiful, and you are very happy to be taking a ride on the rainbow train. You smile as you think to yourself that you are very, very thankful to be experiencing what it is like to ride on a rainbow train!

You do not have to leave your lovely train ride just yet if you don't want to. You can spend as long as you want here and you can come back here anytime you'd like.

You can create anything you want in your mind. Imagine where you want to go and build the picture in your mind. Be sure to imagine how you want it to smell, taste, hear, and feel. The more detailed you can make your mental picture, the more you will enjoy being there.

It is all up to you. Perhaps as you drift off to sleep, you may find yourself back on the rainbow train, speeding down the tracks as you take in the beautiful scenery on a lovely spring day.

Chapter 22:
Back in Time with the Dinosaurs

Do you like learning about dinosaurs? They are so cool to think and learn about, aren't they? Well, what if I told you that you didn't have to only wonder about them, you could actually go back in time and see what they were really like?

You really can- In your mind! Your mind is capable of doing many incredible things, including something called Visualization.

To begin your visualization practice, close your eyes. Really, close your eyes (unless you are the one reading this, of course!) To build a very strong visualization, it is usually helpful to first center yourself and be sure you are giving your brain the very best tools it needs to work with. In this case, that means oxygen, and oxygen means taking some good, deep breaths.

You are going to take some slow, deep breaths now, following along with my instruction: Breathe in very slowly, 1 – 2 – 3 – 4. Now breathe out, very slowly, 1 – 2 – 3 – 4. Excellent. Now again very slowly, 1 – 2 – 3 – 4 and breathe back out very slowly, 1 – 2 – 3 – 4 very nice. Once more, very slowly in 1 – 2 – 3 – 4 and back out very slowly, 1 – 2 – 3 – 4. Great!

Take a moment to review how you feel. Are you comfy and feeling good? Okay, great.

Imagine yourself, in your mind's eye, standing in the middle of a clearing in a forest. You are surrounded by trees and plants you've never seen before. The trees are very tall and thick, and the plants have exotic looking flowers and berries that are not familiar to you.

You bend over to inspect one of the flowers nearest you. It is a bright and vivid orangish-pink color, and it smells strongly of what seems to be a cross between an orange and a strawberry. You notice that behind each bright and vivid orangish-pink flower is a giant orangish-pink fruit. It's beautiful!

Just then, you hear a noise behind you and see a giant lizard making its way toward you. This lizard is bigger than any lizard you've ever seen before... it's as tall as you are! It doesn't seem to take much notice of you as it quickly brushes past you and plucks one of the brightly colored fruits off of the tree that you've been admiring. This lizard is walking upright on its two back legs and is using its smaller front legs like arms. All you can think of is that it seems like this isn't just any lizard... this looks like a dinosaur!

Just then, the ground begins to shake with big booming noises accompanying each tremor of the earth below you. The lizard next to you pauses its fruit-eating and seems to be on alert as it listens and waits. You listen and wait too, wondering what on earth could be making the earth shake like that!

The booming noises are getting louder, and the earth is shaking even more, so you reach out and grab ahold of the fruit tree beside you to keep your balance. Just then, the booming and shaking stops, and you see something come rushing down toward through the treetops above you, from high in the sky.

Oh, my goodness! It's a dinosaur head! A dinosaur with what seems to be an extraordinarily long neck is reaching through the treetops and down towards you! At first, you are frozen in fear, but the dinosaur only seems interested in the fruit tree beside you, and it grabs several of the brightly colored fruits and its branches in its mouth before rising back up and continuing on its way.

Your heart is racing as you realize that you have somehow gone back in time with the dinosaurs! The giant lizard that is still beside you munching on the fruit tree isn't just any giant lizard! It must be a dinosaur too. Wow, this is so cool!

You decide that since this fruit tree is apparently so popular with the dinosaurs, you will try one too. You pull one of the brightly colored fruits off of the tree. It is the size of a large grapefruit, and it has a thick peel on it. You manage to work off a section of the peel using your fingernails, and you are able to expose the pink pulp inside.

The moment you opened the peel, the orange and strawberry smell became incredibly strong, and you hope that it tastes even half as good as it smells! You take one small bite, and your taste buds go crazy! This fruit is the sweetest, juiciest fruit you have ever tasted in your entire life. You happily munch on this delicious dinosaur fruit, and the dinosaur beside you seems to almost smile at you with his toothy, dinosaur grin. You feel so happy and thankful that you are getting to experience dinosaurs so up close like this!

Your new dinosaur friend by your side, you are thoroughly enjoying your visit to the past. You do not have to leave this amazing place just yet if you don't want to. You can spend as long as you want here and you can come back here anytime you'd like.

You can create anything you want in your mind. Imagine where you want to go and build the picture in your mind. Be sure to imagine how you want it to smell, taste, hear, and feel. The more detailed you can make your mental picture, the more you will enjoy being there.

It is all up to you. Perhaps as you drift off to sleep, you may find yourself back in prehistoric times, munching on dinosaur fruits with the dinosaurs!

Chapter 23:
Meet a Sloth

Have you seen a sloth before? They're cool creatures, aren't they? Well, have you ever had an opportunity to actually meet a sloth before? What if I told you that right now, at this moment, you could actually meet a sloth for yourself? You really can- In your mind! Your mind is capable of doing many incredible things, including something called Visualization.

To begin your visualization practice, close your eyes. Really, close your eyes (unless you are the one reading this, of course!) To build a very strong visualization, it is usually helpful to first center yourself and be sure you are giving your brain the very best tools it needs to work with. In this case, that means oxygen, and oxygen means taking some good, deep breaths.

You are going to take some slow, deep breaths now, following along with my instruction: Breathe in very slowly, 1 – 2 – 3 – 4. Now breathe out, very slowly, 1   2   3   4. Excellent. Now again very slowly, 1 – 2 – 3 – 4 and breathe back out very slowly, 1 – 2 – 3 – 4 very nice. Once more, very slowly in 1 – 2 – 3 – 4 and back out very slowly, 1 – 2 – 3 – 4. Great!

Take a moment to review how you feel. Are you comfy and feeling good? Okay, great.

Imagine yourself, in your mind's eye, in a beautiful jungle. Look around you and see all of the beautiful jungle trees and exotic plants that are surrounding you. You take a deep breath in and can smell something that is very fragrant. Perhaps it is flowers?

You look around where you are standing again and notice a beautiful jungle bush that you hadn't noticed before. It is thick with deep green star-shaped leaves that are arranged in clusters, and each cluster has a flower in the middle. The flower in each cluster is spectacularly vivid, beginning with a deep reddish-orange in the center and extending out into brilliant sunshine yellow at each tip.

You move closer to better inspect these gorgeous flowers, and the smell of these flowers is absolutely intoxicating! It smells like a cross between a wild rose and a lilac bush, and you know that you have never smelled anything so wonderfully fragrant in your entire life.

Now you hear a noise behind you, like leaves gently rustling. You turn around and see the branches and leaves of a low bush being moved gently around, almost as if someone was lightly rummaging about inside of it. Then you see a furry paw extend out from underneath the bush, with long, curved nails, slowly moving to grip the ground below.

You are very curious, but not afraid. Whatever this creature is, it seems to be moving so slow you know you don't have to be scared of it! There is another rustling noise, and now there is a second furry paw extending out from underneath the bush, and again, its long, curved nails reach out to dig in and grip the ground below. Again, you hear rustling in the bush as if something is carefully moving around inside, and this time, you can see the leaves of the bush parting slowly to reveal a fuzzy head.

As this fuzzy head slowly emerges from the bush, you see that it is pulling itself out of the bush by the paws that are gripping the ground below. You are quivering with curiosity now, what on earth could this creature be?

Again, you hear the gentle rustling from the bush as this critter seems to be pulling itself finally out, and you first notice how very long its arms are! The lanky arms that have worked so hard to pull this creature out of the bush are now pushing the rest of its body up and out of the bush.

As this creature straightens its body up, its head finally raises, and you can see now that you are standing right next to a sloth! His sleepy eyes meet yours, and his mouth slowly moves into what you are sure is a smile, and you return the smile, so thrilled that you are standing right next to what is certainly one of the cutest animals on the planet!

You get an idea. You reach out to the flower bush with the magnificent flowers and pluck one from its leaf cluster. You take a step towards the sloth that is watching you with great interest now. Holding the flower out towards the sloth, you smile and wait.

This sweet little sloth moves so slow, each movement taking an extraordinary amount of time, but he reaches his furry paw out towards you and finally grasps the flower, then bringing it up towards his nose where he takes a long, deep breath in, smiling a big, happy smile at the gesture.

You return the smile again and are so happy that you can now say that you have met a sloth! You are so thankful that you can now say you have a sweet little sloth friend.

You do not have to leave your sloth friend just yet if you don't want to. You can spend as long as you want here and you can come back anytime you'd like.

You can create anything you want in your mind. Imagine where you want to go and build the picture in your mind. Be sure to imagine how you want it to smell, taste, hear, and feel. The more detailed you can make your mental picture, the more you will enjoy being there.

It is all up to you. Perhaps as you drift off to sleep, you may find yourself back in this jungle clearing, sharing a beautiful flower with your new friend, the sloth.

Chapter 24:
Magic Flowers

Do you like flowers? Most people do like flowers, but most flowers are pretty similar, aren't they? Well, what if there was a flower that was unlike any other flower you had ever seen? What if there was a flower that was magic, and even better yet, you could see it? You really can- In your mind! Your mind is capable of doing many incredible things, including something called Visualization.

To begin your visualization practice, close your eyes. Really, close your eyes (unless you are the one reading this, of course!) To build a very strong visualization, it is usually helpful to first center yourself and be sure you are giving your brain the very best tools it needs to work with. In this case, that means oxygen, and oxygen means taking some good, deep breaths.

You are going to take some slow, deep breaths now, following along with my instruction: Breathe in very slowly, 1 – 2 – 3 – 4. Now breathe out, very slowly, 1 – 2 – 3 4. Excellent. Now again very slowly, 1 – 2 – 3 – 4 and breathe back out very slowly, 1 – 2 – 3 – 4 very nice. Once more, very slowly in 1 – 2 – 3 – 4 and back out very slowly, 1 – 2 – 3 – 4. Great!

Take a moment to review how you feel. Are you comfy and feeling good? Okay, great.

Picture yourself, in your mind's eye, in a meadow on a beautiful, sunny day. The sky is blue above you, and you can hear birds chirping in the distance. The meadow is wide and vast, filled with tall meadow grasses and wildflowers.

You take a deep breath in and can smell the sweet meadow grasses and wildflowers all around you. It smells like spring in the country, and you smile as you look around you.

There are so many different kinds of wildflowers all around you! There is a light spring breeze that is gently blowing the wildflowers and meadow grasses from side to side. Some are tall and skinny, and some are short and fat. It seems to you as if there is every color of the rainbow all around you as they sway back and forth in the gentle spring breeze. You can see reds and yellows, purples and oranges, blues and… oh my goodness! What is that over there that you see!

Beyond the tall and skinny wildflowers over to the left of you is something that you don't think you have ever seen before. It is a flower, but it is… different. It is not as tall as some of the tallest wildflowers, but oh boy, does it stick out of the crowd!

You lean over and wonder if you are really seeing what you think you could be seeing with this flower. It is unlike any flower you have ever seen before because this flower isn't just one single color… No, this flower is somehow every color, all at once!

Not only does this flower appear to have every color of the rainbow, but it is pulsating with a light that does not seem to really be natural. This is no regular flower. You lean over towards it to inspect it further and notice that this flower is not only pulsating with a rainbow light of every color, it is sending out sparkles of rainbow color all around it, and now the grasses down below it are also rainbow colored!

You can hardly believe it, and you reach down to pick some of the magical rainbow-colored blades of grass. They continue to sparkle in your hand, and you sit back on your knees in disbelief. This is a magic flower, and it is in your meadow! How lucky you are. You decide that you will continue walking around in this meadow, looking to see what other magical flowers you might find.

The beautiful rainbow sparkles of light that are pulsating off of this brilliant wildflower are coating everything they touch. Your own hands are even now sparkling with this beautiful rainbow-colored magic! You can't wait to see if there are any more magical wildflowers in this meadow for you to find. You are feeling so grateful that you have had the opportunity to discover magical wildflowers!

You do not have to leave your magic flower just yet if you don't want to. You can spend as long as you want here and you can come back anytime you'd like.

You can create anything you want in your mind. Imagine where you want to go and build the picture in your mind. Be sure to imagine how you want it to smell, taste, hear, and feel. The more detailed you can make your mental picture, the more you will enjoy being there.

It is all up to you. Perhaps as you drift off to sleep, you may find yourself back in this spring meadow, searching for magic flowers.

Chapter 25:
Apple Picking Fun

Have you ever been apple picking before? It is a fabulous autumn activity! What if I told you that right now, you can go apple picking? You really can- In your mind! Your mind is capable of doing many incredible things, including something called Visualization.

To begin your visualization practice, close your eyes. Really, close your eyes (unless you are the one reading this, of course!) To build a very strong visualization, it is usually helpful to first center yourself and be sure you are giving your brain the very best tools it needs to work with. In this case, that means oxygen, and oxygen means taking some good, deep breaths.

You are going to take some slow, deep breaths now, following along with my instruction: Breathe in very slowly, 1 – 2 – 3 – 4. Now breathe out, very slowly, 1 – 2 – 3 – 4. Excellent. Now again very slowly, 1 – 2 – 3 – 4 and breathe back out very slowly, 1 – 2 – 3 – 4 very nice. Once more, very slowly in 1 – 2 – 3 – 4 and back out very slowly, 1 – 2 – 3 – 4. Great!

Take a moment to review how you feel. Are you comfy and feeling good? Okay, great.

Picture yourself, in your mind's eye, outside on a crisp autumn day. The wind is blowing gently, and there is a bit of a chill to the air, but you don't mind because you have on the perfect autumn clothing that will keep you toasty warm on this crisp autumn day.

You are standing in front of a grove of trees that look tall and strong. You can see that each tree has strong and sturdy branches that are thick with deep green leaves and seem to be bursting with splotches of varying hues of bright reds, and you realize that this is an apple orchard.

At the base of each tree is a ladder with a simple wooden bucket beside it. You rush over to the nearest tree and pick up the wooden bucket and move it closer to the ladder. You climb up the sturdy ladder, and as you get closer to the tree branches, you can smell the sweet and appley aroma of the ripe fruit. It smells like autumn and apple pie!

You inspect the apples you can now see up close. Each of them looks so juicy and fresh! You've never seen apples that look so juicy and fresh, and you are excited to get to pick these. Leaning over, you firmly grasp the first apple and give it a little pull. It easily separates from the tree, and you hug it towards yourself and make your way back down the ladder to the bucket below, where you gently place it in, careful to not bruise it.

Back up the ladder you go, to find your next apple. You land your sights on one that is a deep and vivid red, and you have to balance yourself very carefully and stretch your upper body off the ladder to reach it, your fingers barely able to close around it and give it the tug it needs to be released from the tree. You make your way again back down the ladder to place it in the wooden collection bucket. You are so happy to be here picking apples on this beautiful autumn day.

Several trips later and your wooden bucket is full of ripe, juicy apples. You take a long, deep breath in and appreciate the way the crisp autumn air mixes with the intoxicating aroma of the sweet apples in the bucket. There is a beautiful autumn gust that is blowing through the apple orchard, making the branches that are heavy with fruit and thick green leaves rustled pleasantly. You are so excited to have fresh apples to make your autumn treats with! You are so thankful for this awesome fall apple picking experience.

You do not have to leave your apple orchard just yet if you don't want to. You can spend as long as you want here and you can come back anytime you'd like.

You can create anything you want in your mind. Imagine where you want to go and build the picture in your mind. Be sure to imagine how you want it to smell, taste, hear, and feel. The more detailed you can make your mental picture, the more you will enjoy being there.

It is all up to you. Perhaps as you drift off to sleep, you may find yourself back in this apple orchard, gathering the sweetest, juiciest apples you've ever seen.

Chapter 26:
Flying Unicorn

What is it about unicorns that are so fun to think about? They're magical horses, basically, and they always look so beautiful in pictures. Well, what if you could actually meet and fly on a unicorn yourself? You really can- In your mind! Your mind is capable of doing many incredible things, including something called Visualization.

To begin your visualization practice, close your eyes. Really, close your eyes (unless you are the one reading this, of course!) To build a very strong visualization, it is usually helpful to first center yourself and be sure you are giving your brain the very best tools it needs to work with. In this case, that means oxygen, and oxygen means taking some good, deep breaths.

You are going to take some slow, deep breaths now, following along with my instruction: Breathe in very slowly, 1 - 2 - 3 - 4. Now breathe out, very slowly, 1 - 2 - 3 - 4. Excellent. Now again very slowly, 1 - 2 - 3 - 4 and breathe back out very slowly, 1 - 2 - 3 - 4 very nice. Once more, very slowly in 1 - 2 - 3 - 4 and back out very slowly, 1 - 2 - 3 - 4. Great!

Take a moment to review how you feel. Are you comfy and feeling good? Okay, great.

Imagine yourself, in your mind's eye, standing at the edge of a beautiful forest. This forest is full of evergreens, and you can smell the fresh pine scent of the trees in the forest. You listen carefully and can hear birds chirping but also something else in the background; maybe the sound of running water?

You decide to investigate and walk into the forest, following the sound of the water. You don't have to travel far before you discover what it is making the sound... it's a waterfall!

You have ended up in a clearing with a magnificent waterfall, and you admire the powerful rushing water that is falling from such a great height into this beautiful little pond below when you realize that you are actually not alone. On the other side of this clearing is a spectacular sight- a unicorn!

You are in shock. You have never seen a unicorn before! This unicorn is white, and her horn is sparkling with pinks and purples. You call out hello, and before you know it, this unicorn has floated up into the air and began flying over towards you!

Oh, my goodness, you can barely believe it. You have heard of flying unicorns before, but you never dreamed you would actually see one. This majestic creature gently settles down beside you and nuzzles you gently with her snout. You lightly stroke her nose and thank her for coming over towards you. She extends her wings out a bit and motions with her nose for you to hop on.

You are in disbelief and ask her if it is really okay for you to climb on. The beautiful unicorn nods her head yes and nickers softly to you in reply. You are grinning from ear to ear as you climb on her back.

Once you have settled, she begins to gently move upwards in the air, her wings lightly moving up and down. She waits to be sure that you have steadied yourself on her back before she really takes off, and you suddenly find yourself soaring swiftly through the air on her back! You are not afraid because this flying unicorn feels very safe and secure underneath you.

The unicorn flies you up, up, and up over towards the waterfall, and you get to see the beautiful, clear stream up above that is feeding the waterfall. You are so close to the waterfall that droplets of the cool, fresh water splash on your body. You giggle because it tickles as water droplets fall on your nose and cheeks.

The flying unicorn doubles back and forth past the waterfall, and you smile as you enjoy the warm sun on your face, the refreshing mist from the waterfall, and the relaxing sound of the waters rushing below you. The flying unicorn feels safe and strong below you, and you smile because you are so grateful that you are getting the chance to ride on a flying unicorn!

You do not have to leave your flying unicorn ride just yet if you don't want to. You can spend as long as you want here and you can come back anytime you'd like.

You can create anything you want in your mind. Imagine where you want to go and build the picture in your mind. Be sure to imagine how you want it to smell, taste, hear, and feel. The more detailed you can make your mental picture, the more you will enjoy being there.

It is all up to you. Perhaps as you drift off to sleep, you may find yourself back here on your flying unicorn ride, listening to the rushing water of the waterfall.

Chapter 27:
Fun on the Farm

Have you ever been to a farm? There are many different kinds of farms, but farms are places where crops and animals grow. Do you know that you can go visit a farm right now? You really can- In your mind! Your mind is capable of doing many incredible things, including something called Visualization.

To begin your visualization practice, close your eyes. Really, close your eyes (unless you are the one reading this, of course!) To build a very strong visualization, it is usually helpful to first center yourself and be sure you are giving your brain the very best tools it needs to work with. In this case, that means oxygen, and oxygen means taking some good, deep breaths.

You are going to take some slow, deep breaths now, following along with my instruction: Breathe in very slowly, 1 – 2 – 3 – 4. Now breathe out, very slowly, 1 – 2 – 3 – 4. Excellent. Now again very slowly, 1 – 2 – 3 – 4 and breathe back out very slowly, 1 – 2 – 3 – 4 very nice. Once more, very slowly in 1 – 2 – 3 – 4 and back out very slowly, 1 – 2 – 3 – 4. Great!

Take a moment to review how you feel. Are you comfy and feeling good? Okay, great.

Imagine yourself, in your mind's eye, standing in front of a red barn. It is a beautiful sunny day, and you take a deep, long breath in. You can smell fresh hay and some sort of animal. Hmm, wonder what it could be? You hear something from behind you and turn around just in time to see a white, fluffy sheep making its way towards you!

The sheep rubs its body against you, wanting you to pet it! Oh, my goodness, this sheep has the softest, fluffiest wool you have ever felt before. It feels like you are petting a cloud! As you are petting the sheep, you notice little baby squeaking noises, but you have no idea what it might be.

You look around you and think that it must be coming from the side of the bar. You walk around the bales of hay until you reach the side of the bar. There is a gaggle of baby ducklings! They are soft, yellow, fuzzy babies, and you are instantly in love with them.

You kneel down beside them in the soft hay and reach out to touch one. It is covered in a fine, baby-soft fur and it makes sweet little baby squeak noises as you pet its little head. As you are petting one, the rest of the group come over and surround you, trying to hop into your lap!

You are now entirely surrounded by sweet little fluffy soft baby ducklings, and they are squeaking at you as they give you their best little baby quacks! These baby ducklings are so friendly and seem to love you. You have to laugh a little because the baby ducklings do not want you to leave as you get up and make your way back over to the front of the bar.

As you arrive at the front of the barn, you see there is a tractor with a trailer hooked up to it, and the trailer is full of hay! It is a hayride! The driver of the tractor motions for you to hop on, so you do. The hay bales are warm from sitting in the summer sun, and you settle in comfortably as the tractor begins to move. You get to take a tour of the farm!

You see to your left a pigpen with one big, fat mama pig and her three little baby piglets. The piglets are splashing about and playing in the mud, trying to keep cool. They look like they are having such a fun time!

To your right, you can see a pasture full of horses. The horses have their heads down and are eating grass, but a few of them look up at you as you pass as if to say hello. You wave to them and swear that a few of them have nodded back hello to you!

The hayride continues around the farm, and you get to see cows and donkeys, too. The weather is perfect, and the animals are adorable. You are so happy to have been able to visit the farm. You feel so thankful for your awesome day at the farm!

You do not have to leave the farm just yet if you don't want to. You can spend as long as you want here and you can come back anytime you'd like.

You can create anything you want in your mind. Imagine where you want to go and build the picture in your mind. Be sure to imagine how you want it to smell, taste, hear, and feel. The more detailed you can make your mental picture, the more you will enjoy being there.

It is all up to you. Perhaps as you drift off to sleep, you may find yourself back here on the hayride, on a tour of the animals of the farm.

Chapter 28:
Caught in the Snowstorm

Do you like being caught in snowstorms? You know, snow swirling all around you, and you get to watch as it blankets everything it touches? Well, what if I told you that you can go be caught in a snowstorm right now? You really can- In your mind! Your mind is capable of doing many incredible things, including something called Visualization.

To begin your visualization practice, close your eyes. Really, close your eyes (unless you are the one reading this, of course!) To build a very strong visualization, it is usually helpful to first center yourself and be sure you are giving your brain the very best tools it needs to work with. In this case, that means oxygen, and oxygen means taking some good, deep breaths.

You are going to take some slow, deep breaths now, following along with my instruction: Breathe in very slowly, 1 – 2 – 3 – 4. Now breathe out, very slowly, 1 – 2 – 3 – 4. Excellent. Now again very slowly, 1 – 2 – 3 – 4 and breathe back out very slowly, 1 – 2 – 3 – 4 very nice. Once more, very slowly in 1 – 2 – 3 – 4 and back out very slowly, 1 – 2 – 3 – 4. Great!

Take a moment to review how you feel. Are you comfy and feeling good? Okay, great.

Imagine yourself, in your mind's eye, walking along a snowy path. It is the middle of winter, and the blustery winter wind is blowing hard today! You are bundled up well against the cold with your warm winter coat, a soft and fuzzy scarf, your thick woolen hat, and your snug winter gloves, so you aren't too cold on your journey.

You look around you and notice that it is starting to snow. Light, feather-soft snowflakes are falling from the sky, and you stick your tongue out to catch one. The cold snow melts the moment it hits your tongue, and you smile because you love the snow. You can hear the wind howling through the evergreen trees that line the path you are on.

You continue on your walk and enjoy the feeling of the slippery snow beneath your heavy boots as it blankets the ground. You love this part of winter, watching everything become blanketed in snow! You pause a moment to admire the shrubs on the side of the path as the bright white snow covers its evergreen leaves.

You take in a deep, long breath and can smell the fresh, clean scent of a winter's snow. The snow seems to just refresh everything it touches in the wintertime! You notice the snowflakes are getting thicker now. Instead of light, feather-soft snowflakes, they are now fat drops of snow that are coming down from the sky, much quicker than before.

The winter's wind continues to blow, and the thick, heavy snow is swirling around you with each gust of wind. You pause a moment to watch the way the snowflakes catch the daylight as they blow past you. You see that the trees on either side of the path are now almost completely blanketed in this thick winter snow. Continuing on, you notice the snow underfoot has accumulated quickly, and you hear a very satisfying crunch as your boot comes down with each step.

You love the sounds of winter! The crunch of snow underfoot, the blustery wind howling as it rushes through the snow-covered trees, and the satisfying silence of the world around you once it is blanketed with snow.

As long as you are warmly dressed, you are always happy to be out in a beautiful snowstorm like the one you're in right now. You are so grateful that you get to enjoy the beautifully peaceful winter wonderland like this.

You do not have to leave this swirling snowstorm just yet if you don't want to. You can spend as long as you want here and you can come back anytime you'd like.

You can create anything you want in your mind. Imagine where you want to go and build the picture in your mind. Be sure to imagine how you want it to smell, taste, hear, and feel. The more detailed you can make your mental picture, the more you will enjoy being there.

It is all up to you. Perhaps as you drift off to sleep, you may find yourself back in this winter wonderland, enjoying the peaceful beauty of a snowstorm.

Chapter 29:
Confetti Party

Do you like confetti? There are so many different kinds of confetti. Some are sparkly, some are shiny, some can be smaller, some can be bigger... Confetti usually comes out when there is a party, but have you ever been to a confetti party? A party just for confetti? Well, you can go to one right now if you want. You really can- In your mind! Your mind is capable of doing many incredible things, including something called Visualization.

To begin your visualization practice, close your eyes. Really, close your eyes (unless you are the one reading this, of course!) To build a very strong visualization, it is usually helpful to first center yourself and be sure you are giving your brain the very best tools it needs to work with. In this case, that means oxygen, and oxygen means taking some good, deep breaths.

You are going to take some slow, deep breaths now, following along with my instruction: Breathe in very slowly, 1 - 2 - 3 - 4. Now breathe out, very slowly, 1 - 2 - 3 - 4. Excellent. Now again very slowly, 1 - 2 - 3 - 4 and breathe back out very slowly, 1 - 2 - 3 - 4 very nice. Once more, very slowly in 1 - 2 - 3 - 4 and back out very slowly, 1 - 2 - 3 - 4. Great!

Take a moment to review how you feel. Are you comfy and feeling good? Okay, great.

Imagine yourself, in your mind's eye, standing in a hallway, outside of a door with a sign on it. On the sign, it says only: "Confetti Party." You have no idea what that is! You have never been to a confetti party before. You definitely would like to see what one is like, so you slowly open the door.

You step in and are immediately shocked by what you see... There is confetti everywhere! Falling from the ceiling is what appears to be yellow, blue, and orange confetti pieces about the size of grapes made out of some sort of foam substance. You catch a few pieces in your hand and give them a little squeeze. Definitely foam!

The room you are in isn't very big, but each wall has its own special kind of confetti being blown out from it. You walk to the wall to your left and are amazed to see that the confetti is being blown out from vents in the ceilings AND the walls! The confetti over is hot pink and sparkly black. The confetti is made of the same foam material that the overhead confetti is made from, but this confetti is so sparkly that as it falls and catches the light, it reflects around the room like a disco ball!

You move to the next wall and see that this wall has confetti coming down that is made of the same light foam material, but this confetti is multicolored. It seems to be every color of the rainbow, and it's coming down from not just the ceiling and the wall over here, but also from a vent on the floor that is shooting the confetti up and out!

Moving to the next wall, you see the confetti over here is shaped like different zoo animals. You see a little foam giraffe, a little foam zebra, a little foam elephant, a little foam ostrich... all sorts of cute little foam animals, multicolored and floating and flying through the air over here! You love it; it is so cute!

The last wall is the wall that the door you came through is on, and you notice now that this wall has two huge fans on either side of the door. The fans are blowing the different confetti all around, and it feels like you are in a confetti blizzard! It's like being at an amazing party that is being thrown just for you.

You go to stand in the middle of the room, and you do a little twirl as you watch the colorful confetti swirling around you and reflecting the lights off of each foam shape. You are dancing now in a sea of colors and fun, and the little foam confetti shapes fall against your body with a satisfying thud before they bounce back off of you to be caught again in the wind of the fans.

This confetti party is awesome, and you are so happy you are here! You never knew confetti could be so fun. You are so thankful that you are getting to see what it is like to be in the middle of a swirling, crazy confetti party!

You do not have to leave this confetti party just yet if you don't want to. You can spend as long as you want here and you can come back anytime you'd like.

You can create anything you want in your mind. Imagine where you want to go and build the picture in your mind. Be sure to imagine how you want it to smell, taste, hear, and feel. The more detailed you can make your mental picture, the more you will enjoy being there.

It is all up to you. Perhaps as you drift off to sleep, you may find yourself back at this confetti party, twirling around as multicolored confetti floats all around you.

Chapter 30:
Fluffy Room

Have you ever been in a room that is totally and completely made up of soft and fluffy surfaces? A room where you could bounce off of a trampoline in any direction you wanted to, and it would be perfectly fine because every single surface is fluffy and soft? Well, you can go to one right now if you want. You really can- In your mind! Your mind is capable of doing many incredible things, including something called Visualization.

To begin your visualization practice, close your eyes. Really, close your eyes (unless you are the one reading this, of course!) To build a very strong visualization, it is usually helpful to first center yourself and be sure you are giving your brain the very best tools it needs to work with. In this case, that means oxygen, and oxygen means taking some good, deep breaths.

You are going to take some slow, deep breaths now, following along with my instruction: Breathe in very slowly, 1 - 2 - 3 - 4. Now breathe out, very slowly, 1 - 2 - 3 - 4. Excellent. Now again very slowly, 1 - 2 - 3 - 4 and breathe back out very slowly, 1 - 2 - 3 - 4 very nice. Once more, very slowly in 1 - 2 - 3 - 4 and back out very slowly, 1 - 2 - 3 - 4. Great!

Take a moment to review how you feel. Are you comfy and feeling good? Okay, great.

Picture yourself, in your mind's eye, standing on a trampoline. This trampoline is a little different from other trampolines that you may have been on before. You see, this trampoline is covered with fluff! This isn't just a fluffy fabric on this trampoline, no, this trampoline is covered with a fluffy substance that reminds you almost of the fluffiest clouds you've ever seen in the sky.

In fact, this entire room is covered in this fluff! The trampoline is covered with this fluff, the floor all around the trampoline is covered with this fluff, the walls are covered with this fluff, and even the ceiling is covered with this fluff.

You crouch down and touch this fluff below you on the trampoline. You feel like you have stuck your hand inside of a marshmallow! It is soft and squishy and oh so fluffy! You decide to give it a little test bounce. You do a quick bounce up, and when your feet touch back down on the fluffy trampoline surface, you are catapulted up in the air higher than you've ever been before!

You feel like you are flying through the air, and you come back down again, this time landing on your back. Your body lands with a soft squish into this fluffy, white substance, and you are entirely enclosed inside fluffiness! You can see inside of this fluffiness, but it looks like what you would imagine looking inside a cloud would be like.

You sit up and are ready to do it again! This fluff is totally awesome, and you decide to see what will happen if you jump from the fluffy trampoline to the wall this time. You do another little bounce, and once again, the fluffy trampoline catapults you through the air, and you laugh as you point yourself towards the wall. You sail through the air towards the fluffy wall, and your body bounces off of it the same way a marshmallow would bounce off of another marshmallow.

This is great! You climb back up on the fluffy trampoline and decide to this time, dive down in the fluff below. You perch yourself on the edge of the fluffy trampoline and look down into the white fluffy pool all around you. It looks so deliciously soft, and so you spring off with your feet and slide into the fluffiness with your hands and arms first, the rest of your body quickly slipping through.

The fluffiness all around you feels so comfortable. You feel like you are almost weightless! Every move you make, this soft fluffy stuff gently caresses you, and it sounds like what you would imagine a cloud touching another cloud would sound like. You think you could take a lovely nap in this fluff if you wanted to. It is the softest, fluffiest stuff you have ever touched! You are so happy to be in this fluffy room as you rest yourself back on a fluffy cloud. You are so grateful to get to experience this fluffiness like this!

You do not have to leave this fluffy room just yet if you don't want to. You can spend as long as you want here and you can come back anytime you'd like.

You can create anything you want in your mind. Imagine where you want to go and build the picture in your mind. Be sure to imagine how you want it to smell, taste, hear, and feel. The more detailed you can make your mental picture, the more you will enjoy being there.

It is all up to you. Perhaps as you drift off to sleep, you may find yourself back in this fluffy room, sailing through the air with each jump and landing in the fluffy clouds below.

Chapter 31:
Chocolate River

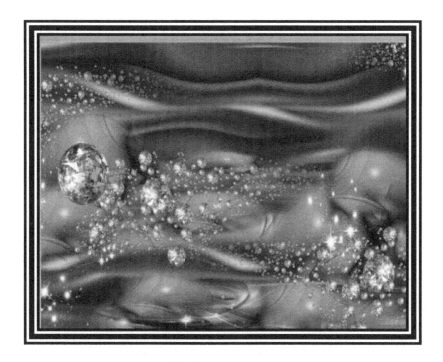

Do you know what a chocolate river looks like? You know, where the chocolate for your chocolate candy comes from? Well, there isn't really a chocolate river in real life, but there is one in your imagination! That's right, and you can go there right now. You really can- In your mind! Your mind is capable of doing many incredible things, including something called Visualization.

To begin your visualization practice, close your eyes. Really, close your eyes (unless you are the one reading this, of course!) To build a very strong visualization, it is usually helpful to first center yourself and be sure you are giving your brain the very best tools it needs to work with. In this case, that means oxygen, and oxygen means taking some good, deep breaths.

You are going to take some slow, deep breaths now, following along with my instruction: Breathe in very slowly, 1 - 2 - 3 - 4. Now breathe out, very slowly, 1 - 2 - 3 - 4. Excellent. Now again very slowly, 1 - 2 - 3 - 4 and breathe back out very slowly, 1 - 2 - 3 - 4 very nice. Once more, very slowly in 1 - 2 - 3 - 4 and back out very slowly, 1 - 2 - 3 - 4. Great!

Take a moment to review how you feel. Are you comfy and feeling good? Okay, great.

Imagine yourself, in your mind's eye, standing beside a river. You take a deep and long breath in and notice that the air where you're standing smells very sweet. In fact, the air smells sweet and rich and very familiar. You look around you and notice that the trees near this river are very unique.

The bark on these trees is very interesting. They don't seem as rough as the bark on most trees you have ever seen. You reach out a hand to lightly touch one of the trees and pull it back with shock.

That isn't tree bark! It felt smooth to the touch, and even a little pliable, like you could push on it and leave an indentation with your finger! Hmm. You move closer to inspect it further and notice that it smells absolutely heavenly.

It smells milky and sweet, and that's when you notice the fruit that is growing on this interesting tree.

Each tree branch has beautiful green leaves covering each branch, but the fruit hanging off of it is unlike any fruit you have ever seen. They are little drop shapes and almost remind you of chocolate candy kisses. You tentatively lean forward to pluck one-off and inspect it closer. That's when you realize that each piece of fruit on this tree IS a chocolate candy kiss!!!

You go back over to the bark of the tree and scratch off a little bit with your fingernail and then gingerly give it a little taste with your tongue. Oh, my goodness, it is delectable dark chocolate that melts in your mouth! Chocolate bark! On a tree!

You spin around, amazed at what you are seeing all around you. It looks as if there is chocolate as far as you can see! There are chocolate candy kiss trees all around you, and you think that you can even see a tree that looks like it might be a coconut tree! You go over to it and pluck one of the coconuts from a branch. You are able to crack open the coconut easily and find that instead of coconut and coconut milk inside, it has melted milk chocolate inside! You take a sip of it, and it is the most delectable chocolate coconut candy you have ever tasted in your entire life!

You are beyond excited. You have somehow stumbled on this amazing chocolate world! Then you remember, weren't you standing by a river before? You rush back over towards the river, thinking that there just would be no way that the river would possibly be made out of... Oh! But look! It is!!!!

It is a chocolate river, and you watch the sweet milk chocolate flow past you as you stand in disbelief on the banks. You crouch down beside the river, daring to dip a finger in for a quick taste. The chocolate river is warm and smooth, and the liquid chocolate clings to your finger when you bring it up from the river towards your mouth.

You give it a little taste, and your taste buds go absolutely berserk. You've never tasted milk chocolate quite like this before! It is the sweetest, smoothest, silkiest milk chocolate you have ever tasted, and you can hardly believe it is real. In fact, this entire chocolate world seems like a fantasy dream come true! You are so grateful that you have had this incredible experience in this chocolate dream world!

You do not have to leave this chocolate fantasy world just yet if you don't want to. You can spend as long as you want here and you can come back anytime you'd like.

You can create anything you want in your mind. Imagine where you want to go and build the picture in your mind. Be sure to imagine how you want it to smell, taste, hear, and feel. The more detailed you can make your mental picture, the more you will enjoy being there.

It is all up to you. Perhaps as you drift off to sleep, you may find yourself back in this world of milk chocolate rivers and chocolate candy kiss trees, back to explore and enjoy the chocolatey goodness again.

Chapter 32:
Magic Dancing Shoes

Do you know what magic dancing shoes are? Well, they are kind of like regular dancing shoes... but much more magical! Would you like to know what it is like to wear magic dancing shoes? Well, you can find out right now, without having to move a single muscle. You really can- In your mind! Your mind is capable of doing many incredible things, including something called Visualization.

To begin your visualization practice, close your eyes. Really, close your eyes (unless you are the one reading this, of course!) To build a very strong visualization, it is usually helpful to first center yourself and be sure you are giving your brain the very best tools it needs to work with. In this case, that means oxygen, and oxygen means taking some good, deep breaths.

You are going to take some slow, deep breaths now, following along with my instruction: Breathe in very slowly, 1 – 2 – 3 – 4. Now breathe out, very slowly, 1 2 3 4. Excellent. Now again very slowly, 1 – 2 – 3 – 4 and breathe back out very slowly, 1 – 2 – 3 – 4 very nice. Once more, very slowly in 1 – 2 – 3 – 4 and back out very slowly, 1 – 2 – 3 – 4. Great!

Take a moment to review how you feel. Are you comfy and feeling good? Okay, great.

Picture yourself, in your mind's eye, in a dance studio. The room is long and wide with a light oak floor and mirrors on every wall so you can always see every move you are making. It smells fresh and clean in here, like light oak paneling and clean floors. You are practicing your dance moves, but you feel your body getting tired.

Your instructor asks you if you have tried the magic dance shoes yet. You laugh a little because you have never heard of such a thing! You think this must be a silly joke of some sort, but your dance instructor assures you that it is not and brings you over a pair of shiny black dance shoes.

You are still unsure what to think, but you figure you might as well give them a try. You take off your dance shoes and set them off to the side. The dance shoes your instructor has given you are the shiniest dance shoes you have ever seen. You slide them on your feet and fasten them on to you, smiling a little to yourself about the idea of magic dancing shoes. They fit perfectly as if they were created just for you!

Once the shoes are fastened to your feet, you begin to stand up but find that your legs fly out from underneath you, and you leap up and into the air without you even trying! Your legs spread out into the perfect mid-air splits, and you land gracefully on one foot. Your mouth drops open, and you are in shock for a moment. How did you just do that?

You look at your instructor, dumbfounded, and your instructor just nods with encouragement for you to keep going. You think that you will attempt a quick twirl, but before you can even move a single muscle, your body is again leaping up and into the air, your legs tucking in and spinning as you do a perfect twirl through the air. Again, you land gracefully on one foot. How is this happening, you wonder?

Suddenly, you are whirling and twirling through the air with no conscious effort on your part. You feel as though you are flying, and your feet are so quick and sure! You relax into the moment and let your dancing shoes take the lead as your body soars through the air gracefully.

You are doing dance moves you never dreamed of attempting before! Your legs and arms are no longer tired as they seamlessly perform complicated dance moves that you haven't even been taught yet! You watch yourself in the long mirrors along the walls, in awe at how graceful you seem as you twirl and whirl through the air! You tell yourself to remember how this feels because someday you will dance like this without the magic dance shoes, you just know it.

Your magic dancing shoes are leading the way as you take a running start across the dance studio, leap high up into the air, and then perform mid-air, a full-body flip that you would never dream of attempting in your wildest dreams! In fact, you've never even seen someone do a dance move like this before in all your years dancing. You come out of this full-body flip and land perfectly down below in the splits, your legs stretching out easily along the shiny, light pine floor.

You are breathing heavily now, but not out of effort! The dancing shoes have done all the hard work for you, but you are extremely excited to have this opportunity to see what your body can do with some hard work and practice. These dancing shoes have really opened your eyes to what you can accomplish if you just keep at it. You are so thankful for this very cool experience with these magic dancing shoes.

You do not have to leave your magic dancing shoes behind just yet if you don't want to. You can spend as long as you want here and you can come back anytime you'd like.

You can create anything you want in your mind. Imagine where you want to go and build the picture in your mind. Be sure to imagine how you want it to smell, taste, hear, and feel. The more detailed you can make your mental picture, the more you will enjoy being there.

It is all up to you. Perhaps as you drift off to sleep, you may find yourself back in this dance studio, soaring through the air with your magic dancing shoes leading the way.

Chapter 33:
Magical Mermaid Potion

Have you ever wondered what it would be like to be a mermaid, swimming under the deep blue sea? What if there was some secret way that you could become a mermaid, just for a little while? Maybe you can... with a magical mermaid potion. You really can- In your mind! Your mind is capable of doing many incredible things, including something called Visualization.

To begin your visualization practice, close your eyes. Really, close your eyes (unless you are the one reading this, of

course!) To build a very strong visualization, it is usually helpful to first center yourself and be sure you are giving your brain the very best tools it needs to work with. In this case, that means oxygen, and oxygen means taking some good, deep breaths.

You are going to take some slow, deep breaths now, following along with my instruction: Breathe in very slowly, 1 – 2 – 3 – 4. Now breathe out, very slowly, 1 – 2 – 3 – 4. Excellent. Now again very slowly, 1 – 2 – 3 – 4 and breathe back out very slowly, 1 – 2 – 3 – 4 very nice. Once more, very slowly in 1 – 2 – 3 – 4 and back out very slowly, 1 – 2 – 3 – 4. Great!

Take a moment to review how you feel. Are you comfy and feeling good? Okay, great.

Imagine yourself, in your mind's eye, standing on a long, wooden pier out over the sea. The sea is a deep blue-green, and it extends as far as your eye can see. You take in a deep, long breath and smell the fresh, salty sea air as the sea breeze gently flows over and around you.

It is a lovely day to be out exploring by the sea! The sun is shining overhead, and you enjoy hearing the steady whoosh of each wave as it gently crashes into the shore. You think you might be just about ready to take a little dip in the water, now that you've gotten nice and toasty warm out on the dock of the pier. You walk back to the sandy beach, your footsteps making a satisfying plunking noise on each wooden section of the pier. Your footsteps seem to echo around the wide-open seascape, and you pause for a moment as you notice a seagull swooping down beside you to pluck a fish out of the sea.

The sea is always both an exciting and peaceful place to be for you. There are plenty of interesting things to see and do and have fun, but there is also an easy relaxation that happens while you are here, too. You take another long, deep breath in of salty sea air as you take your next step to hop off of the pier on to the sandy beach when you feel your toe brush against something hard and smooth in the sand.

You crouch down to inspect what you've brushed against and see that it is a tiny glass bottle with a cork stopper in it and a tiny note attached. You read the note while your toes sink satisfyingly down into the sand, and it says, "Magical Mermaid Potion: Drink me." The liquid inside is a shimmery, iridescent purplish-blue and as you lift the bottle up to the sunlight to get a closer look at it, the potion inside seems to shimmer and shine in the sun.

You wonder what on earth a magical mermaid potion does! You take a few steps through the warm sand of the beach to reach the water. The cool, clear saltwater feels refreshing on your feet. You are still holding on to the clear glass bottle, thinking to yourself that you really should try it. After all, isn't the beach an excellent place for fun and adventure?

You pull the tan cork out of the mouth of the bottle with a satisfying pop and put the clear glass bottle up to your mouth. You very cautiously take the teeniest, tiniest sip of the shimmery purplish-blue liquid. It tastes sweet and fresh, like the juice from a freshly picked pineapple! It is delicious, you think, as you turn the bottle upside down and drink down the rest of it. Hmm, you think, as you put the cork back in the bottle and set it back down in the sand. You don't feel any different!

Suddenly, you feel yourself falling forward into the water, unable to stand upright. You go to step out one of your feet for balance while you look down to see in amazement that you do not have any feet! Instead, you have a mermaid tail!!!!

You land in the water with a huge splash, and you are shocked that the huge emerald green fins that you had just seen where your feet should have been begun naturally flipping back and forth and propelling through the water! You easily glide through the clear and cool seawater, and you feel like you are flying through the water! Wow!

You dive deep beneath the surface of the water and realize that just like a mermaid, you can breathe underwater, too! You swiftly and easily swim through the water without having to worry about coming up for air. You are so excited to realize that now that you have mermaid fins and can breathe underwater, you will be able to explore parts of the sea that you have never been able to see before. You are so grateful that you have been able to have this experience.

It really is true. You never know what a visit to the beach might mean! You do not have to come out of the clear, beautiful sea just yet if you don't want to. You can spend as long as you want here and you can come back anytime you'd like.

You can create anything you want in your mind. Imagine where you want to go and build the picture in your mind. Be sure to imagine how you want it to smell, taste, hear, and feel. The more detailed you can make your mental picture, the more you will enjoy being there.

It is all up to you. Perhaps as you drift off to sleep, you may find yourself back at the seashore, ready to drink another little bottle of magical mermaid potion.

Chapter 34:
Freeze Time, Freeze

Have you ever wondered what it would be like to have supernatural powers? You know, like the ability to fly or see through walls? Well, what if you could freeze time and stop it in its tracks anytime you want? You really can- In your mind! Your mind is capable of doing many incredible things, including something called Visualization.

To begin your visualization practice, close your eyes. Really, close your eyes (unless you are the one reading this, of

course!) To build a very strong visualization, it is usually helpful to first center yourself and be sure you are giving your brain the very best tools it needs to work with. In this case, that means oxygen, and oxygen means taking some good, deep breaths.

You are going to take some slow, deep breaths now, following along with my instruction: Breathe in very slowly, 1 – 2 – 3 – 4. Now breathe out, very slowly, 1 – 2 – 3 – 4. Excellent. Now again very slowly, 1 – 2 – 3 – 4 and breathe back out very slowly, 1 2 3 4 very nice. Once more, very slowly in 1 2 – 3 – 4 and back out very slowly, 1 – 2 – 3 – 4. Great!

Take a moment to review how you feel. Are you comfy and feeling good? Okay, great.

Imagine yourself, on a warm summer day, standing outside in a green, grassy field. You are surrounded by sounds of nature all around you. You can hear the singing and warbling of birds all around you as they call to each other from the trees. You can hear the distant sound of gurgling water, perhaps from a nearby stream or brook.

You take a step forward and can feel the tall grass underfoot as it is being pressed down with your step; it makes a satisfying pressure on the bottom of your shoe. You continue to move forward across the grassy field in the direction of the water sounds, curious to see where it is coming from.

You are daydreaming today, thinking of the many cool superhero powers that superheroes in stories can have. You think of what it might be like to have superhero powers yourself. For example, what if you could freeze time in its tracks? That would be a pretty neat superhero power, wouldn't it?

Suddenly you hear a disturbance in the trees. It sounds as if something has startled the birds there, and you hear the sounds of several birds flapping their wings quickly and all at once as they leave their perches in the trees to fly up and away from whatever has startled them. As the group of birds becomes visible, you are excited to see how colorful they are!

The birds set off to fly over the very field you are standing in, and you are intrigued by the beautiful colors you see, but it is hard to see them well because they are moving so fast. You think that you wish you could freeze time and see them closer and... Whoa!!!!

Right when you thought that, the birds froze in their flight above you! In mid-air! Just completely stopped in the exact positions they were in, no movement whatsoever. You are surprised as you stand below them, your mouth hanging open in shock. Did you just freeze time? Like a superhero???

Well, you can definitely see the birds and their beautiful colors now! You can see some of the birds have deep reds and oranges, and some of the birds are light blues and greens. Some of these birds are even yellow! It is a stunning group of birds, and you can see them all in exquisite detail because they are frozen in flight, wings extended, just hanging out above you about a hundred feet up in the air or so.

You think to yourself that you don't know how to make time start again, and you want the birds to be able to continue on their journey. The moment you have that thought, the birds start again as if nothing had happened! They are flying over you, wings flapping as usual as they continue on their way. Wow!

You notice the sound of the nearby stream again and continue your way across the field, pressing the tall grasses down underfoot with every step. There is a lovely summer breeze blowing across the field now, and you notice that the weather seems to be shifting a bit. It looks like it might even rain. You decide to pick up the pace a little and begin jogging across the field, your legs feeling strong and sturdy as you run.

You finally reach the stream, the sounds of the water rushing over and around rocks is much louder now. It is a lovely sound, and you crouch down by the water's edge and put a hand into the water. It feels cool and refreshing as the water moves quickly over and around your hand.

You hear a loud clap of thunder in the distance and think, oh no! It's going to storm; you have got to get to shelter. You look up and see the dark gray rain-filled clouds moving quickly towards you, and you look around to see where you can go to get out of the storm. There really isn't anywhere near you to shelter, and you wish that the storm would just stop and... oh my goodness!

The dark gray rain-filled clouds that were moving so quickly towards you a moment ago have stopped! Looking up, the sky directly above you is the bright blue of a summer day, and the over in the distance is the dark gray sky of a thunderstorm. You have done it again. You have frozen time!

The water in the stream has stopped moving, as well. You can see the little waves and bubbles that the water makes as it churns and travels along the river bank with excellent detail now as everything has frozen perfectly in place. You stand up and step back from the bank.

You can hardly believe your eyes. You can stop time! You can freeze it in its tracks, just by wishing it! You are so excited to imagine all of the fun things you can see and explore and do by freezing time and you decide that you better take off for home before you have to unfreeze this storm, but you will be freezing time everywhere you go! You are so thankful that you have this incredible superpower that can you use!

You do not have to stop freezing time if you don't want to. You can spend as long as you want here and you can come back anytime you'd like.

You can create anything you want in your mind. Imagine where you want to go and build the picture in your mind. Be sure to imagine how you want it to smell, taste, hear, and feel. The more detailed you can make your mental picture, the more you will enjoy being there.

It is all up to you. Perhaps as you drift off to sleep, you may find yourself having this superhero power to freeze time again, able to freeze time anywhere and anytime you choose.

Chapter 35:
Trampoline Tricks

Have you ever wondered what it would be like to jump on a massive trampoline? You know, like a trampoline that is basically as big as a house? Well, you can, right now, without even moving a muscle. You really can- In your mind! Your mind is capable of doing many incredible things, including something called Visualization.

To begin your visualization practice, close your eyes. Really, close your eyes (unless you are the one reading this, of course!) To build a very strong visualization, it is usually helpful to first center yourself and be sure you are giving your brain the very best tools it needs to work with. In this case, that means oxygen, and oxygen means taking some good, deep breaths.

You are going to take some slow, deep breaths now, following along with my instruction: Breathe in very slowly, 1 – 2 – 3 – 4. Now breathe out, very slowly, 1 – 2 – 3 – 4. Excellent. Now again very slowly, 1 – 2 – 3 – 4 and breathe back out very slowly, 1 – 2 – 3 – 4 very nice. Once more, very slowly in 1 – 2 – 3 – 4 and back out very slowly, 1 – 2 – 3 – 4. Great!

Take a moment to review how you feel. Are you comfy and feeling good? Okay, great.

Imagine yourself, in your mind's eye, standing outside on a clear and sunny day. The weather is absolutely perfect. It is not too hot and not too cold, and there is a light breeze that is gently rustling the leaves in the trees around you. You are in a beautiful backyard with flowers, shrubbery, and trees all around you.

Up ahead is something that is very large and round. It is so big that it is almost as big as the backyard you are standing in. You take a few steps closer in your bare feet, feeling the soft and plush green grass squish underfoot with each step. You realize it is a trampoline that is taking up so much space back here!

Wow! This trampoline is huge! You've never seen a trampoline so large, and you go running up to it. You climb the ladder to get on as quickly as you can, the surface of the trampoline is cool and slick under your bare feet.

You love trampolines, and this trampoline is incredible! Looking out across the taut black surface, you are full of excitement. You take a few tentative steps forward across the trampoline, your feet bouncing back up with the tension of the trampoline surface with every step.

You decide to give it a little test jump, and you bend your legs ever so slightly and let yourself do a bit of a jump just to see how bouncy this thing is. You spring up into the air with amazement and think, wow! This is the bounciest trampoline you've ever been on!

You decide to really start jumping now, and with every jump you make, you are flung higher and higher up into the air. You look around you, and you realize that you can see everything around you from up here. You can see the tops of bushes and the flower beds, with their deep greens, bright reds and pinks, and vivid oranges and yellows. You can see up and into the trees around you. You can even see birds in the branches!

You twist around to look behind you and realize that you can even almost see the roof of the house!!! Every bounce seems to take you higher, and you can hear the air whooshing around you as your body moves so quickly you can barely even make out details of everything around you as the world around you is a bit of a blur as you jump so high and so fast.

You decide to try a flip, and as you bend and tuck your body into a flip, you realize you can do several flips in the time you spend in the air on this super trampoline. You land on your feet, spring back up into the air, tuck your body into itself, and feel yourself doing one, two, three, four, five, six, even seven intervals through the air before your feet touch the trampoline again. You are amazed! This trampoline is incredible.

You decide to take advantage of the width of this super trampoline and to jump the entire way across. You take a running start and spring off with your legs into a flying leap. You are sprung so high up in the air that you feel like you are practically flying as you leap across this giant trampoline. You land on the other side with a laugh because this is the most incredible trampoline you have ever been on, and you are so happy you are here. You are so grateful to whoever decided to build this massive trampoline!

You do not have to leave this super trampoline right now if you don't want to. You can spend as long as you want here and you can come back anytime you'd like.

You can create anything you want in your mind. Imagine where you want to go and build the picture in your mind. Be sure to imagine how you want it to smell, taste, hear, and feel. The more detailed you can make your mental picture, the more you will enjoy being there.

It is all up to you. Perhaps as you drift off to sleep, you may find yourself back on this giant trampoline, flipping and leaping so far up into the air that you feel like you are flying.

Chapter 36:
Build a Snow Fort

Have you ever built a snow fort before? An epic fort made out of snow made in the middle of winter? Well, you can build one right now without having to ever move a single muscle. You really can- In your mind! Your mind is capable of doing many incredible things, including something called Visualization.

To begin your visualization practice, close your eyes. Really, close your eyes (unless you are the one reading this, of course!) To build a very strong visualization, it is usually helpful to first center yourself and be sure you are giving your brain the very best tools it needs to work with. In this case, that means oxygen, and oxygen means taking some good, deep breaths.

You are going to take some slow, deep breaths now, following along with my instruction: Breathe in very slowly, 1 - 2 - 3 - 4. Now breathe out, very slowly, 1 - 2 - 3 - 4. Excellent. Now again very slowly, 1 - 2 - 3 - 4 and breathe back out very slowly, 1 - 2 - 3 - 4 very nice. Once more, very slowly in 1 - 2 - 3 - 4 and back out very slowly, 1 - 2 - 3 - 4. Great!

Take a moment to review how you feel. Are you comfy and feeling good? Okay, great.

Imagine yourself, in your mind, standing outside in the middle of a swirling snowstorm. Everywhere you look, you see a glittering white wonderland.

It is cold outside, but you are warm because you are completely bundled up against the cold. You have your heaviest, snuggliest winter coat on, your softest scarf wrapped around your neck, your wooliest hat on your head, and your thickest gloves on your hands. You have your warm long johns on underneath your snowsuit, and you have not one, but two pairs of snuggly warm socks on your feet! You are well armored against the bitter winter cold.

The winter winds are blowing snow in from all directions, but you love winter and do not mind much. You take a deep breath in and enjoy the crisp, clean smell of freshly fallen snow.

You are excited because you are going to build a snow fort! You have a shiny metal shovel, and you begin by first digging out the trench that your snow fort will be built around. The snow is heavy and densely packed together, so you have to use your arm and back muscles to dig in and move the snow out of the way for the trench, but it feels good for your muscles to get to work. It warms you up from the inside out.

Once you have dug out your trench, you take a step back to survey the space. It is just wide enough for probably two or three people to sit in, but that is perfect for a snow fort because you want it to be small enough that you can keep the heat in. You begin to work on your snow bricks next. Using your thickly gloved fingers, you shape each snow brick diligently and begin to stack them up, row by row. The snow is really coming down all around you, and this inspires you to move even quicker.

You first build up the first three rows and then decide to make a window on one side to see out of. You very carefully stack the bricks around the window. You will build and carefully scoop out the excess snow on either side. You are getting excited because your snow fort only needs the top two rows of snow bricks to be built up and come together on the top, and then it will be done!

You place the final snow bricks and voila! Just like that, you have built your snow fort. You step back to admire your handiwork and notice that the wind is really kicking up out here, and you are starting to feel a bit chilly. Time to test out your snow fort!

You climb in through the door and immediately notice the temperature difference. The inside of your snow fort perfectly shelters you from the cold winter winds outside, and you sit directly under the window so you can enjoy the gentle winter light coming in. Looking around, the outside light coming through the window and the door is reflecting off of the snow bricks inside and making it look as though they are glowing with winter light.

You are warm and toasty inside your snow fort and so proud of all your hard work! You have built a fabulous snow fort, and it will be an excellent shelter for you to stay warm and protected from the winter storm that is raging on around you. You are so grateful for this cozy snow fort that you were able to build.

You do not have to leave your cozy snow fort right now if you don't want to. You can spend as long as you want here and you can come back anytime you'd like.

You can create anything you want in your mind. Imagine where you want to go and build the picture in your mind. Be sure to imagine how you want it to smell, taste, hear, and feel. The more detailed you can make your mental picture, the more you will enjoy being there.

It is all up to you. Perhaps as you drift off to sleep, you may find yourself back in this winter storm, enjoying the toasty warm snow fort you built for yourself.

Chapter 37:
Tree House Building

Do you have a treehouse? Have you ever wondered what it would be like to build your very own treehouse that you could go in anytime you wanted to? Well, you can do that right now without moving a single muscle. You really can- In your mind! Your mind is capable of doing many incredible things, including something called Visualization.

To begin your visualization practice, close your eyes. Really, close your eyes (unless you are the one reading this, of course!) To build a very strong visualization, it is usually helpful to first center yourself and be sure you are giving your brain the very best tools it needs to work with. In this case, that means oxygen, and oxygen means taking some good, deep breaths.

You are going to take some slow, deep breaths now, following along with my instruction: Breathe in very slowly, 1 – 2 – 3 – 4. Now breathe out, very slowly, 1 – 2 – 3 – 4. Excellent. Now again very slowly, 1 – 2 – 3 – 4 and breathe back out very slowly, 1 – 2 – 3 – 4 very nice. Once more, very slowly in 1 – 2 – 3 – 4 and back out very slowly, 1 – 2 – 3 – 4. Great!

Take a moment to review how you feel. Are you comfy and feeling good? Okay, great.

Picture yourself, in your mind's eye, standing outside on a beautiful spring day. The sky is blue above you, and you can hear the sounds of birds singing and chirping to each other in the trees around you. You are in a backyard, standing before a mighty oak tree.

The mighty oak tree is tall and strong, with branches that are so thick they could be trees themselves! The leaves on the tree are the light, fresh, vibrant green that you see in spring while the world is growing fresh and new. You take a big, long, deep breath in and smell the flowers that are freshly blooming along the fence nearby. What a lovely day, you think!

You notice that there is a spot up in this big, beautiful oak tree where two branches separate as they extend out from the tree, and you think it would be the perfect spot to put a treehouse!

That's when you notice all the materials you need to build a treehouse are right there next to the tree. There are planks of sturdy wood, a tool belt with a hammer and nails, and rope to build a rope swing! Perfect, you think.

You attach the tool belt to yourself and set off to work. There are five perfectly cut smaller planks of wood that you are able to easily attach to the trunk of the tree going up to where you will place the base of your treehouse. The sound of the hammer as it drives the nails into the tree is like music to your ears as you are satisfied to step back and admire the steps you have built that will let you easily climb up and down the tree!

Once the steps are complete, it is time to build the platform of the treehouse. You begin with the first plank, attaching it carefully between the two branches that extend out from the tree. Once the first plank is firmly attached to the branches, it is easy to keep adding the other planks side by side that will make up the floor of your treehouse. One by one, you hammer the nails into the planks that safely attach and secure them to the tree. Before long, you have the entire floor completed!

Now that the floor is completed, you can start working on the walls! You decide that you will do walls that go up to your waist and leave the top part completely open so you will be able to see in all directions while you are up in your treehouse. Just as you did with the floor, you carefully and steadily place each wooden beam where it belongs and use the hammer and nails to securely attach them in place.

You finally place the final beam and get the last of the nails driven in. You climb down from the platform, and once you are standing on the ground, take a few steps back so you can look up at your handiwork. Wow! You have built yourself a fabulous treehouse.

Now it is time to attach the rope swing. You decide that you will put the rope swing on the opposite side of the treehouse, so if you decide you would like to, you can simply climb on the rope swing and swing out and over into your treehouse. You climb up the opposite side of the mighty oak tree, the bark of the tree trunk and its branches rough against your hands. You attach the rope swing and give it a gentle tug to be sure it is firmly attached.

Feels okay, you think, but you know you need to test it more. Well, what better way to test it than to just go ahead and try it out? You go ahead and climb on to it, and it holds you perfectly as you sway out and away from the tree. You use your feet to kick back against the tree trunk and swing-out wider and higher. This time as you swing back towards the mighty oak, you decide to go ahead and see if you can land in your treehouse.

Success! You are able to swing into your treehouse, no problem. You let go of the rope swing, and your feet land firmly on the floor of your treehouse with a very satisfying thud. You stand in the middle of the floor that you have just built and look around.

The view from your treehouse is spectacular! Just as you've planned, you can see out in every direction with your half walls, and there is even a lovely spring breeze coming through the tree that makes your treehouse feel absolutely perfect. You smile with satisfaction as you are very proud of yourself and all the hard work you've done to build this awesome treehouse. You are so thankful that you were able to build a cool treehouse that you can enjoy whenever you want.

You do not have to leave the fabulous treehouse you have built just yet if you don't want to. You can spend as long as you want here and you can come back anytime you'd like.

You can create anything you want in your mind. Imagine where you want to go and build the picture in your mind. Be sure to imagine how you want it to smell, taste, hear, and feel. The more detailed you can make your mental picture, the more you will enjoy being there.

It is all up to you. Perhaps as you drift off to sleep, you may find yourself back on this gorgeous spring day, enjoying the awesome treehouse you built for yourself.

Chapter 38:
Speaking Animal:

Have you ever wondered what it might be like to be able to speak to animals? What if you could understand them and they could understand you? Wouldn't that be cool! Well, you can actually do that right now, without having to even move a single muscle. You really can- In your mind! Your mind is capable of doing many incredible things, including something called Visualization.

To begin your visualization practice, close your eyes. Really, close your eyes (unless you are the one reading this, of course!) To build a very strong visualization, it is usually helpful to first center yourself and be sure you are giving your brain the very best tools it needs to work with. In this case, that means oxygen, and oxygen means taking some good, deep breaths.

You are going to take some slow, deep breaths now, following along with my instruction: Breathe in very slowly, 1 - 2 - 3 - 4. Now breathe out, very slowly, 1 - 2 - 3 - 4. Excellent. Now again very slowly, 1 - 2 - 3 - 4 and breathe back out very slowly, 1 - 2 - 3 - 4 very nice. Once more, very slowly in 1 - 2 - 3 - 4 and back out very slowly, 1 - 2 - 3 - 4. Great!

Take a moment to review how you feel. Are you comfy and feeling good? Okay, great.

Imagine yourself, in your mind's eye, standing outside on a sidewalk by a park. You are walking along the sidewalk, feeling the smooth concrete under your feet. It is a lovely fall day, and the air is crisp and cool. You look around you and notice how beautiful the leaves on the trees are as they change their colors. You can see bright and vivid colors of orange, yellow, red, and many colors in between.

A light fall breeze blows through, and some of the leaves from the trees surrounding the park flutter past you as they fly off the trees. You take a long, slow, deep breath in and say "I love Fall!" quietly and under your breath, to yourself as you walk under a tree by the entrance of the park, only to hear a response of, "I would too if it wasn't so much work!"

You are surprised because there is no one here in the park right now! You look all around you, to your left, to your right, behind you and in front of you, and don't see anyone at all, but you know you just heard someone respond. What on earth?

Just then, you hear the voice again, this time saying "up here!" from just above you. You take a tentative step back away from the tree and look up, still not seeing who this voice belongs to. That's when you see a bushy tail twitching back and forth on a branch of the tree and see the dark brown squirrel that is perched there, tail swishing back and forth as it sits and looks out at you.

You laugh out loud at yourself because for a moment there, you thought maybe it was the squirrel! Squirrels can't talk, that would be ridiculous, right? Out loud, you say, "I could've sworn I heard a voice, but all I see is you, Mr. Squirrel! I know you can't talk, so..." as you make a silly expression on your face and turn to go. You stop dead in your tracks when you hear the same small voice say again, "Just because you've never talked to a squirrel doesn't mean you need to be rude about it!"

You slowly turn back around and see the squirrel now leaning back on its hind legs with its little arms crossed across his chest. He is looking right at you! Your eyes wide as saucers, you stammer out "You??? Are you actually talking to me, Mr. Squirrel???"

"Well, yeah! You said you love Fall. I would probably love Fall, too, if I didn't have to spend it preparing so much for winter! I have to gather enough acorns to last me through the winter, so fall is nothing but hard work for me!" the little brown squirrel said animatedly.

You are trying to get over your shock that this furry little animal is talking to you- and you can actually understand it- when you hear another little voice from the other side of the tree.

"Well, it's no walk in the park for us, either. We are getting ready for our long journey south. Trust me, that kind of a flight and your wings get pretty tired!"

"Who is that?!" you ask excitedly as you peer around the tree. You see no one and look back up at the squirrel, who is now pointing up at the branch on the other side of the tree from him. There you see a pair of two beautiful little blue jays, perched carefully together. The two birds raise their wings and wave at you!

"Oh, my goodness! You can talk too!" you stammer out. The birds look at each other and laugh at this. "Well, of course, we do, silly! How else would we communicate?"

"I've never been able to hear you before," you answer. The birds laugh again before answering, "Well, you do! Humans hear birds just fine. Only most of the time, you only hear it as whistles and chirps. Every now and then a human can hear more."

The squirrel is nodding at this. "Yup, usually humans just hear squirrels as chittering and squeaking. Only sometimes can you understand us."

You are so amazed! You had no idea that you would ever be able to communicate with animals! It's like speaking a new language. Animalese, maybe! You are so glad that you have had this incredible experience. You are so thankful that these cute little critters decided to talk to you today!

You do not have to leave your new animal friends just yet if you don't want to. You can spend as long as you want here and you can come back anytime you'd like.

You can create anything you want in your mind. Imagine where you want to go and build the picture in your mind. Be sure to imagine how you want it to smell, taste, hear, and feel. The more detailed you can make your mental picture, the more you will enjoy being there.

It is all up to you. Perhaps as you drift off to sleep, you may find yourself back in this park, chatting it up in animalese to your new animal friends.

Chapter 39:
Trip to the Zoo

Have you been to the zoo before? It's always so fun to see the different exotic animals, isn't it? Well, would you like to go visit the zoo right now? You can do this without moving a single muscle. You really can- In your mind! Your mind is capable of doing many incredible things, including something called Visualization.

To begin your visualization practice, close your eyes. Really, close your eyes (unless you are the one reading this, of course!) To build a very strong visualization, it is usually helpful to first center yourself and be sure you are giving your brain the very best tools it needs to work with. In this case, that means oxygen, and oxygen means taking some good, deep breaths.

You are going to take some slow, deep breaths now, following along with my instruction: Breathe in very slowly, 1 - 2 - 3 - 4. Now breathe out, very slowly, 1 - 2 - 3 - 4. Excellent. Now again very slowly, 1 - 2 - 3 - 4 and breathe back out very slowly, 1 - 2 - 3 - 4 very nice. Once more, very slowly in 1 - 2 - 3 - 4 and back out very slowly, 1 - 2 - 3 - 4. Great!

Take a moment to review how you feel. Are you comfy and feeling good? Okay, great.

Now, picture yourself, in your mind's eye, standing in front of a large, black wrought iron gate. This huge gate has the word "Zoo," written in massive letters at the top. You push the gate forward, and it easily opens for you as you walk through.

It is a lovely summer day, and the sun is shining. There is a gentle breeze blowing the air that helps to keep you cool. Take a long, deep breath in and notice that it smells like water. You look around, squinting your eyes a bit in the bright sun.

That's when you notice that directly to your left, you see a lovely pond area that is surrounded by a fence. You walk along the concrete path that runs beside the fence, wondering what is in there. You are standing on your tiptoes now as you scan the area, wondering what could possibly be in there when you are suddenly face-to-face with a fuzzy bird face!

Oh! You take a step back with a laugh. You are separated by a chain-link fence, but just about a foot or so away from you is an ostrich, craning its head from side to side, quizzically, as it looks you up and down. Behind the ostrich are more ostriches now in view, approaching the edge of the pond to get a drink.

Their faces are very expressive, and their eyes are wide and interesting as they peer out at you. When they bend down to get a drink in the pond, you giggle at the feathers on their bums as they flounce up and down with every movement.

There is a rock in the middle of the pond that you didn't notice before. It's not very big, but it... Wait, it is getting bigger somehow. Oh, wait! No, it is not getting bigger, but it is moving because it is not really a rock at all!

The large gray mound emerges out of the water completely, and you see it is a huge, dark gray hippopotamus! The water cascades down the sides of the hippo, and it stretches its large, blocky head up towards the sun before it opens its wide mouth into a massive yawn! Wow, look at those teeth!

Continuing on the concrete path, you enjoy the feeling of the sun as it warms your skin. Suddenly, there is a shadow overhead, and you realize the path you are on has led you to an entrance of a cave! Interesting! You enter in tentatively, your eyes needing to adjust from the bright sunshine outside to the darkness of the cave.

Inside, there is a wide-open area in the middle surrounded by walls of glass all around you. On the other side of the glass is something that causes you to exclaim out loud because it almost looks like you are all right in the same space together, but you remember then that you are protected by the glass.

Beautifully majestic lions lounge around on the other side of the glass. You see some lions laying on top of giant rocks, sunning themselves, and some lions down below in the shade, cleaning themselves with their massive tongues just like a housecat!

You are directly in the middle of them and can spin around in circles, watching these beautiful lions as they go about their day. Suddenly some commotion from behind causes you to whip around and see what it is, and you get to see two adorable baby lion cubs as they frolic and play together. The two baby lion cubs approach a lion that is stretched out near them, napping.

The lion cubs look at each other and quickly pounce on the older lion stretched out nearby, and the startled and surprised look on the older lion's face makes you laugh out loud! Those sweet little lion cubs are funny. You are so glad that you are here, and you feel so thankful to be at the zoo.

You are loving that you get to see these interesting animals, so up close. You do not have to leave this zoo just yet if you don't want to. You can spend as long as you want here and you can come back anytime you'd like.

You can create anything you want in your mind. Imagine where you want to go and build the picture in your mind. Be sure to imagine how you want it to smell, taste, hear, and feel. The more detailed you can make your mental picture, the more you will enjoy being there.

It is all up to you. Perhaps as you drift off to sleep, you may find yourself back at the zoo, exploring the trails and looking at interesting animals.

Chapter 40:
Go Kart Race

Have you ever had the chance to ride in a go-kart before? How about racing a go-kart? Well, don't worry if you never have before because you are going to get a chance to ride in a go-kart race right now without having to move a single muscle. You really can- In your mind! Your mind is capable of doing many incredible things, including something called Visualization.

To begin your visualization practice, close your eyes. Really, close your eyes (unless you are the one reading this, of

course!) To build a very strong visualization, it is usually helpful to first center yourself and be sure you are giving your brain the very best tools it needs to work with. In this case, that means oxygen, and oxygen means taking some good, deep breaths.

You are going to take some slow, deep breaths now, following along with my instruction: Breathe in very slowly, 1 – 2 – 3 – 4. Now breathe out, very slowly, 1 – 2 – 3 – 4. Excellent. Now again very slowly, 1 – 2 – 3 – 4 and breathe back out very slowly, 1 – 2 – 3 – 4 very nice. Once more, very slowly in 1 – 2 – 3 – 4 and back out very slowly, 1 – 2 – 3 – 4. Great!

Take a moment to review how you feel. Are you comfy and feeling good? Okay, great.

Picture yourself, in your mind's eye, standing outside of a huge race track. It is a beautiful spring day. The sky is bright blue up above you, and the spring sun is gently warming the air.

You look down and see you are dressed in racing gear from head to foot! You have a helmet on, leather racing gloves, and a full-body racing suit. Wow!

Just in front of you is a cherry red go-kart. You climb in, and you are safely strapped in with the seat belt. On either side of your go-kart are large flags with your name written on them! Just right there, for everyone to see, your name!

Now you notice that there are people in bleachers and stands all around the track. They are clapping excitedly, and you see that there is another person climbing into a go-kart right beside you, and they are getting carefully seat belted in. You both look up at each other and give each other the thumbs-up sign.

You are so excited! You are going to get to race go-karts!!! Alright, looks like you are ready to race. There is a black and white checkered flag that is directly in front of the two go-karts, and it is waving back and forth before you hear a loud popping sound as the black and white kart is raised and you know that means it is time to drive!

You push down with your right foot against the accelerator, and off you go! Your body is pressed back against the seat as your go-kart is speeding up as it travels along the track. You feel great as you fly down the track! The people sitting in the bleachers around you are a blur to you as you are now going so fast you can't really make out details.

You know the other go-kart is nearby, but you are having such a fantastic time you don't even really care if you will win or lose, you are just happy to be here racing! The rumble of the engine underneath you is getting stronger the faster you go. You can feel it vibrating throughout your entire body now!

You are vaguely aware of the other go-kart nearby, and you are not really sure is ahead right now. It doesn't seem to even really matter when you are having such a great time racing around this track! You can see something up ahead and in the distance that looks like it might have lights on it. Yes, you can see it now! It is the finish line, and it is lit up with strings of lights that go over and across the entire track.

You are so close! You can still hear the cheering from the crowd around you, but you are zoned in now on the finish line. You know you are getting closer and closer, and you push the gas pedal down completely to the floor of the go-kart as you know you need to really push it in this final stretch.

Your go-kart leaps forward, and you are aware, out of the corner of your eye, of the other go-kart being left behind you as you finally race across the lit-up finish line. You have won the race!

Your go-kart rolls to a stop, and the other go-kart rolls to a stop beside you. You feel exhilarated and happy. You unbuckle and begin to climb out of the go-kart and can see the other driver beside you doing the same. Once you are both out, you reach over and shake hands, telling each other that it was a great race.

The crowd is growing wild and cheering your name! You look around and can see everyone clapping and cheering loudly. You are so proud of the race you won, and you smile broadly as you stand in the sun, arms stretched up and out in triumph. You are so happy and thankful that you have been able to participate in this incredible race!

You do not have to leave this go-kart track just yet if you don't want to. You can spend as long as you want here and you can come back anytime you'd like.

You can create anything you want in your mind. Imagine where you want to go and build the picture in your mind. Be sure to imagine how you want it to smell, taste, hear, and feel. The more detailed you can make your mental picture, the more you will enjoy being there.

It is all up to you. Perhaps as you drift off to sleep, you may find yourself back at the track, racing around in your go-kart as the crowds' cheer and call out your name.

Chapter 41:
Country Road Bike Riding

Do you like to ride bikes? How about riding your bike out in the country where there are no other cars around, and you can really ride in the wide-open? What if I told you that you can go country road bike riding right this very moment, without having to move a single muscle? You really can- In your mind! Your mind is capable of doing many incredible things, including something called Visualization.

To begin your visualization practice, close your eyes. Really, close your eyes (unless you are the one reading this, of course!) To build a very strong visualization, it is usually helpful to first center yourself and be sure you are giving your brain the very best tools it needs to work with. In this case, that means oxygen, and oxygen means taking some good, deep breaths.

You are going to take some slow, deep breaths now, following along with my instruction: Breathe in very slowly, 1 – 2 – 3 – 4. Now breathe out, very slowly, 1 – 2 – 3 – 4. Excellent. Now again very slowly, 1 – 2 – 3 – 4 and breathe back out very slowly, 1 – 2 – 3 – 4 very nice. Once more, very slowly in 1 – 2 – 3 – 4 and back out very slowly, 1 – 2 – 3 – 4. Great!

Take a moment to review how you feel. Are you comfy and feeling good? Okay, great.

Imagine yourself, in your mind's eye, out under a deep blue sky, surrounded by cornfields and tall grasses? You are out in the country, and there is a dusty dirt road beneath your feet, and you are right next to a beautiful aqua blue bike. You take in a deep, long breath in and you smell the clean, fresh air of the country.

The road beneath you is a caramel-colored brownish tan, and it is lined with tall, spring green meadow grasses. You are so ready to ride! You climb on to the aqua blue bike and take a moment to enjoy the gentle summer breeze and the warm summer sun that is washing over you.

With a smile on your face, you begin to pedal forward. You can feel the muscles in your legs and feet as they begin to warm up with the effort of pedaling, and it feels so good to be able to use your strong and capable muscles in this way.

Pedaling forward, your aqua blue bike rolls along. You are out in the country, far, far away from other houses, businesses, buildings, or anything at all, really, so there is no one out on the road. You are completely free to do anything you want out here! You are able to go as fast as you want or as slow as you want because there is no one else out on the road with you.

The tires on your bike are aired up completely, and they ride like a dream. This bike ride is one of the smoothest bike rides you have ever been on as this country road is smooth and made of dirt that has been packed down from years and years of use. It is like riding on a cloud!

You look around you at the tall, strong stalks of corn growing in the fields on both sides of you. The summer breeze makes the corn stalks sway back and forth, and you can hear the gentle rustling of their rough, green stalks. It is the music of a country road cornfield.

The summer sun is soaking into your exposed skin, and you feel revitalized in the sun. The warm summer air washes over you as you fly on your bike down this beautiful country road. It feels so freeing to be riding your bike out here in the great, wide-open of a backcountry road. It is wonderful to not have to worry about traffic or traffic stops.

You love seeing the tall meadow grasses that line the country road gently sway in the summer breeze. Occasionally there is a patch of wildflowers mixed in, and the splashes of yellows, oranges, and purple look like a watercolor painting as you fly by on your bike.

You are completely at ease and feel relaxed and calm. You are happy to be spending a beautiful summer day out riding in the country, amongst the cornfields. You don't have to worry about time or traffic. You are just peaceful and calm. You are so grateful that you get to enjoy this kind of beautiful, peaceful experience.

You do not have to leave these lovely country roads just yet if you don't want to. You can spend as long as you want here and you can come back anytime you'd like.

You can create anything you want in your mind. Imagine where you want to go and build the picture in your mind. Be sure to imagine how you want it to smell, taste, hear, and feel. The more detailed you can make your mental picture, the more you will enjoy being there.

It is all up to you. Perhaps as you drift off to sleep, you may find yourself back out here in the wide-open country, pedaling your bike down these country roads in total freedom.

Chapter 42:
Rollerblading by the River

Have you ever been rollerblading before? If you have not, that's perfectly okay, because you are going to get to experience rollerblading right now, by the river, without moving a single muscle. You really can- In your mind! Your mind is capable of doing many incredible things, including something called Visualization.

To begin your visualization practice, close your eyes. Really, close your eyes (unless you are the one reading this, of course!) To build a very strong visualization, it is usually helpful to first center yourself and be sure you are giving your brain the very best tools it needs to work with. In this case, that means oxygen, and oxygen means taking some good, deep breaths.

You are going to take some slow, deep breaths now, following along with my instruction: Breathe in very slowly, 1 – 2 – 3 – 4. Now breathe out, very slowly, 1 – 2 – 3 – 4. Excellent. Now again very slowly, 1 – 2 – 3 – 4 and breathe back out very slowly, 1 – 2 – 3 – 4 very nice. Once more, very slowly in 1 – 2 – 3 – 4 and back out very slowly, 1 – 2 – 3 – 4. Great!

Take a moment to review how you feel. Are you comfy and feeling good? Okay, great.

Picture yourself, in your mind's eye, standing on a well-paved stretch of walkway, in a pair of rollerblades. These rollerblades are pretty cool looking, too, because these rollerblades are actually a deep, indigo blue color with sparkles! Not only do these rollerblades sparkle, but they actually light up as you roll along!

You move your feet back and forth a bit to test out these rollerblades and yup! There they are, lighting up with movement. Neat!

It is a beautiful spring day, and everywhere you look you can see the signs of spring. You take a long, slow, deep breath in and smell the freshly cut spring grass. You can see that there are beautiful flower beds that have been carefully planted on either side of the walkway that stretch completely along the riverwalk, and you can smell the light fragrant scent of their newly budding flower petals.

The riverwalk you are standing at the top of extends all the way along the river, as far as your eye can see. You are enthralled at the chance to travel on this pathway because you are at the top of a decent sized hill and know that once you start rolling, you will probably fly pretty quickly along the pathway.

Well, you decide, there's no better time than the present! With that thought, you take off, pushing off on one foot and sending yourself gliding along the pathway down the hill. The hill is easy to roll down on your rollerblades, and you don't have to do much work yourself, but it still feels good to your legs as your muscles are strong, and you are easily able to rollerblade along this path.

From where you are on the hill, you can see out over the river. It is gleaming in the sun and looks like the sunshine is sparkling out across the serene and still water of the river. You can see the deep, vibrant green of the trees on the opposite side of the river, lining the bank. There is a lush forest over there on the other bank, and you can see that some of the trees have giant white flowers on them- they must be Magnolia trees!

Now that you have seen the Magnolia trees, you realize you can smell them in the air too. Their scent is heavy, heady, and floral, and you take in a deep, long breath as you appreciate their lovely smell.

Gliding along the smooth path in your sparkly blue light-up rollerblades, you feel like you could be flying! You stretch your arms out to your sides and feel the sweet spring breeze flow over and around your arms, and you are half-tempted to close your eyes to enjoy this feeling even more. You laugh at yourself for the thought because you are riding down a hill on rollerblades, and closing your eyes would probably be terribly dangerous!

You keep your arms outstretched beside you as you soar down the pathway, the freshly planted flowers that line the riverwalk are a colorful blur to you now as you fly path them. The spring breeze gently flows over and around your entire body, and you smile because it feels so wonderful. The sun is shining, the flowers are blooming, and everything feels perfectly well in the world where you are.

Right now, you feel perfectly content. Your legs are strong, and your muscles feel great as you glide easily along the riverwalk path. You are happy and confident in your abilities, and you are so thankful to be out gliding along this river that is sparkling in the sunshine on this lovely spring day. You are thankful to be out here enjoying this beautiful riverwalk rollerblading experience.

You do not have to leave this beautiful riverwalk rollerblading experience just yet if you don't want to. You can spend as long as you want here and you can come back anytime you'd like.

You can create anything you want in your mind. Imagine where you want to go and build the picture in your mind. Be sure to imagine how you want it to smell, taste, hear, and feel. The more detailed you can make your mental picture, the more you will enjoy being there.

It is all up to you. Perhaps as you drift off to sleep, you may find yourself back out here, gliding along the riverwalk on your sparkly blue light-up rollerblades again.

Chapter 43:
Carriage Ride in the Snow

Have you ever been on a carriage ride? You know, with a pair of horses pulling the carriage along? How about a carriage ride through the snow on a sleigh? Well, what if I told you that you can go on a carriage through the snow right now without having to move a single muscle? You really can- In your mind! Your mind is capable of doing many incredible things, including something called Visualization.

To begin your visualization practice, close your eyes. Really, close your eyes (unless you are the one reading this, of course!) To build a very strong visualization, it is usually helpful to first center yourself and be sure you are giving your brain the very best tools it needs to work with. In this case, that means oxygen, and oxygen means taking some good, deep breaths.

You are going to take some slow, deep breaths now, following along with my instruction: Breathe in very slowly, 1 – 2 – 3 – 4. Now breathe out, very slowly, 1 – 2 – 3 – 4. Excellent. Now again very slowly, 1 – 2 – 3 – 4 and breathe back out very slowly, 1 – 2 – 3 – 4 very nice. Once more, very slowly in 1 – 2 – 3 – 4 and back out very slowly, 1 – 2 – 3 – 4. Great!

Take a moment to review how you feel. Are you comfy and feeling good? Okay, great.

Picture yourself, in your mind's eye, standing beside a snow-covered road. Snow is falling lightly all around you- big, fat snowflakes that swirl and blow around with the gentle winter breeze. You are cozy and warm in your winter weather clothes, and you pull your knitted wool cap down further over your head and ears for maximum warmth.

On the snow-covered road is a horse-drawn carriage led by two very large, very strong, and very sweet horses. You approach them because you have something to give to each one. The first horse is a large, dark brown mare- a girl horse. You come up to her side, speaking softly to her that you would like to give her a little treat before the ride. The dark brown mare knickers a soft hello back to you as she looks you over with her kind brown eyes. You reach out to stroke her long, dark mane, and she nods her head a little in your direction to lean into you.

You smile at this sweet horse and tell her that you have her treat for her. You are convinced she understands this because her pointy ears perk up and lean forward at the word "treat," and she looks at you expectantly. You giggle as you offer her a crisp red apple. She eagerly takes it from your gloved hand with an enthusiastic nod of gratitude, and you giggle again as you believe you have made a lovely new horse friend.

You now approach the horse beside her, a beautiful jet-black mare with a glossy black mane and kind brown eyes, just like her friend. You offer her a quiet hello and hold out a crisp red apple for her, and she gives a soft little knicker as she nods her head and steps lightly with her front hoofs, as if doing a little happy dance! You giggle at this big, beautiful horse doing a happy dance as she carefully plucks the apple out of your warmly gloved hand. As she munches, you stroke her glossy black mane and remark to yourself how silky smooth it is!

Now that the horses have been fed their treats, you are ready to climb into the back of the carriage. There is a large step up to get into the carriage, and you have to grip the side rails before you are able to make the giant step up to get in. You use your strong arm and leg muscles to pull yourself upward and push yourself forward and finally you are in!

The seat in the back is well-padded, and you let yourself sink into it comfortably. There is a nest of blankets all around it, and you pull the soft and fuzzy blankets up and around you, and you are instantly ensconced in warmth. Just then, the drive of the carriage gives the signal to the horses to begin moving forward, and suddenly the carriage is moving forward smoothly across the snowy road.

You lean back into the comfy seat and pull the soft and fuzzy blankets tighter around you. The snow is falling steadily now, and the big, fat snowflakes are piling up on top of each other all around you and even on top of you. You blink a couple of times because the snow is sticking to your eyelashes and it makes them heavy and hard to keep open, so you brush them off and pull the blankets up around and over the top of your head to make yourself a little cloak to keep the snow from falling on your lashes.

The scene beyond the carriage is growing more and more beautiful by the moment. The snow on the evergreen trees is piling up, and the fluffy white snow stacked on the forest green branches looks like something you would see on a holiday card. There is a twinkling of lights through the snow as you can see where people in the distance have decorated their home for the winter holidays, and the twinkling lights are shining through the dusting of white snow.

You are so happy in this beautiful winter wonderland! You are grateful to be on this amazing carriage ride in the snow, enjoying the beauty of winter all around you.

You do not have to leave this beautiful carriage ride just yet if you don't want to. You can spend as long as you want here and you can come back anytime you'd like.

You can create anything you want in your mind. Imagine where you want to go and build the picture in your mind. Be sure to imagine how you want it to smell, taste, hear, and feel.

The more detailed you can make your mental picture, the more you will enjoy being there.

It is all up to you. Perhaps as you drift off to sleep, you may find yourself back out here riding through this winter wonderland in a horse-drawn carriage.

Chapter 44:
Magic Hammock

What do you think a magic hammock would be? Well, it is a bit like a regular hammock, only this magic hammock is... well, it is magic! You can see for yourself, if you'd like, without moving a single muscle. You really can- In your mind! Your mind is capable of doing many incredible things, including something called Visualization.

To begin your visualization practice, close your eyes. Really, close your eyes (unless you are the one reading this, of course!) To build a very strong visualization, it is usually helpful to first center yourself and be sure you are giving your brain the very best tools it needs to work with. In this case, that means oxygen, and oxygen means taking some good, deep breaths.

You are going to take some slow, deep breaths now, following along with my instruction: Breathe in very slowly, 1 - 2 - 3 - 4. Now breathe out, very slowly, 1 - 2 - 3 - 4. Excellent. Now again very slowly, 1 - 2 - 3 - 4 and breathe back out very slowly, 1 - 2 - 3 - 4 very nice. Once more, very slowly in 1 - 2 - 3 - 4 and back out very slowly, 1 - 2 - 3 - 4. Great!

Take a moment to review how you feel. Are you comfy and feeling good? Okay, great.

Picture yourself, in your mind's eye, outside in a beautiful grassy area on a sweet, spring day. The weather is light and breezy, and the sun is shining down from above, and you are enjoying this lovely spring weather! You take a long, slow, deep breath in and smell the flowers that have just recently bloomed. You love spring.

Across the grass is a hammock that you have never seen before. Oh, wonderful! Today is the perfect kind of day to enjoy swinging in a hammock. You walk towards the hammock, your bare feet enjoying the feel of the soft and squishy spring grass beneath you. The hammock is a beautiful swirl pattern of greens and blues and reminds you of the waves in the sea. You reach out and touch it, and the material is a soft, thin, gauzy kind of material. You rub your fingertips back and forth against it, and you wonder how it could be so soft against your skin.

You decide to give it a try, and you ease yourself into the hammock carefully, leaning your body back until you are entirely inside of it. You put your hands behind your head as a pillow, and your bare feet are comfortably kicked up on the other end. You scrunch your toes a few times and marvel at how wonderful they feel against this soft and gauzy fabric. It is soft but perfectly light to the touch.

Looking up into the large sycamore tree above you, you let your thoughts drift a bit. This hammock is very comfortable, and the gentle spring breeze is causing it to sway back and forth lightly. As it sways, you watch the leaves in the tree above you as they gently flutter back and forth in the breeze. You think the leaves look like they are almost dancing in the wind, and you wonder what it feels like to dance like that in the wind.

Suddenly, you feel the hammock lift up, and you drift slowly but steadily up towards the branches of the sycamore tree up above you! You are almost in shock, and you are frozen in place as you are moving closer and closer to the branches of the giant sycamore. Your hammock comes to a stop on one of the lower branches, and you feel like you are hanging off of this big sycamore tree branch, just like a giant leaf of some sort!

A gust of wind blows through, and you feel your hammock flutter in the breeze, just as you watched the leaves do from below, and you gently sway back and forth and back and forth. You feel so light and breezy up here in the tree, and the spring breeze continues to rock the hammock gently back and forth. You relax into the experience of fluttering like a leaf in the breeze and look up at the bright blue sky through the branches and leaves above you.

The sky is a vividly bright blue that you find in beautiful spring mornings, and you can see that the sky is full of fluffy white clouds floating by. You think how wonderfully fluffy and full they look, and you wonder what it would be like to be floating like a cloud in the breeze.

Just then, you are suddenly floating out from beneath the tree branches of the sycamore, and you are completely suspended out in midair! You aren't quite sure what to think, but there's not much you can do as this magic hammock steers you out and up. You are floating up, up, and up towards the white fluffy clouds above, and again, you are shocked and amazed by this magic hammock! Your hammock comes to a stop on the top of a fluffy white cloud!

Surrounded by thick and full white fluff, your hammock is again gently swaying back and forth in the breeze, but when the spring wind gusts, this time you are also gliding through the air on the cloud below you! You are basically riding a fluffy, white cloud in this magic hammock, and you cannot help smiling at this amazing and magical adventure. You are so grateful that you have been given the opportunity to see what it is like to flutter like a leaf in the breeze or to sail like a cloud in the sky.

You do not have to leave this magic hammock just yet if you don't want to. You can spend as long as you want here and you can come back anytime you'd like.

You can create anything you want in your mind. Imagine where you want to go and build the picture in your mind. Be sure to imagine how you want it to smell, taste, hear, and feel. The more detailed you can make your mental picture, the more you will enjoy being there.

It is all up to you. Perhaps as you drift off to sleep, you may find yourself back out here sailing through the sky on your magic hammock in the clouds.

Chapter 45:
Finding A Magic Wand

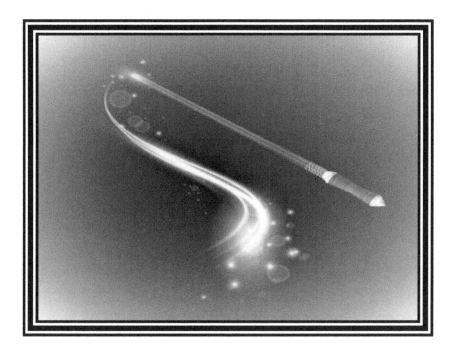

Have you ever let yourself wonder about what it would be like to have a magic wand? Just let your imagination run wild and think about all the cool things you could do with a magic wand? Well, what if I told you that you could experience what it is like to have a magic wand right now, without moving a single muscle? You really can- In your mind! Your mind is capable of doing many incredible things, including something called Visualization.

To begin your visualization practice, close your eyes. Really, close your eyes (unless you are the one reading this, of course!) To build a very strong visualization, it is usually helpful to first center yourself and be sure you are giving your brain the very best tools it needs to work with. In this case, that means oxygen, and oxygen means taking some good, deep breaths.

You are going to take some slow, deep breaths now, following along with my instruction: Breathe in very slowly, 1 – 2 – 3 – 4. Now breathe out, very slowly, 1 – 2 – 3 – 4. Excellent. Now again very slowly, 1 – 2 – 3 – 4 and breathe back out very slowly, 1 – 2 – 3 – 4 very nice. Once more, very slowly in 1 – 2 – 3 – 4 and back out very slowly, 1 – 2 – 3 – 4. Great!

Take a moment to review how you feel. Are you comfy and feeling good? Okay, great.

Picture yourself, in your mind's eye, walking along a sidewalk. It is a beautiful autumn day, and the wind is gently blowing the freshly fallen leaves around as you walk. It is like walking through an autumn-colored vortex as the leaves of red, yellow, and orange crunch below your feet and swirl around below and around your ankles with every fresh gust of wind.

You love this weather! You take a long, deep, slow breath in and notice how crisp and clear this autumn day is. It smells like freshly fallen leaves, and you use your feet to kick the leaves out of the way, loving the way the leaves feel and sound as you kick through them. You love the crispy, crunchy, crinkly sounds the leaves make as you... Wait a moment. That wasn't a leaf you just kicked.

Your foot just connected with something that was heavier and harder than an autumn leaf, and you heard the gentle thud it made as it landed just a bit ahead of you. You are curious and want to know what the heck that was that you just kicked, so you go up to where you heard the thud and lightly move the leaves around with the tip of your foot. The leaves are moved out of the way, and below it, you see what it was you kicked: just a stick.

But just wait for a second here, what kind of a stick is that? You pick it up and notice that it is not just a stick, but rather a tool of some sort. It is made of wood but has been smoothly whittled into a pointed shape with a clear crystal medallion at the tip. Interesting! You inspect it closely and see that there are words carved into the side: "The Westis Wand." What the heck does that mean, you wonder? Pretty cool fake wand, you think, and you imagine maybe it is a movie prop or something because it certainly looks too nice to be just a toy.

You point it at the empty sidewalk in front of you and say, "Westis Wand, I want a chocolate milkshake!" You are shocked and amazed when there is a zap of what looks like lightning that comes out of the end of the wand, and an actual, real-life chocolate milkshake is actually floating in the air right in front of you!!!

Whoa! You tentatively reach out and pull the magically floating chocolate milkshake out of the air where it hovers before you and take a sip. Oh my gosh, yes! It is a delicious chocolate milkshake. This magic wand is REAL!

You decide to test it further. Chocolate milkshake still in one hand, you use the other hand to point the wand at the leaf pile you pulled it out of and said, "Westis Wand, make these leaves dance!" Again, there is a zap of what looks like lightning that comes out of the end of the wand, and suddenly, the crunchy autumn leaves are coming up and off of the sidewalk and are dancing through the air.

The leaves are swirling around you, and you are in the middle of their dance, the reds, oranges, and yellows of the autumn leaves floating and swirling gently around you as you stand in disbelief with a delicious chocolate shake in one hand and a MAGIC WAND IN THE OTHER!

You are so thrilled to have found a magic wand. You have no idea what you will do with it next, but you are so grateful to have found it and to be able to do incredible, magical things with it!

You do not have to leave your magic wand just yet if you don't want to. You can spend as long as you want here and you can come back anytime you'd like.

You can create anything you want in your mind. Imagine where you want to go and build the picture in your mind. Be sure to imagine how you want it to smell, taste, hear, and feel. The more detailed you can make your mental picture, the more you will enjoy being there.

It is all up to you. Perhaps as you drift off to sleep, you may find yourself back out here in the middle of a swirling dance of autumn leaves, holding a magic wand and a chocolate milkshake.

Chapter 46:
Science Time Fun

Do you like science? Science experiments can be so fun! Would you like to do a science experiment right now? What if I told you that you can do a science experiment right now without having to move a single muscle. You really can- In your mind! Your mind is capable of doing many incredible things, including something called Visualization.

To begin your visualization practice, close your eyes. Really, close your eyes (unless you are the one reading this, of course!) To build a very strong visualization, it is usually helpful to first center yourself and be sure you are giving your brain the very best tools it needs to work with. In this case, that means oxygen, and oxygen means taking some good, deep breaths.

You are going to take some slow, deep breaths now, following along with my instruction: Breathe in very slowly, 1 - 2 - 3 - 4. Now breathe out, very slowly, 1 - 2 - 3 - 4. Excellent. Now again very slowly, 1 - 2 - 3 - 4 and breathe back out very slowly, 1 - 2 - 3 - 4 very nice. Once more, very slowly in 1 - 2 - 3 - 4 and back out very slowly, 1 - 2 - 3 - 4. Great!

Take a moment to review how you feel. Are you comfy and feeling good? Okay, great.

Picture yourself, in your mind's eye, wearing a long white lab coat in front of a metallic counter. You look around and see that you are in a laboratory. The walls are clean white, and the counters are all made of stainless steel. You take a deep, long breath in and notice that it smells like an antiseptic cleaning solution in here, and you think, wow, this is definitely a laboratory, all right!

You see that the metallic counter in front of you seems to be prepped for a science experiment. It has labels on it: Step 1, Step 2, Step 3, and Step 4. Cool!

Well, no better time than the present, you think! You move closer to inspect the Step 1 section. Step 1 looks like it begins with safety protocol, cool! There are wide science safety goggles for you to put on, so you put those on, carefully adjusting them to be sure they are securely fastened over your eyes. The next item laid out on Step 1 is a pair of purple latex gloves. Cool! You pull those on, feeling excited about this science experiment that you are getting ready for!

Now on to Step 2. Step 2 appears to have two parts. The first part is labeled with instructions to scoop some of the powder from the first clear see-through container into the second clear see-through container. You study the containers for a moment. The first container is filled with what looks like a very coarsely ground yellow powder, almost like yellow sand of some sort. The second container is filled with what looks like a very finely ground red powder, and it reminds you of baking powder or corn starch!

The instructions state to scoop four complete scoops from the first container into the second container, so you pick up the metal scoop and measure out four complete scoops, transferring the coarsely ground yellow powder into the container with the finely ground red powder: one, two, three, four.

Okay, done with that step. You move to the Step 3 station and note it says to bring the newly combined powders from Step 2 over to the Step 3 station, so you pick up the see-through container with its yellow and red powder in it and bring it to the Step 3 station. Here there is a measurement tool that looks like a giant eyedropper, but it is called a pipette, and it is used to add very small amounts of liquid. Okay, what does this step say?

It says to use the pipette to transfer four drops of liquid from container A to container B. Okay. Container A is a round bowl with a yellow liquid that is very thick, like paint. Container B is a tall, clear cylinder that is filled with what looks like water. You very carefully take the pipette and begin dropping the four drops of liquid from container A to container B: One, two, three, four.

Alright! The thick, yellow paint-like liquid is swirling itself around in the tall, clear cylinder, and you watch it for a moment as it seems to be making beautiful art all on its own! Very neat. Alright, on to step number four.

Step number four states that you must bring the tall cylinder with the orange swirling liquid inside and the yellow-orange powder from step two over to the step four station. Alright, easy enough. You bring the containers over and see here that there is a large, clear, see-through square box, probably as big as a microwave, sitting here at this station. Hmm! Wonder what that is for.

The instructions at this station tell you to begin by very carefully pouring the orange swirling liquid out of the tall cylinder into the clear square box. You do this and watch as the orange swirling liquid seems to become even more active in the larger box than it was in the tall cylinder. The next step calls for you to add the yellow-orange powder to it, but it has a safety warning. It says that once you pour the yellow-orange powder into the square, you will only have ten seconds to move to the other side of the lab so you can safely watch the chemical reaction unfold. Cool!!!!

Very carefully, but quickly, you pour the yellow-orange powder into the square, see-through box, and then you set down the empty container and run to the other side of the laboratory while you count down from ten: Ten, nine, eight, seven, six, five, four, three, two, one and then there is a loud BOOM, and there is a puff of yellow-orange smoke coming from the box, and you wonder if that was it.

As the smoke clears, you see that there is something hovering in the air above the box. It looks like a cloud! You have created a cloud, somehow! It is a bright tangerine-orange cloud, and it looks like it is raining back into the clear square box and forming a tangerine-orange lake! It is beautiful. You can see the tangerine-orange liquid in the clear box evaporating back up into the cloud, the cloud becoming dense and raining back into the box, and you realize that your scientific experiment created the water cycle! You can watch it happen just as it does outside when it rains. How cool!

You are so happy that you got to do this awesome experiment, and you are so grateful that you can see science in action like this.

You do not have to leave the science lab just yet if you don't want to. You can spend as long as you want here and you can come back anytime you'd like.

You can create anything you want in your mind. Imagine where you want to go and build the picture in your mind. Be sure to imagine how you want it to smell, taste, hear, and feel. The more detailed you can make your mental picture, the more you will enjoy being there.

It is all up to you. Perhaps as you drift off to sleep, you may find yourself back in this awesome science lab, conducting another cool science experiment.

Chapter 47:
Butterfly Metamorphosis

Do you know that a butterfly is not born a butterfly? First, a butterfly is actually a caterpillar, which then spins a cocoon around itself before it transforms into a butterfly. Super cool, right? This process is called metamorphosis. What if you could experience your own metamorphosis? What if you could do that right now, without having to move a single muscle? You really can- In your mind! Your mind is capable of doing many incredible things, including something called Visualization.

To begin your visualization practice, close your eyes. Really, close your eyes (unless you are the one reading this, of course!) To build a very strong visualization, it is usually helpful to first center yourself and be sure you are giving your brain the very best tools it needs to work with. In this case, that means oxygen, and oxygen means taking some good, deep breaths.

You are going to take some slow, deep breaths now, following along with my instruction: Breathe in very slowly, 1 - 2 - 3 - 4. Now breathe out, very slowly, 1 - 2 - 3 - 4. Excellent. Now again very slowly, 1 - 2 - 3 - 4 and breathe back out very slowly, 1 - 2 - 3 - 4 very nice. Once more, very slowly in 1 - 2 - 3 - 4 and back out very slowly, 1 - 2 - 3 - 4. Great!

Take a moment to review how you feel. Are you comfy and feeling good? Okay, great.

Picture yourself, in your mind's eye, out playing in the grass. You are just running around, kicking a ball, having fun outside. It is a beautiful spring morning, and you are enjoying the fabulous spring weather. The sun is shining above you, and there is a gentle spring breeze blowing through the yard.

You decide that it is just a little bit chilly out here, so you go ahead and pick up the hooded sweatshirt that you brought out just in case you might need it, and you pull it on over your arms and shoulders, zipping it all the way up. You even pull the hood up and over your head and take a moment to consider how warm and cozy you are now- it's like your own personal cocoon, you think.

You start to feel an intense urge to stretch, and you reach your arms way up high towards the sky, but you realize that your sweatshirt is keeping your arms from being able to stretch all the way out. You unzip your sweatshirt and take it back off and try to stretch again, letting your arms really, really stretch up and out, and all of a sudden, you notice that where you once had arms, you now have wings!

Whoa!!! Your arms are now beautiful butterfly wings! They are blue and purple, and you give them a little wiggle on each side as you stare in disbelief. What on earth has happened? Did you just transform into a butterfly???

Shocked and amazed, you stretch your new butterfly wings out and let them flap up and down a few times. A gentle spring gust of wind blows through the yard, and you are suddenly floating upwards in the air!

You are flying! You keep flapping your wings gently, going up and up and up towards the sky. It is a beautiful, clear blue-sky kind of day, and you are amazed to see the world below you from this point of view! You feel so light and free.

You are soaring through the sky with your new butterfly wings, marveling at how free and fun this is. Your wings are shimmering in the spring sunlight, and you are warmed by the lovely sun so near to you. Flapping your wings feels glorious, and you continue swooping and soaring through the sky.

You feel light and free, and your wings are rippling in the breeze. You smile because the sun on your face and the breeze under your magnificent wings feel so good together, and you wonder if this is how all butterflies feel when they soar through the sky? You are happy and content.

You are so excited that you get to experience flying like a butterfly. You are ready to explore the world from a butterfly's point of view, and you are so grateful that you get to experience what it's like to go through a butterfly metamorphosis.

You do not have to stop flying with your fancy new butterfly wings just yet if you don't want to. You can spend as long as you want here and you can come back anytime you'd like.

You can create anything you want in your mind. Imagine where you want to go and build the picture in your mind. Be sure to imagine how you want it to smell, taste, hear, and feel. The more detailed you can make your mental picture, the more you will enjoy being there.

It is all up to you. Perhaps as you drift off to sleep, you may find yourself back up in the sky, soaring and swooping in the sweet spring sunlight with your beautiful butterfly wings.

Chapter 48:
Waterfall Trip

Have you had a chance to explore a waterfall before? Some are small, and some are tall, but all the waterfalls are beautiful, aren't they? Well, what if I told you that you can go explore a waterfall right now, without having to move a single muscle? You really can- In your mind! Your mind is capable of doing many incredible things, including something called Visualization.

To begin your visualization practice, close your eyes. Really, close your eyes (unless you are the one reading this, of course!) To build a very strong visualization, it is usually helpful to first center yourself and be sure you are giving your brain the very best tools it needs to work with. In this case, that means oxygen, and oxygen means taking some good, deep breaths.

You are going to take some slow, deep breaths now, following along with my instruction: Breathe in very slowly, 1 – 2 – 3 – 4. Now breathe out, very slowly, 1 – 2 – 3 – 4. Excellent. Now again very slowly, 1 – 2 – 3 – 4 and breathe back out very slowly, 1 – 2 – 3 – 4 very nice. Once more, very slowly in 1 – 2 – 3 – 4 and back out very slowly, 1 – 2 – 3 – 4. Great!

Take a moment to review how you feel. Are you comfy and feeling good? Okay, great.

Picture yourself, in your mind's eye, standing on a bank of a river. It is a crystal-clear blue river, and it is surrounded by rocks. You can see to the bottom of this river bed. The water is so clear! Take a long, deep in and notice how fresh and clean the air here smells. What is that you hear? It is the sound of rushing water.

You decide to follow the river up towards the sound of the rushing water. You are wearing the perfect hiking boots for this journey because the rocks that line the river require you to climb up and over each one to get to the next, but you don't mind because you love to climb and stretch your strong muscles. It reminds you of how capable you are of doing whatever it is you want to do, and it feels good to be strong and able.

It is a warm summer's day, but it feels nice and is cool down here by the river. There is a densely wooded forest on either side beyond the rocks, and it feels like you are in a secret, magical spot of the forest here as you follow the river bed towards the rushing water sound. You think it is getting louder and louder as the river bed has a steep curve around this dense cluster of trees here. You cannot see beyond it until you climb up over this particularly large rock.

The rock is cool and rough beneath your hands as you use your hands and feet to climb up and over this boulder to get to the other side, and as you near the top, you notice that there are tiny water droplets that seem to be coming from the other side. You finally reach the top and are greeted with a spectacular sight: It is a waterfall!

You scramble over the top of the boulder and marvel at this giant waterfall! It stretches up high over the treetops. You just couldn't see it with the thick forest of trees before it. You continue making your way along the river bed towards where the waterfall empties into it, and the mist from the waterfall splashes your skin and feels refreshing and cool on this warm summer's day.

Soon you are standing before this mighty waterfall, craning your neck backward as you look up, up, up where it begins so high above. The summer's sun is reflecting off of the water as it pours over the cliff above, and it gives the appearance of a shimmering and sparkling waterfall. The water here where the waterfall crashes into the river is just as clear, and you can see the rocks that line the river are covered in a soft and fuzzy moss here. You reach down and touch this fuzzy moss, amazed at how soft and springy it is.

You take another long, deep breath in, amazed at how clean and fresh the waterfall smells. You decide to sit on one of these rocks that are covered by this soft, springy moss and to enjoy the beautiful waterfall up close. You are so grateful that you have had the opportunity to see and experience the beauty of a waterfall so close. The spray from the waterfall cools and refreshes you, and you feel perfectly at peace.

You do not have to leave this beautiful waterfall just yet if you don't want to. You can spend as long as you want here and you can come back anytime you'd like.

You can create anything you want in your mind. Imagine where you want to go and build the picture in your mind. Be sure to imagine how you want it to smell, taste, hear, and feel. The more detailed you can make your mental picture, the more you will enjoy being there.

It is all up to you. Perhaps as you drift off to sleep, you may find yourself back here on this moss-covered rock, enjoying the sights and sounds of a beautiful waterfall.

Chapter 49:
In Your Invisibility Cape

Do you know what an invisibility cape is? It is a cape that makes anyone that wears it invisible! What if you could try on an invisibility cape? Where would you go, and what would you do? What if I told you that you could try on an invisibility cape right now, without having to move a single muscle? You really can- In your mind! Your mind is capable of doing many incredible things, including something called Visualization.

To begin your visualization practice, close your eyes. Really, close your eyes (unless you are the one reading this, of course!) To build a very strong visualization, it is usually helpful to first center yourself and be sure you are giving your brain the very best tools it needs to work with. In this case, that means oxygen, and oxygen means taking some good, deep breaths.

You are going to take some slow, deep breaths now, following along with my instruction: Breathe in very slowly, 1 – 2 – 3 – 4. Now breathe out, very slowly, 1 – 2 – 3 – 4. Excellent. Now again very slowly, 1 – 2 – 3 – 4 and breathe back out very slowly, 1 – 2 – 3 – 4 very nice. Once more, very slowly in 1 – 2 – 3 – 4 and back out very slowly, 1 – 2 – 3 – 4. Great!

Take a moment to review how you feel. Are you comfy and feeling good? Okay, great.

Imagine yourself, in your mind's eye, playing dress-up. You are in a room with racks upon racks upon racks of different kinds of costumes, and you are trying on many different kinds of costumes. Look at this! It is an old-fashioned top hat, like the kind that people wore to fancy parties a long time ago. You pull it on and laugh at your reflection in the huge dressing room mirror. So funny!

What is this here that you see? You reach out and touch some material that is incredibly soft and smooth, like a silky smooth. Your skin slides over the fabric softly, and you lift it up, and off of the hook, it was on. It looks like a cape of some sort. It is midnight black, and you think you definitely want to try this on!

You remove the top hat and hang it back up before tying the cape on you with a grand gesture- how else can you put on a cape, really- and you look in the mirror to inspect your image only... there is nothing there!!! Nothing at all! You cannot see the cape, and you cannot see yourself!!!

You are startled and confused, and you look down at yourself and realize you can't see yourself at all, in the mirror, or in real life! You quickly rip off the cape and throw it to the floor, feeling a little nervous. Instantly, you can see yourself both in the mirror and in real life. What in the world???

You pick up the cape again, inspecting it thoroughly. Finally, you find a small label on the inner lining, and it reads: "Invisibility Cape"

What the heck? An actual invisibility cape?? Wow! Now that you understand what is happening, you quickly pull it back on yourself. You look in the mirror again and yup! You are invisible! Wow! You giggle a little as you begin to daydream about all the fun you can have with this thing!

You are excited to play with this invisibility cape and so grateful that you have found it. You can't wait to play with it! What kinds of fun things will you do with it?

You do not have to leave your invisibility cape just yet if you don't want to. You can spend as long as you want here and you can come back anytime you'd like.

You can create anything you want in your mind. Imagine where you want to go and build the picture in your mind. Be sure to imagine how you want it to smell, taste, hear, and feel.

The more detailed you can make your mental picture, the more you will enjoy being there.

It is all up to you. Perhaps as you drift off to sleep, you may find yourself back here in your invisibility cape, ready to play and have all sorts of fun, invisible adventures!

Chapter 50:
Dancing on the Moon

What do you think it would be like to dance on the moon? What if I told you that you could experience dancing on the moon right now without having to move a single muscle? You really can- In your mind! Your mind is capable of doing many incredible things, including something called Visualization.

To begin your visualization practice, close your eyes. Really, close your eyes (unless you are the one reading this, of course!) To build a very strong visualization, it is usually helpful to first center yourself and be sure you are giving your brain the very best tools it needs to work with. In this case, that means oxygen, and oxygen means taking some good, deep breaths.

You are going to take some slow, deep breaths now, following along with my instruction: Breathe in very slowly, 1 - 2 - 3 - 4. Now breathe out, very slowly, 1 - 2 - 3 - 4. Excellent. Now again very slowly, 1 - 2 - 3 - 4 and breathe back out very slowly, 1 - 2 - 3 - 4 very nice. Once more, very slowly in 1 - 2 - 3 - 4 and back out very slowly, 1 - 2 - 3 - 4. Great!

Take a moment to review how you feel. Are you comfy and feeling good? Okay, great.

Imagine yourself, in your mind's eye, standing on a silvery smooth surface. Look around you and see that the silvery smooth surface extends out as far as you can see! You look down at yourself and notice that you are in a spacesuit. You are standing on the moon!

All around you, there is a stillness and empty space. It is extraordinarily peaceful and relaxing here, and you can see twinkling stars way up and out in the distance. You take a long, deep breath in and relax into the moment. It is your first time in outer space, and you give a little hop of excitement, and you are immediately reminded that there is no gravity in outer space!

Your body floats easily up and off of the surface of the silvery moon, gently traveling upward, upward, upward. You feel as light as a feather out here! Your body very slowly floats back down, your space boots lightly touching the silvery surface beneath you as you land. You decide to do a little twirl around to see what it might feel like, and your body twirls around slowly and lightly. It makes you feel like an autumn leaf dancing in the breeze!

Any tiny, concentrated movement you make out here is immediately magnified by the lack of gravity, and you feel like a balloon full of air! Every step you take is a bounce, and every turn you take becomes a twirl as your body reacts to the lack of gravity.

Looking around you out in the dark, midnight black of the universe, you are in awe of the beauty of the twinkling stars that look so bright and beautiful. It is as if you are surrounded by thousands of shimmering, twinkling lights. It is a beautiful experience, and you are so grateful that you are getting to explore the moon like this.

You do not have to leave this peaceful, silvery moonscape just yet if you don't want to. You can spend as long as you want here and you can come back anytime you'd like.

You can create anything you want in your mind. Imagine where you want to go and build the picture in your mind. Be sure to imagine how you want it to smell, taste, hear, and feel. The more detailed you can make your mental picture, the more you will enjoy being there.

It is all up to you. Perhaps as you drift off to sleep, you may find yourself back out here in outer space, enjoying the peaceful twinkling of a thousand stars.

Bonus Chapter:
Superpower Grounding

Do you know that you have a superpower? It's true, you really do! You have the superpower to calm yourself down anytime you want, no matter what is happening around you. That means that even if you are scared, or worried, or angry about something that is happening to you or around you, you have the superpower ability to do something calling Grounding.

It works like this: When you are upset by something, your brain gets a little scrambled by your feelings. It can be very easy to end up acting out and saying and doing things you do not really mean to do when your brain is feeling scrambled like that.

The good news here is that there is a way to unscramble your feelings by grounding yourself, and you can do it by yourself! It works because it calms your brain down. Once you learn how to do this grounding exercise, you will see that you can be more in control of yourself, even when you are very upset, just by connecting your brain and body in a purposeful manner.

Hold up one hand. You are going to tap your thumb and index finger together while counting up to five, and then you will repeat with your thumb and middle finger, your thumb and ring finger, and then your thumb and pinky finger. Once you get to your thumb and pinky finger, you will begin counting back down from five while tapping your thumb and pinky finger together, then your thumb and ring finger, then your thumb and middle finger, then your thumb and index finger, all while counting down from five.

So, counting up would be tapping each finger while counting 1, 2, 3, 4, 5, and back down would be 5, 4, 3, 2, 1. Let's try it together.

Tapping your thumb and index finger together: 1, 2, 3, 4, 5

Tapping your thumb and middle finger together: 1, 2, 3, 4, 5

Tapping your thumb and ring finger together: 1, 2, 3, 4, 5

Tapping your thumb and pinky finger together: 1, 2, 3, 4, 5

Now back down!

Tapping your thumb and pinky finger together: 5, 4, 3, 2, 1

Tapping your thumb and ring finger together: 5, 4,3, 2, 1

Tapping your thumb and middle finger together: 5, 4, 3, 2, 1

Tapping your thumb and index finger together: 5, 4, 3, 2, 1

Easy, right? Doing this will calm your brain down and allow you to unscramble the upset feelings you may be having. You can do this superpower ANYWHERE at all, too! You can do it at school, at the dentist, at the park, anywhere at all. You can count out loud or in your head, whatever works for you.

Give it a try; you will be amazed at how quickly this superpower grounding will help you!

Chapter 1:
Astronaut for a Day

Have you ever wondered what it would be like to be an astronaut? Wouldn't it be amazing to go explore another planet, even if just for a day? What if I told you that you could, without moving a single muscle? You really can- In your mind! Your mind is capable of doing many incredible things, including something called Visualization.

To begin your visualization practice, close your eyes. Really, close your eyes (unless you are the one reading this, of course!) To build a very strong visualization, it is usually helpful to first center yourself and be sure you are giving your brain the very best tools it needs to work with. In this case, that means oxygen, and oxygen means taking some good, deep breaths.

You are going to take some slow, deep breaths now, following along with my instruction: Breathe in very slowly, 1 – 2 – 3 – 4. Now breathe out, very slowly, 1 – 2 – 3 – 4. Excellent. Now again very slowly, 1 – 2 – 3 – 4 and breathe back out very slowly, 1 – 2 – 3 – 4 very nice. Once more very slowly in 1 – 2 – 3 – 4 and back out very slowly, 1 – 2 – 3 – 4. Great!

Take a moment to review how you feel. Are you comfy and feeling good? Okay, great.

Picture yourself, in your mind's eye, standing before the white, shiny, metal door of a space ship. Peering through the small window of the door in front of you, you can see that you are standing inside the space ship, looking out at the surface of another planet!

Looking down, you see that you are suited up in an astronaut's uniform: the thick, white material is completely covering your arms and legs and you even have on thick, white, protective gloves. You reach up to touch your face and realize you have the protective astronaut headgear on as well! Looks like you are perfectly suited up to step outside of this space ship and explore the surface of this planet.

The door of the space ship opens briskly with a whishing sound. You take a few steps forward and step out of the spaceship, your space boots connecting with the ground of this planet with a light thud.

Wow! Looking around you, you can see that the ground of this planet is a glittery gold color. Everywhere around you, you can feel the effects of being on a planet with no gravity. Your body feels light and full of air, almost like you are a balloon filled with helium!

You look up and notice there is very little up above you in this planet's atmosphere. There are wispy purple things that seem somewhat like the clouds that are found on Earth, but these wispy purple clouds seem like they are less dense than the clouds back on Earth. In fact, these wispy purple clouds remind you of something else entirely, you just can't quite put your finger on what.

You decide to collect a specimen for scientific research and you reach into the pocket of your space suit and pull out a glass vial that is about the size of a drinking cup. You crouch down to gather some of the soil like substance that is on the surface of this planet and you are amazed at how glittery it is!

Pulling the cork out of the top of the smooth glass vial, you hear a satisfying "pop" sound as it releases. You run the glass vial across the glittery gold surface of this planet and the shimmery, glittery soil-like substance easily scoops into the specimen collection vial. Once it is full, you carefully put the cork back in to be sure that none of this beautiful glittery gold soil is lost before you can get it back to study it!

Having collected the specimen that you needed from the surface of this planet, you stand up and stretch yourself out a bit after you've placed the now full glass vial back into your special space suit pocket. As you stretch your arms out and back behind you, you look up again at the atmosphere of this beautiful planet.

Now you see it! That's what it reminds you of! You realize that these purple wispy clouds remind you of something very specific: cotton candy! They look like they could be the exact same texture as the wispy spun sugar that you get at carnivals that melts in your mouth into a sticky mess when it gets wet. You don't know if this planet's atmosphere has rain or not, but you don't want to stick around to find out!

You walk back over to the space ship door and step back inside. You close the space ship door again with a "whish" shut behind you. From safely inside the space ship, you look out one last time at this incredible planet. Purple wisp cotton candy clouds and glittery gold soil. What a magical place!

You pull the glass vial out of your space suit pocket and hold it up in the light, watching as the glittery gold swirls around with the movement and sparkles and shines in the light. You cannot wait to properly investigate this stuff!

You are ready to go get yourself buckled in for your return trip to Earth. You are so grateful that you have had this incredible experience of being an astronaut for a day! Plus, you have a pretty cool souvenir here in your space suit pocket.

You do not have to leave your space ship on the purple and gold glittery planet just yet if you don't want to. You can spend as long as you want here and you can come back anytime you'd like.

You can create anything you want in your mind. Imagine where you want to go and build the picture in your mind. Be sure to imagine how you want it to smell, taste, hear and feel. The more detailed you can make your mental picture, the more you will enjoy being there.

It is all up to you. Perhaps as you drift off to sleep, you may find yourself back here in your space suit, ready to go out on another fun space adventure.

Chapter 2:
Ready, Set, Soar Like a Bird!

Have you ever wondered what it would be like to fly like a bird? Not just fly a little bit from tree to tree, but to really and truly soar through the wide-open sky like a bird? Well, what if I told you that you can actually feel what that would be like right now without having to move a single muscle? You really can- In your mind! Your mind is capable of doing many incredible things, including something called Visualization.

To begin your visualization practice, close your eyes. Really, close your eyes (unless you are the one reading this, of course!) To build a very strong visualization, it is usually helpful to first center yourself and be sure you are giving your brain the very best tools it needs to work with. In this case, that means oxygen, and oxygen means taking some good, deep breaths.

You are going to take some slow, deep breaths now, following along with my instruction: Breathe in very slowly, 1 - 2 - 3 - 4. Now breathe out, very slowly, 1 - 2 - 3 - 4. Excellent. Now again very slowly, 1 - 2 - 3 - 4 and breathe back out very slowly, 1 - 2 - 3 - 4 very nice. Once more very slowly in 1 - 2 - 3 - 4 and back out very slowly, 1 - 2 - 3 - 4. Great!

Take a moment to review how you feel. Are you comfy and feeling good? Okay, great.

Picture yourself, standing outside on a beautiful summer's day. You are standing out in what looks like a giant field, and the sky is a vivid, deep blue with fluffy white clouds. You are barefoot and the grass is lush and soft underfoot. You squish your toes a little bit to feel the soft green grass as it pushes back against your toes.

You take a long, deep breath in and notice how fresh and clear the air around you smells. It is a lovely summer's day and you feel strong and healthy. You stretch your arms up and over your head, feeling the muscles of your arms as they tighten briefly and then release. Bringing your arms back down, you have the thought that you feel so good right now, you almost feel like you could fly.

You look out over the huge field you are standing in and decide that it would be wonderful to go for a long, lovely run through it. You break out first in a sprint, lightly running, but the muscles in your legs feel so strong and powerful that it quickly turns into a run and you are running, running, running, your bare feet loving the feel of the lush, green grass underfoot.

You are running so fast now that it feels like your feet are barely touching the grass. You are moving so quickly that it is almost like you are flying over the grassy field rather than running through it! That is when you realize you cannot even feel the grass beneath your feet anymore and you feel exhilarated and light and you don't even really feel the muscles in your legs working that hard anymore, especially not for how quickly you are racing across this field.

You stretch your arms out to your sides in total happiness and you immediately feel a gust of air underneath you, lifting you up, and you are suddenly airborne! Your mouth is open in total shock as you realize that while you are still going forward, you are also going up, up, and up even further! You are flying! Really, truly flying!!!!

Your legs and your arms are now being carried on what feels like a breeze as your body continues forward and upward. You are now as high as the trees that line the field, but still, you are traveling upward. The wind is passing over and around you and it feels like a cool, refreshing caress on your face as you fly up, up, and up.

You are now well over the tree line, and you continue to soar forward and up. You realize that you are easily able to steer by simply shifting your body weight a little in one direction or another and you begin to play with this ability by dipping a little to the left, your entire body going sideways so it feels like you are laying on your side in the sky!

You are now as high as the clouds! You are approaching a beautifully dense, white fluffy cloud and you decide to steer yourself right into it. Up this close, it looks like a giant marshmallow! You reach your arms out towards it so your fingers touch it first and you are amazed at how soft and smooth this white fluffy cloud is! Your entire body easily slides in and through it and you decide to roll over to your back.

You feel like you have flopped down on to a giant marshmallow and your entire body is encased in this soft, smooth, fluffy cloud. You even put your hands behind your head as an extra pillow and you feel so relaxed and content! Your body is so comfortable and your mind is so elated as you relax back into this fluffy white pillow. You lay here for a few moments, letting all of the muscles in your body completely relax into the fluffy softness of this cloud. You feel limp, like a rag doll, in the very best way!

You are ready to return to the grassy field now, so you let yourself start drifting back down. It isn't hard to do at all, all you had to do was think that that is what you wanted to do, and your body began to slowly float back downward. You feel like a balloon that is slowly, very slowly, losing its helium as it drifts back down from the sky.

As you are nearing the lush, green field below you, you think that you are so grateful that you have had this amazing experience of soaring through the sky like a bird.

You do not have to leave this green, grassy field where you can fly just yet if you don't want to. You can spend as long as you want here and you can come back anytime you'd like.

You can create anything you want in your mind. Imagine where you want to go and build the picture in your mind. Be sure to imagine how you want it to smell, taste, hear and feel. The more detailed you can make your mental picture, the more you will enjoy being there.

It is all up to you. Perhaps as you drift off to sleep, you may find yourself back here on this lush, green grass, ready to take off and soar through the sky like a bird.

Chapter 3:
Your Royal Highness

Have you ever wondered what it might be like to be royalty? Like, actual royalty that lives in a castle? Well, what if I told you that you could experience what it is like to be a royal highness? You really can- In your mind! Your mind is capable of doing many incredible things, including something called Visualization.

To begin your visualization practice, close your eyes. Really, close your eyes (unless you are the one reading this, of course!) To build a very strong visualization, it is usually helpful to first center yourself and be sure you are giving your brain the very best tools it needs to work with. In this case, that means oxygen, and oxygen means taking some good, deep breaths.

You are going to take some slow, deep breaths now, following along with my instruction: Breathe in very slowly, 1 - 2 - 3 - 4. Now breathe out, very slowly, 1 - 2 - 3 - 4. Excellent. Now again very slowly, 1 - 2 - 3 - 4 and breathe back out very slowly, 1 - 2 - 3 - 4 very nice. Once more very slowly in 1 - 2 - 3 - 4 and back out very slowly, 1 - 2 - 3 - 4. Great!

Take a moment to review how you feel. Are you comfy and feeling good? Okay, great.

Picture yourself, in your mind's eye, standing in front of a large picture window. It is a gigantic window and you are standing before it, looking out. You can see that it looks like you are up high, maybe in some sort of building on a hilltop or a cliff, because spread out below, as far as you can see, seems to be a village. You can see the tiny homes and the many people walking through and around.

You notice that the village is on the edge of the sea and that there are many large ships docked in the harbor. The sea is a beautiful sparkling blue color as the sun gleams down across the still water. You take a step back from the window and look around you.

The room you are in is very, very large, and it seems to be made entirely of stone. The walls are stone, the floor is stone, the ceiling even appears to be made of stone! There are vividly bright colored rugs on the ground and richly patterned tapestries along the walls. There is a huge fireplace on the opposite side of the room, with a roaring fire that is crackling and popping as it settles.

You continue to look around this room in amazement and you realize that you must be in a castle! Just then the large door on the far side of this giant room opens and in comes a much older man with white hair, wearing a formal red coat with brass buttons on it. He is carrying a tray but before he even takes a single full step into the room, he nods in your direction and says "Your Royal Highness" before continuing to enter into the room.

You gasp and for the first time, look down at yourself. You see now that you are wearing what does look royal attire! You are dressed in deep blues and purples and that's when you notice that all of the beautiful tapestries on the walls are also this same rich shade of deep blue and vivid indigo purple. Your eyes then notice something on the wall that you had not seen before: a picture of you, completely dressed in what looks like the finest royal frippery and a small crown on your head, to boot!

The servant- you assume it must be a servant- has set the contents of the tray he was carrying out on a table beside the fire. You cross the large room and thank him and he smiles and says, "Of course, Your Royal Highness," before quickly exiting the room.

You look at what he has set out and you can hardly believe your eyes! There appears to be every delicious treat you could possibly imagine here! There is a chocolate donut with sprinkles, a blueberry muffin with dusted sugar on top, a few pieces of milk chocolate fudge with what looks like a caramel swirl, and an assortment of salted nuts and cheeses. There is a large mug also that appears to have a warm liquid in it with whipped cream and chocolate shavings on top. You pick it up, the warm mug feeling wonderfully cozy in your hands, and you can smell immediately that it must be hot cocoa!

You sit yourself down in the well-cushioned chair beside the table, relaxing against the over-stuffed back, the warm mug still between your hands. You lift it up to your lips and take a cautious first sip, not sure how warm the liquid inside is. You are pleasantly surprised to find that it is absolutely perfect! Warm and soothing but not too hot to drink, by any means, so you eagerly sip the luxuriously rich hot cocoa within, noticing the whipped cream and chocolate shavings on top are sticking to your upper lip!

You laugh a bit as you catch sight of yourself in a mirror beside the fireplace as you can see the whipped cream mustache you have given yourself! You lick it clean, the sweet and fluffy cream being the perfect accompaniment for the rich hot chocolate. You notice that there is a stack of books and magazines beside your chair so you carefully set your mug down and pick up a few and flip through them. They are the exact kinds of books and magazines that you love!

You relax back into this oversized, comfy chair and look around you at the table full of delightful treats and the roaring fire that is offering you its cozy warmth and you feel so incredibly grateful to be a Royal Highness.

You do not have to leave this beautiful castle where you are royalty just yet if you don't want to. You can spend as long as you want here and you can come back anytime you'd like.

You can create anything you want in your mind. Imagine where you want to go and build the picture in your mind. Be sure to imagine how you want it to smell, taste, hear and feel. The more detailed you can make your mental picture, the more you will enjoy being there.

It is all up to you. Perhaps as you drift off to sleep, you may find yourself back here on your comfy chair in your castle, enjoying your day as a Royal Highness.

Chapter 4:
Magician for a Day

Have you ever considered what it might be like to be a magician? You could make people say "ooooh" and "aaaaaah" as you did your tricks and maybe you could even make someone disappear and then reappear somewhere else! Well, what if I told you that you can be a magician for a day, and you wouldn't even have to move a single muscle. You really can- In your mind! Your mind is capable of doing many incredible things, including something called Visualization.

To begin your visualization practice, close your eyes. Really, close your eyes (unless you are the one reading this, of course!) To build a very strong visualization, it is usually helpful to first center yourself and be sure you are giving your brain the very best tools it needs to work with. In this case, that means oxygen, and oxygen means taking some good, deep breaths.

You are going to take some slow, deep breaths now, following along with my instruction: Breathe in very slowly, 1 – 2 – 3 – 4. Now breathe out, very slowly, 1 – 2 – 3 – 4. Excellent. Now again very slowly, 1 – 2 – 3 – 4 and breathe back out very slowly, 1 – 2 – 3 – 4 very nice. Once more very slowly in 1 – 2 – 3 – 4 and back out very slowly, 1 – 2 – 3 – 4. Great!

Take a moment to review how you feel. Are you comfy and feeling good? Okay, great.

Imagine yourself, standing on a large wooden platform, with lights all around you. You look around yourself and see that this isn't just any platform, it is a stage! There are people that are sitting out beyond the lights: an audience!

Beside you is a large black table. The table has several items on it: a tall black silk hat, a large velvet, midnight blue bag, and what appears to be a giant button. The button is cherry red and it says in large letters: FINALE. That must mean it is supposed to be pushed at the very end.

Looking out at the audience, you realize that they are here for a show. You are the only person up here on this stage, so it looks like you are the magician today!

You begin by picking up the tall black silk hat. You pick it up and it feels like a normal hat, nice and light, nothing in it that you can see. You step towards the audience and show it to them, inside and out. Then you reach inside the tall black silk hat and you are very surprised when your hand feels something that is furry! You root around a bit in there until you are confident that your hand is around something that you can grab and you pull.

Out appears a fluffy gray bunny rabbit! The audience bursts out in applause as you hold this cute fluffy gray bunny rabbit up in the air for all to see. This cute little bunny rabbit even has his own tall black silk hat on! How cute.

As you are holding the fluffy gray bunny rabbit up in the air, you notice his tall silk black hat moves a little bit. You reach one hand up and pull his tall black silk hat off of him, only to reveal an even tinier fluffy gray bunny rabbit under his hat!!!! The audience erupts into more applause and you can tell they really have liked this trick!

You carefully set the two fluffy gray bunnies down on the stage, where they sit quietly. Now you go over to the large velvet midnight blue bag. Just as you did with the tall black silk hat, you assume that you should reach inside this one too, so you do. You first put your hand in tentatively, as this bag is large and looks full of things, but you have to keep putting more and more of your arm in to look for what is inside.

Still, nothing! You now have both arms in this large bag, completely up to your neck, and you still can't feel anything inside! Perplexed, you pull yourself back out and look out at the audience, stumped. The audience erupts into laughter, and that's when you realize that there are bubbles floating out of the bag and all along and off of your arms! The effect makes it look like your arms are bubble wands and you can feel the slippery bubble solution as it rolls along your skin and produces hundreds and hundreds of bubbles.

The stage is quickly filling with bubbles and you raise your arms in the air triumphantly. You decide to try the bag again so you reach back into the velvet bag and immediately touch something solid. It feels like a tube of some sort and you pull it out very carefully as you have no idea what this thing is. As the tube is being pulled from the bag, it begins setting off what looks like fireworks of some sort, but instead of fireworks, you realize it is glitter! You point it towards the audience and they are showered with shiny, shimmery glitter of every color imaginable and you can hear the audience as they "ooooh" and "aaaaaah" over how beautiful the glitter looks as it rains down on them from above.

You are grinning widely now as you know the audience has enjoyed your magic show. You are ready now to push the big red "FINALE" button. You take a quick bow for the audience and you push the button. There is a loud BOOM sound and suddenly, you have disappeared from the stage! The audience gasps in surprise and you are now suddenly looking down at the stage you were just on! You are somehow now on a platform above the stage.

After a moment of listening to the audience as they murmur amongst themselves and wonder where you've gone, you are then being lowered carefully down on the platform you are standing on, and as the audience sees you coming back to the stage, they burst into thunderous applause. You can see your audience is even giving you a standing ovation and you can hear whistles and whoops of enjoyment. You are so grateful that you have had the opportunity to be a magician for a day!

You do not have to leave this stage where you are a magician just yet if you don't want to. You can spend as long as you want here and you can come back anytime you'd like.

You can create anything you want in your mind. Imagine where you want to go and build the picture in your mind. Be sure to imagine how you want it to smell, taste, hear and feel. The more detailed you can make your mental picture, the more you will enjoy being there.

It is all up to you. Perhaps as you drift off to sleep, you may find yourself back here on stage, pulling fluffy gray bunnies out of a tall black silk hat.

Chapter 5:
Swim with the Dolphins

Have you ever thought about what it would be like to go swimming with dolphins? Do you know that dolphins are mammals, just like us? They are very smart animals and they can be a lot of fun to swim with. What if I told you that you could see what it is like to go swimming with dolphins right now, without moving a single muscle? You really can- In your mind! Your mind is capable of doing many incredible things, including something called Visualization.

To begin your visualization practice, close your eyes. Really, close your eyes (unless you are the one reading this, of course!) To build a very strong visualization, it is usually

helpful to first center yourself and be sure you are giving your brain the very best tools it needs to work with. In this case, that means oxygen, and oxygen means taking some good, deep breaths.

You are going to take some slow, deep breaths now, following along with my instruction: Breathe in very slowly, 1 – 2 – 3 – 4. Now breathe out, very slowly, 1 – 2 – 3 – 4. Excellent. Now again very slowly, 1 – 2 – 3 – 4 and breathe back out very slowly, 1 – 2 – 3 – 4 very nice. Once more very slowly in 1 – 2 – 3 – 4 and back out very slowly, 1 – 2 – 3 – 4. Great!

Take a moment to review how you feel. Are you comfy and feeling good? Okay, great.

Picture yourself, in your mind's eye, sitting on a sandy beach. You are enjoying the sunny warmth of this beautiful summer's day and the sand is gritty and warm beneath you. You have been out here in the sunshine for a while now, watching the gentle sea waves as they lightly crash on the shore.

You take in a long, deep breath and smell the seawater. It smells fresh and salty and you are starting to think it might be time to go swimming as your skin is really feeling warm from all this sun.

Standing up, you brush the gritty sand off of your legs, squirming your toes and letting them squish into the cool sand a bit as you survey the water. The water is very clear and calm and you are excited to go swim! You take a few steps forward to test the temperature and are very pleased to feel how perfect the temperature is on this hot, sunny day. It is cool, but not cold.

You decide it is time and you go rushing out into the water, letting your body flop out into the water. The seawater makes you very buoyant and you float easily as you take a few strokes out to get further out to sea. The water is very refreshing and you flip back on to your back to float for a bit.

You are floating comfortably, just relaxing in the water, when you hear a little chittering noise nearby. You open your eyes and look around you and that's when you see that you are not alone out here in the sea! You look around you and see that there are several dolphins around you! Whoa!

The dolphin nearest to you that had just made the chittering noise dives under, nose-first. You wonder where he went when suddenly, right beside you, he comes shooting out of the water where he flies up and out before landing back near you with a giant splash! The dolphin resurfaces and he and all of the other dolphins now make the little chittering noise and you think it sounds like laughter, almost.

The other dolphins now are also now diving deep only to come flying back up and out of the water and they are splashing all around you! Each time they land, all the dolphins chitter and you are laughing now, too. The dolphins' bluish-gray skin is so shiny in the sun when they surface and you tentatively reach out your hand to touch one. It is sleek and slippery, but also soft, and this dolphin seems to like being petted by you!

You decide to do your best dolphin impression and you dive down, as deep as you can, and then kick your feet and legs as hard as you can to try and get some speed so you can also come soaring out of the water. Unfortunately, you are a human and your attempt to come flying out of the water wasn't as spectacular as a dolphin, until the very last moment when your new dolphin friend came underneath you and used his nose to help hoist you out of the water!

You are able to soar up and out of the water just like a dolphin and you land with a splash among your dolphin friends. They all chitter and you laugh. You are so grateful that you have met these dolphin friends and had the opportunity to swim with them! It is an experience you will never forget.

You do not have to leave your new dolphin friends just yet if you don't want to. You can spend as long as you want here and you can come back anytime you'd like.

You can create anything you want in your mind. Imagine where you want to go and build the picture in your mind. Be sure to imagine how you want it to smell, taste, hear and feel. The more detailed you can make your mental picture, the more you will enjoy being there.

It is all up to you. Perhaps as you drift off to sleep, you may find yourself back out here in the cool, refreshing sea, swimming with your new dolphin friends.

Chapter 6:
Elephant Friends

Have you ever wondered what it might be like to get to know an elephant? Maybe even what it might be like to be friends with an elephant? Well, what if I told you that you could see what it is like to be friends with an elephant, and you can do it without moving a single muscle? You really can- In your mind! Your mind is capable of doing many incredible things, including something called Visualization.

To begin your visualization practice, close your eyes. Really, close your eyes (unless you are the one reading this, of course!) To build a very strong visualization, it is usually helpful to first center yourself and be sure you are giving your brain the very best tools it needs to work with. In this case, that means oxygen, and oxygen means taking some good, deep breaths.

You are going to take some slow, deep breaths now, following along with my instruction: Breathe in very slowly, 1 – 2 – 3 – 4. Now breathe out, very slowly, 1 – 2 – 3 – 4. Excellent. Now again very slowly, 1 – 2 – 3 – 4 and breathe back out very slowly, 1 – 2 – 3 – 4 very nice. Once more very slowly in 1 – 2 – 3 – 4 and back out very slowly, 1 – 2 – 3 – 4. Great!

Take a moment to review how you feel. Are you comfy and feeling good? Okay, great.

Imagine yourself, in your mind's eye, standing on a grassy plain. Below the grass is red clay dirt that vividly contrasts with the light olive green, reed-thin grasses that are all around you. The sky is a bright blue above and the sunshine is beaming down brightly, illuminating the beautiful trees that are clustered in a grove nearby. The trees are tall with trunks that bend dramatically halfway up and you think this all looks like something you've seen in safari pictures.

Beyond the grove of twisting, spindly trees, you can see something moving. What is back there? You take a few steps towards the grove only to be stopped short in your tracks when you are all of a sudden face to face with a baby elephant! The baby elephant is a dusty gray color and he is holding something green and bushy in his trunk.

"Uh, hi!" You say, never having met an elephant before. The baby elephant steps backwards a couple of steps in surprise and raises and lowers his trunk a few times as he looks you up and down, accidentally dropping what he had held in his trunk. The baby elephant is looking at you intently with curious but somewhat suspicious eyes as it seems as if he is trying to figure out if you are a friend or enemy.

"You dropped this, buddy," you say as you pick up the green bushy bundle off of the ground and offer it back towards to the baby elephant. The baby elephant's giant floppy ears flap back and forth and you can tell that he is thinking about this. The baby elephant takes a small step towards you, moving slowly and carefully. He leans forward tentatively, reaching out to the bushel with his trunk. Once he is close enough, he quickly plucks the bushel out of your hands and takes a quick step back.

He took it! You are so happy that this sweet baby elephant trusts you. You smile widely at him and give him a little wave of your hand as he chomps on his bushel, thoughtfully watching you. Once he finishes the bushel, he lifts his trunk up to you and gives you a little wave back! You are so excited by this sweet baby elephant that you jump up in the air and clap a little from happiness, only to be amazed when the baby elephant does the very same back at you!!!!

Wow, you think. This baby elephant is playing with me! You decide to do a little spin around where you stand, with your arms stretched out above you. You turn back to the baby elephant just in time to see him also spinning himself around; his trunk stretched high up in the air. You laugh at how sweet and cute your baby elephant friend is!

You stomp your feet a little and are very surprised that when your baby elephant friend does it, the red dirt underfoot is kicked up and seems to swirl all around him. The baby elephant seems to like this and he sways back and forth in the red dust, letting it coat his gray, leathery skin. You realize that he probably does this to keep the mosquitos and other bugs off of him.

You have an idea! You bend down and touch the red clay dirt below you. It is cool and soft to the touch and you pick it up and rub it together in your hands. You laugh as you take it and use it to paint your face and arms! Your baby elephant friend seems to enjoy this very much as he is nodding and shaking his head back and forth as if he just heard a joke! You are having so much fun with your baby elephant friend and you feel very grateful that you met him.

You do not have to leave your new elephant friend just yet if you don't want to. You can spend as long as you want here and you can come back anytime you'd like.

You can create anything you want in your mind. Imagine where you want to go and build the picture in your mind. Be sure to imagine how you want it to smell, taste, hear and feel. The more detailed you can make your mental picture, the more you will enjoy being there.

It is all up to you. Perhaps as you drift off to sleep, you may find yourself back out here on the plains of the savannah, playing with your new baby elephant friend.

Chapter 7:
Firefighter for a Day

Have you ever wondered what it might be like to be a firefighter? They have a pretty cool job, don't they? They get to ride on a shiny red fire truck and go help people and put out fires! What if I told you that you could actually be a firefighter for a day, without having to move a single muscle? You really can- In your mind! Your mind is capable of doing many incredible things, including something called Visualization.

To begin your visualization practice, close your eyes. Really, close your eyes (unless you are the one reading this, of course!) To build a very strong visualization, it is usually helpful to first center yourself and be sure you are giving your brain the very best tools it needs to work with. In this case, that means oxygen, and oxygen means taking some good, deep breaths.

You are going to take some slow, deep breaths now, following along with my instruction: Breathe in very slowly, 1 – 2 – 3 – 4. Now breathe out, very slowly, 1 2 3 4. Excellent. Now again very slowly, 1 – 2 – 3 – 4 and breathe back out very slowly, 1 – 2 – 3 – 4 very nice. Once more very slowly in 1 – 2 – 3 – 4 and back out very slowly, 1 – 2 – 3 – 4. Great!

Take a moment to review how you feel. Are you comfy and feeling good? Okay, great.

Imagine yourself, in your mind's eye, standing outside on a beautiful spring day. The birds are chirping, the sun is shining, and the weather is absolutely perfect. The sky is blue overhead and you don't see a single cloud in the sky.

You are standing outside of a fire station. You can see the giant garage where they keep the fire trucks, but the garage doors are closed. Just then, one of the doors opens and a firefighter in their full gear comes out towards you and she asks if you would like to see what it is like to be a firefighter for a day. Of course, you answer yes!

The firefighter leads you into the spot where you will put the firefighter uniform on over your regular clothes. The firefighter uniform is bright yellow and you ask the firefighter why? She answers that this is because they want to be sure they can see each other through heavy smoke while they are fighting fires together. That makes sense!

You pull the heavy and thick firefighter pants on over yours, very surprised at how thick and heavy they are. The firefighter explains to you that their uniforms have to be thick because they have to protect their clothes and skin beneath from being burnt while they are fighting fires. Once you have the pants on, the firefighter helps you put the uniform top on and you can now really feel the weight of this uniform. You realize that firefighters must be so strong to be able to work in these!

The next step is to put on the heat resistant firefighter boots. These are also heavy and thick. You have just gotten dressed up like a firefighter and you already feel like you've got a workout! The firefighter that is helping you tells you that this is exactly why she and all the other firefighters have to be in excellent physical condition. Their entire job depends on it!

Just as you are finishing putting on the last boot, the entire garage is filled with the loud wailing of an alarm. You are startled and you look around as all of a sudden, the garage is full of firefighters, pulling on their uniforms quickly. The firefighter that has helped you has quickly pulled her uniform on and tells you that you can ride along. She helps you climb up into the truck very fast and you are soon seated in the back of the fire truck, surrounded by firefighters.

The fire truck takes off out of the garage with a leap and is soon moving swiftly down the road, the lights blazing and the siren sounding. You watch in awe as all of the other traffic on the road around you moves out of the way quickly, and you even wave to the cars as they pull off to the side. Some of the cars have kids in them and they look very surprised to see a kid firefighter waving at them from the fire truck!

The fire truck is coming to a stop now and you try to see where the fire is. That's when you see it: a farmer been burning a leaf pile that looks like it has gone a bit out of control and could be headed towards their barn. The firefighters quickly jump off of the truck and get to work, pulling hoses and other equipment out fast. You climb off of the truck after them, trying to stay out of the way.

The firefighters use teamwork to quickly put the fire out, and the farmer thanks them over and over again for saving his barn and all of the animals in it. The firefighters tell him that they are happy they were able to help, and one of the firefighters even invites you down next to them to have a chance to spray the hose.

The fire is out now, but the farmer says that he wouldn't mind if the barn got hosed down and cleaned off a little if you want and so that is where they set you up. You are holding on to the nozzle and the firefighters tell you that this is a very, very, very strong hose. Once they turn the switch, the water will come bursting out of the end and you will have to hold tight and use your muscles to aim at the barn.

You take a deep breath, tighten your arms and hands and nod that you are ready. Suddenly it feels like the hose in your hands has come alive and the long length of the hose behind you is kicking around like it is a wild snake trying to escape capture! You hold tight, using all of your muscles and all of your strength and keep the hose aimed right at the barn, washing the soot and ash from the fire off of it.

Once you are done, the water is turned off and all of your new firefighter friends and the farmer applaud for you! You are so grateful that you have been able to have this experience as a firefighter for a day.

You do not have to stop being firefighter for a day just yet if you don't want to. You can spend as long as you want here and you can come back anytime you'd like.

You can create anything you want in your mind. Imagine where you want to go and build the picture in your mind. Be sure to imagine how you want it to smell, taste, hear and feel. The more detailed you can make your mental picture, the more you will enjoy being there.

It is all up to you. Perhaps as you drift off to sleep, you may find yourself back out here on this farm, being firefighter for a day.

Chapter 8:
Acrobat in the Circus

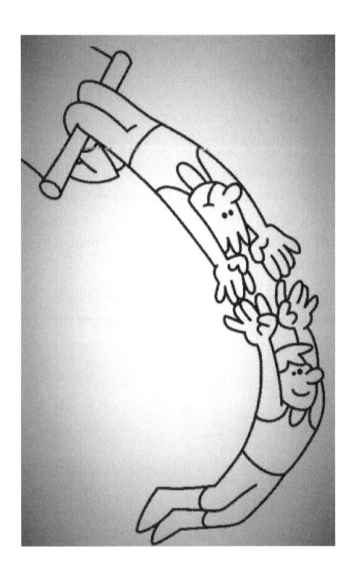

Have you ever been to the circus and seen the acrobats perform? They do incredible stunts from hundreds of feet way up in the air. What if I told you that you could see what it is like to be an acrobat in the circus, flipping and flying through the air, without having to move a single muscle? You really can- In your mind! Your mind is capable of doing many incredible things, including something called Visualization.

To begin your visualization practice, close your eyes. Really, close your eyes (unless you are the one reading this, of course!) To build a very strong visualization, it is usually helpful to first center yourself and be sure you are giving your brain the very best tools it needs to work with. In this case, that means oxygen, and oxygen means taking some good, deep breaths.

You are going to take some slow, deep breaths now, following along with my instruction: Breathe in very slowly, 1 - 2 - 3 - 4. Now breathe out, very slowly, 1 - 2 - 3 - 4. Excellent. Now again very slowly, 1 - 2 - 3 - 4 and breathe back out very slowly, 1 - 2 - 3 - 4 very nice. Once more very slowly in 1 - 2 - 3 - 4 and back out very slowly, 1 - 2 - 3 - 4. Great!

Take a moment to review how you feel. Are you comfy and feeling good? Okay, great.

Picture yourself, in your mind's eye, standing below a giant, red and white striped circus tent. You are in the circus ring, surrounded by other performers all around you. You can see someone riding on a gigantic bicycle, and there is someone else doing a performance where they juggle with fire! Wow!

You take a deep, long breath in and can smell the hay under your feet and popcorn and other circus foods out beyond. You look down at yourself and see that you are in a sparkly emerald green performer's outfit!

All of a sudden the lights in the circus tent dim and everything gets quiet as the other performers slowly make their way off to the sides. There is an announcement coming over the loudspeaker PA system: "Attention everyone! You are in for a treat. You have watched our performers juggle fire and ride giant bicycles; you have watched incredible feats that are exciting and rare! For our next performer, the stunts are far more than anyone would dare. Please welcome our Amazingly Marvelous Acrobat!" With that, a spotlight is suddenly on you and you realize... You are the acrobat!!!

You are feeling a little nervous but very, very, very excited as you realize that this means that you get to put on a fantastic acrobat show! A drumroll starts in the distance and the audience starts clapping rhythmically in sync with an air of expectation. The spotlight slowly moves off of you and towards a ladder.

You take a few tentative steps towards the ladder, following the spotlight. Once you arrive at the bottom of the ladder, you look up... and up...and up and up and up!!!! This ladder is very, very high, leading to some sort of platform. You gulp, swallowing hard as you summon your strength to reach out and grab on to the first rung. You can do this, you tell yourself, you know you can.

Tentatively, you reach out for the first rung. The moment your fingers touch the rung of the ladder, the audience explodes into applause and cheers. Wow! They are so excited to see this acrobat show, you think. Feeling very determined and capable, you continue up the ladder, confidently grasping on each new rung and steadfastly placing each foot as you climb higher, higher, and higher.

You are nearing the top now and the crowd below is still cheering and applauding you. You feel so excited as you get closer and closer to the top. You are on your very last rung now and you can see out over the platform. Wow! Those are trapeze bars!!!

You climb up and out on to the platform, pausing for a moment to turn and wave to the crowd, who is still excitedly cheering for you. The trapeze looks like a giant swing and you are feeling a little nervous about being so high up in the air on it, but you know that you are capable and you are brave. You know it is okay to feel a little scared about trying something new, but you can do it anyway!

You climb out onto the giant swing, firmly grasping the sides. You take a long, deep breath in as you push off of the platform and feel yourself soar outwards over the crowd! The crowd is going wild, cheering excitedly and clapping loudly for you. The breeze washes over you as you are soaring out through the air with the red and white circus tent so close to you above that you can feel like you could almost touch it. You are so proud of yourself and grateful that you have had this experience to be an acrobat for a day.

You do not have to leave this circus tent where you are acrobat for a day just yet if you don't want to. You can spend as long as you want here and you can come back anytime you'd like.

You can create anything you want in your mind. Imagine where you want to go and build the picture in your mind. Be sure to imagine how you want it to smell, taste, hear and feel. The more detailed you can make your mental picture, the more you will enjoy being there.

It is all up to you. Perhaps as you drift off to sleep, you may find yourself back up here on your acrobat swing as the crowds below you cheer for you.

Chapter 9:
Garden Gnomes

Do you know what garden gnomes are? They are the cute little statues that you see sometimes sitting outside on people's lawns and in their gardens. Most garden gnomes have tall, pointy hats they wear and they are usually painted wearing brightly colored clothing that looks whimsical and fun. Have you ever wondered what it might be like to be able to paint your very own garden gnomes? What if I told you that you could paint your very own garden gnomes to put out in your garden right now, without having to move a single muscle? You really can- In your mind! Your mind is capable of doing many incredible things, including something called Visualization.

To begin your visualization practice, close your eyes. Really, close your eyes (unless you are the one reading this, of course!) To build a very strong visualization, it is usually helpful to first center yourself and be sure you are giving your brain the very best tools it needs to work with. In this case, that means oxygen, and oxygen means taking some good, deep breaths.

You are going to take some slow, deep breaths now, following along with my instruction: Breathe in very slowly, 1 – 2 – 3 – 4. Now breathe out, very slowly, 1 – 2 – 3 – 4. Excellent. Now again very slowly, 1 – 2 – 3 – 4 and breathe back out very slowly, 1 – 2 – 3 – 4 very nice. Once more very slowly in 1 – 2 – 3 – 4 and back out very slowly, 1 – 2 – 3 – 4. Great!

Take a moment to review how you feel. Are you comfy and feeling good? Okay, great.

Picture yourself, in your mind's eye, outside on a beautiful spring day. The sky is a pale blue above you and the sun is warming you where you sit. You have an artist's workspace set up with a wooden table that is about the same height as your waist, stocked with paints and paintbrushes of every color and every size. There are also several garden gnome statues beside the table, all the same light gray color of unpainted pottery.

You take a long, deep breath in and notice how fresh and clean the spring air is and you think to yourself that today is a spectacular day to be outside doing a lovely paint project. You look down and notice that you have on a long, black apron. Perfect! Now you won't have to worry about getting paint on your clothes.

You lean down to inspect the garden gnomes. Each one is unique and different. Some are smiling and others are making funny faces. Some are standing with their hands on their hips and some are crouched down petting a bunny rabbit or holding a little frog. There is even a garden gnome that is picking his nose!!! You laugh a little at this, gross!

That's when you see it: the perfect garden gnome for you! This garden gnome is wearing the typical pointy gnome hat but with a twist: it has a super-wide brim, like a sun hat and his hands are up in the air with his fingers outstretched like he is at a party or something! You know it will be so fun to paint and decorate this little guy.

You lifted the fun party garden gnome up and set him on the table. You take a couple of steps back, wondering what color you should paint his hat. You pull a paint palette out and inspect the color options: there is a light aqua blue, tangerine orange, bright cherry red, pale buttercream yellow, and a sparkly midnight black color. So many awesome choices, but you think that this little gnome needs a fun party hat, so you decide to start with the bright cherry red!

You look at the many paintbrushes available and decide that the hat needs one that is a decent size, so you pick up a paintbrush that is about as wide as a quarter. You dip it into the cherry red, swirling the color on to the paintbrush. You begin to paint the awesome party hat and smile as you watch the vivid cherry red slowly cover the entire hat.

Now it's time to move on to the garden gnome's outfit. Hmm. You look at your palette and decide that sparkly midnight black color would be the perfect color for the shirt, so you choose another wide paintbrush and dip it into the midnight black color, loving how sparkly it is! You begin to paint the gnome's shirt, watching in awe as the sparkly midnight black seems to glitter more and more with every stroke of your paintbrush. You love it!

The next step is to paint the little shorts, and you think that the tangerine orange would be perfect, so you select another paintbrush and begin to paint the gnome's shorts a beautiful tangerine orange. You think that the tangerine orange is such an awesome color, you will keep the same paintbrush and just dip it right into the pale buttercream yellow to create a deep yellow-orange for the gnome's little shoes.

Now that you've painted your garden gnome's clothes, you step back from the table to look him over. His cherry-red hat, his sparkly midnight black shirt, tangerine orange shorts, and yellow-orange shoes are absolutely perfect! He is colorful and bright and looks like the perfect addition to your garden. You look over at all the other garden gnomes waiting to be painted and are very thankful that you get to paint all these cute garden gnomes. Next gnome is the one picking his nose!

You do not have to leave your garden gnomes just yet if you don't want to. You can spend as long as you want here and you can come back anytime you'd like.

You can create anything you want in your mind. Imagine where you want to go and build the picture in your mind. Be sure to imagine how you want it to smell, taste, hear and feel. The more detailed you can make your mental picture, the more you will enjoy being there.

It is all up to you. Perhaps as you drift off to sleep, you may find yourself back here with your paints and your garden gnomes, enjoying this beautiful spring day.

Chapter 10:
Fun with Desert Friends

Have you ever been out in the desert? The desert has a very dry climate and only special animals and plants can live there that don't need as much water as other animals and plants do. Would you like to go explore the desert and make new desert friends? What if I told you that you could do this without having to move a single muscle? You really can- In your mind! Your mind is capable of doing many incredible things, including something called Visualization.

To begin your visualization practice, close your eyes. Really, close your eyes (unless you are the one reading this, of course!) To build a very strong visualization, it is usually helpful to first center yourself and be sure you are giving your brain the very best tools it needs to work with. In this case, that means oxygen, and oxygen means taking some good, deep breaths.

You are going to take some slow, deep breaths now, following along with my instruction: Breathe in very slowly, 1 – 2 – 3 – 4. Now breathe out, very slowly, 1 – 2 – 3 – 4. Excellent. Now again very slowly, 1 – 2 – 3 – 4 and breathe back out very slowly, 1 – 2 – 3 – 4 very nice. Once more very slowly in 1 – 2 – 3 – 4 and back out very slowly, 1 – 2 – 3 – 4. Great!

Take a moment to review how you feel. Are you comfy and feeling good? Okay, great.

Picture yourself, in your mind's eye, standing outside. The ground is sandy beneath your feet, but it is hard-packed sand that is easy to walk on. Looking around you, you can see that you are in the desert! You can see many different kinds of cactus, or cacti, and the ground is wide and flat for as far as you can see!

You take a long, deep breath in and notice how dry and warm the air here in the desert is. The sun is shining brightly above and it is very, very hot here where you are. The desert is an interesting environment because it is typically very, very hot during the day and then very, very cool at night. There's not a lot of places to shelter from either the hot sun during the day or the cool air at night, so animals and plants that live in the desert have to be very tough and resilient.

You have on a wide-brimmed sun hat and plenty of sunscreen lotion to protect yourself from the sun and you have plenty of water in your backpack, so you feel ready and prepared to set out on your desert adventure.

You take a few steps towards a particularly large cactus that is nearby. Many of the cacti that you see out in the desert are fairly small, your size or smaller. This cactus, however, is HUGE! You walk up to it and it towers overhead. You are amazed at how huge this thing is, completely covered in spindly spines.

The cool thing about cacti is that they are able to take the very, very small amount of rainfall and moisture that happens in the desert and they are able to store it inside of their prickly trunks and use just a little tiny bit every few weeks until it rains again. This is very different from the way most plants and animals work, right? Most living things need water every single day.

Knowing this, you don't expect that you will see very many animals out here in the desert, so you are very excited when movement catches your eye on the huge cactus. It is a beetle with a shiny black shell that reflects the sunshine that is beaming down. You watch the beetle with interest as it scuttles across the surface of the cactus, weaving in and out of the large, spiny needles. It looks like this little beetle is on some kind of obstacle course, the way it has to dodge the spiny needles of the cactus as it scurries along until…

WHOA! From out of nowhere a long, sticky tongue appears and scoops the shiny black beetle up. What on earth?? You look and can't see where this tongue came from, all you see is the green cactus that… oh wait, you do see it now! It is a chameleon and he is camouflaged! He has turned himself the exact same shade of green as the cactus so he can hunt without being seen. Very cool!

The chameleon suddenly jumps from the cactus down to the desert floor and you are amazed at how quickly he is able to camouflage into the gray sand of the desert floor. What a neat trick, you think, as the chameleon cranes his neck back and forth as he looks up at you quizzically. You laugh because he looks so funny as he bobs back and forth when you are startled by something running past you.

What the heck was that? It ran by so quickly! You search the landscape around you and that's when you see it. It is a funny-looking bird with a long, curved beak, tall head feathers, and very, very long tail feathers that stick way up in the air. Now you know what that was; it is a roadrunner! They are known for how fast they are.

The roadrunner is peering at you, trying to figure out what kind of desert animal you are. You laugh again because you have made a lot of new desert animal friends today, but you are not a desert animal, are you? You are very thankful that you have had the opportunity to explore the desert plants and animals.

You do not have to leave your desert friends just yet if you don't want to. You can spend as long as you want here and you can come back anytime you'd like.

You can create anything you want in your mind. Imagine where you want to go and build the picture in your mind. Be sure to imagine how you want it to smell, taste, hear and feel.

The more detailed you can make your mental picture, the more you will enjoy being there.

It is all up to you. Perhaps as you drift off to sleep, you may find yourself back out here in the desert, exploring the amazingly tough desert plants and animals.

Chapter 11:
Fairies in the Forest

Have you ever wondered what it would be like to see fairies? What if you could see fairies playing out in the forest? What if you could actually see fairies playing out in the forest right now, without having to move a single muscle? You really can- In your mind! Your mind is capable of doing many incredible things, including something called Visualization.

To begin your visualization practice, close your eyes. Really, close your eyes (unless you are the one reading this, of

course!) To build a very strong visualization, it is usually helpful to first center yourself and be sure you are giving your brain the very best tools it needs to work with. In this case, that means oxygen, and oxygen means taking some good, deep breaths.

You are going to take some slow, deep breaths now, following along with my instruction: Breathe in very slowly, 1 - 2 - 3 - 4. Now breathe out, very slowly, 1 - 2 - 3 - 4. Excellent. Now again very slowly, 1 - 2 - 3 - 4 and breathe back out very slowly, 1 - 2 - 3 - 4 very nice. Once more very slowly in 1 - 2 - 3 - 4 and back out very slowly, 1 - 2 - 3 - 4. Great!

Take a moment to review how you feel. Are you comfy and feeling good? Okay, great.

Picture yourself, in your mind's eye, standing at the edge of a forest. You are going to go on a forest walk. You take a deep, long breath in and smell the woody pine fresh scent from all around you. It is a beautiful spring day and there is a gentle breeze that is blowing through the air around you.

You take your first steps into the forest and immediately appreciate the way the sunlight is streaming through the tree canopy above you, giving the forest an ethereal look. The trees in this forest are tall and thin and the tree limbs and leaves above are a deep and dark green. You stop to inspect one of the tree trunks and see that it is covered in a soft and downy green moss. You gently touch it and realize that it is almost pillow-soft!

This deep green moss is all over each of the trees and you realize that it makes the trees like something out of a fairy tale. You continue your walk through the beautiful forest, the ground beneath you soft and squishy beneath your shoes and you realize that the ground is also covered in moss! Wow! You are enjoying the cushioned walk when you see something that stops you dead in your tracks: a fairy circle! If you have never heard of a fairy circle before, it is a circle of toadstool mushrooms that legend says is where fairies meet.

You very carefully walk around the fairy circle, smiling and thinking that it is just perfect to see a fairy circle out here because this beautiful forest seems like just the sort of place that fairies would be. You come to a tree that is a little bit wider than the others and you have to walk around it. As you walk around the tree, you see something that makes you crouch down and you hide immediately...

On the other side of this wide tree is another fairy circle on the mossy ground, but this one has actual fairies on it! You can hardly believe your eyes and you try to count how many fairies you see in this clearing, but there are too many to count, or maybe it is just difficult to count something that is twinkling and flitting all around!

Each fairy is sparkly and twinkling in the sunlight as it streams through the tree leaves above, and they flit so quickly back and forth that if you weren't sure what you were looking at, you might think that they were just specks of dust dancing in the sunlight. You notice that the fairies have taken some of the moss and arranged it into little couches and beds and there are some fairies that seem to be lounging about and relaxing on the mossy resting areas before flitting back up and out in a twinkle of light.

The fairies are flitting about so quickly and you really want to get a better look so you try and shift your weight very quietly and carefully to get a better view, but your foot slips and you make a rustling noise. Just like that, in a single moment, the fairies all flit up and out of view. You look up at the sunlight as it streams through the trees, searching for the fairies, but all you can see from this space are twinkles of light. Just like that, the fairies were gone.

You go and look at their cute little moss beds and couches, set around the toadstool mushrooms, and you smile because it looks like such a lovely place to be. You wonder what it is like to be a fairy out here in this ethereal forest and you are grateful that you've had this awesome experience.

You do not have to leave this fairy filled forest just yet if you don't want to. You can spend as long as you want here and you can come back anytime you'd like.

You can create anything you want in your mind. Imagine where you want to go and build the picture in your mind. Be sure to imagine how you want it to smell, taste, hear and feel. The more detailed you can make your mental picture, the more you will enjoy being there.

It is all up to you. Perhaps as you drift off to sleep, you may find yourself back out here in this fairy tale forest, looking for the lovely twinkling fairies and their fairy circles.

Chapter 12:
Library Book Adventure

Do you like to go to the library? A library is a magical place because there are thousands and thousands of books there and each book has its own adventure. All you have to do is open it up to step inside. What if I told you that you could go step inside a library book adventure right now if you wanted to, without moving a single muscle? You really can- In your mind! Your mind is capable of doing many incredible things, including something called Visualization.

To begin your visualization practice, close your eyes. Really, close your eyes (unless you are the one reading this, of course!) To build a very strong visualization, it is usually helpful to first center yourself and be sure you are giving your brain the very best tools it needs to work with. In this case, that means oxygen, and oxygen means taking some good, deep breaths.

You are going to take some slow, deep breaths now, following along with my instruction: Breathe in very slowly, 1 – 2 – 3 – 4. Now breathe out, very slowly, 1 – 2 – 3 – 4 Excellent. Now again very slowly, 1 – 2 – 3 – 4 and breathe back out very slowly, 1 – 2 – 3 – 4 very nice. Once more very slowly in 1 – 2 – 3 – 4 and back out very slowly, 1 – 2 – 3 – 4. Great!

Take a moment to review how you feel. Are you comfy and feeling good? Okay, great.

Imagine yourself, in your mind's eye, standing outside of a massive brick building. It is summertime and the weather is very warm. You see there is a sign above the door and it says "Library." You love libraries so you decide to head on in and cool off.

You step inside and the entire interior is painted with bright, beautiful colors like yellow, orange, blue, green, purple, and red. It is bright and sunny with lots of windows on every single wall and it looks like there are couches and bean bag chairs all over for people to sit in and relax at.

You keep walking in, looking for the children's section, but it is not hard to find because the entrance to this library's children's section has a rainbow carpet that leads the way into it. You follow the rainbow carpet into the children's section and begin looking at the books there.

The first book you pull out has a beautiful cover on it of a child bundled up in a swirling snowstorm and the title is, "Playing in the Snow." You decide to take it over to one of the nearby beanbag chairs. You plop yourself down into the soft, squishy chair and open your book.

Suddenly, you are standing outside with snow swirling all around you! It is just like the cover of the book. You are bundled up just like the child on the cover was so you are not cold, but you are amazed that you have somehow stepped inside of this book! You reach down to touch the snow that is covering the ground and your boots and you can really touch it; it is real snow! Wow!

You begin rolling the snow into three balls; a huge ball of snow for the bottom, a medium ball of snow for the middle, and then a smaller ball of snow for the top. Now you have made a snowman! You step back and admire your snowman work and then suddenly, you find yourself sitting back in the beanbag chair of the library.

"Well, I guess that was one way to cool off!" you think as you get up and go to see what other books you can find. Your eye settles on a very pretty book cover. This one has a kid completely covered in autumn leaves, their head the only part sticking out. You head back over to the beanbag chair and settle back in.

You open the book and suddenly you can't see anything at all! You move your arms around a bit and the leaves that were covering your face and eyes fall away. You are completely covered in a giant pile of autumn leaves, with only your head sticking out! This is exactly like the book cover, you think, and you roll your body back and forth in the crunchy, crispy leaves, listening to them crackle with your movement.

An autumn breeze blows through and scatters the leaves that are on top of you and suddenly, you are back in the library, snuggled into the beanbag chair and holding the book in your hands.

You are so happy and thankful that you have had this library adventure. Anytime you open a book, you can imagine yourself right there in it. Every book you read can be a fun adventure wherever you are!

You do not have to leave your library adventure just yet if you don't want to. You can spend as long as you want here and you can come back anytime you'd like.

You can create anything you want in your mind. Imagine where you want to go and build the picture in your mind. Be sure to imagine how you want it to smell, taste, hear and feel. The more detailed you can make your mental picture, the more you will enjoy being there.

It is all up to you. Perhaps as you drift off to sleep, you may find yourself back in this beautiful library, ready to hop into another fun book adventure.

Chapter 13:
Swimming in the Clouds

Do you ever lay outside on a cloudy day and wonder what clouds feel like? Especially the extra fat and fluffy clouds, would they feel as soft and squishy as they look? What if you could go swimming through the clouds, what would that feel like? What if I told you that you could go swimming in the clouds, right now, without moving a single muscle? You really can- In your mind! Your mind is capable of doing many incredible things, including something called Visualization.

To begin your visualization practice, close your eyes. Really, close your eyes (unless you are the one reading this, of course!) To build a very strong visualization, it is usually

helpful to first center yourself and be sure you are giving your brain the very best tools it needs to work with. In this case, that means oxygen, and oxygen means taking some good, deep breaths.

You are going to take some slow, deep breaths now, following along with my instruction: Breathe in very slowly, 1 – 2 – 3 – 4. Now breathe out, very slowly, 1 – 2 – 3 – 4. Excellent. Now again very slowly, 1 – 2 – 3 – 4 and breathe back out very slowly, 1 – 2 – 3 – 4 very nice. Once more very slowly in 1 – 2 – 3 – 4 and back out very slowly, 1 – 2 – 3 – 4. Great!

Take a moment to review how you feel. Are you comfy and feeling good? Okay, great.

Picture yourself, in your mind's eye, sitting outside on a beautiful summer day. The sun is warm and you feel perfectly comfortable in this lovely summer weather. The sky is a bright, vivid blue and it is full of white, fluffy clouds. You are watching as the clouds slowly drift by.

You take a long, deep breath in and smell the fresh air and the summer smells around you: fresh cut grass, blooming flowers, and maybe even the smell of someone cooking out on a grill nearby. The clouds above are so thick today that you think it looks like they are solid. You wonder what it would feel like to try and lay back on a cloud...

Suddenly, you are surrounded by white. You are confused and try and get your bearings, looking all around you. When you look up, you can see some blue, but below you is something that is fluffy, cushiony, and soft. It is a cloud! You are laying in a cloud.

Wow! You can hardly believe it; you are really in a cloud. Against your skin, the cloud feels like something that is light and airy, but also cool and moist, and thick and fluffy, too, all at once! You move your arm back and forth in disbelief and it almost feels like how it feels to move your arm underwater. This gives you an idea!

You begin to move your arms back and forth how you would if you were trying to swim in a swimming pool and you are immediately propelled forward, wow! It really is like swimming in a pool! You continue to work your arms like you are doing the breaststroke, your arm going up high over your head and forward until it cuts back through the thickest, fluffiest part of the cloud.

You feel like you are in a dream, in a thick, white, fluffy dream! You continue to move forward, forward, forward through the soft, fluffy cloud and then you decide to roll on your back and see if you can do the backstroke.

Easily rolling onto your back, you begin to reach up again through the fluffy white substance and this time, you bring your arm up and back behind you, your body easily floating backward now through the clouds. The cloud is both supportive and soft, holding your body weight up easily, but allowing you to sink into it like you are floating inside of a jello mold of some kind!

You continue to backstroke through the cloud, your legs kicking up and down as well. It is just like swimming but instead of water resistance, you have cloud resistance! You stop your arms and legs for a moment and just let yourself float in the clouds. You feel so incredibly relaxed and supported up here in the clouds. You are so grateful that you get to experience what it is like to swim through the clouds and you will always remember this, every time you look up and see the clouds above you.

You do not have to stop swimming through the clouds just yet if you don't want to. You can spend as long as you want here and you can come back anytime you'd like.

You can create anything you want in your mind. Imagine where you want to go and build the picture in your mind. Be sure to imagine how you want it to smell, taste, hear and feel. The more detailed you can make your mental picture, the more you will enjoy being there.

It is all up to you. Perhaps as you drift off to sleep, you may find yourself back up here in the fluffy clouds, swimming through the sky.

Chapter 14:
Butterfly Garden

Do you know what a butterfly garden is? It is a special garden where all of a butterfly's favorite plants and flowers are grown, and butterflies will come from all around to hang out and rest there. Do you know that you can go and see a butterfly garden right now, without having to move a single muscle? You really can- In your mind! Your mind is capable of doing many incredible things, including something called Visualization.

To begin your visualization practice, close your eyes. Really, close your eyes (unless you are the one reading this, of

course!) To build a very strong visualization, it is usually helpful to first center yourself and be sure you are giving your brain the very best tools it needs to work with. In this case, that means oxygen, and oxygen means taking some good, deep breaths.

You are going to take some slow, deep breaths now, following along with my instruction: Breathe in very slowly, 1 – 2 – 3 – 4. Now breathe out, very slowly, 1 – 2 – 3 – 4. Excellent. Now again very slowly, 1 – 2 – 3 – 4 and breathe back out very slowly, 1 – 2 – 3 – 4 very nice. Once more very slowly in 1 – 2 – 3 – 4 and back out very slowly, 1 – 2 – 3 – 4. Great!

Take a moment to review how you feel. Are you comfy and feeling good? Okay, great.

Picture yourself, in y our mind's eye, sitting on a bench in a beautiful garden. It is a spring morning and the weather is lovely. The morning sunshine is bathing the garden in lovely spring light. Everywhere you look there are plants and flowers.

Some plants are large with big, wide leaves and some are small, with thin, reed-like leaves. Some flowers are tall, with long, skinny stems and big, full blooms at the top. Some are small and close to the ground, with thick and full stems that all seem to connect with one another as they are clustered beside each other. It seems like there are flowers and plants of just about every color you can possibly imagine.

The bench you are sitting on is made of stone and you sit up a little bit and look at the back, as there is something engraved here. It is a picture of a butterfly, carved right into the rock. How neat! You stand up from the bench and follow the smooth pebble path beneath your feet a few steps and that's when you realize that these plants and flowers aren't just colorful all by themselves; they are colorful also because they have butterflies on them!

Immediately to your right is an iris patch. Irises are flowers with tall, thin stems and large blue blooms at the top, and they easily sway back and forth in the breeze. These irises are swaying steadily back and forth, but there isn't much of a breeze today. It appears these irises are swaying due to the visitors that are crawling on each bloom! You stop to inspect the iris that is closest to you.

There is an orange monarch butterfly on this iris bloom. Orange monarchs have large, bright orange wings that have large dark circles on them that almost look like eyes from a distance. This beautiful orange monarch is holding on tight to this beautiful iris bloom as it drinks in its nectar, slowly and gently swaying side to side as the weight of this butterfly keeps the flower in motion.

This particular iris patch has butterflies of all different colors, it seems. You see butterflies that are orange, some that are blue like the iris itself, some that are purple, and some that are yellow. Each butterfly is busy enjoying a good meal.

You continue down the path and come to a beautiful trellis tunnel. It is a wrought-iron gate trellis tunnel that extends several feet along the path and it is covered in a beautiful flowering vine. The flowers on this vine are yellow and orange, but it has attracted butterflies of every color here. As you walk through this beautiful flower tunnel, the butterflies flitting and flying around your head as they move between flowers on either side. It is almost like being inside of some kind of butterfly wind tunnel!

You pause a moment to examine an especially vividly colored viceroy butterfly that is a violet-blue that you have never seen in a butterfly before. Perched on the edge of a buttercream yellow flower, this violet-blue purple looks like something out of a picture book. As you appreciate this beautiful little butterfly, you get a surprise visitor that perches right on the tip of your finger!

It is a zebra-striped swallowtail butterfly! Just as their name suggests, this butterfly has black and white stripes, just like a zebra, and a long, billowy set of wings that ripple as it flutters. You are in awe of this beautiful creature and try to remain still as it sits and flaps its wings right on your finger! You are so excited to have such a close-up view of these beautiful butterflies.

The beautiful zebra-striped swallowtail decides to flutter off out from under the trellis tunnel and you follow along behind it. You watch it as it comes out of the tunnel and flies up, up, and up into the lovely blue morning sky. Wow, you think. What a beautiful butterfly and what a lovely experience this has been. You are so grateful that you have had the chance to see and examine these butterflies so closely.

You do not have to leave this beautiful butterfly garden just yet if you don't want to. You can spend as long as you want here and you can come back anytime you'd like.

You can create anything you want in your mind. Imagine where you want to go and build the picture in your mind. Be sure to imagine how you want it to smell, taste, hear and feel.

The more detailed you can make your mental picture, the more you will enjoy being there.

It is all up to you. Perhaps as you drift off to sleep, you may find yourself back out here in the butterfly garden, following a zebra-striped swallowtail out into the sun.

Chapter 15:
Paddling the Canoe

Have you ever had a chance to go floating along a river in a canoe? How about actually paddling a canoe? It can be a ton of fun to be the one in charge of the oars as you make your way down a river. What if I told you that you can actually paddle in a canoe right now, without having to move a single muscle? You really can- In your mind! Your mind is capable of doing many incredible things, including something called Visualization.

To begin your visualization practice, close your eyes. Really, close your eyes (unless you are the one reading this, of

course!) To build a very strong visualization, it is usually helpful to first center yourself and be sure you are giving your brain the very best tools it needs to work with. In this case, that means oxygen, and oxygen means taking some good, deep breaths.

You are going to take some slow, deep breaths now, following along with my instruction: Breathe in very slowly, 1 - 2 - 3 - 4. Now breathe out, very slowly, 1 - 2 - 3 - 4. Excellent. Now again very slowly, 1 - 2 - 3 - 4 and breathe back out very slowly, 1 - 2 - 3 - 4 very nice. Once more very slowly in 1 - 2 - 3 - 4 and back out very slowly, 1 - 2 - 3 - 4. Great!

Take a moment to review how you feel. Are you comfy and feeling good? Okay, great.

Picture yourself, in your mind's eye, standing on a muddy bank of a river. The weather is warm and the sky is blue and the sunshine that is coming down from the summer sun is heating you up quickly. You are standing above a canoe and the canoe and the water below it look very inviting on this hot summer's day.

You step into the canoe from the muddy bank very carefully, first one foot, and then the other. Once you are in the canoe, you pick up one of the oars and use it to gently push off of the muddy bank so you can float down the river. Once you are in the river's current, you relax back a little bit and take in a long, deep breath. You can smell the clean, clear, and fast-moving water of the river and the muddy banks on either side.

On the shores beyond the muddy banks are trees. You are entirely surrounded by a beautiful forest on both sides and as you float down the river gently, you enjoy the sounds of the forest you can hear around you: there are frogs croaking and crickets chirping nearby. Somewhere close is a bird chirping its song and you can hear its partner chirping back its response somewhere out in the distance.

You smile and feel so content to be out here on this lovely river. You pick up the other oar and begin to help the canoe to move forward. You dip one oar in and bring it back, then the other oar, bringing it back at the same time the other is moving forward. You find a rhythm and your arms are feeling strong and steady as you continue to move forward. Now that you are rowing, there is a lovely breeze coming through as you are moving quickly now.

The breeze washes over you, refreshing you. Your arms are strong and steady and the wind is moving quickly over and around you as you continue to paddle on, faster and faster. Up ahead, you can see that the river narrows and the trees on either side of the shores have grown up and over the river, forming a beautiful natural tunnel. As you approach this natural tunnel, you decide to stop rowing for a moment.

Letting your arms rest and your body relax, you feel the shade that the leaf-filled branches above you offer and you take another long, deep breath in. The summer's sun is shielded entirely from you here and you relish the feeling of cool air. Your muscles feel strong and capable and you are proud of how well you do when you work hard at something you want. You know that you can do anything you put your mind to, as long as you work hard for it.

You decide to take up the oars again and begin to move faster, steadily forward, forward, letting the muscles in your strong, steady arms propel you forward, out into the summer's sunshine. You feel grateful that you are strong and capable of rowing.

You do not have to leave this lovely river just yet if you don't want to. You can spend as long as you want here and you can come back anytime you'd like.

You can create anything you want in your mind. Imagine where you want to go and build the picture in your mind. Be sure to imagine how you want it to smell, taste, hear and feel. The more detailed you can make your mental picture, the more you will enjoy being there.

It is all up to you. Perhaps as you drift off to sleep, you may find yourself back out here in this canoe, rowing yourself down the river.

Chapter 16:
Berry Picking Fun

Have you ever been berry picking before? There are so many different kinds of berries out there: strawberries, raspberries, blueberries, boysenberries, razzle-dazzle berries... well, razzle-dazzle berries are probably not real, but whatever kind of berry you like, picking them is half the fun! What if I told you that you can actually go berry picking right now, without having to move a single muscle? You really can- In your mind! Your mind is capable of doing many incredible things, including something called Visualization.

To begin your visualization practice, close your eyes. Really, close your eyes (unless you are the one reading this, of course!) To build a very strong visualization, it is usually helpful to first center yourself and be sure you are giving your brain the very best tools it needs to work with. In this case, that means oxygen, and oxygen means taking some good, deep breaths.

You are going to take some slow, deep breaths now, following along with my instruction: Breathe in very slowly, 1 - 2 - 3 - 4. Now breathe out, very slowly, 1 - 2 - 3 - 4. Excellent. Now again very slowly, 1 - 2 - 3 - 4 and breathe back out very slowly, 1 - 2 - 3 - 4 very nice. Once more very slowly in 1 - 2 - 3 - 4 and back out very slowly, 1 - 2 - 3 - 4. Great!

Take a moment to review how you feel. Are you comfy and feeling good? Okay, great.

Imagine yourself, in your mind's eye, in a beautiful clearing in the forest. It is a lovely summer day and it is still early enough in the day that the weather is not too hot yet. You have been on a lovely hike through this forest, but you are also on a mission! You are looking for an elusive berry species: the razzle-dazzle berry!

The razzle-dazzle berry has just been discovered and it is very difficult to find. You have been out hiking every day for the last few days looking for this very elusive berry type. You have a field guide that shows what kind of berry you are looking for and this is very important because you wouldn't want to pick the wrong berry and find out that it is poisonous!

You consult your field guide. The razzle-dazzle berry is bright pink and it has a property that no other berries have: it sparkles! That's right, razzle-dazzle berries have tiny seeds all over the outside of its fruit and they reflect whatever light they are in, so when you look at a razzle-dazzle berry, you are dazzled by its sparkle! You review the other information you have about it: it grows on vines in thickets and it usually grows near running water, so any sort of streams or rivers is usually a good place to start.

Today, you are hopeful because you are heading to a waterfall and you think there is a good chance you might finally find yourself a razzle-dazzle berry patch! You take a moment to get your bearings, taking a long, deep breath in and smelling the clean, fresh air of the forest. You can hear birds chirping all around you as they sing to each other, but now there is something else that you can also hear; what is that? It sounds like running water!

You continue on your path, much quicker now, following the sound of the water. It isn't long before you stumble across exactly what you've been looking for. It is a waterfall! The waterfall is beautiful and the spray of the water as it lands in the stream bounces up and into your face and you smile because it is perfectly refreshing. You are on a mission, however, so you walk along the bank of the stream, hunting for the razzle-dazzle berries that you hope are here.

Nothing. You are starting to feel a little worried that perhaps you might not find them when you scramble up and over a particularly large boulder, only to find on the other side something that stops you immediately in your tracks! It is a thicket of sparkling, bright pink berries growing on what appears to be a cluster of vines; you have found the razzle-dazzle berries!

You consult your field guide and check the pictures and the descriptions and make sure that they match with the berries you have found, but the most distinctive part of these berries is impossible to miss, and that is the sparkle! These berries are so bright and sparkly that you almost need sunglasses to come close!

You go to pick your first razzle-dazzle and you realize that not only is this berry beautiful, but it is also velvety soft and you gently roll it back and forth between your index finger and your thumb. You decide to give it a little taste and you pop it into your mouth. It is an explosion of flavor! This berry is sweet and tart and almost effervescent in your mouth- it feels like your mouth is sparkling now, too!

You are so thrilled that you have found the razzle-dazzle berries, and you move along, gently but eagerly plucking the berries from their vines, sampling a berry every few minutes. You are so happy that you found the razzle-dazzle berries and you feel grateful that you have had this experience.

You do not have to leave the razzle-dazzle berries just yet if you don't want to. You can spend as long as you want here and you can come back anytime you'd like.

You can create anything you want in your mind. Imagine where you want to go and build the picture in your mind. Be sure to imagine how you want it to smell, taste, hear and feel. The more detailed you can make your mental picture, the more you will enjoy being there.

It is all up to you. Perhaps as you drift off to sleep, you may find yourself back out here beside the waterfall, picking sparkling razzle-dazzle berries.

Chapter 17:
Horseback Riding Fun

Have you ever been on a horse? It is so fun to go horseback riding. What if I told you that you could go horseback riding right now without having to move a single muscle? You really can- In your mind! Your mind is capable of doing many incredible things, including something called Visualization.

To begin your visualization practice, close your eyes. Really, close your eyes (unless you are the one reading this, of

course!) To build a very strong visualization, it is usually helpful to first center yourself and be sure you are giving your brain the very best tools it needs to work with. In this case, that means oxygen, and oxygen means taking some good, deep breaths.

You are going to take some slow, deep breaths now, following along with my instruction: Breathe in very slowly, 1 – 2 – 3 – 4. Now breathe out, very slowly, 1 – 2 – 3 – 4. Excellent. Now again very slowly, 1 – 2 – 3 – 4 and breathe back out very slowly, 1 – 2 – 3 – 4 very nice. Once more very slowly in 1 2 – 3 – 4 and back out very slowly, 1 – 2 – 3 – 4. Great!

Take a moment to review how you feel. Are you comfy and feeling good? Okay, great.

Imagine yourself, in your mind's eye, standing in a green, grassy field. It is a beautiful autumn day and the leaves in the trees beyond the field are changing colors already. You take a long, deep breath in and can smell the crisp, cool fall air, and there is something else that you smell as well... it reminds you of being on a farm!

You look around you and see that you are standing beside a wooden fence that appears to lead into a pasture, and inside the pasture is a beautiful, chestnut brown mare! You walk into the pasture, calling out to the horse in a friendly tone of voice to let her know that you would like to be friends.

As you approach her, you can see that she has a very shiny, rich brown coat. Her mane is silky smooth and looks like it has just been brushed. You say hello to her softly as you slowly put your hand up to pet her neck, taking your time so you can get to know each other. Her large brown expressive eyes seem to look you over as if she is trying to gauge if you two will be friends or not. You lightly stroke her mane and tell her what a beautiful horse she is and she knickers in soft reply back to you, so you guess this must mean that you are friends!

As you are petting and talking to her, you notice that she has a name etched on her bridle, "Oh, that's your name- Celia," you say to her and she gives a sweet little knicker in response as her ears perk up at her name. You see she has her harness on and looks ready to ride, so you ask her if she would mind and she seems to nod back at you with her smiling brown eyes so you decide to go ahead and climb on up.

Once you have slid yourself into place, you give Celia a little nudge with your heels to let her know you're ready, and off you two go! Celia is calmly trotting along the pasture fence with you on her back. Way up high on this gorgeous mare's back, you feel like you are on top of the world! She is a strong horse and riding on her back makes you feel strong, too. You hold on to the leather reins firmly between your hands and you decide to lead her on out of the fenced-in pasture out to the wide-open field.

Celia exits the pasture with you on her back and once you have exited the fence, you give her another little nudge with your feet to let her know you would like to go a little faster and she immediately responds for you. Now she is galloping and you hold tighter to the reigns, feeling exhilarated by the quick movement. You can feel Celia's strong muscles beneath you and you are all smiles as she continues galloping across the open field.

The scenery on this ride is stunning as you pass by the medley of fall colors on the trees. The leaves are burnt gold and rust orange and occasionally there is a scarlet red burst of color and everything is absolutely beautiful. You can tell Celia is also enjoying getting a chance to really stretch her legs and use her muscles.

The autumn wind is bracing and refreshing against your skin and you are smiling and happy. You feel so grateful that you have been able to come out and meet a new horse friend and go for a ride.

You do not have to leave your horseback ride just yet if you don't want to. You can spend as long as you want here and you can come back anytime you'd like.

You can create anything you want in your mind. Imagine where you want to go and build the picture in your mind. Be sure to imagine how you want it to smell, taste, hear and feel. The more detailed you can make your mental picture, the more you will enjoy being there.

It is all up to you. Perhaps as you drift off to sleep, you may find yourself back out here in the wide-open field, galloping along with your new horse friend, Celia.

Chapter 18:
Puppy Hero

Do you like playing with puppies? Well, of course! Who wouldn't? What if you could play with puppies right now, without having to move a single muscle? You really can- In your mind! Your mind is capable of doing many incredible things, including something called Visualization.

To begin your visualization practice, close your eyes. Really, close your eyes (unless you are the one reading this, of

course!) To build a very strong visualization, it is usually helpful to first center yourself and be sure you are giving your brain the very best tools it needs to work with. In this case, that means oxygen, and oxygen means taking some good, deep breaths.

You are going to take some slow, deep breaths now, following along with my instruction: Breathe in very slowly, 1 – 2 – 3 – 4. Now breathe out, very slowly, 1 – 2 – 3 – 4. Excellent. Now again very slowly, 1 – 2 – 3 – 4 and breathe back out very slowly, 1 – 2 – 3 – 4 very nice. Once more very slowly in 1 – 2 – 3 – 4 and back out very slowly, 1 – 2 – 3 – 4. Great!

Take a moment to review how you feel. Are you comfy and feeling good? Okay, great.

Imagine yourself, standing outside, barefoot in the grass. You are in a fenced in backyard and it is one of those lovely summer's days with the sun shining and the birds chirping and the air smelling clean and sweet. You look around and notice that there are tiny toys all over this yard. You lean down to pick one up; it is a tiny fake hot dog and you give it a little squeeze and hear it "squeak, squeak." Aww, it's a squeaker toy!

Do you hear something from around the corner of the fence, a slight rustling perhaps? All of a sudden, rushing out together from around the fence, appear a tiny little pack of puppies! Oh my goodness, they are so adorable! There are five puppies and they are a goldish tan color with floppy ears almost as big as their entire bodies!

They come racing across the yard towards you, so excited to see you! You bend down to pet the first few that arrive and you are immediately bombarded with wet, sloppy, furry puppy kisses! They are so lovable and they wriggle and wriggle and wriggle their warm and soft bodies as they try to climb on to your lap, up your back, and into your arms.

You laugh because it is impossible to pet and love on all of them at one time but that is what they want you to do. You toss the hot dog across the yard, squeezing it before you let it go, and two of the pups go racing after it. You pick up another toy, a little rope chew toy, and you fling that across the yard too, which sends the other three scampering after it.

Now the first two have returned, fighting over the squeaky hot dog. These puppies are so cute! You keep up the game, picking up new toys and tossing them, the dogs delighted in chasing after them and playing fetch. You have just picked up the squeaky hot dog to toss it again when suddenly there is a loud clap of thunder. You have been so busy playing with these sweet pups that you did not even notice there was a storm brewing. The puppies immediately surround you, trying again to climb in your lap, up to your back, and in your arms, as the thunder has frightened them. You stand up and lead them towards the door of the house, opening it up for them so they can feel safe.

Once you are in, the pups look up at you in awe and gratitude. They are so precious and you are so happy and grateful that you have been able to play with them, and now you are a puppy hero!

You do not have to leave your adorable puppy friends just yet if you don't want to. You can spend as long as you want here and you can come back anytime you'd like.

You can create anything you want in your mind. Imagine where you want to go and build the picture in your mind. Be sure to imagine how you want it to smell, taste, hear, and feel. The more detailed you can make your mental picture, the more you will enjoy being there.

It is all up to you. Perhaps as you drift off to sleep, you may find yourself back here with these sweet puppy dogs, playing the hero.

Chapter 19:
Turtle Home

Do you know much about turtles and the habitats that they live in? Well, if you were going to build a turtle home, you would need to know this. What if I told you that you could build a fabulous turtle home right now, without having to move a single muscle? You really can- In your mind! Your mind is capable of doing many incredible things, including something called Visualization.

To begin your visualization practice, close your eyes. Really, close your eyes (unless you are the one reading this, of

course!) To build a very strong visualization, it is usually helpful to first center yourself and be sure you are giving your brain the very best tools it needs to work with. In this case, that means oxygen, and oxygen means taking some good, deep breaths.

You are going to take some slow, deep breaths now, following along with my instruction: Breathe in very slowly, 1 – 2 – 3 – 4. Now breathe out, very slowly, 1 – 2 – 3 – 4. Excellent. Now again very slowly, 1 – 2 – 3 – 4 and breathe back out very slowly, 1 – 2 – 3 – 4 very nice. Once more very slowly in 1 2 – 3 – 4 and back out very slowly, 1 – 2 – 3 – 4. Great!

Take a moment to review how you feel. Are you comfy and feeling good? Okay, great.

Picture yourself, in your mind's eye, standing in front of an empty aquarium. There is nothing in this aquarium, but you have a turtle that is next to it in a lonely cardboard box. This turtle friend needs a much better home than a lonely cardboard box, so you will build him one!

To begin, you start by investigating what materials you might have. You notice that there are several different sizes of rocks, pebbles, and twigs in a box near the aquarium, so you decide to begin there. You choose a couple of large rocks and place them on either side of the aquarium. One rock has a smooth, flat top, and this will be perfect for your turtle friend to climb up on and dry out when he needs to.

Next, you choose a large twig that stretches from one side of the aquarium to the other, and you prop some other rocks against it so you can create a lovely little cave-like space for your turtle friend to hang out in when he wants some privacy.

Next, you take the pebbles and scatter them about the bottom, making sure it is fully covered with pebbles.

Now you will need to add some water! You pick up the pitcher of water that is lying beside the aquarium and you very carefully pour it in, being sure to leave the top of the smooth, flat rock dry so the turtle has a dry place to hang out. Now you can add your turtle friend.

You pick him up out of the lonely cardboard box and place him in his new turtle home. He looks very happy as he goes for a quick swim before making his way up to the cave. You are so grateful that you have been able to help your turtle friend.

You do not have to leave your turtle friend just yet if you don't want to. You can spend as long as you want here and you can come back anytime you'd like.

You can create anything you want in your mind. Imagine where you want to go and build the picture in your mind. Be sure to imagine how you want it to smell, taste, hear and feel. The more detailed you can make your mental picture, the more you will enjoy being there.

It is all up to you. Perhaps as you drift off to sleep, you may find yourself back here with your turtle friend, helping to build him a home he will love.

Chapter 20:
Surf's Up

Have you ever been surfing? Riding the waves out in the open sea? Well, what if I told you that you could go surfing right now without having to move a single muscle?

You really can- In your mind! Your mind is capable of doing many incredible things, including something called Visualization.

To begin your visualization practice, close your eyes. Really, close your eyes (unless you are the one reading this, of

course!) To build a very strong visualization, it is usually helpful to first center yourself and be sure you are giving your brain the very best tools it needs to work with. In this case, that means oxygen, and oxygen means taking some good, deep breaths.

You are going to take some slow, deep breaths now, following along with my instruction: Breathe in very slowly, 1 – 2 – 3 – 4. Now breathe out, very slowly, 1 – 2 – 3 – 4. Excellent. Now again very slowly, 1 – 2 – 3 – 4 and breathe back out very slowly, 1 – 2 – 3 – 4 very nice. Once more very slowly in 1 – 2 – 3 – 4 and back out very slowly, 1 – 2 – 3 – 4. Great!

Take a moment to review how you feel. Are you comfy and feeling good? Okay, great.

Imagine yourself, in your mind's eye, standing on the seashore. You look out over across the deep blue ocean and watch as the waves build up over the water and come crashing at the shore. You take a deep, long breath in, enjoying the clean and fresh salt air and the beautiful sunshine that is beaming down from above.

Beside you is a long, tangerine orange surfboard. You are going to go out and check out these waves for yourself! You take a few steps into the cool, refreshing ocean water with your surfboard before laying on it, stomach first. You use your arms to paddle out further into the water. There is a wave coming towards you but you know you haven't made it out far enough yet so using all the muscle power you have in your arms, you paddle, paddle, paddle and get up and over this little wave.

You turn and look back and you see that you are now a good distance away from the shore. The next wave that comes, you will be able to ride. You very carefully balance yourself on your tangerine orange surfboard into a standing up position as you watch as the next wave building out in the ocean is rapidly approaching you.

You get yourself ready by crouching down low and keeping your body strong and steady in the center of the board. The wave is here now and you feel the swell lift you and your board up and over and you are riding the wave back towards the shore! The power of the sea beneath you is awesome and you feel like you are a part of nature as you ride this wave as it curves and rushes back to shore.

The sun above you and the saltwater spray all around you is lovely and you smile wide as you think how wonderful it is to be able to be out here riding waves. You look behind you and are surprised to see another wave coming so soon, but you crouch down low again and strengthen your muscles to brace for it and this wave lifts you and your board again and once more you feel like you a part of the ocean, even if only for a moment.

You are so grateful to have the chance to be out here riding the ocean waves.

You do not have to stop riding these ocean waves just yet if you don't want to. You can spend as long as you want here and you can come back anytime you'd like.

You can create anything you want in your mind. Imagine where you want to go and build the picture in your mind. Be sure to imagine how you want it to smell, taste, hear and feel.

The more detailed you can make your mental picture, the more you will enjoy being there.

It is all up to you. Perhaps as you drift off to sleep, you may find yourself back out here on the sea, riding the waves on your surfboard.

Chapter 21:
Rock Climbing Fun

Have you ever been rock climbing before? It is so fun to be standing in front of a large boulder, ready to jump on and climb over. What if I told you that you could go rock climbing right now without having to move a single muscle? You really can- In your mind! Your mind is capable of doing many incredible things, including something called Visualization.

To begin your visualization practice, close your eyes. Really, close your eyes (unless you are the one reading this, of

course!) To build a very strong visualization, it is usually helpful to first center yourself and be sure you are giving your brain the very best tools it needs to work with. In this case, that means oxygen, and oxygen means taking some good, deep breaths.

You are going to take some slow, deep breaths now, following along with my instruction: Breathe in very slowly, 1 – 2 – 3 – 4. Now breathe out, very slowly, 1 – 2 – 3 – 4. Excellent. Now again very slowly, 1 – 2 – 3 – 4 and breathe back out very slowly, 1 – 2 – 3 – 4 very nice. Once more very slowly in 1 – 2 – 3 – 4 and back out very slowly, 1 – 2 – 3 – 4. Great!

Take a moment to review how you feel. Are you comfy and feeling good? Okay, great.

Picture yourself on a sunny summer's morning. You are out on a hike through the woods to get to a rock climbing spot. You take a long, deep breath in and smell the fresh woodsy scent of the forest and you enjoy the way the sun feels as it is beaming down on you.

You finally see it: a big, beautiful gray boulder that is a perfect climbing boulder. You admire it from a distance before you approach because with the morning sunshine beaming down on it, it glistens in the light. You move closer and sit down beside the boulder, pulling your backpack off of your back and digging your special climbing shoes out to change into. Your climbing shoes fit very snugly, as they are supposed to, but they have a special grip on the bottom that helps with climbing. Once your shoes are on, you stand up and look over the boulder.

You see the route you would like to take immediately and reach out to touch the surface of the rock. It is cool to the touch as this particular spot is shaded from the summer's sun above, and the combination of cool but rough feels very pleasant to your skin. Using your weight to push against this spot with one hand, you reach up with the other to take a hold of a bit of an outcropping above you as you put your foot in place to push off and lift yourself further up.

You continue up the boulder-like this, your hands finding holds in the rocky surface wherever it can and your feet finding small grooves or outcroppings to rest on and push against. The rock is cool in the places it is shaded but very warm in the spots where the sun is touching and you enjoy the back and forth between cool and warm under your hands.

You have your full attention on each move because you have to be alert and focused to find each new spot that you will place your hands and feet. It feels so good to use your muscles like this and you feel strong and capable as you near the top.

This is your final extension and you stretch your upper body as far as you can to grasp on to the top of the boulder and pull yourself the rest of the way up. You are on top of the boulder now and you stand proudly with your hands on your hips and enjoy the view from up here. It's not that terribly high, because to boulder without gear you cannot go too high or you would risk serious injury, but it is high enough to give you an amazing view of the woods around you.

You take a long, deep breath in, feeling happy and proud of your accomplishment. You are grateful that you have had this amazing experience.

You do not have to leave this boulder just yet if you don't want to. You can spend as long as you want here and you can come back anytime you'd like.

You can create anything you want in your mind. Imagine where you want to go and build the picture in your mind. Be sure to imagine how you want it to smell, taste, hear and feel. The more detailed you can make your mental picture, the more you will enjoy being there.

It is all up to you. Perhaps as you drift off to sleep, you may find yourself back out here in the woods, about to climb another boulder.

Chapter 22:
Swimming in the Sea

Do you like to swim? How about swimming in the salty sea? Well, what if I told you that you could go swim in the sea right now, without having to move a single muscle? You really can- In your mind! Your mind is capable of doing many incredible things, including something called Visualization.

To begin your visualization practice, close your eyes. Really, close your eyes (unless you are the one reading this, of

course!) To build a very strong visualization, it is usually helpful to first center yourself and be sure you are giving your brain the very best tools it needs to work with. In this case, that means oxygen, and oxygen means taking some good, deep breaths.

You are going to take some slow, deep breaths now, following along with my instruction: Breathe in very slowly, 1 – 2 – 3 – 4. Now breathe out, very slowly, 1 – 2 – 3 – 4. Excellent. Now again very slowly, 1 – 2 – 3 – 4 and breathe back out very slowly, 1 – 2 – 3 – 4 very nice. Once more very slowly in 1 – 2 – 3 – 4 and back out very slowly, 1 – 2 – 3 – 4. Great!

Take a moment to review how you feel. Are you comfy and feeling good? Okay, great.

Picture yourself, in your mind's eye, standing on the seashore. The water is mostly calm, with a few small waves sending the water towards you as it laps up and over your toes. Take a long, deep breath in and smell the salty sea air as the refreshing water washes over your toes.

You are excited to be here at the sea because you love to swim in saltwater. Swimming in saltwater means that you float easier and floating is your very favorite thing to do while swimming in the sea. You have been standing out under the summer sunshine for long enough for it to have sufficiently warmed your skin and you are now more than ready to cool off in the salty sea so you make your way into the water.

The seawater cools you off immediately as you lower yourself in. Once you are in entirely, you do a few backstrokes, enjoying the way the cool water glides over your skin as you slice through the water. There aren't too many waves, just enough that you enjoy being able to swim through and over them when they come.

The seawater makes you feel so light and you roll completely on to your back and let your arms and legs float to the top of the water. The seawater below you feels like a soft and welcoming space and you let all of your muscles relax and release their tension.

Your entire body is mostly submerged, with just spots of the tops of your legs and arms and your face. You close your eyes, feeling completely at peace as you rest in the calm, salty waters of the sea. You take a long, deep breath in and notice how refreshingly clean the sea air is out here and the gentle spray of the light rippling waves around you feels wonderful.

You feel perfectly at peace out here, swimming in the sea and you are so content and grateful that you have been able to enjoy floating around in the salty sea.

You do not have to leave the salty sea just yet if you don't want to. You can spend as long as you want here and you can come back anytime you'd like.

You can create anything you want in your mind. Imagine where you want to go and build the picture in your mind. Be sure to imagine how you want it to smell, taste, hear and feel. The more detailed you can make your mental picture, the more you will enjoy being there.

It is all up to you. Perhaps as you drift off to sleep, you may find yourself back out here in the calm sea waters, floating and relaxing.

Chapter 23:
Finger Painting Fun

Do you like to finger paint? It is so fun to put your fingers into the paint and use it to make cool pictures, isn't it? Well, what if I told you that you could fingerpaint right now without having to move a single muscle? You really can- In your mind! Your mind is capable of doing many incredible things, including something called Visualization.

To begin your visualization practice, close your eyes. Really, close your eyes (unless you are the one reading this, of course!) To build a very strong visualization, it is usually helpful to first center yourself and be sure you are giving your brain the very best tools it needs to work with. In this case, that means oxygen, and oxygen means taking some good, deep breaths.

You are going to take some slow, deep breaths now, following along with my instruction: Breathe in very slowly, 1 – 2 – 3 – 4. Now breathe out, very slowly, 1 – 2 – 3 – 4. Excellent. Now again very slowly, 1 – 2 – 3 – 4 and breathe back out very slowly, 1 – 2 – 3 – 4 very nice. Once more very slowly in 1 – 2 – 3 – 4 and back out very slowly, 1 – 2 – 3 – 4. Great!

Take a moment to review how you feel. Are you comfy and feeling good? Okay, great.

Picture yourself, in your mind's eye, standing outside on a patio. You have before you a giant blank canvas on a huge easel. It is definitely the largest easel you have ever seen. If you laid the canvas that is on the easel on the ground and laid beside it, it might even be bigger than you! Beside this huge blank canvas is an assortment of beautiful color pods. There are oranges and yellows, reds and purples, pinks and blues, greens and grays, blacks and silvers, golds and whites and just about every color combination you can imagine.

You take in a long, deep breath and enjoy the feeling of the fresh air filling your lungs as you step closer to the blank canvas. You waste no time in getting started as you plunge your fingers into a canary yellow color, the paint squishy and wet on your fingers. You swirl your fingers about a bit in the paint pod and then bring them up to the canvas, tentatively touching the surface at first. This beautiful yellow is easily transferred to the canvas and you make a sweeping motion across the upper right corner of the space for the sun.

You wipe your fingers clean using the towel hanging on the easel and then decide to dip into a light aqua blue, again enjoying the wet and squishy paint on your fingers as you scoop up the perfect amount you need. You use your fingers to streak this light, clean aqua blue across the top half of the blank canvas for the sky, loving the look of the blue and the yellow together.

Wiping off your fingers again, you decide this time to go for beautiful, pale spring green, dipping your fingers into the paint pod and this time using little fanning motions to transfer the paint on to the bottom portion of the canvas, making the grass. You dip your fingers back into this same pod again and make large, sweeping, sticks along the middle of the canvas- there will be the flower stalks for your large flowers.

Once your flower stalks have been placed, you wipe your fingers clean and begin placing the colorful blooms on each stalk: cherry red, tangerine orange, violet purple, lavender-blue, fuschia pink, and on. Soon your canvas is full of color and you take a step back to examine your work.

You have painted a beautiful fingerpaint landscape. The colors are all vibrant and fun and you are proud of the work you've done and grateful that you have had this opportunity to fingerpaint.

You do not have to leave your finger painting just yet if you don't want to. You can spend as long as you want here and you can come back anytime you'd like.

You can create anything you want in your mind. Imagine where you want to go and build the picture in your mind. Be sure to imagine how you want it to smell, taste, hear and feel. The more detailed you can make your mental picture, the more you will enjoy being there.

It is all up to you. Perhaps as you drift off to sleep, you may find yourself back out here with your giant blank canvas, ready to finger paint some more.

Chapter 24:
Roasting Marshmallows

Isn't camping fun? The tents, the campfire, and of course, roasting marshmallows! What if I told you that you could go do this right now without having to move a single muscle? You really can- In your mind! Your mind is capable of doing many incredible things, including something called Visualization.

To begin your visualization practice, close your eyes. Really, close your eyes (unless you are the one reading this, of

course!) To build a very strong visualization, it is usually helpful to first center yourself and be sure you are giving your brain the very best tools it needs to work with. In this case, that means oxygen, and oxygen means taking some good, deep breaths.

You are going to take some slow, deep breaths now, following along with my instruction: Breathe in very slowly, 1 - 2 - 3 - 4. Now breathe out, very slowly, 1 - 2 - 3 - 4. Excellent. Now again very slowly, 1 - 2 - 3 - 4 and breathe back out very slowly, 1 - 2 - 3 - 4 very nice. Once more very slowly in 1 - 2 - 3 - 4 and back out very slowly, 1 - 2 - 3 - 4. Great!

Take a moment to review how you feel. Are you comfy and feeling good? Okay, great.

Picture yourself, in your mind's eye, sitting on a camp chair that is sat around a campfire. It is dusk and the sun is sinking slowly in the sky and the air is cool and crisp. You take a long, deep breath in and smell the smoky scent of the campfire. Beside you is a bag full of goodies. You pick up the bag to investigate and pull out a huge bag of marshmallows!

Opening the bag, you pull a fluffy, sticky marshmallow out of the bag. You pierce the marshmallow with a sharpened stick and hold the stick out and over the campfire. The flames of the campfire dance and sparkle beneath your marshmallow, the heat warming both your marshmallow and yourself.

You decide to let your marshmallow dip down a bit into the flames and you inch it very slowly down into the fire. The flames of the campfire dance underneath and all-around your marshmallow until it finally catches on fire itself!

Oh no, you think, as you pull the marshmallow up quickly towards yourself to blow it out. You inspect your very well roasted marshmallow and see that it was only on fire for a moment so rather than being too burnt, it is instead nicely crackled and hardened on the outside. You think this might actually end up being a perfectly roasted marshmallow!

You reach into the bag beside you and pull out a paper plate. Very, very carefully, you use the paper plate to grasp the very hot marshmallow and pull it off of your stick. Once it is on the plate, you have to admire it for a moment as the roasted marshmallow has now been well squished and you can see the marshmallow fluff on the inside exploding out on every side.

You can hardly wait to taste it, but you know it will be extra hot right now, so you hold the paper plate up to your mouth and blow on it as hard as you can, long, slow, blowing breaths out onto the marshmallow.

You can't wait for it anymore; you have to try it! Very carefully, you inch the marshmallow towards your mouth and take a very tiny and tentative bite with just your very front teeth. The marshmallow is still very warm, but it is not too hot to eat! The roasted marshmallow melts in your mouth, the smoky hardened shell giving way to the sweet and sticky fluffy interior. You close your eyes for a moment and just think how thankful you are for this delicious roasted marshmallow. You are so grateful that you have had this experience. You gobble up the rest of the marshmallow and reach back in the bag for another!

You do not have to leave your marshmallow roasting just yet if you don't want to. You can spend as long as you want here and you can come back anytime you'd like.

You can create anything you want in your mind. Imagine where you want to go and build the picture in your mind. Be sure to imagine how you want it to smell, taste, hear and feel. The more detailed you can make your mental picture, the more you will enjoy being there.

It is all up to you. Perhaps as you drift off to sleep, you may find yourself back out here by the campfire, getting ready to roast another delicious marshmallow.

Chapter 25:
Washing the Car

Do you like to help wash your parent's car? Isn't it fun to get all soapy and sudsy and wash away all the dirt and grime until the car is sparkly and good as new? Well, what if you could do that right now, without having to move a single muscle? You really can- In your mind! Your mind is capable of doing many incredible things, including something called Visualization.

To begin your visualization practice, close your eyes. Really, close your eyes (unless you are the one reading this, of

course!) To build a very strong visualization, it is usually helpful to first center yourself and be sure you are giving your brain the very best tools it needs to work with. In this case, that means oxygen, and oxygen means taking some good, deep breaths.

You are going to take some slow, deep breaths now, following along with my instruction: Breathe in very slowly, 1 – 2 – 3 – 4. Now breathe out, very slowly, 1 – 2 – 3 – 4. Excellent. Now again very slowly, 1 – 2 – 3 – 4 and breathe back out very slowly, 1 – 2 – 3 – 4 very nice. Once more very slowly in 1   2 – 3 – 4 and back out very slowly, 1 – 2 – 3 – 4. Great!

Take a moment to review how you feel. Are you comfy and feeling good? Okay, great.

Picture yourself, in your mind's eye, standing outside in a driveway, beside a car. This car is FILTHY! There is a lot of dust and dirt all over it. Luckily, there is a bucket full of super sudsy soapy water and a giant scrubber here too, so you reach into the sudsy water and pull the scrubber on out and get to work.

You take a long, deep breath in and think that this summer's day is the perfect day to wash the car. The sun is shining, the birds are chirping, and this car needs you to wash it! You begin by standing on your tiptoes to reach the very top of the car, using the giant scrubber to make large circles of bubbles on top. You continue this way along the top of the car, down the back windows, the trunk, and then back up to the front windshield and on to the hood of the car, making giant circles of bubbles.

You dip your giant scrubber back into the sudsy soapy bucket and let the scrubber fill back up with bubbles and bring it back up to the car, this time starting on the car doors and making your way quickly around the car. It feels so good to be using your muscles to scrub this car clean. You finally finish scrubbing the last door clean and you are excited because it is finally time for your favorite part!

You put the scrubber back in the bucket and walk over to the spigot on the side of the house and turn the hose on, getting ready for the water. The water begins to spray forcefully out of the hose and you aim it at the car, letting the water rinse away each and every scrub bubble. As the bubbles are rinsed away, you can see how sparkling clean the car is now that you have scrubbed it. You are proud of the job you've done and are grateful that you can work hard when you need to.

You do not have to leave your excellent work just yet if you don't want to. You can spend as long as you want here and you can come back anytime you'd like.

You can create anything you want in your mind. Imagine where you want to go and build the picture in your mind. Be sure to imagine how you want it to smell, taste, hear and feel. The more detailed you can make your mental picture, the more you will enjoy being there.

It is all up to you. Perhaps as you drift off to sleep, you may find yourself back out here with the giant scrub brush, ready to get this car back to sparkling clean.

Bonus Chapter: Gratitude List

Gratitude List:

Do you know that there is a way to instantly make yourself feel better? It doesn't matter what is happening in your life: you may be scared of trying something new, or maybe you are worried about taking a test, or it might be that you just woke up from a bad dream, but no matter what is happening, there is something that you can do to make yourself feel better instantly.

It is called the Gratitude List, and it is something you can do in your head or out loud anywhere you are. You will make a list with your hands, either using one hand to count five things or two hands to count ten, but either way you will use your fingers to count them off.

To begin, hold up one finger and name something that you are grateful for. It can be anything at all: your parents, your pet, your toy, your shirt, the snack you just ate, absolutely anything. All that matters is that it is something that you are genuinely thankful for. You will hold up each finger and name a thing that you are grateful for, either counting five things or ten things, depending on how big you want your list to be.

You will find that as you count off the things you are grateful for, your mind will settle and you will begin to feel better, no matter what is going on in your life. This is because when you remind yourself of all the things you have to be grateful for, your mind begins to focus on the good and it can be really difficult to feel bad when your mind is thinking of the good things in y our life!

Some people like to practice making this list at night before they go to sleep because it puts them in a good mood before they go to sleep and can help them have happy dreams. It doesn't matter what time of day you do the gratitude list, but you will find that the more you do the gratitude list, the more that your mind will search for things every day to be thankful for! It is amazing how our brains help us to see what we are looking for, isn't it?

Try the gratitude list right now, up to five: Hold up your first finger and think of one thing you are grateful for. Now, hold up the next finger and think of one thing you are grateful for. Now, hold up the third finger and think of one thing you are grateful for. Hold up the fourth finger and think of one thing you are grateful for. Finally, the last finger, and think of one thing you are grateful for.

Doesn't that feel great to focus your attention on the things you are thankful for? You will notice that the more you do it the quicker it will work for you. Just like any skill, practice will make you better!

Chapter 1:
Tree House

Have you ever had your own tree house before? Your own special place to go to, high up in a tree? Well, what if I told you that you could go to your very own treehouse right now, without having to move a single muscle? You really can- In your mind! Your mind is capable of doing many incredible things, including something called Visualization.

To begin your visualization practice, close your eyes. Really, close your eyes (unless you are the one reading this, of course!) To build a very strong visualization, it is usually helpful to first center yourself and be sure you are giving your

brain the very best tools it needs to work with. In this case, that means oxygen, and oxygen means taking some good, deep breaths.

You are going to take some slow, deep breaths now, following along with my instruction: Breathe in very slowly, 1 – 2 – 3 – 4. Now breathe out, very slowly, 1 – 2 – 3 – 4. Excellent. Now again very slowly, 1 – 2 – 3 – 4 and breathe back out very slowly, 1 – 2 – 3 – 4 very nice. Once more, very slowly in 1 – 2 – 3 – 4 and back out very slowly, 1 – 2 – 3 – 4. Great!

Take a moment to review how you feel. Are you comfy and feeling good? Okay, great.

Picture yourself, in your mind's eye, standing outside on a beautiful spring day. The weather is warm, and the sun is shining and there is a light spring breeze. You take in a long, deep breath and smell the freshly cut grass and the blooming spring flowers all around you.

You are beneath a large oak tree; the trunk of this large oak tree is probably the biggest tree you have ever seen! This is a very special tree to you because this tree is the tree that you have built your treehouse in.

You go to the other side of the tree and begin climbing up the rope ladder that you have hung down for yourself. You climb up, up, up, your hands gripping on to the rough rungs of the rope ladder. Once you make it to the platform, you pull yourself up and through the opening.

The floor of your treehouse is made of wooden pallet slats, and they are cool and smooth against your hands. You push yourself up to stand up on the platform and look around your treehouse. Your treehouse even has a platform hallway that stretches all the way around the tree so you can walk all the way around and see in every direction you want.

You follow along the platform walkway, ducking under some of the low-hanging branches of the oak. The branches and their leaves give you shade and privacy. Plus, you get to pick acorns off of the tree and collect them to make crafts with.

You reach up in one of the branches and pluck a few of the acorns down from the branch. Carefully, you carry them back over the main platform of your treehouse and put them in the basket of acorns you keep by the entrance. Once you have filled your acorn basket up, you will begin painting them as decorations for your room at home. You decide to have a seat and check out your acorn collection, so you let yourself settle back into the bean bag chair in the corner with the basket of acorns.

You are excited that you have almost filled this basket up. You put your hand in the basket and rifle through the acorns, letting your imagination run wild with ideas about how you will decorate them. You might even have to pull out the glitter paint for some of these! You are so grateful that you have an awesome treehouse to play in that you can come back to anytime you want.

You do not have to leave your treehouse just yet if you don't want to. You can spend as long as you want here and you can come back anytime you'd like.

You can create anything you want in your mind. Imagine where you want to go and build the picture in your mind. Be sure to imagine how you want it to smell, taste, hear, and feel.

The more detailed you can make your mental picture, the more you will enjoy being there.

It is all up to you. Perhaps as you drift off to sleep, you may find yourself back here in your treehouse, enjoying the space that has been built just for you.

Chapter 2:
Magic School

Have you ever wondered what it would be like to be able to cast magic spells? Wouldn't it be neat if you could just wave a wand and have whatever you wanted to appear, appear? Well, what if I told you that you could go to magic school and learn how to do these things without having to move a single muscle? You really can- In your mind! Your mind is capable of doing many incredible things, including something called Visualization.

To begin your visualization practice, close your eyes. Really, close your eyes (unless you are the one reading this, of course!) To build a very strong visualization, it is usually helpful to first center yourself and be sure you are giving your

brain the very best tools it needs to work with. In this case, that means oxygen, and oxygen means taking some good, deep breaths.

You are going to take some slow, deep breaths now, following along with my instruction: Breathe in very slowly, 1 – 2 – 3 – 4. Now breathe out, very slowly, 1 – 2 – 3 – 4. Excellent. Now again very slowly, 1 – 2 – 3 – 4 and breathe back out very slowly, 1 – 2 – 3 – 4 very nice. Once more, very slowly in 1 – 2 – 3 – 4 and back out very slowly, 1 – 2 – 3 – 4. Great!

Take a moment to review how you feel. Are you comfy and feeling good? Okay, great.

Imagine yourself, in your mind's eye, standing on a gravel driveway. The ground is bumpy and hard beneath your feet, and you are standing before a massive stone building. This building towers above you, but the front door is wide open and waiting for you to walk in. You take a long, deep breath in, shivering with excitement as a loud, clear bell tinkles as you walk in, announcing your presence.

You walk through the front door and are immediately in a very large hall. The carpet is a vivid, wine red, and there are candles burning on the walls on both sides. This hallway is enormous! You take a few steps forward and realize that there are even mirrors on the ceiling in this place. How fancy!

Finally, you reach a large mahogany desk, and the person seated behind the desk is dressed in long, navy blue robes with silver tassels hanging down. He has a long, gray-white beard speckled with silver and a tall hat of navy blue, also with silver tassels. He looks like a wizard. You see the plaque on the front of his desk, and it says, "The Silver Wizard." Wow! He really is a wizard.

The Silver Wizard welcomes you to magic school and gives you a map to your classroom. The map is written on old, yellowed parchment paper that crinkles when you touch it, and you see that the path that you are supposed to take follows along with a series of dots and dashes, but you don't know where the map begins. That is, of course, until you see that once you start moving your feet, the dots and dashes of where you are at start disappearing! It is like some sort of a magical treasure hunt but you are hunting for your classroom.

You continue on with one foot in front of the other, following the series of dots and dashes as they disappear behind you. They lead you to what looks like a dead end. You look up and around, but there is nothing in front of you other than a heavy, wooden end table with a very elaborate and expensive-looking bronze lamp on it. You look behind you and realize that you have come a very, very long way. You consult the map again, but there are no more dots and dashes. What on earth can this mean, you think?

You reach out to touch the desk with the lamp, but your hand goes right through it! It is a mirage! You try to touch the lamp, and it too is a mirage. You take a tentative step forward and walk right through the desk, lamp, and even the wall behind it, and you end up suddenly in a classroom!

The classroom is full of students sitting at their desks and a teacher at the front, another wizard, from the looks of him. You are invited to find your seat. This was your first magic lesson! Still excited from the magical map adventure that got you here, you slide into your seat, feeling grateful that you are at a magic school and ready to learn some magic!

You do not have to leave your magic school just yet if you don't want to. You can spend as long as you want here and you can come back anytime you'd like.

You can create anything you want in your mind. Imagine where you want to go and build the picture in your mind. Be sure to imagine how you want it to smell, taste, hear, and feel. The more detailed you can make your mental picture, the more you will enjoy being there.

It is all up to you. Perhaps as you drift off to sleep, you may find yourself back here in your magic school, ready to learn how to do magic for yourself.

Chapter 3:
Crime Fighters

Have you ever thought it would be cool to be a crime fighter? You know, to be a real-life hero? What if I told you that you could see what it was like to be a crime fighter right now, without having to move a single muscle? You really can- In your mind! Your mind is capable of doing many incredible things, including something called Visualization.

To begin your visualization practice, close your eyes. Really, close your eyes (unless you are the one reading this, of course!) To build a very strong visualization, it is usually helpful to first center yourself and be sure you are giving your brain the very best tools it needs to work with. In this case,

that means oxygen, and oxygen means taking some good, deep breaths.

You are going to take some slow, deep breaths now, following along with my instruction: Breathe in very slowly, 1 – 2 – 3 – 4. Now breathe out, very slowly, 1 – 2 – 3 – 4. Excellent. Now again very slowly, 1 – 2 – 3 – 4 and breathe back out very slowly, 1 – 2 – 3 – 4 very nice. Once more, very slowly in 1 – 2 – 3 – 4 and back out very slowly, 1 – 2 – 3 – 4. Great!

Take a moment to review how you feel. Are you comfy and feeling good? Okay, great.

Picture yourself, in your mind's eye, standing in a park. You are on a sidewalk beside a pond. It is early morning, and the wildlife here in the park is just waking up. You take a long, deep breath in and enjoy the fresh air as you watch as a mama duck leads her baby ducklings along behind her. They are waddling along the path on the opposite side of the pond as you watch as the little fluffy ducklings try and keep up with mama duck.

Suddenly a stiff breeze comes whistling through the trees, blowing the crisp fall leaves through the air. You pull your sweater tighter around yourself as you can feel that the fall weather is getting colder and colder, and it likely won't be too much longer before there is the first snowfall of winter.

You continue to stroll along the sidewalk, and you watch as the parks and recreation employees spread pine needles out around the smaller trees and shrubbery to keep their roots warm for the cold weather to come. You notice that one of the workers is mixing pine needles and hay into a wooden crate that is turned on its side. You wonder what it is for, so you head over to him and ask. He tells you that it will be a winter home for the mama duck and her baby ducklings and that they will place it over by the pond for them to have a place to warm up as it gets cold.

You love this, and you continue on your walk around the park, thinking how nice it will be for the mama duck and the baby ducklings to have a warm place for the winter. You listen to the songs of the last of the birds in the trees before they fly south for winter, and you enjoy the way the steady breeze blows the colorful autumn leaves through the air.

The park is beautiful this time of the year with the golden yellows and fiery reds of the falling trees dancing in the breeze, and you finally make your way back over to the opposite side of the pond and you see where the workers placed the crate for the mama duck and her baby ducklings. You smile again at the thought of the duck family having a nice place to keep warm this winter. You hear a scraping noise that you can't quite place and then you see something strange that stops you in your tracks. The crate is moving… by itself!

You cautiously step towards it, trying to figure out how it is moving by itself! The ducks are swimming around in the pond, clueless that their winter home is being tampered with. You look around for the workers, but they have already finished and left. It is just you here.

Well, you will not let the ducks' winter home be taken by whoever is inside of that crate. That would be a crime! You are now finally close enough that you can peer inside the crate, and now you see a furry little black, white, and gray face peering back out of you. It's a raccoon!

What on earth is this raccoon trying to do? It looks like it is trying to push the crate into the forest, maybe as a home for itself? Well, that certainly will not do. A raccoon is perfectly capable of finding its own winter shelter, but this duck family is not. You grab a stick that is laying nearby and begin tapping loudly on the top of the crate to spook the raccoon- it works!

The raccoon scampers out quickly, looking back at you and chittering angrily before running back into the forest. That raccoon can be just as mad as it wants to be, but you are a crime fighter today! You will not let a critter's home be stolen out here on your watch.

You look around to see if there's any way to help keep the ducks home safe from this happening again and that is when you see it; there is a small boulder nearby that is just large enough to keep the crate from being moved by another animal like the raccoon was able to do, but small enough to still provide plenty of room for the duck family. In fact, the boulder will probably even help keep the crate even more snuggly warm because it will help block some of the winter wind.

You step back and admire your work and hear a "quack quack" from behind you. You turn around and see the mama duck leading her baby ducklings towards the crate, so you step out of the way and watch as they file into the crate and settle in.

It may not seem like much, but you are grateful that you were able to stop an active crime in progress and be a hero for this duck family. You are glad you were here to be a crime fighter!

You do not have to leave your duckling friends just yet if you don't want to. You can spend as long as you want here and you can come back anytime you'd like.

You can create anything you want in your mind. Imagine where you want to go and build the picture in your mind. Be sure to imagine how you want it to smell, taste, hear, and feel. The more detailed you can make your mental picture, the more you will enjoy being there.

It is all up to you. Perhaps as you drift off to sleep, you may find yourself back here in the park, fighting crime wherever you see it.

Chapter 4:
Camping in the Forest

Have you ever been camping in the forest before? It can be so much fun to set up a campsite deep out in the forest and spend a night just enjoying being out in nature. What if I told you that you could go camping in the forest right now, without having to move a single muscle? You really can- In your mind! Your mind is capable of doing many incredible things, including something called Visualization.

To begin your visualization practice, close your eyes. Really, close your eyes (unless you are the one reading this, of course!) To build a very strong visualization, it is usually helpful to first center yourself and be sure you are giving your brain the very best tools it needs to work with. In this case, that means oxygen, and oxygen means taking some good, deep breaths.

You are going to take some slow, deep breaths now, following along with my instruction: Breathe in very slowly, 1 – 2 – 3 – 4. Now breathe out, very slowly, 1 – 2 – 3 – 4. Excellent. Now again very slowly, 1 – 2 – 3 – 4 and breathe back out very slowly, 1 – 2 – 3 – 4 very nice. Once more, very slowly in 1 – 2 – 3 – 4 and back out very slowly, 1 – 2 – 3 – 4. Great!

Take a moment to review how you feel. Are you comfy and feeling good? Okay, great.

Picture yourself, in your mind's eye, walking a wooded trail on a beautiful summer's day. It is late afternoon, and you have finally made your way to a lovely little clearing in the forest that will make for an ideal campsite. You take a long, deep breath and notice how clean and clear the air is out here.

You set down your camping gear and take a look around you. This spot will be perfect! You pull out your tent and begin to place the poles together, one by one, connecting them and stretching the canvas fabric across the poles to create your tent. You set your tent up in no time.

Once your tent is up, you decide to start gathering the firewood you will need for your campfire. You head back out into the woods, picking up sticks that are dry and brittle enough to serve as firewood and leaving ones that are too fresh behind. You trek back and forth between the woods and your campsite, depositing the sticks you've collected there in a pile. Once you've collected enough, you begin to arrange the sticks into the perfect shape for a campfire.

You have to build a pyramid shape with your firewood, so you stack the sticks up against each other in a pyramid, leaving an open space at the bottom where you will put the kindling to start the fire. You look up and around you and notice that it is now dusk, and the sun is setting. It will be getting dark very soon and you will need your fire to provide light and warmth out here in the dark woods.

You purposefully place the small, broken pieces of dry and brittle wood into the space left at the bottom of the pyramid and pull out the Firestarter that you have, very carefully lighting it under the pyramid, taking special care to not knock over your well-built pyramid or burn yourself. The pieces at the bottom catch fire immediately and light the rest of the pyramid, in turn, and you now have a beautiful campfire going. You pull out a bag of marshmallows and carefully pierce one of the fluffiest marshmallows with the special spear that you brought along to cook with before you put it out and over the hot and crackling flames.

You watch as the marshmallow toasts above the campfire, the outside forming a hard and crispy shell while the inside becomes even hotter and stickier. Once you have finished toasting your marshmallow, you let it cool a bit before you begin taking small, cautious bites off it, knowing that it will be incredibly hot still. It is delicious, and you enjoy your toasted marshmallow as you watch the campfire you've built burn in the dark of night.

You look up and see that the night is clear, and you can see thousands of twinkling silver stars above you. You hear an owl "hooting" in the distance and you think to yourself that you are so very proud that you have been able to set up such a nice campsite and you are grateful that you have had the opportunity to go camping.

You do not have to leave your lovely campsite just yet if you don't want to. You can spend as long as you want here and you can come back anytime you'd like.

You can create anything you want in your mind. Imagine where you want to go and build the picture in your mind. Be sure to imagine how you want it to smell, taste, hear, and feel. The more detailed you can make your mental picture, the more you will enjoy being there.

It is all up to you. Perhaps as you drift off to sleep, you may find yourself back here in the woods, watching the stars twinkle above you as you sit beside the campfire.

Chapter 5:
Kid Spy

Are you good at following clues? Do you think that you would maybe make a good spy if you tried? Well, what if I told you that you could be a kid spy right now without having to move a single muscle? You really can- In your mind! Your mind is capable of doing many incredible things, including something called Visualization.

To begin your visualization practice, close your eyes. Really, close your eyes (unless you are the one reading this, of course!) To build a very strong visualization, it is usually helpful to first center yourself and be sure you are giving your brain the very best tools it needs to work with. In this case,

that means oxygen, and oxygen means taking some good, deep breaths.

You are going to take some slow, deep breaths now, following along with my instruction: Breathe in very slowly, 1 – 2 – 3 – 4. Now breathe out, very slowly, 1 – 2 – 3 – 4. Excellent. Now again very slowly, 1 – 2 – 3 – 4 and breathe back out very slowly, 1 – 2 – 3 – 4 very nice. Once more, very slowly in 1 – 2 – 3 – 4 and back out very slowly, 1 – 2 – 3 – 4. Great!

Take a moment to review how you feel. Are you comfy and feeling good? Okay, great.

Picture yourself, in your mind's eye, standing at the entrance of a park, with a notebook and pencil in hand. It is a cool winter's day, and while it has snowed recently, the snow is melting quickly under the bright winter sun of this day, so there are wet puddles everywhere. You are prepared with long, waterproof snow boots. You know you don't want to get wet today out in this cold, especially when you have a super-secret spy mission to complete. You take a long, deep breath in and appreciate the clean, cool winter air.

In your notebook is a list of instructions for your super-secret spy mission. You take a quick look around you to be sure no one is looking over your shoulder, and then you open your notebook to see what the first instruction is.

"If you want to reach your treat, your first clue awaits you at the highest snowy peak" is what it reads. Hmm! The highest snowy peak. You look around you, narrowing your eyes in the best super spy way you can. The park is pretty flat, but still mostly covered in snow. There are trees surrounding the park, but there are a ton of those, and they are mostly the same size, so you don't think that trees would be the highest snowy peak... hmm.

You continue to look around you when you realize the slide on the playground has a tall, pointed roof, and it is still covered in snow! You run over to the playground equipment and climb up the ladder to the slide. You look all around you, but you don't see anything that could be a clue. All you see is snow melting... oh, wait! You can see your next clue! The snow is melting and you can see beneath some of the snow that is melting. There is a stick with something tied to it that was mostly hidden beneath the snow. It is a clue.

You pick up the clue that is tied to the stick, and you examine it. There is nothing there! You turn it over, again and again, wondering what it means. That's when you realize that it might be invisible ink! Hmm, how can you make invisible ink appear? Oh, that's right: heat!

You cup the small card in your warm and toasty hands and blow warm air into the space that is in between. The ink quickly appears! Your next clue is this: "When winter winds blow and bluster, where is the place that feathered friends gather under?"

Hmm. Feathered friends have to be some sort of animal. So, where do animals go to get out of the winter winds in this park? You look out over the park at the trees, the pond, and...that's it! You know exactly where to go! You slide down the slide and race over to the pond, or rather the spot right beside the pond that has been set up to be a shelter for a mama duck and her baby ducklings.

You see the clue immediately, attached to the backside of the shelter. All this clue says is, "Spy kids everywhere agree, treats are best enjoyed beneath a tree." Beneath a tree? You scan the park with your super-spy eyes. There are trees completely surrounding the park; it would take forever to search under each tree. But wait, only one tree has a bench beneath it! You will start there.

You race away from the pond towards the bench, your snow boots coming in handy as you splash through newly formed puddles of melting snow. The winter sun is coming out, and you are grateful to feel it warming you up. There is the bench, with a sliver of winter sun beaming down on to it through the tree branches above, and there on the bench is a small white bag with a label: "Spy Kids Only."

You sit in the sun on the bench and peek inside. It is your favorite snack! You are so excited to get to enjoy your favorite snack in the winter sunshine, and you are grateful that you could be a spy kid today.

You do not have to leave your winter spy kid adventure just yet if you don't want to. You can spend as long as you want here and you can come back anytime you'd like.

You can create anything you want in your mind. Imagine where you want to go and build the picture in your mind. Be sure to imagine how you want it to smell, taste, hear, and feel. The more detailed you can make your mental picture, the more you will enjoy being there.

It is all up to you. Perhaps as you drift off to sleep, you may find yourself back here in the park, enjoying another spy kid adventure.

Chapter 6:
Fairy Friends

Do you ever wonder what it might be like to meet a fairy? What if you could even be friends with one? Wouldn't that be cool? Well, what if I told you that you could be friends with a fairy if you only knew where to look? You really can- In your mind! Your mind is capable of doing many incredible things, including something called Visualization.

To begin your visualization practice, close your eyes. Really, close your eyes (unless you are the one reading this, of course!) To build a very strong visualization, it is usually helpful to first center yourself and be sure you are giving your brain the very best tools it needs to work with. In this case, that means oxygen, and oxygen means taking some good, deep breaths.

You are going to take some slow, deep breaths now, following along with my instruction: Breathe in very slowly, 1 - 2 - 3 - 4. Now breathe out, very slowly, 1 - 2 - 3 - 4. Excellent. Now again very slowly, 1 - 2 - 3 - 4 and breathe back out very slowly, 1 - 2 - 3 - 4 very nice. Once more, very slowly in 1 - 2 - 3 - 4 and back out very slowly, 1 - 2 - 3 - 4. Great!

Take a moment to review how you feel. Are you comfy and feeling good? Okay, great.

Picture yourself, in your mind's eye, walking through the woods on a warm summer's day. The sun is shining above you, but the woods are shaded and nice and cool. You make your way through and around the huge trees with their trunks and their twisted root systems that you have to carefully step up and over to not trip on!

You take a moment to appreciate how beautiful it is in these woods as the sunlight streams through the branches with tendrils of light that illuminate sections of the trees and the ground below. You are on the hunt for something quite specific, so you keep moving, taking a deep, long breath, and enjoying how fresh and clean the air in the woods is.

You have to go around a particularly large tree trunk when you finally see it, exactly what you are looking for: a fairy circle! If you have never seen a fairy circle before, it is a circle of toadstool mushrooms, and they are a popular place for fairies to hang out. You crouch down for a closer look when suddenly in your ear, you hear the smallest, tiniest voice you have ever heard saying, "Hello there! What are you looking for?"

You stand up and look around you, but you don't see anyone. "I'm right here, silly," the same tiny voice says, and you scratch your head, again looking around but seeing no one.

"Okay, close your eyes," the tiny voice tells you. You do, wondering what the heck this is about. "Okay, now open!"

You open your eyes, and right in front of you, flitting back and forth is the sparkliest, shiniest, ball of light you have ever seen! "What am I look ing at? Oh my goodness, are you a fairy???" you ask in disbelief.

"Yes! I am. Human eyes cannot see us very well, but here we are! You were looking at our fairy circle. Do you need something?" the tiny voice asks.

"Well, no. I just love reading stories about fairies and wanted to see if I could see one for myself... why can't I see you?" you ask as you squint your eyes at the sparkling and shimmering ball of light that is flitting back and forth in front of you still.

"Well, fairies live very different lives than humans! We are always on the move. In fact, even when fairies are sitting still, we are still technically moving because we sparkle and shimmer like this no matter what! Would you like to see?" the fairy asks you, and you, of course, answer yes.

Your eyes follow the sparkling, shimmering ball of light down to the fairy circle, and what she said was true. Even though she was technically sitting still on a toadstool mushroom, all you could see was her sparkling and shimmering. "Wow!" you say as she flitters and flutters back up to your eye level.

"So you can see how easy it is for us fairies to fly right under the radar. You humans usually don't see us, even when we are right by you! I have actually seen you before. You like to come out here and walk in the woods, don't you?" the fairy asks.

"Yes, I do! I usually hunt for these fairy circles because I think they are so neat. I've always wanted to meet a fairy!" you say.

"Well, now you have! Maybe we can even be friends, what do you say?" the fairy asks. You reply with excitement, "Absolutely!"

"Well, okay! I will be sure to say hello to you the next time I see you. Have fun on your walk through the woods!" your fairy friend tells you as she flits and flutters away.

"You too!" you call after her, watching her sparkling and shimmering light fly through the branches of the trees. Wow. You are so happy that you were able to meet an actual fairy, and you are grateful that you now have a fairy friend.

You do not have to leave these fairy-filled woods just yet if you don't want to. You can spend as long as you want here and you can come back anytime you'd like.

You can create anything you want in your mind. Imagine where you want to go and build the picture in your mind. Be sure to imagine how you want it to smell, taste, hear, and feel. The more detailed you can make your mental picture, the more you will enjoy being there.

It is all up to you. Perhaps as you drift off to sleep, you may find yourself back here in the woods, meeting up with your new fairy friend.

Chapter 7:
Baking Cookies

Do you like to bake? It can be so fun to mix a bunch of separate ingredients together to form something super delicious! What if I told you that you could actually have a baking adventure right now, without having to move a single muscle? You really can- In your mind! Your mind is capable of doing many incredible things, including something called Visualization.

To begin your visualization practice, close your eyes. Really, close your eyes (unless you are the one reading this, of course!) To build a very strong visualization, it is usually helpful to first center yourself and be sure you are giving your brain the very best tools it needs to work with. In this case,

that means oxygen, and oxygen means taking some good, deep breaths.

You are going to take some slow, deep breaths now, following along with my instruction: Breathe in very slowly, 1 – 2 – 3 – 4. Now breathe out, very slowly, 1 – 2 – 3 – 4. Excellent. Now again very slowly, 1 – 2 – 3 – 4 and breathe back out very slowly, 1 – 2 – 3 – 4 very nice. Once more, very slowly in 1 – 2 – 3 – 4 and back out very slowly, 1 – 2 – 3 – 4. Great!

Take a moment to review how you feel. Are you comfy and feeling good? Okay, great.

Picture yourself, in your mind's eye, standing in a kitchen. This kitchen has a long, shiny counter with cookie baking ingredients on it! You approach the counter and take a look. There is flour, sugar, eggs, and of course, chocolate chips! Awesome!

You see, the mixing bowl has a recipe card beside it so you take a look. The recipe card is labeled, "The World's Fluffiest, Yummiest, Chocolate Chip Cookies." Sounds good to you!

Step number one is to measure out the flour. The recipe says it needs two and a half cups of flour, so you pick up a measuring cup and dip it into the bag of flour, scooping out the two and a half cups of flour that the recipe calls for. You dump it into the mixing bowl, watching as the powdery flour hits the bottom of the bowl, and flour dust flies up into the air. It looks like it is snowing in your bowl!

You look at the recipe card. Step number two is to measure out the sugar. The recipe calls for one cup of sugar. That seems simple enough, you think. You pick up the bag of sugar and very carefully pour one cup of sugar from the bag to the measuring cup, listening as the sugar granules hit the bottom of the cup. Then you add the white sugar to the flour and look to the recipe card again.

The next step is to add two eggs. You pull two eggs out of the carton and look for a good spot to crack them open. You know you need a hard surface to crack them on, so you suppose the steel counter will work just fine. You firmly, but carefully, crack the first egg. Once the egg has the crack in it, you use your thumbs to push in and peel the eggshell back, letting the slippery inside of the egg fall in the mixing bowl. You repeat with the second egg, feeling very proud when you realize that you didn't get a single bit of shell into your cookie dough batter!

You are very proud of this as you go to the nearby sink to wash your hands thoroughly. Once your hands are washed, you return to your recipe card. Awesome, it is time to add the chocolate chips! You look at the chocolate chip options. There is a bag of milk chocolate chips, a bag of dark chocolate chips, a bag of white chocolate chips, and even a bag of butterscotch chips! How on earth will you ever decide which kind to add?

Hmm. Well, you probably can't go wrong if you just add them all, right? You add some milk chocolate chips, some dark chocolate chips, some white chocolate chips, and some butterscotch chips before you pick up the large mixing spoon to begin combining these ingredients. You mix the flour, sugar, eggs, and chips in well, and the cookie dough batter begins to thicken.

Once the batter is well mixed, you begin to shape the small dough balls that will become the cookies, placing them on the greased cookie sheet beside you. Once that is done, all you have to do is put the cookies in the oven, set a timer, and wait!

The waiting is always the hardest part, but you clean up the cookie-making mess while you wait, so the time passes quickly. You hear the ding of the timer just as you wash the last dish, and you spin around with excitement, the smell of freshly-baked cookies in the air. You have an adult help you get the cookies out of the oven and off of the hot cookie sheet and you look them over as they cool on a plate on the corner.

They are a golden-brown and look so fluffy stuffed full of the different flavors of chocolate chips. Oh, it is so hard to wait for a taste! You pick one up and take a tiny cautious nibble to see if it has cooled enough to eat. Your taste buds explode with excitement! These are delicious! You are so grateful that you have been able to make these cookies. The recipe was right; these really are The World's Fluffiest, Yummiest, Chocolate Chip Cookies!

You do not have to leave your delicious cookies just yet if you don't want to. You can spend as long as you want here and you can come back anytime you'd like.

You can create anything you want in your mind. Imagine where you want to go and build the picture in your mind. Be sure to imagine how you want it to smell, taste, hear, and feel. The more detailed you can make your mental picture, the more you will enjoy being there.

It is all up to you. Perhaps as you drift off to sleep, you may find yourself back here in this kitchen, baking up a fresh batch of The World's Fluffiest, Yummiest, Chocolate Chip Cookies.

Chapter 8:
Playing in the Band

Have you ever wondered what it might be like to play an instrument and create your own music? Wouldn't it be fun to be able to create music and play any instrument you want? Well, what if I told you that you could actually try out different instruments right now without having to move a single muscle? You really can- In your mind! Your mind is capable of doing many incredible things, including something called Visualization.

To begin your visualization practice, close your eyes. Really, close your eyes (unless you are the one reading this, of course!) To build a very strong visualization, it is usually helpful to first center yourself and be sure you are giving your brain the very best tools it needs to work with. In this case,

that means oxygen, and oxygen means taking some good, deep breaths.

You are going to take some slow, deep breaths now, following along with my instruction: Breathe in very slowly, 1 – 2 – 3 – 4. Now breathe out, very slowly, 1 – 2 – 3 – 4. Excellent. Now again very slowly, 1 – 2 – 3 – 4 and breathe back out very slowly, 1 – 2 – 3 – 4 very nice. Once more, very slowly in 1 – 2 – 3 – 4 and back out very slowly, 1 – 2 – 3 – 4. Great!

Take a moment to review how you feel. Are you comfy and feeling good? Okay, great.

Picture yourself, in your mind's eye, standing in a music room. This music room has dark purple walls and a dark purple ceiling and white tile floors. Looking around you, you see several instruments you recognize and even some that you don't. You take a few steps and hear the awesome echo of your footsteps on the floor. You walk up to a drum set and take a look. It has several different drum heads and two sticks sitting on the seat.

You pick up the smooth, wooden sticks and have a seat. You are going to try these drums out! You tentatively tap on one of the large drum heads nearest to you, and it answers back with a forceful "TAP" sound and you smile. Wow! You decide to go ahead and just see what each different drum head sounds like, so you begin tapping on each one in order, listening carefully as some of them make deeper sounds and others are thinner and tinnier sounding. You close it all off with a direct hit to the double cymbal, sending a loud "crash" sound reverberating out into the room.

The drums were fun, but what's next? Your eye settles on the guitar stand nearby. That guitar looks great; you think as you get up and walk over to it. This guitar is an acoustic guitar and it is a deep reddish-brown color. You pick it up carefully and take a seat nearby. You run your fingers over the strings before thoughtfully plucking the one that is closest to you. The sound rings out through the music studio. You like that! You continue plucking the different strings and then you try strumming them all at once. What a beautiful sound this guitar makes!

You look up and around the music room to see what other instruments are in here. What about the piano on the other side of the room? You're sure that will be fun! You walk over and have a seat on the wooden piano bench before lifting the cover off of the keys. You lightly run your fingertips over the white and black piano keys, enjoying the feel of the smooth ivory against your skin. You decide to push a few of the keys and are immediately delighted with the rich sounds that fill the music room. It is beautiful!

You look around the music room and are grateful that you get to try out all of these fun instruments.

You do not have to leave this awesome music room just yet if you don't want to. You can spend as long as you want here and you can come back anytime you'd like.

You can create anything you want in your mind. Imagine where you want to go and build the picture in your mind. Be sure to imagine how you want it to smell, taste, hear, and feel. The more detailed you can make your mental picture, the more you will enjoy being there.

It is all up to you. Perhaps as you drift off to sleep, you may find yourself back here in this music room with the dark purple walls, ready to explore the different instruments again.

Chapter 9:
Play Ball!

Do you like to play sports? Sometimes it can be a lot of fun to just head out to a wide-open space and kick around a ball, right? Well, what if I told you that you could do that right now without having to move a single muscle? You really can- In your mind! Your mind is capable of doing many incredible things, including something called Visualization.

To begin your visualization practice, close your eyes. Really, close your eyes (unless you are the one reading this, of course!) To build a very strong visualization, it is usually helpful to first center yourself and be sure you are giving your brain the very best tools it needs to work with. In this case,

that means oxygen, and oxygen means taking some good, deep breaths.

You are going to take some slow, deep breaths now, following along with my instruction: Breathe in very slowly, 1 – 2 – 3 – 4. Now breathe out, very slowly, 1 – 2 – 3 – 4. Excellent. Now again very slowly, 1 – 2 – 3 – 4 and breathe back out very slowly, 1 – 2 – 3 – 4 very nice. Once more, very slowly in 1 – 2 – 3 – 4 and back out very slowly, 1 – 2 – 3 – 4. Great!

Take a moment to review how you feel. Are you comfy and feeling good? Okay, great.

Picture yourself, in your mind's eye, outside in a large field on a beautiful summer's day. The sky is blue, and the sun is shining and you feel great! You take a long, deep breath in and enjoy the smell of the fresh-cut grass of the field you are in.

The field you are in is surrounded by groves of trees on each side, but the field itself is very large. It is a beautiful day out here, and you have brought just the thing to enjoy this beautiful summer's day: a soccer ball!

You decide to practice some of your footwork, so you begin by lightly tapping the soccer ball back and forth between each foot, using the edges of your feet to volley the ball back and forth as you lightly jog across the field. The weight of the ball as it catches the sides of your feet feels great, and you enjoy the light sound of your feet knocking the ball back and forth.

Your leg muscles are starting to warm up, and you feel strong and capable as you pick up speed. Now you are quickly running across the field, still passing the ball between each foot, feeling quick and coordinated. You love doing this because it feels good to be outside using your muscles and practicing this skill.

You are nearing the edge of the field, so you begin to circle back around, but you stop for a moment to catch your breath. The birds are singing their summer songs in the trees around you and you think to yourself that it is a lovely day to be out here with your soccer ball. You want to see how far you can kick this thing down the field, so you step back and away from the ball for a moment, looking out across this giant field, and think to yourself that you bet you can make it all the way across this field!

You make a bit of a running start before your foot connects solidly with the ball and sends it sailing through the air and across the field. "Yes!" you call out, but you don't stand there to watch; instead, you take off down the field after it. Your legs feel strong and powerful as you chase after your kick.

Finally, you make it down to the other end of the field, and you start to volley the ball back and forth again with the edges of your feet, but you think that maybe you should kick the ball up now and see if you can do any tricks. Using the toe of your shoes, you flip the ball up into the air and then catch it again, using only your feet, enjoying the "bap, bap" sound the ball makes each time you connect with the ball.

You practice this for a while, kicking the ball gently up, practicing your control and coordination. It feels good to focus on an activity and work hard to improve. You smile because this is a beautiful day to be out on a field playing ball, and you are grateful that you have this opportunity.

You do not have to leave this grassy field just yet if you don't want to. You can spend as long as you want here and you can come back anytime you'd like.

You can create anything you want in your mind. Imagine where you want to go and build the picture in your mind. Be sure to imagine how you want it to smell, taste, hear, and feel. The more detailed you can make your mental picture, the more you will enjoy being there.

It is all up to you. Perhaps as you drift off to sleep, you may find yourself back out here on this perfect summer's day, practicing your soccer skills.

Chapter 10:
Modeling Clay

Do you like to make things with your hands? It can be a lot of fun to use different kinds of clay to be artistic, especially something like modeling clay that can be so easily shaped into whatever kind of thing you want to make! What if I told you that you could use modeling clay right now without having to move a single muscle? You really can- In your mind! Your mind is capable of doing many incredible things, including something called Visualization.

To begin your visualization practice, close your eyes. Really, close your eyes (unless you are the one reading this, of course!) To build a very strong visualization, it is usually helpful to first center yourself and be sure you are giving your brain the very best tools it needs to work with. In this case, that means oxygen, and oxygen means taking some good, deep breaths.

You are going to take some slow, deep breaths now, following along with my instruction: Breathe in very slowly, 1 – 2 – 3 – 4. Now breathe out, very slowly, 1 – 2 – 3 – 4. Excellent. Now again very slowly, 1 – 2 – 3 – 4 and breathe back out very slowly, 1 – 2 – 3 – 4 very nice. Once more, very slowly in 1 – 2 – 3 – 4 and back out very slowly, 1 – 2 – 3 – 4. Great!

Take a moment to review how you feel. Are you comfy and feeling good? Okay, great.

Picture yourself, in your mind's eye, sitting at a smooth, wood table. On the table are several different jars and a basket that has many different art tools and supplies. You take a seat, excited to see what else is in the jars.

You realize that these jars are full of different colors of modeling clay- cool! You pick up the jar that is closest to you and peer inside while using your fingers to pull the clay out of the jar. It is a light mint green color, and the squishy modeling clay sticks to the side of the jar as you pull it out.

You use your fingers to pinch and mold the modeling clay, enjoying the way it feels under your fingers as it easily gives away to the pressure of your hands. If you listen very carefully, you can hear the squish sound the clay makes as it is pushed together. You decide to flatten it out completely under your hand, laying the mint green clay out on the table and then using your hands to firmly press it down, down, down with all of your muscles. The clay flattens easily until it looks like you are trying to make a modeling clay pizza pie!

You look in the basket of tools to see what is there, and your eye settles on a wooden pizza cutter looking tool. You pull it out and then holding it by the handle, you begin to roll the wooden wheel over and across the giant clay circle, back and forth, back and forth. Once you've cut into several of the areas of the clay, you begin to peel it up with your fingernails, enjoying the feeling of the thick clay building up underneath.

You begin rolling the clay around the table, picking up the tiny pieces that have stuck from the modeling clay pizza pie. Once you have gathered all of the mint green modeling clay, you reach for the next jar and dig out the cherry red modeling clay inside.

You use your fingers to pinch the clay together and then pull it back apart, watching as the clay stretches across the distance as you pull your hands away. You hold it up in front of you, stretching your hands apart as the cherry red clay becomes so thin that you can see through it right before it breaks apart with a light snapping sound.

You set the cherry red clay aside and pull modeling clay out of the remaining bins until you have a rainbow assortment of clay on the table in front of you. You take the different colored clays and make different shapes. You make a cherry-red heart, a mint green star, a tangerine orange ball, a silver triangle, a navy-blue square, and so on. Eventually, you cover the table in front of you with a rainbow of shapes.

Working the modeling clay into different shapes is so relaxing for you. You are so grateful that you have had the opportunity to use the modeling clay, and you are going to start imagining what kinds of things you might make with them next time.

You do not have to leave your modeling clay art just yet if you don't want to. You can spend as long as you want here and you can come back anytime you'd like.

You can create anything you want in your mind. Imagine where you want to go and build the picture in your mind. Be sure to imagine how you want it to smell, taste, hear, and feel. The more detailed you can make your mental picture, the more you will enjoy being there.

It is all up to you. Perhaps as you drift off to sleep, you may find yourself back here at this table, using your imagination to create whatever modeling clay art you want.

Chapter 11:
Growing a Garden

Do you like to garden? It can be so much fun to get your hands dirty as you work in the soil, planting seeds, carefully tending to your plants, and watching them grow. What if I told you that you could plant your own garden to grow right now, without having to move a single muscle? You really can-In your mind! Your mind is capable of doing many incredible things, including something called Visualization.

To begin your visualization practice, close your eyes. Really, close your eyes (unless you are the one reading this, of

course!) To build a very strong visualization, it is usually helpful to first center yourself and be sure you are giving your brain the very best tools it needs to work with. In this case, that means oxygen, and oxygen means taking some good, deep breaths.

You are going to take some slow, deep breaths now, following along with my instruction: Breathe in very slowly, 1 – 2 – 3 – 4. Now breathe out, very slowly, 1 – 2 – 3 – 4. Excellent. Now again very slowly, 1 – 2 – 3 – 4 and breathe back out very slowly, 1 – 2 – 3 – 4 very nice. Once more, very slowly in 1 – 2 – 3 – 4 and back out very slowly, 1 – 2 – 3 – 4. Great!

Take a moment to review how you feel. Are you comfy and feeling good? Okay, great.

Picture yourself, in your mind's eye, outside on a warm spring day. The sun is shining above you, the birds are happily singing in the nearby trees, and you are kneeling down in the grass beside a garden space. You have all of the gardening tools you might need beside you and several different kinds of seeds. You are going to plant some seeds and transplant some baby plants that were started from seed indoors already.

You look at the packet of seeds that you have. It is for watermelons! You open the packet and peer in. Each seed is so tiny; it is a wonder that someday that teeny tiny seed will become a huge watermelon! The instructions on the back of the packet say to make a mound of dirt to plant the watermelon seeds in, so that is what you do.

With your hands deep in the rich, brown soil, you begin shaping the soil into a long mound. The soil is soft and cool in your hands as you form the long mound that you will plant the seeds into. Once you have your mound made, you pick up the packet of seeds again. The instructions say to plant each seed one inch deep into the soil mound, so you begin by making a small one-inch indentation into the soil mound, scooping the soil out of the way to make what looks like a little bowl.

Perfect, you think, and you place the first seed inside very carefully, gently covering it back up with the rich, brown soil. You continue doing this along the mound, first scooping out a little bowl, placing a seed inside, then covering it back up with the displaced soil. You enjoy planting these seeds, knowing that it is up to you to plant them well so they can have all they need to grow.

Once you have planted all the seeds, you sit back on your heels and take a look at your garden. The birds chirping nearby are serenading you as you garden. On the far side of the garden is a spot that you have reserved for the marigold transplants that are ready to be planted outside. You pick up a small carton of little baby plants, remembering how these also started from a teeny, tiny seed. These will also need the perfect little home for them to grow up in, so you begin to scoop out little homes for these as well, just as you did for the watermelon seeds.

The marigold plants need more space than the watermelon seeds because the marigold plants already have a little root ball growing, so you are sure to make enough space for the little tangle of roots that each marigold has. Once you have made space for them, you pick the first one up and out of its container, exposing its root ball. You take a moment to look at how interesting the root structures of plants are because they go deep down into the soil to help gather nutrients for the plant, and they are very, very important, but most of the time, they are completely hidden!

You gently and carefully place each marigold root ball into its new space, moving the soil back over and around the base of the plant, careful to not bury any of the fragile leaves of the marigold. Someday these plants will be tall, orange flowers, but right now, they are just little green plants with a long way to go.

Once you have finished transplanting the marigolds to their new outdoor home, you sit back again to admire your work. The mound of watermelon seeds and the marigold transplants look wonderful, but now you need to go through and weed your garden. You have to pull weeds because they will take all of the nutrition from the soil that your seeds and transplants need, if not. You hunt along the mound, and the transplants, carefully pulling the stray plants out that don't belong. This way, your watermelons, your marigolds, will have everything they need to grow big and strong. You love working in the garden and you are grateful that you have a chance to get your hands dirty in the soil.

You do not have to leave your lovely garden just yet if you don't want to. You can spend as long as you want here and you can come back anytime you'd like.

You can create anything you want in your mind. Imagine where you want to go and build the picture in your mind. Be sure to imagine how you want it to smell, taste, hear, and feel.

The more detailed you can make your mental picture, the more you will enjoy being there.

It is all up to you. Perhaps as you drift off to sleep, you may find yourself back here in the garden, tending to the freshly planted watermelon and marigold plants.

Chapter 12:
The Sunflower Maze

Have you ever been to a sunflower field? Many times, sunflowers are grown all together in giant fields, and farmers can do fun things like build sunflower mazes with their sunflowers because sunflowers are huge! They grow to be the size of a fully grown adult, even taller in some cases. What if I told you that you could go to a sunflower maze right now, without moving a single muscle? You really can- In your mind! Your mind is capable of doing many incredible things, including something called Visualization.

To begin your visualization practice, close your eyes. Really, close your eyes (unless you are the one reading this, of course!) To build a very strong visualization, it is usually helpful to first center yourself and be sure you are giving your brain the very best tools it needs to work with. In this case, that means oxygen, and oxygen means taking some good, deep breaths.

You are going to take some slow, deep breaths now, following along with my instruction: Breathe in very slowly, 1 – 2 – 3 – 4. Now breathe out, very slowly, 1 – 2 – 3 – 4. Excellent. Now again very slowly, 1 – 2 – 3 – 4 and breathe back out very slowly, 1 – 2 – 3 – 4 very nice. Once more, very slowly in 1 – 2 – 3 – 4 and back out very slowly, 1 – 2 – 3 – 4. Great!

Take a moment to review how you feel. Are you comfy and feeling good? Okay, great.

Picture yourself, in your mind's eye, standing outside on a crisp autumn day. You are standing at the entrance of a sunflower maze, and you are very, very excited because you have never been to one before! In fact, you have never seen such giant sunflowers before.

Taking a step closer to the sunflowers that surround the entrance, you take a closer look. The stalk of the sunflower is a deep olive green, and it is so wide that it is probably the size of a stalk of celery. The sunflower stalk and its leaves are fuzzy, too! They have teeny tiny hairs all over them. Following the fuzzy green stalk up, your eye settles on the brilliant yellow of the actual sunflower above. It is so large and heavy that the thick stalks seem to bend over slightly under the weight of it, and every time the autumn wind blows, the sunflowers sway heavily back and forth.

You are so excited to check out this sunflower maze! You know it is very large, and you know it will be very beautiful. You take a long, deep breath in, smelling the sweet scent of the sunflowers as a stiff autumn breeze blows through, sending the sunflowers to sway back and forth as though they are dancing.

You enter through the dancing sunflowers at the entrance and are immediately struck by how well these sunflowers make walls! The stalks are thick, and they have lots of leaves, so it is difficult to see through the sunflowers. This maze will be so much fun, you think! You walk forward until you run into a wall of the thick, fuzzy green stalks and leaves and have to make a choice: will you go to the left, or will you go to the right? Hmm, you wonder.

You decide to go to the right, and the sunflower maze path takes you in what almost feels like a circle, and then suddenly, it spits you out right back at the entrance! You laugh because obviously, the right was not the way to go!

You plunge back through the sunflower entrance, and when you come to the sunflower wall dead end again, this time, you make a left. Your left turn takes you first to the left, but then back to the right, and then back to the left again, cutting back and forth. Again, you come to a sunflower wall and you are face to face with the fuzzy green stalks and leaves that obscure just enough of your vision that you can't peek through to see which way you should go!

Hmm, you think, as you listen to the sound, the sunflower stalks and leaves make as they sway in the autumn breeze. Last time you went left and that was the correct way, so surely this time you must be meant to go right, so that is what you do. You follow the sunflower path to the right and it very quickly leads you to a wide-open spot in the sunflower maze that has several hay bales for resting and in the very center of it all, the largest sunflower you have ever seen in your life!

You slowly walk up to it and look up, and up, and up! This sunflower is so very tall that you think it is as tall as your house! Well, maybe not that tall, really, but it is very, very tall and very beautiful. You take a step back and look at all of the beautiful sunflowers all around you in this sunflower maze and you are so grateful to be here surrounded by these gorgeous yellow flowers.

You do not have to leave this spectacular sunflower maze just yet if you don't want to. You can spend as long as you want here and you can come back anytime you'd like.

You can create anything you want in your mind. Imagine where you want to go and build the picture in your mind. Be sure to imagine how you want it to smell, taste, hear, and feel. The more detailed you can make your mental picture, the more you will enjoy being there.

It is all up to you. Perhaps as you drift off to sleep, you may find yourself back out here on this beautiful autumn day, exploring a spectacular sunflower maze.

Chapter 13:
Dancing in the Rain

Have you ever danced in the rain before? Not just run to get out of the rain when it starts, but really, truly, staying outside and dancing in the rain as it falls? It is so refreshing and feels so wonderful! What if I told you that you could dance in the rain right now, without moving a single muscle or getting wet? You really can- In your mind! Your mind is capable of doing many incredible things, including something called Visualization.

To begin your visualization practice, close your eyes. Really, close your eyes (unless you are the one reading this, of course!) To build a very strong visualization, it is usually

helpful to first center yourself and be sure you are giving your brain the very best tools it needs to work with. In this case, that means oxygen, and oxygen means taking some good, deep breaths.

You are going to take some slow, deep breaths now, following along with my instruction: Breathe in very slowly, 1 – 2 – 3 – 4. Now breathe out, very slowly, 1 – 2 – 3 – 4. Excellent. Now again very slowly, 1 – 2 – 3 – 4 and breathe back out very slowly, 1 – 2 – 3 – 4 very nice. Once more, very slowly in 1 – 2 – 3 – 4 and back out very slowly, 1 – 2 – 3 – 4. Great!

Take a moment to review how you feel. Are you comfy and feeling good? Okay, great.

Picture yourself, in your mind's eye, outside on a beautiful summer's day. You are standing in a meadow. The meadow is full of tall wildflowers and meadow grasses, some even as tall as you are! You take a long, deep breath in, enjoying the fresh scent of the meadow grass and the beautiful wildflowers all around you.

You are lazily walking through the meadow and enjoying this beautiful sunny summer's day and listening to the birds singing their songs in the nearby trees. You glance up and see that there seem to be some clouds forming. Hmm, you wonder if it might rain? The wildflowers and meadow grasses would certainly love it if it did!

You continue slowly and languidly walking along when you spot a wildflower that is a beautiful deep purple color. You stop to take a closer look, bending over so you can closely inspect the deep purples of the petals. You take a long, deep breath in and smell the sweet, floral scent. What a beautiful flower!

You stand up and stretch your arms up and over your head, thinking to yourself how good it feels to stretch your body on this lazy summer's day. You even start to yawn while you are stretching your body, and as your mouth opens wide into a very satisfying yawn, something drops down into your mouth. Startled, your eyes pop open wide and you are immediately hit by a few more drops of something, landing on your arms and face.

These are raindrops, you realize! They are big, fat, cool raindrops and they are falling faster now. You stretch your arms out wide to the side as the rain steadily falls around you, cooling you and the summer air. You smile a wide and happy smile and do a little twirl in the rain, enjoying the feel of the fat raindrops as they plop on your skin.

The rain is invigorating to you, and you do not feel like it is a lazy summer's day anymore! You decide to go skipping through the meadow, enjoying the feel of the tall meadow grasses, now damp, as they whip against your legs. The rain is refreshing you and these beautiful meadow grasses and wildflowers.

You look out over and across the meadow and think how happy all of the plant life looks now! Everything looks so fresh and green. You continue skipping through the meadow toward the paved sidewalk nearby. You are heading toward the tree line because you love watching the way the rain cascades off of the tree branches like a waterfall.

The rain is really coming down now, and you see that the rain is now cascading off the tree branches like waterfalls, and you can hear it as it splashes on to the ground with a satisfying splat. As you get closer, you realize the water is pooling there on the pavement and now there are rain puddles! Awesome!

You look down and realize you are already getting pretty wet out here in the rain, so why worry about getting even wetter now? Exclaiming happily, you leap up into the air and then land solidly in the middle of one particularly deep puddle, sending the water splashing up and out of the puddle!

You continue jumping from rain puddle to rain puddle, grinning widely. You are so grateful to be out here on this rainy summer day, enjoying the awesome weather.

You do not have to leave this rainy summer day just yet if you don't want to. You can spend as long as you want here and you can come back anytime you'd like.

You can create anything you want in your mind. Imagine where you want to go and build the picture in your mind. Be sure to imagine how you want it to smell, taste, hear, and feel. The more detailed you can make your mental picture, the more you will enjoy being there.

It is all up to you. Perhaps as you drift off to sleep, you may find yourself back out here in this lovely meadow, enjoying a rainy summer's day.

Chapter 14:
Painting the Fence

Have you ever painted a fence before? It is something that might not seem like it would be a lot of fun, but do you know that it really is? You get to watch as the fence is completely transformed by the new paint color, and you get to feel so proud that you are the one doing it! What if I told you that you could paint a fence right now, without having to even move a single muscle? You really can- In your mind! Your mind is capable of doing many incredible things, including something called Visualization.

To begin your visualization practice, close your eyes. Really, close your eyes (unless you are the one reading this, of course!) To build a very strong visualization, it is usually helpful to first center yourself and be sure you are giving your brain the very best tools it needs to work with. In this case, that means oxygen, and oxygen means taking some good, deep breaths.

You are going to take some slow, deep breaths now, following along with my instruction: Breathe in very slowly, 1 – 2 – 3 – 4. Now breathe out, very slowly, 1 – 2 – 3 – 4. Excellent. Now again very slowly, 1 – 2 – 3 – 4 and breathe back out very slowly, 1 – 2 – 3 – 4 very nice. Once more, very slowly in 1 – 2 – 3 – 4 and back out very slowly, 1 – 2 – 3 – 4. Great!

Take a moment to review how you feel. Are you comfy and feeling good? Okay, great.

Picture yourself, in your mind's eye, standing outside on a cool autumn day. It is early fall, and the leaves are changing colors on the trees but have not yet begun to fall. There is a lovely autumn breeze blowing and you are perfectly comfortable outside.

It's a good thing that it is such a perfectly comfortable day outside, too, because you have some work ahead of you! You are standing in front of a fence that is a sad, grayish-brown color. This fence definitely looks like it has seen better days!

This is where you come in. Beside the fence, there is a bucket of paint and a paint pan with a long roller brush in it. You have the important task of painting this fence and making it look fresh and fun! You actually don't even know what color you are painting it, only that it is supposed to be a fun and happy color. Any color will be an improvement on this dull grayish-brown color, you think.

You take a long, deep breath in and smell the crisp autumn air. You are excited to get started on this fence, so you go over to the paint can and pull the lid off. It is definitely a light color but you know that you won't really be able to see it completely until you mix it up properly with the paint stick because the bright color always settles to the bottom of the paint can. What a fun surprise this will be!

You crouch down beside the paint bucket and pick up the paint stick laying on the ground next to it. You dip it into the thick paint and begin to stir, the paint so thick that you have to really use your arm muscles to get in there and mix the paint around. You can see the color coming up from the bottom, and you can now see that this color is going to be an orange color of some sort, wow! Using your arm muscles, you keep mixing, mixing, mixing, watching as more of the bright tangerine color shows up at the top of the paint can.

Time to pour the paint can into the paint pan! You very carefully lift the paint can up and gently begin to pour the paint into the paint pan. The colors mixed together beautifully, and you can really appreciate the sweet tangerine color as it folds into the can.

Now, for the fun part! You pick up the long roller brush and begin carefully rolling the brush through the tangerine orange paint, watching as the paint sticks to the roller, completely covering it in light and bright orange. Once you have completely coated the roller brush, you pick it up and begin rolling it on to the old, grayish-brown fence. Using long and purposeful strokes, you are amazed as you watch how each section transforms from dull and gray to fun and orange!

Diligently you continue on, covering each section of the old, grayish-brown fence with the new, bright tangerine orange paint. The new color is so fun and bright that it makes the fence look like it is brand new again! You are feeling so proud of yourself when you step back and take a look at what your hard work has done.

You are on the very last section of the fence now, and as you apply the final strokes of beautiful tangerine orange paint to cover the old grayish-brown, you think how grateful you are that you were able to refresh this old fence and make it look fun and happy again!

You do not have to leave your beautiful, freshly painted fence just yet if you don't want to. You can spend as long as you want here and you can come back anytime you'd like.

You can create anything you want in your mind. Imagine where you want to go and build the picture in your mind. Be sure to imagine how you want it to smell, taste, hear, and feel. The more detailed you can make your mental picture, the more you will enjoy being there.

It is all up to you. Perhaps as you drift off to sleep, you may find yourself back out here with your beautiful tangerine orange paint, ready to refresh another old, dull fence.

Chapter 15:
Bounce House Fun

Have you ever been to a bounce house before? They are so fun! It is an entire place that is specially made just for kids to bounce around in and have fun in; what is there not to love about them? What if I told you that you could go have fun in a bounce house right now, without having to even move a single muscle? You really can- In your mind! Your mind is capable of doing many incredible things, including something called Visualization.

To begin your visualization practice, close your eyes. Really, close your eyes (unless you are the one reading this, of course!) To build a very strong visualization, it is usually helpful to first center yourself and be sure you are giving your

brain the very best tools it needs to work with. In this case, that means oxygen, and oxygen means taking some good, deep breaths.

You are going to take some slow, deep breaths now, following along with my instruction: Breathe in very slowly, 1 – 2 – 3 – 4. Now breathe out, very slowly, 1 – 2 – 3 – 4. Excellent. Now again very slowly, 1 – 2 – 3 – 4 and breathe back out very slowly, 1 – 2 – 3 – 4 very nice. Once more, very slowly in 1 – 2 – 3 – 4 and back out very slowly, 1 – 2 – 3 – 4. Great!

Take a moment to review how you feel. Are you comfy and feeling good? Okay, great.

Picture yourself, in your mind's eye, standing outside in a field on a spring day. The sun is shining down above you, and it is the perfect temperature outside. You take a long, deep breath in, appreciating the cool and clear spring air, but the thing you are most excited about is what you are standing directly in front of, which is a bounce house!

Now, this is not just any bounce house. This is a Super Huge Mega Colossal bounce house! This thing is truly massive! There are supposed to be three different bounce houses here, all connected to each other, and kids can bounce from one to the other. It is your first time here, and you are so very excited!

You sit down in front and pull off your shoes, setting them carefully by the front entrance. Once your shoes are off, you climb up the ramp to get in, and you push the first curtain aside with your head and fall into the bounce house bouncy bottom. Wow! You look around and the very first thing you notice is how very colorful this bounce house is. It is a rainbow of colors all around you and you feel like you are in a kaleidoscope or something with how beautiful and bright this room is.

You push yourself up to standing and begin to jump up and down, your leg muscles quickly warming up. You bounce up and down and up and down and up and down, enjoying the way it feels when the bouncy bottom of the bounce house bounces you way high up in the air. You love bounce houses!

This room is pretty cool, but this mega bounce house has three rooms to it, so you decide to go check the others out. There is a passageway beside you, but you cannot see through it because it looks like when you climb up into it, all you can see is the tunnel. Intriguing, you think! You climb up and into the passageway. The passageway is the same rainbow colors as the first room was, and it is beautiful to be completely surrounded by a rainbow-like this.

You come to the end of the tunnel and see why you couldn't see through to the other side. The other end of the tunnel drops off below! It looks like this bouncy house is also rainbow-colored, but something looks a little different about the bouncy floor of this bouncy house, but you can't quite make out what it is. You decide to go ahead and drop into this side, and you very quickly discover what it is that made it look so different: this bouncy house is full of soft, foam, rainbow-colored balls!

You laugh out loud as you roll around in the soft and squishy foam balls in this bouncy house room. They are so fun! You stand up and begin to bounce, the rainbow-colored foam balls bouncing along with you. It feels like you are being popped with rainbow-colored popcorn kernels all around you!

You jump for a little while longer with the soft and squishy foam balls, enjoying the way your leg muscles feel as they work hard. Then you remember that there is another room in this place that you need to check out. You look around you for the passage to the next room, but you don't see it right away. It is camouflaged in the corner of this bouncy house room under all of those foam balls because this room has a little door you have to open to enter into it. Neat!

You make your way through the foam balls and open the door and are amazed by what you see. It looks like another passage, but this passage is pitch black except for the glow in the dark star stickers all over the ceiling and walls! Wow! You follow along with the stickers very carefully, and it leads you to the final room, completely pitch black except for the glow in the dark star stickers and a black light overhead!

Black lights are so awesome because they make everything, even a person's skin, glow in the dark! As you bounce in this room, you realize there is a mirror on the ceiling where you can look up and see how cool you look as you bounce under the blacklight, your skin, hair, and clothing glowing in the dark!

Wow, you think as you jump in this incredible bounce house room. This has been the coolest bounce house you've ever been in, and you are so grateful that you have had the opportunity to check out this Super Huge Mega Colossal bounce house!

You do not have to leave this awesome bounce house just yet if you don't want to. You can spend as long as you want here and you can come back anytime you'd like.

You can create anything you want in your mind. Imagine where you want to go and build the picture in your mind. Be sure to imagine how you want it to smell, taste, hear, and feel. The more detailed you can make your mental picture, the more you will enjoy being there.

It is all up to you. Perhaps as you drift off to sleep, you may find yourself back out here in this Super Huge Mega Colossal bounce house again.

Chapter 16:
The Tallest Slide

Have you ever had a chance to ride down one of the super tall slides at a fair or carnival? The kind of slide where you can look out over the entire fair when you're way up at the top? They are so fun! Well, what if I told you that you could slide down the very tallest slide right now, without having to move a single muscle? You really can- In your mind! Your mind is capable of doing many incredible things, including something called Visualization.

To begin your visualization practice, close your eyes. Really, close your eyes (unless you are the one reading this, of course!) To build a very strong visualization, it is usually helpful to first center yourself and be sure you are giving your brain the very best tools it needs to work with. In this case, that means oxygen, and oxygen means taking some good, deep breaths.

You are going to take some slow, deep breaths now, following along with my instruction: Breathe in very slowly, 1 - 2 - 3 - 4. Now breathe out, very slowly, 1 - 2 - 3 - 4. Excellent. Now again very slowly, 1 - 2 - 3 - 4 and breathe back out very slowly, 1 - 2 - 3 - 4 very nice. Once more, very slowly in 1 - 2 - 3 - 4 and back out very slowly, 1 - 2 - 3 - 4. Great!

Take a moment to review how you feel. Are you comfy and feeling good? Okay, great.

Picture yourself, in your mind's eye, standing in the middle of a carnival. The summer sun is shining down overhead, and it is a lovely summer day. The sights and sounds of the carnival are all around you. There are children running, laughing, and shouting as they run from ride to ride and you can see all kinds of different carnival rides and attractions around you.

You take a long, deep breath in and can smell the delicious carnival food that is being served: cotton candy, funnel cakes, corn dogs! Yum! As delicious as all that food smells, there is something that you have to do before you go eat any yummy carnival food or ride any other carnival rides: you want to slide down the tallest slide.

The tallest slide at this carnival is a really, really, really tall slide. It is the very tallest slide you have ever seen! You want to ride on it because you know that it will be so fun to ride down it, but you also know that you are very nervous about climbing up that high. That is okay. You can be nervous but still do it anyway!

You approach the person who is running the slide, and you give him the tickets that it costs, and he directs you to the blanket looking potato sacks that they have you use to slide down on. You pull one off of the pile, and its rough and scratchy texture surprises you. Your potato sack in hand, you walk towards the steps.

There are people ahead of you already making their way up, and you stop for a moment to watch. Lots of people, including kids, are already climbing up these steps. There are even kids much smaller than you already heading up! You look over at the slide and watch a few people slide down. Everyone that comes down this tall, tall slide has such a huge smile on their face! You know this is what you want, too, so you take a moment to build your courage up again.

You pull your shoulders back and stand up straight and strong. You take a deep breath and remember how much fun it will be to come down this very tall slide, and you know that you are ready to take your first step up the stairs.

One foot in front of the other and one step at a time. That is what you keep telling yourself as you climb higher and higher up. This tall, tall slide has so many stairs! You look out over the rail and see that you are really getting up high now. Even though you are a little nervous to be going up so very high, you remind yourself that you can be nervous about doing something but still do it anyway. You can be brave and do the things you want to do, even if they scare you.

You keep climbing higher and higher, and you can see the platform that you will walk across to get on the slide- you are so close! There is one person in front of you, a kid about your age. You watch as they set their potato sack up and carefully sit down on it. They turn around and give you a thumbs-up sign before they slide down, and you flash a thumbs-up sign right back at them!

It is your turn now, and you slowly walk across the platform, your heart beating very fast. You carefully arrange your potato sack at the top and sit on top, looking out across the carnival. You can see everything from way up here! You feel like you are sitting on top of the world way up here. With a huge smile on your face, you use your hands to push off from the platform, and just like that, you are off!

The potato sack on the tall, tall slide goes racing down, and you realize you are giggling as the air goes rushing around your face. You are so grateful that you were brave enough to go on the tallest slide!

You do not have to leave the tallest slide just yet if you don't want to. You can spend as long as you want here and you can come back anytime you'd like.

You can create anything you want in your mind. Imagine where you want to go and build the picture in your mind. Be sure to imagine how you want it to smell, taste, hear, and feel. The more detailed you can make your mental picture, the more you will enjoy being there.

It is all up to you. Perhaps as you drift off to sleep, you may find yourself back out here at the carnival, ready to climb up to the top of the tallest slide again.

Chapter 17:
Animal Rescue

Do you know what an Animal Rescue is? It is a special animal hospital for animals that needed to be saved and taken care of. Animal Rescue's are very special places, and they often rely on people to volunteer to help care for the animals they have taken in. It is wonderful to volunteer and help to take care of animals in need. What if I told you that you could go volunteer at an Animal Rescue right now, without having to even move a muscle? You really can- In your mind! Your mind is capable of doing many incredible things, including something called Visualization.

To begin your visualization practice, close your eyes. Really, close your eyes (unless you are the one reading this, of course!) To build a very strong visualization, it is usually helpful to first center yourself and be sure you are giving your brain the very best tools it needs to work with. In this case, that means oxygen, and oxygen means taking some good, deep breaths.

You are going to take some slow, deep breaths now, following along with my instruction: Breathe in very slowly, 1 – 2 – 3 – 4. Now breathe out, very slowly, 1 – 2 – 3 – 4. Excellent. Now again very slowly, 1 – 2 – 3 – 4 and breathe back out very slowly, 1 – 2 – 3 – 4 very nice. Once more, very slowly in 1 – 2 – 3 – 4 and back out very slowly, 1 – 2 – 3 – 4. Great!

Take a moment to review how you feel. Are you comfy and feeling good? Okay, great.

Picture yourself, in your mind's eye, standing in front of a large brick building. The words "Animal Rescue" are on a sign beside the door, and you know you are in the right place. You walk in and tell the person at the front desk that you are here to help take care of animals, and they are very happy that you are here.

They walk you back through the front room to the first care room. You are introduced to the woman in charge of this care room. She is tall with short, dark hair and she is very excited that you have come to help. She explains that this room is where animals come to stay that need special help eating.

You look around the room. There is white tile on the floors, and the walls are painted a light blue color. There are several crates in this room, each one with a different critter. The first crate that you are taken to is full of blankets and bedding, but you don't see any animal inside. You ask what it is, and you are told that it is a baby squirrel that was separated from its mom and needs special help eating out of a bottle. It likes to burrow into the blankets to stay warm, so that is why you can't see him!

You are given a teeny tiny baby bottle with milk inside, and you are told that if you drop a few drops of the milk into the crate, the baby squirrel will smell it and come out to eat. You do this and you see and hear a quick commotion under the blankets as the baby squirrel quickly makes his way out towards the bottle.

He is so tiny! He is probably about half of the size of your hand, but he is fast as he scurries over towards the bottle tip. He reaches up and latches on to the bottle tip that you have in the crate, and you watch in awe as this teeny tiny baby squirrel works to get milk out of this bottle. He eats very sloppily, making little squeak noises, too, as he watches you through the crate while he eats.

Once the little baby squirrel has finished his bottle, you move on to the next crate. In this crate, you are told, is a very special new arrival. This little arrival is another baby, but this is a baby bird, and it has a very special diet. Do you know what baby birds eat? Yup, they eat worms!

You are given the container with the baby bird food in it, and you are surprised to see that the little tiny worms in the container are actually still alive and wriggling around! It is explained to you that that is how the mama bird would feed the baby, so that is how the baby birds are fed here at the Animal Rescue, too.

You pick up the tweezers in the container and get the first worm for the baby bird. The baby bird is in a little makeshift bird nest that is made of hay and grass, and you are surprised to see how little hair this teeny tiny baby bird has! It has just a little fluff of hair on the top of its head and just a little fuzz on its body, and that is it. You put the worm down near the baby bird's nest and it begins to flutter its tiny wings excitedly as it hops around a few times while holding its baby beak open. You giggle because this baby bird is so excited it can barely keep still enough to eat the worm you have for it!

The baby bird finally manages to grab on to a worm from the end of the tweezers and you clap with delight as this baby bird finally gets a nice meal. You know that taking care of these animals that need help at the Animal Rescue is so important, and you feel so grateful that you were able to help.

You do not have to leave the Animal Rescue just yet if you don't want to. You can spend as long as you want here and you can come back anytime you'd like.

You can create anything you want in your mind. Imagine where you want to go and build the picture in your mind. Be sure to imagine how you want it to smell, taste, hear, and feel. The more detailed you can make your mental picture, the more you will enjoy being there.

It is all up to you. Perhaps as you drift off to sleep, you may find yourself back here at the Animal Rescue, helping to take care of the animals that need help the most.

Chapter 18:
Hike in the Woods

Do you like to go hiking? It can be so much fun to go for a nice long walk and have an adventure in the woods. You never know what you might see while you are there! What if I told you that you could go for a hike in the woods right now without having to move a single muscle? You really can- In your mind! Your mind is capable of doing many incredible things, including something called Visualization.

To begin your visualization practice, close your eyes. Really, close your eyes (unless you are the one reading this, of

course!) To build a very strong visualization, it is usually helpful to first center yourself and be sure you are giving your brain the very best tools it needs to work with. In this case, that means oxygen, and oxygen means taking some good, deep breaths.

You are going to take some slow, deep breaths now, following along with my instruction: Breathe in very slowly, 1 – 2 – 3 – 4. Now breathe out, very slowly, 1 – 2 – 3 – 4. Excellent. Now again very slowly, 1 – 2 – 3 – 4 and breathe back out very slowly, 1 – 2 – 3 – 4 very nice. Once more, very slowly in 1 – 2 – 3 – 4 and back out very slowly, 1 – 2 – 3 – 4. Great!

Take a moment to review how you feel. Are you comfy and feeling good? Okay, great.

Picture yourself, in your mind's eye, standing at the edge of a forest. It is a lovely fall day, and you take a long, deep breath in, enjoying the crisp, clean smell of autumn. The trees at the edge of this forest are changing color for the season and there are burnt oranges and golden yellow colors everywhere you look.

There is a clearing here in the trees, and it looks like the perfect path to head off on, so you begin your hike by following this path in the woods. You can tell it is well-traveled because there are no branches or bushes in the way, and most of the autumn leaves have even been kicked off to the side. You continue walking on, your feet plodding along the well-worn path.

You can hear the sounds of the autumn wind as it whips through the trees of the forest and rustles the remaining leaves on the trees. Occasionally the wind blows hard enough that some of the autumn leaves blow off the trees and are swirling around you in a beautiful mix of orange and gold. What a lovely day for a hike, you think.

You continue on the path until you reach a log that is stretched out across the clearing. You are climbing over it when you hear a loud and guttural croaking sound. What on earth could that be, you wonder? As you slide your legs over to the other side of the log, you see what made that noise. It is a bullfrog!

The bullfrog croaks at you again from its spot on the other side of the log. You laugh a little because this little green guy sure did startle you! You say hello to the bullfrog before continuing on your hike. Before long, you get to a place on the path where the path splits. You can either go to the left or the right.

Hmm. You look to the right and notice how the path is well-cleared. It looks like lots of people go that way. You look to the left and notice that there are lots of leaves strewn across that path, which probably means not as many people take that path. You decide that you would like to check out the path that is less traveled.

Heading down the path on the left, you enjoy the crisp rustling sound that your shoes make as they crunch the leaves below your feet. The sound is very relaxing to you, and you are enjoying listening to it when you realize that there is another sound that you hear, too, but you are not sure what it is, so you stop for a moment to listen.

It is water! You continue on the path, and the water noise gets louder and louder until you see a clearing up ahead with a giant, flat rock. You think that looks like the perfect spot to take a bit of a break. As you get closer to the rock, you are amazed to see the source of the water sound is right here!

Below you, down a rocky ravine, is a lovely little babbling brook. The water is gurgling as it rushes over the rocks in the brook. You take a seat on the smooth, flat rock and relax, enjoying the lovely music of the babbling brook below. You take a long, deep breath in of the crisp autumn air and think to yourself that you are so grateful that you found this beautiful spot on your lovely hike in the woods.

You do not have to leave this beautiful spot in the woods just yet if you don't want to. You can spend as long as you want here and you can come back anytime you'd like.

You can create anything you want in your mind. Imagine where you want to go and build the picture in your mind. Be sure to imagine how you want it to smell, taste, hear, and feel. The more detailed you can make your mental picture, the more you will enjoy being there.

It is all up to you. Perhaps as you drift off to sleep, you may find yourself back out here in the woods, enjoying the babbling brook on a beautiful autumn day.

Chapter 19:
Airplane Ride

Have you ever had the chance to fly in an airplane? It is so fun! You get to experience what it feels like to go soaring through the air, way high up in the sky, just like a bird. What if I told you that you could go an airplane ride right now, without having to move a single muscle? You really can- In your mind! Your mind is capable of doing many incredible things, including something called Visualization.

To begin your visualization practice, close your eyes. Really, close your eyes (unless you are the one reading this, of course!) To build a very strong visualization, it is usually helpful to first center yourself and be sure you are giving your brain the very best tools it needs to work with. In this case, that means oxygen, and oxygen means taking some good, deep breaths.

You are going to take some slow, deep breaths now, following along with my instruction: Breathe in very slowly, 1 - 2 - 3 - 4. Now breathe out, very slowly, 1 - 2 - 3 - 4. Excellent. Now again very slowly, 1 - 2 - 3 - 4 and breathe back out very slowly, 1 - 2 - 3 - 4 very nice. Once more, very slowly in 1 - 2 - 3 - 4 and back out very slowly, 1 - 2 - 3 - 4. Great!

Take a moment to review how you feel. Are you comfy and feeling good? Okay, great.

Picture yourself, in your mind's eye, standing in a long line of people. This isn't just any line, of course. This is a very special line! This is the line to board an airplane. The line is moving pretty quickly, and you hold your boarding pass in your hands. It is almost your turn, and you are getting very excited as the person in front of you is now handing over their boarding pass for the airport employee to scan, because you know it is almost your turn!

The person in front of you steps out of the line and into the hallway that leads to the plane, and your stomach is full of excited butterflies as you proudly hand the airport employee your boarding pass to scan. The employee thanks you with a big smile and motions for you to follow the long hallway to the airplane, and you are now so excited you can hardly stand it!

You follow the long, wide hallway to the airplane, your backpack on your back, the only thing you are carrying with you. Once you make it to the end of this long, wide hallway, the captain of the airplane and the flight attendants that will help during the flight welcome you onboard. You thank them and step onto the blue-carpeted airplane. There are two rows of seats and you carefully walk down the hallway in between, hunting for the seat number on your boarding pass.

Here it is! You found your seat number and slide into your seat. You are seated right next to the window, and you are very excited about this because this means you will get to see everything as you fly! There is a lot of hustle and bustle around you as the other passengers find their seats and get settled.

It isn't long before you hear the voice of the captain come over the loudspeaker for the plane and explain to all of the passengers that take off will be in just a few moments. Passengers are reminded to put their seat belt on, and the captain wishes everyone a happy flight. You are so incredibly excited now that you can hardly stand it!

You remember that you bought chewing gum in your backpack so your ears can easily pop as the plane goes up. You quickly pull out a piece and pop it in your mouth, chewing the hard stick until it softens. Perfect timing, because the plane is beginning to move slowly away from the gate.

At first, the plane moves very slowly away from the gate and then picks up speed until it is practically racing down the runway. You watch out the window as the airport in the distance becomes a blur and then suddenly, there is liftoff! Now the ground below is being left behind, and you continue to watch as the plane rises higher and higher.

Thank goodness for this chewing gum, you think, as you feel your ears popping several times with the altitude! The cars and buildings on the ground below are looking so small, and far away now, you think. You continue looking out your window as you are now flying into the white and wispy clouds. It is absolutely beautiful and you are grateful that you are able to go on an airplane ride and see what it is like to go soaring through the clouds.

Now all you have to do is relax and enjoy the ride.

You do not have to leave your lovely airplane ride just yet if you don't want to. You can spend as long as you want here and you can come back anytime you'd like.

You can create anything you want in your mind. Imagine where you want to go and build the picture in your mind. Be sure to imagine how you want it to smell, taste, hear, and feel. The more detailed you can make your mental picture, the more you will enjoy being there.

It is all up to you. Perhaps as you drift off to sleep, you may find yourself back up here in the clouds, sailing through the sky on an airplane ride.

Chapter 20:
New Kid Next Door

Isn't it fun when you get to meet new people? Especially new friends, right? It's always really fun when the new friends you meet live near you, too, so you can play often. What if I told you that you could meet a new friend that is also a neighbor without having to move a single muscle? You really can- In your mind! Your mind is capable of doing many incredible things, including something called Visualization.

To begin your visualization practice, close your eyes. Really, close your eyes (unless you are the one reading this, of

course!) To build a very strong visualization, it is usually helpful to first center yourself and be sure you are giving your brain the very best tools it needs to work with. In this case, that means oxygen, and oxygen means taking some good, deep breaths.

You are going to take some slow, deep breaths now, following along with my instruction: Breathe in very slowly, 1 – 2 – 3 – 4. Now breathe out, very slowly, 1 – 2 – 3 – 4. Excellent. Now again very slowly, 1 – 2 – 3 – 4 and breathe back out very slowly, 1 – 2 – 3 – 4 very nice. Once more, very slowly in 1 – 2 – 3 – 4 and back out very slowly, 1 – 2 – 3 – 4. Great!

Take a moment to review how you feel. Are you comfy and feeling good? Okay, great.

Picture yourself, in your mind's eye, just waking up for the day. You get yourself up, get dressed, brush your teeth, all of the normal wake-up stuff you do to get ready for your day. Once you've gotten yourself ready for your day, you notice that there is a moving truck pulling in to the house next door. Wow! New neighbors!

You sit down at the table to eat your favorite breakfast, watching as the movers get to work unloading the moving truck next door. There is a team of several movers, so they are moving pretty fast on this sunny summer morning. You see, a couple of couches and some bedroom furniture make its way in, and you are wondering what kind of new neighbors you will have.

The people that lived in the house before had been very nice neighbors, but they were an older family, and there were no kids to play with. It would be so cool to have kids to play with nearby, you think! Plus, your yard and the neighbor's yard both have giant oak trees that grow on either side of the fence, and you've always wondered what it might be like to have a friend that could climb up on their side of the fence and you two could hang out together up in the trees.

You are imagining how cool that would be when you see a bed being pulled out of the moving truck that looks smaller than the other bed that had been taken off. You think that could definitely be a kid bed, but you aren't quite sure just yet. You watch as more furniture is unloaded, but it is just dressers and chairs, and you don't see anything else that clues you into whether or not a new kid is moving in next door.

You get excited when you see the movers unload a bicycle, but it is a full-size adult bike, so you aren't quite sure just yet. You know there are lots of kids that are tall enough to ride a full-size adult bike, but you don't want to get your hopes up for no reason, so you continue to eat your breakfast and watch as the movers unload another full-size adult bike. Okay, so there are at least two bike riders next door. Are they adults or kids?

You get up from the table to grab yourself a napkin, and as you return, you realize you missed whatever the last mover just took off of the truck! Oh no, how will you ever know who is moving in next door? You quickly finish the rest of your breakfast and watch as mostly just boxes are taken off of the truck and then you get up to clear your place.

You had a nice breakfast; now you figure you will go outside to play for a bit. You guess you will meet the neighbors whenever they arrive, and you will have to be patient until then. First, you go to open the front door and bring in the morning paper. As you are opening the front door, there is a commotion over at the new neighbors, so you look over in that direction.

It is a dog running around in circles, barking excitedly! Hey, the new neighbors have a dog, cool! Two people come running out of the house towards the dog and you assume they must be the new neighbors so you give a little wave. They wave back at you as they laugh and try to corral their dog back into the house, but the dog escapes them and runs towards you!

They call out to you that their dog is friendly, just excited, so you are not afraid. You reach out your hand to pet the fluffy, white dog, and this dog begins covering you in kisses! You laugh as the new neighbors make their way over to you and introduce themselves and their dog. You are very happy to meet them as they seem very, very nice. You are a little disappointed that there is no new kid moving in, but you are still happy to have nice, new neighbors with a friendly and fluffy puppy dog!

Just then, a voice pipes up from behind the moving truck, asking if anyone knows where the dog's leash is. It's a kid! Your new neighbors DO have a kid and they introduce you to this new friend. You both smile at each other, excited to have a new friend and neighbor that is your age. You are so grateful that you have made a new friend!

You do not have to leave your new neighbor friend just yet if you don't want to. You can spend as long as you want here and you can come back anytime you'd like.

You can create anything you want in your mind. Imagine where you want to go and build the picture in your mind. Be sure to imagine how you want it to smell, taste, hear, and feel. The more detailed you can make your mental picture, the more you will enjoy being there.

It is all up to you. Perhaps as you drift off to sleep, you may find yourself back here with your new neighbor friend and their fluffy puppy dog.

Chapter 21:
Dance Class

Have you ever taken dance lessons? Dance class is so fun! It is great to learn new ways to move and twist your body. There are so many different ways to dance! What if I told you that you could go to a dance class right now without having to move a single muscle? You really can- In your mind! Your mind is capable of doing many incredible things, including something called Visualization.

To begin your visualization practice, close your eyes. Really, close your eyes (unless you are the one reading this, of course!) To build a very strong visualization, it is usually

helpful to first center yourself and be sure you are giving your brain the very best tools it needs to work with. In this case, that means oxygen, and oxygen means taking some good, deep breaths.

You are going to take some slow, deep breaths now, following along with my instruction: Breathe in very slowly, 1 – 2 – 3 – 4. Now breathe out, very slowly, 1 – 2 – 3 – 4. Excellent. Now again very slowly, 1 – 2 – 3 – 4 and breathe back out very slowly, 1 – 2 – 3 – 4 very nice. Once more, very slowly in 1 – 2 – 3 – 4 and back out very slowly, 1 – 2 – 3 – 4. Great!

Take a moment to review how you feel. Are you comfy and feeling good? Okay, great.

Picture yourself, in your mind's eye, standing in a dance studio. This dance studio is a long, narrow room that has mirrors on each wall so you can always see what your body is doing. The floor is light oak, and the room smells clean and fresh. The lights are bright overhead and there is a bar along one entire wall that is perfect for stretching out your body with.

You take a long, deep breath as you look around this dance studio. There are a dance instructor and other dance students in this class with you, and everyone is excited and glad to be here. The dance instructor tells everyone to begin by taking a seat on the floor and stretching their legs out in front of them, pointing their toes, and bending at the waist to touch their toes.

The instructor tells you how important it is to properly stretch out your muscles before you begin to dance. It is important because if you do not stretch and warm up your muscles, you could get injured when you dance. Besides that, stretching feels wonderful! You love the way it feels when the muscles in your legs and lower back begin to loosen up with the stretch, and you take a long, deep breath in as you enjoy this feeling.

Next, your dance instructor tells you all to bring the bottoms of your feet together and to pull them into you as close as you can and to again, stretch yourself down at the waist, as low as you can, still holding your feet tucked in close against you. Now you feel the stretch up high in your thighs and your lower back, and you close your eyes while you feel these muscles loosening and warming up. You take another long, deep breath in, enjoying your body warming up for dance!

Now the instructor wants everyone to stand up. She tells everyone to stand up as tall as they possibly can and reach way high up in the sky like they are trees trying to grow. You do this and love the way it feels to stretch your arms way up high. Next, the instructor wants everyone to use their arms that are stretched so high up in the air and to sway slowly back and forth with them, like branches swaying in the breeze.

You sway gently back and forth, smiling as you and all the other students sway back and forth, looking like a grove of swaying trees in the mirrors. The instructor has everyone stop swaying and shake their bodies loose, getting ready to dance. You are excited because you know that you will be learning how to leap today.

The instructor shows you all how to leap up and into the air, stretching one leg behind you and one leg in front of you. You are told that you will need to push off with your back leg and follow the leg in front, keeping your toes pointed as best as you can. You watch as the other students go; first, each taking a few running steps before leaping up in the air, legs spread far apart and toes pointed. Everyone looks so strong and graceful as they fly through the air in a leap!

Now, it is your turn. Your instructor reminds you to use your back leg to push off against the ground and that these muscles must be full of power to propel you off of the ground. You nod your head; you are ready. You take a few running steps before you use your back leg to power yourself up and off the ground.

You are leaping! Your legs are spread far apart, both toes pointing, sailing through the air. You catch a quick glimpse of yourself in the mirror and are amazed that you look just as strong and graceful as you felt during your leap. You land with a satisfied smile and feel so proud of yourself for mastering this difficult dance move. You are grateful to be here, learning how to dance.

You do not have to leave the dance studio just yet if you don't want to. You can spend as long as you want here and you can come back anytime you'd like.

You can create anything you want in your mind. Imagine where you want to go and build the picture in your mind. Be sure to imagine how you want it to smell, taste, hear, and feel. The more detailed you can make your mental picture, the more you will enjoy being there.

It is all up to you. Perhaps as you drift off to sleep, you may find yourself back here in the dance studio, watching yourself in the mirrors as you leap across the room.

Chapter 22:
Sledding Through the Snow

Have you ever been sledding down a snowy hill? It is one of the best winter activities for kids! It is so fun to climb up to the very top of a huge snowy hill and then to ride down on a slick path with your sled! What if I told you that you could go sledding through the snow right now, without having to move a single muscle? You really can- In your mind! Your mind is capable of doing many incredible things, including something called Visualization.

To begin your visualization practice, close your eyes. Really, close your eyes (unless you are the one reading this, of course!) To build a very strong visualization, it is usually helpful to first center yourself and be sure you are giving your brain the very best tools it needs to work with. In this case, that means oxygen, and oxygen means taking some good, deep breaths.

You are going to take some slow, deep breaths now, following along with my instruction: Breathe in very slowly, 1 – 2 – 3 – 4. Now breathe out, very slowly, 1 – 2 – 3 – 4. Excellent. Now again very slowly, 1 – 2 – 3 – 4 and breathe back out very slowly, 1 – 2 – 3 – 4 very nice. Once more, very slowly in 1 – 2 – 3 – 4 and back out very slowly, 1 – 2 – 3 – 4. Great!

Take a moment to review how you feel. Are you comfy and feeling good? Okay, great.

Picture yourself, in your mind's eye, standing outside on a cold, blustery winter's day. It is snowing! There are big, thick, fluffy snowflakes falling all around you, and the snow is very thick underfoot. You are glad you are well bundled up against the cold because you are toasty warm with all of your layers and your thick winter coat.

You are standing at the foot of a hill, but this is not just any hill. This is the biggest, tallest, best sledding hill for miles and miles around, and everyone loves it! Big kids, little kids, even adults, too, everyone loves to come to this hill and sled down it.

This is your first time ever coming sledding here, so you are very, very excited! You have a hold of the rope handle of your sled as you begin the trek up the hill. You have to go up the side of the hill; otherwise, you would get taken out by one of the sleds as they race down the hill!

The snow is thick and deep, so it takes a bit to get up to the top of the hill, but eventually, you make it up to the top. You stand at the top of this huge hill, and you look all around you. The snow is still falling and it swirls and whirls with each winter wind and there is a white blanket coating of snow as far as you can see in every direction.

You get your sled ready to put into place at the top of the hill, and suddenly you realize that this hill seems somehow even taller now that you are at the top of it! You feel a little nervous, but you know that you would never let feeling nervous stop you from doing something you really want to do. You are brave.

With that thought, you push forward, and with a whoosh, you are off! Your sled flies down the hill over the slick, hard-pressed snow, and the other kids sledding down around you look like blurs out of the corner of your eyes. You are moving so fast you can't see anything, but you can feel the wind as it whips across your face, and you hold tight to the sled below you.

You are coming to the end, and the sled slows down as the ground evens out. Wow! How exhilarating and exciting that was! You love sledding! You are so grateful that you have had the chance to go sledding down this awesome hill, and you are going to go again.

You do not have to leave this snowy hill just yet if you don't want to. You can spend as long as you want here and you can come back anytime you'd like.

You can create anything you want in your mind. Imagine where you want to go and build the picture in your mind. Be sure to imagine how you want it to smell, taste, hear, and feel. The more detailed you can make your mental picture, the more you will enjoy being there.

It is all up to you. Perhaps as you drift off to sleep, you may find yourself back out here in the snow, getting ready to fly back down the hill on your sled.

Chapter 23:
Ice Skating Fun

Do you like to go ice-skating? It is so fun to go out and glide across the glistening ice on a fresh pair of ice skates! What if I told you that you could go ice skating right now, without having to move a single muscle? You really can- In your mind! Your mind is capable of doing many incredible things, including something called Visualization.

To begin your visualization practice, close your eyes. Really, close your eyes (unless you are the one reading this, of course!) To build a very strong visualization, it is usually

helpful to first center yourself and be sure you are giving your brain the very best tools it needs to work with. In this case, that means oxygen, and oxygen means taking some good, deep breaths.

You are going to take some slow, deep breaths now, following along with my instruction: Breathe in very slowly, 1 – 2 – 3 – 4. Now breathe out, very slowly, 1 – 2 – 3 – 4. Excellent. Now again very slowly, 1 – 2 – 3 – 4 and breathe back out very slowly, 1 – 2 – 3 – 4 very nice. Once more, very slowly in 1 – 2 – 3 – 4 and back out very slowly, 1 – 2 – 3 – 4. Great!

Take a moment to review how you feel. Are you comfy and feeling good? Okay, great.

Picture yourself, in your mind's eye, standing outside on a cold, winter's day. There is a light snow falling all around you, the kind that sticks to your eyelashes but melts right away if you catch it on your tongue. You are not cold because you have your warmest winter clothing on and you feel toasty and warm.

On your feet are ice skates! You are standing beside a thickly frozen pond, and you are ready to go ice skating. It is your first-time ice skating, so you are a little nervous at first. You take a long, deep breath in of the fresh winter air before you take your first step out on to the frozen pond.

You have to use your leg and ankle muscles to keep yourself upright on the ice skates, so you take your first few steps very tentatively while you figure out how to do that exactly. You are feeling a little unsteady still, so you take it easy while you get used to the way the skates feel on the ice, and you watch as other ice skaters glide past.

You study the way they propel themselves forward. They are gliding because they are pushing backward with your legs, you think. It is almost like pushing off against the ice. You decide to try it, and the first time you push forward, you feel your skates wibble and wobble like crazy and you almost fall! You laugh because you feel like a baby deer trying to stand for the first time.

You are determined to learn how to ice skate, so you try again, this time pushing off slowly and carefully. You are amazed when you are easily propelled forward, gliding, just like the other skaters, seem to be doing around you. Wow! You are really doing it.

You continue to glide around the pond, enjoying the way the hard, frozen pond feels underfoot as the blade of your ice skates cuts into it. There is a pale winter sun shining down from above, and you love the way the sunlight is glinting off of both the frozen surface of the pond and the metal blades of the ice skates all around you.

You are gliding easily now, and you feel very graceful and strong. The snow flurries are still falling all around you and you feel like you are in a real-life snow globe. You are so happy to be out here on this beautiful frozen pond and you are grateful that you have learned how to ice skate.

You do not have to leave this frozen pond just yet if you don't want to. You can spend as long as you want here and you can come back anytime you'd like.

You can create anything you want in your mind. Imagine where you want to go and build the picture in your mind. Be sure to imagine how you want it to smell, taste, hear, and feel.

The more detailed you can make your mental picture, the more you will enjoy being there.

It is all up to you. Perhaps as you drift off to sleep, you may find yourself back out here in your ice skates, gliding gracefully in a beautiful snow globe.

Chapter 24:
Building a Bridge

Do you like to play in creek beds? Tiny little streams of water that usually are very shallow are called creeks, and the creek beds they are in can be a lot of fun to play in. One really fun thing to do in a creek bed is to build a bridge out of rocks across the creek. What if I told you that you could build a bridge right now, without having to move a single muscle? You really can- In your mind! Your mind is capable of doing many incredible things, including something called Visualization.

To begin your visualization practice, close your eyes. Really, close your eyes (unless you are the one reading this, of course!) To build a very strong visualization, it is usually helpful to first center yourself and be sure you are giving your brain the very best tools it needs to work with. In this case, that means oxygen, and oxygen means taking some good, deep breaths.

You are going to take some slow, deep breaths now, following along with my instruction: Breathe in very slowly, 1 – 2 – 3 – 4. Now breathe out, very slowly, 1 – 2 – 3 – 4. Excellent. Now again very slowly, 1 – 2 – 3 – 4 and breathe back out very slowly, 1 – 2 – 3 – 4 very nice. Once more, very slowly in 1 – 2 – 3 – 4 and back out very slowly, 1 – 2 – 3 – 4. Great!

Take a moment to review how you feel. Are you comfy and feeling good? Okay, great.

Picture yourself, in your mind's eye, standing outside on a warm summer's day. The sun is shining down above you, and you can hear the birds singing in the nearby trees. You are standing beside a creek bed and the water in this creek bed is running clear and cool.

There are rocks on each side of this creek bed, and there are many different shapes and sizes. You think that this could be a perfect time to build a bridge from one side to the other. You take a long, deep breath in and smell the cool, clear air down here by the creek.

You know that you need to select rocks that are big enough to step on, so you set out in search of the perfect bridge-building rocks. Your eye immediately settles on one that will be the perfect first stepping stone. It is a wide, smooth rock and it will be perfect. You hoist this heavy rock up and carefully carry it over to the creek bed, where you let it fall into the water with a splash.

On to the next rock! It doesn't take you long to find another wide, smooth rock to use for the next step, and you lug this heavy rock over to the spot and plop it into the water as the second step. Now, you only need one more rock to complete your bridge, but it is proving more difficult to find another wide, smooth rock. You might have to create this step out of smaller rocks piled together.

You gather together as many smooth, flat rocks as you can find, and you begin to pile them up together as the last step of the stepping stones. You build a rock platform out of several of the rocks and once you have built this final stepping stone, you step back to examine your handiwork. It looks great, but the real test will be how it works!

You step onto the first step, then the second, and finally, your handmade platform and then off to the other side of the creek. Perfect! You have built a fabulous bridge out here in the creek bed and you are grateful that you had the opportunity to hang out down here by the creek on this lovely summer's day.

You do not have to leave your freshly built bridge just yet if you don't want to. You can spend as long as you want here and you can come back anytime you'd like.

You can create anything you want in your mind. Imagine where you want to go and build the picture in your mind. Be sure to imagine how you want it to smell, taste, hear, and feel. The more detailed you can make your mental picture, the more you will enjoy being there.

It is all up to you. Perhaps as you drift off to sleep, you may find yourself back out here by the creek on this beautiful summer day.

Chapter 25:
Tree Climbing Fun

Do you like to climb trees? It is so fun to use your muscles to climb high up in a tree, isn't it? Well, what if I told you that you could go have some tree climbing fun right now, without having to move a single muscle? You really can- In your mind! Your mind is capable of doing many incredible things, including something called Visualization.

To begin your visualization practice, close your eyes. Really, close your eyes (unless you are the one reading this, of course!) To build a very strong visualization, it is usually helpful to first center yourself and be sure you are giving your brain the very best tools it needs to work with. In this case, that means oxygen, and oxygen means taking some good, deep breaths.

You are going to take some slow, deep breaths now, following along with my instruction: Breathe in very slowly, 1 – 2 – 3 – 4. Now breathe out, very slowly, 1 – 2 – 3 – 4. Excellent. Now again very slowly, 1 – 2 – 3 – 4 and breathe back out very slowly, 1 – 2 – 3 – 4 very nice. Once more, very slowly in 1 – 2 – 3 – 4 and back out very slowly, 1 – 2 – 3 – 4. Great!

Take a moment to review how you feel. Are you comfy and feeling good? Okay, great.

Picture yourself, in your mind's eye, sitting down at the base of a tree. It is a beautiful spring morning, and you are listening to the birds singing and enjoying the fresh spring breeze. You take a long, deep breath in, smelling the freshly blooming spring flowers.

You are sitting below a huge oak tree. You stand up and pat the trunk a little, thanking it for its awesome shade that you were just enjoying. You look up through its branches and realize that this tree would actually be a great climbing tree, too!

You see that there is one branch that is pretty low to the ground, low enough to the ground that you can jump up and grab on to it. You grab on to this branch and then use your feet to climb up the trunk until you can pull yourself all the way up and onto this branch. Now that you are up on the first branch, you can see how there are many branches up here that will be easy to climb!

The tree branches and trunks feel rough against your hands, but it doesn't hurt at all. You like the way it feels against your skin as you continue to climb up and around this gorgeous oak tree. Your leg and arm muscles feel strong and capable as you climb up, up, and up. Ah, there is the perfect spot, you think. There is a spot where three branches come together, and it looks like a great spot to stop and rest.

Once you climb over to this spot and settle in, you look out through the branches. The view is beautiful up here! You can see the entire yard, and you can really listen to the birds singing their songs up here because now you are so close to them! You take a long, deep breath in, again, enjoying this beautiful oak tree on this lovely spring day. You are grateful that you are strong and capable and able to climb trees.

You do not have to leave your perfect spot in this beautiful oak tree just yet if you don't want to. You can spend as long as you want here and you can come back anytime you'd like.

You can create anything you want in your mind. Imagine where you want to go and build the picture in your mind. Be sure to imagine how you want it to smell, taste, hear, and feel. The more detailed you can make your mental picture, the more you will enjoy being there.

It is all up to you. Perhaps as you drift off to sleep, you may find yourself back out here in this oak tree, enjoying this lovely spring day.

Bonus Chapter:
Count Off Centering

Do you know what a centering exercise is? It is what a person can do when they find themselves feeling anxious, scared, or upset in some way. It can also be called grounding, but for this exercise, we are calling it Count Off Centering.

One of the coolest things about centering is that you can do it anytime, anywhere, and no one even has to know you are doing it!

For this exercise, we are going to Count Off. We will begin with the number three and will count off down to one.

The number three we will Count Off with will be three things of a specific color. You can choose any color you like, but for this example, it will be blue. Count Off Blue! You need to find three things around you that are blue and count them off, one, two, three.

Next, you will Count Off two. For this, you need to listen to identify two different sounds. Doesn't matter what the sounds are, but you do need to listen until you can identify two separate sounds, and then you will count them off. Count Off Sounds! Listen for your two sounds around you and count them off, one, two, three.

Next, you will Count Off one. This time, you need to think of one thing that you are touching. It can be something you are wearing on your body, like clothes, or it can be one thing that you are touching with your hand, or even just the hair that might be touching your face. Count Off Touch! What is one thing that you are touching right now?

When you do a centering or grounding practice, you are connecting your brain to your physical body, and this can help you to calm your brain down enough so you can make good choices. Remember this exercise and use it anytime you want to calm yourself down or make yourself feel better.

Conclusion

Thank you for choosing *Bedtime Stories For Kids Vol 1+ Vol 2 + vol 3: A collection of over100 short meditation stories to reduce anxiety, learn mindfulness, increase relaxation, and help children fall to sleep fast (ages 2-6, 6-12, 3-5).* These stories were written to be engaging and useful for children between the ages of two and twelve, but utilizing visualization and meditation techniques for relaxation and mindfulness is useful for people of any age!

These stories can and should be read over and over again and can become a healthy addition to any bedtime routine. An advantage of guided meditation and visualization techniques in a bedtime book is that not only is meditation an excellent primer for bedtime, but the visualization cues and prompts provide excellent inspiration for your child to think about as they drift off to sleep. The prompts are intended to give plenty of space for imagination, and hopefully, great dreams will follow.

It can be helpful to follow up with your children, either immediately after the story has been read or the following morning. This can be a nice moment of connection for parents and their children as they can then discuss together what their personal visualization was like. Asking questions that are both specific and open-ended like, "When you were on the hike in the woods, and you stumbled across the babbling brook, what did you think?" The idea is to ask the child about a specific part of the visualization but to leave the space for the child to fill in their own creative visualization details.

Meditation and visualization are powerful tools that can be employed by anyone of any age. Hopefully, the stories in this book have been useful.

Thank you

Made in the USA
Middletown, DE
23 March 2020